Merciless Legacy

Asha Kade Private Detective Mystery Thriller

Tikiri Herath

Rebel Diva
ACADEMY PRESS

Merciless Legacy

Asha Kade Private Detective Mystery Thriller Series

www.TikiriHerath.com

Copyright ©2021 Tikiri Herath

Library & Archives Canada Cataloging in Publication

E-book ISBN: 978-1-989232-87-3

Paperback ISBN: 978-1-990234-05-7

Hardback ISBN: 978-1-990234-06-4

Audiobook ISBN: 978-1-989232-86-6

Large Print book ISBN: 978-1-990234-00-2

Author: Tikiri Herath

Publisher: Rebel Diva Academy Press

Copy Editor: Stephanie Parent

Back Cover Headshot: Aura McKay

Tikiri

The Red Heeled Rebels Universe

The Red Heeled Rebels universe of mystery thrillers, featuring your favorite kick-ass female characters.

Tanya Stone FBI K9 Mystery Thrillers

Thriller series starring Red Heeled Rebel and FBI Special Agent Tanya Stone, and her loyal German Shepherd K9, Max. These are serial killer thrillers set in Black Rock, a small upscale resort town on the coast of Washington state.

Her Deadly End
Her Cold Blood
Her Last Lie
Her Secret Crime
Her Perfect Murder
Her Grisly Grave
www.TikiriHerath.com/Thrillers

Asha Kade Private Detective Murder Mysteries
Murder mystery thrillers, featuring the Red Heeled Rebels, Asha Kade and Katy McCafferty. Asha and Katy receive one million dollars for their favorite children's charity from a secret benefactor's estate every time they solve a cold case.
Merciless Legacy
Merciless Games
Merciless Crimes
Merciless Lies
Merciless Past
Merciless Deaths
www.TikiriHerath.com/Mysteries

Red Heeled Rebels International Mystery & Crime - The Origin Story
The award-winning origin story of the Red Heeled Rebels characters. Learn how a rag-tag group of trafficked orphans from different places united to fight for their freedom and their lives and became a found family.
The Girl Who Crossed the Line

The Girl Who Ran Away
The Girl Who Made Them Pay
The Girl Who Fought to Kill
The Girl Who Broke Free
The Girl Who Knew Their Names
The Girl Who Never Forgot
www.TikiriHerath.com/RedHeeledRebels

Tikiri's novels and nonfiction books are available in e-book, paperback, and hardback editions, on all good bookstores around the world. These books are also available in libraries everywhere. Just ask your friendly local librarian or your local bookstore to order a copy for you.
www.TikiriHerath.com
Happy reading.

A Surprise For You

Dear reader friend,

Thank you for picking up my book.

I write mystery thrillers that feature feisty female detectives who hunt villains and make them pay. In my books, justice always prevails.

My stories are for smart readers who love pulse-pounding thrills and nail-biting twists. There is no explicit sex, graphic violence, or heavy cursing in my books, and no dog is ever harmed.

I'm not a marketing company or a branding firm that employs ghost writers or artificial engines. I don't hide behind a pen name or a fake avatar. I write my own books.

I'm also a reader, just like you, and I'm delighted to meet you. **Since you picked up this book, I have a gift for you!**

HER DEADLY END is a twisty thriller about a devious serial killer stalking a small seaside town in Washington State, USA. It features the private detectives, Asha Kade & Katy McCafferty, you'll read about here. But the main characters in that book are their friend, Special Agent Tanya (Tetyana) & Max, her adorable German Shepherd K9.

The link to this exclusive gift is at the end of this book. I dare you to guess who the villain is.

Enjoy this read and the gift.

Best wishes,

Tikiri

Vancouver, Canada

PS/ My books use American spelling because most of my readers live in North America. But I'm a Canadian who went to international schools all over the world, so I write in mostly British English. (I know. I'm a mixed up gal.) As soon as I finish writing a book, I run a US English spell checker, and after that, my wonderful (American) editor double checks any remaining errors. But words are insidious. And sneaky.

If you see a funny-looking word, please report it. Rest assured, they will be given a sound talk to and banished from my books.

There is no explicit sex, heavy cursing, or graphic violence in my books. There is, however, a closed circle of suspects, twists and turns, and nail-biting suspense.

NO DOG IS EVER HARMED IN THESE BOOKS. But the villains always are.

Tropes you'll find in this murder mystery thriller series: female protagonists, women sleuths, private investigators, small town, crime, murder, missing, kidnapping, dark secrets, creepy cabins, revenge, vengeance, vigilante justice, family life, lies, psychological suspense, twists and turns, intrigue, and thriller mysteries.

Merciless Legacy

A Manor of Secrets. A Killer on the Loose. A Detective Trapped.

In the heart of the White Mountains, a chilling secret lies within the walls of an old-money manor.

Asha Kade, a fierce private detective with a haunted past, is drawn into a web of deception and danger by a cryptic deathbed wish.

"Find my children and tell them I did it for love."

As a merciless storm isolates the mansion from the outside world, a brutal murder shatters the silence. The killer is lurking among them, picking off the family members one by one.
Asha, marked next on the killer's list, must unravel the family's dark past to expose the truth.
But time is running out.
With every tick of the clock, the killer draws closer.
Can Asha unmask the murderer before they strike again? Or will she be the next victim?
Trust no one. Fear everything. The hunt is on.

The Anonymous Letter

"If you tell anyone what you saw that day, I will cut your throat while you're sleeping and leave you to bleed to death. Don't ever think I can't do it."

Chapter One

"Watch out!" shouted Tetyana.

I swerved the car and struggled to straighten the vehicle. I glanced at my rearview mirror, my heart pounding.

"What was that?" I asked.

"A pothole the size of Mexico," replied my friend, who was sitting in the passenger seat next to me. "Slow down, Asha. We're not in a NASCAR rally."

"We're running late. We have to get there by five thirty."

I peeked through the windshield.

There was still some afternoon light left.

New Hampshire's magnificent White Mountains gazed down at us, their peaks glistening against the setting sun on the distant horizon. This was a beautiful place. But I couldn't help but feel those mountains were warning me.

This was dangerous terrain.

We wouldn't want to get lost here.

Or get stuck.

In the dark.

"At this rate, we'll never get there," grumbled Tetyana. "Should have rented an all-wheel drive."

"We're driving in style," piped Katy from the back, pushing her head in between the front seats. "They don't even make these cars anymore."

"Give me function over form any day," said Tetyana gruffly.

I had to agree.

The back of this vehicle was so small, Katy's tall and curvaceous frame and fiery red hair obscured my view through the back window. I knew we shouldn't have asked her to choose our ride.

When we arrived at the airport rental company, and she'd squealed with delight to see this retro machine designed like a 1930s gangster getaway car, I hadn't had the heart to say no to my BFF.

But now, as I navigated this unpaved road through this unfamiliar mountain pass at dusk, I wondered if we'd made a big mistake.

"Everyone will know we're out-of-towners," Tetyana groused.

"What's your problem?" said Katy.

"The official vehicle in this state is a super-duty truck with a gun rack in the back."

"Do you know what I think—"

"We're in horse country, that's for sure," I said, trying to deflect the argument brewing between my two best friends. "Breathe that fresh air in, will you? It's good for your health."

I turned to them and grinned.

"We made it, girls. Finally. From New York to Twin Mountain. From Twin Mountain to Falcon Hills. We're almost there."

"How long before we get to Cedar Cottage?" asked Katy. "It's getting a bit dark, isn't it?"

Tetyana looked down at her phone. "We're already on the estate grounds," she said, zooming in on the GPS map.

"I saw a *Private* sign when we turned from the main road about five minutes ago," I said.

"My GPS says ETA in fifteen minutes."

"Sit back and relax," I said, looking at Katy through my rearview mirror, "and enjoy the view."

"It's stunning here. I'll give you that," she said, leaning back in her seat with a sigh.

"You needed the break, hun," I said.

Katy's life had turned upside-down recently. I knew she hadn't been sleeping well for weeks, so it was good to see her smile again.

"Plus, you only turn thirty once. We need to celebrate."

"That was three days ago."

"It's your birthday *week*, girlfriend."

Katy finally cracked a smile.

"These mountains remind me of home," said Tetyana, gazing out her window. She sounded wistful, unusual for her.

"Ukraine, you mean?" I asked.

She nodded.

"My brother and I used to ride our horses to the glacier streams every Sunday. We even caught a few fish for supper." She paused and her voice dropped several octaves. "At least, we used to, until the Russians came."

The car fell silent.

Tetyana hadn't just lost a brother to the brutal Russian militia, but her mother, too.

"Why don't we go on a mountain hike this weekend?" I said, hoping to distract her from her dark memories. "Maybe they have a riding stable at the estate. Our job shouldn't take that long. It's not like we're trying to catch child traffickers this time."

"Don't speak too fast," replied Tetyana, her voice somber. "I have a feeling this assignment of yours is bigger than you think."

Tetyana always looked at the harsher side of life. Given her past, I didn't blame her. Katy and I hadn't escaped our childhoods unscathed either, but we were more optimistic.

It was overkill to bring along a former rebel-soldier-turned-weapons-trainer for this simple job. But David, my fiancé, who had his own top-secret military past, almost had a panic attack when I told him I would solve this case of poison pen letters all by myself. And drive up to a mysterious mansion in the woods in another state, all by myself.

I'm a grown woman, for goodness' sake, I told him, but he only relaxed after Tetyana promised to accompany me and Katy.

The more I drove into the heart of this remote mountain region, the more I was glad she was sitting next to me with her subcompact Glock on her belt.

I didn't realize it then, but it would come in handy soon.

Chapter Two

"I bet you a hundred bucks this is all about rich folk fighting with each other," said Tetyana.

"I think it's a jealous ex-lover," said Katy, poking her head in between the seats again. "Blackmail. Gossip. Small-town families with small-town problems. That's what we're going to find at Cedar Cottage."

"She sounded terrified," I said, recalling the telephone call I'd got from a Mrs. Robinson only three days ago.

"Death threats are never fun," said Tetyana. "What I can't figure out is how she got your number. People call you for cakes and crumpets, not crime."

"Remember the nasty call we got the other day?" piped up Katy from the back. "This is probably just another prank like that."

I swallowed something bitter.

A stranger had called my bakery in Harlem seven days ago. Rosalie, one of the sous chefs, had picked up the phone thinking it was a regular client, but then came the heavy-breathing.

Rosalie had caught a few words just before the anonymous caller had hung up abruptly.

I found you. I know who you all are.

But Rosalie hadn't been sure she had heard it right. Had it been a prank? Or had someone from our past resurfaced in New York?

If so, who were they and what did they want? Was there a connection between that weird call and this case?

I shook my head to clear it.

I was over-thinking again. That call had to be a stupid gag made by a bored kid from their mother's basement. I had more important matters to attend to.

I turned my attention back to the case at hand.

Something nagged at the back of my mind. Mrs. Robinson had called me exactly forty-eight hours after Madame Bouchard's death. I knew there was a connection between these two women.

"Madame Bouchard's playing with us from the grave," I said. "Some days I wonder if she's really dead. Remember, no one was invited to her funeral?"

"A sham burial?" said Katy. "That sounds expensive."

"If anyone had the means to do it, it was her."

None of us had been fond of this woman who'd played games with us for years. She'd known we were refugees escaping haunted pasts. She'd known we had nowhere to go and no one to turn to, except for each other.

And she'd taken full advantage of that.

Even if Madame Bouchard had had good intentions, she'd tricked us, never letting on about her true motivations. Now she was finally dead, taking her secrets with her.

But even with her dying breath, she'd summoned me over and played me like a puppet.

I'd made two promises at her deathbed.

The first was to step up to anyone who called us at my New York bakery asking for help. For every problem we resolved, for every cold case we cleared, her lawyer would deposit a million dollars in the bank account of our foundation for trafficked orphans.

There was a glint in her dying eyes when she told me this.

She knew I'd have helped anyone who truly needed it for free. We all would have. Yet, it was hard to say no to a million-dollar donation. So, I agreed, though I knew everything she gave came at a price. I just didn't know what it was yet.

Her second dying wish had been even more ominous.

"Find my children and tell them I did it because I loved them," she'd whispered.

I had wanted to ask her what she meant, but she'd turned away and closed her eyes. Her breaths became raspy and shallow. The cancer in her bone marrow was winning. This wasn't the time for questions.

Within seconds, the hand that had clutched my arm slackened and her nurse ushered me out the door.

"I don't care if Madame Bouchard's alive somewhere, if she's cryogenically frozen and her lawyer's pulling all the strings," said Tetyana, "I'll do whatever it takes for a million dollars for our orphanages. Better for the kids."

"Me too," said Katy. "Where can you get that amount of charity money anymore? All we have to do is stop someone from getting hate mail? Count me in, Miss Marple."

I had to agree, but that nagging feeling refused to leave me.

When my found-family arrived on the shores of America ten years ago, we'd been overjoyed at the chance of starting a fresh new life. It felt good to leave our dark pasts behind.

We'd set up an upscale bakery in the now gentrified Harlem. We'd opened orphanages to help those who were going through what we'd suffered in our messed-up youths.

I had a good crew at my shop. Luc, my head baker, apprenticed under me for a decade and could now take over the job at a moment's notice. Bibi, Sarah, and Rosalie kept the place in top shape, which garnered five-star reviews from our discerning clients.

Win, our computer genius and Luc's bride, now worked for the largest cyber security company in the city. Peace was about to make partner at a prestigious New York law firm. And David ran a popular martial arts dojo next door to the bakery with Tetyana as his head instructor.

Without this family of mine, I'd never have survived the traffickers who'd hounded us through our childhood.

Things were finally settling in.

Things were looking up.

But life had a funny way of turning upside down when you least expected it.

If I'd learned anything from my nomadic life, first in Africa, next in Asia, and then in Europe, it was to take nothing for granted.

"It's hard to see the downside," I said. "We get paid handsomely to solve problems for wealthy folk. Before the year ends, we can open an orphanage in every state—"

"Hey, slow down," said Tetyana, her voice urgent.

I took my foot off the accelerator and peered through the windshield. Tetyana was leaning forward, eyes trained on something on the road in front of us.

"What is it?" I said.

"Stop the car!" she yelled.

But it was too late.

A loud thump under my tires told me everything. I clutched the steering wheel firmly as the car shuddered and fishtailed from side to side.

"What's going on?" cried Katy.

"I hit something!"

I was losing control.

Fast.

"Brakes!" said Tetyana, grabbing the wheel.

I pumped the brakes and came to a screeching stop.

"What the heck was that?" I said, craning my neck to check the road behind me, my heart pounding.

"Felt like we drove over a dead body," said Katy.

Tetyana jumped out of the car.

With an exasperated sigh, I got out and joined her. She was bent over the back tire, her fingers brushing against the shredded rubber.

"My goodness," I said. "What did that?"

"This is useless now," she replied, shaking her head.

I glanced behind me to see what I'd driven over. But there was nothing. I squatted to see if anything had caught on the undercarriage.

Nothing.

Strange.

I was sure I hadn't imagined that loud thud and bump. I certainly didn't imagine the shredded tire.

"I swear I had my eyes on the road," I said. "I saw nothing."

But Tetyana was already opening the trunk to haul out the spare. She rolled the extra tire toward the back of the car.

"Let's fix this thing and figure out what happened later," she said as she leaned the tire against the side panel and wiped her hands. "We're already running late."

The back door opened and Katy jumped out. She joined me as I watched Tetyana jack up the car, standing by to help her. Katy looked over her shoulder and nudged me.

"It's a little creepy out here, now the sun's going down, don't you think?"

I swiveled my head. Dusk was settling around us, giving the woods a menacing and mysterious tinge.

When we'd landed at the tiny airport in the nearby town, I'd thought we'd have a little mountain vacation after we finished our job. But now, stuck on this desolate road in the heart of a pine forest, this place didn't feel like a tourist destination anymore.

In the dusky distance, the White Mountains looked like they were frowning at me in disapproval for getting the flat.

"This was a professional job," said Tetyana, not looking up.

Katy and I exchanged alarmed looks.

Tetyana wasn't one to make petty statements or run her mouth. But when she spoke, I paid attention.

"Who would do something like that?" I said. "Out here, of all places?"

Without answering, she got up and walked down the road we came on. Katy and I followed, wondering what she was up to.

She stopped when she got to five yards from our car and kneeled to scrutinize the ground.

I peered at the dirt, looking for clues, but saw nothing. Then again, my vocation was baking for high society, not tracking "professional jobs." That was Tetyana and David's department.

With a shake of her head, Tetyana turned back to the car.

"I'll finish the wheel. Give me ten minutes, would you?"

I nodded, my mind wandering back to Mrs. Robinson. I hated being late for appointments. I couldn't mess up my first million-dollar call.

"Wow. That's beautiful."

I spun around to see Katy staring at a maple tree whose leaves had turned to warm golds and reds.

Fall was already on its way.

From somewhere deep in the woods, I could hear rushing water. There must be a river or a large stream nearby.

"Gorgeous, aren't they?" said Katy, pulling out her phone.

She stepped closer to the roadside ditch and picked an Instagram-worthy red leaf from the ground and snapped a picture. Before I could reply, she jumped over the ditch to take another photo of another leaf.

Then another.

I was about to tell her to come back and get in the car when I saw it.

There was a shadow among the trees.

Chapter Three

"Katy?" I whispered.

But she didn't hear me, her focus on getting the perfect picture of that red maple leaf.

The shadow was moving away from her now, heading deeper into the woods. I wondered if they'd spotted us.

I glanced behind me.

Tetyana was by the car, head down, busy with the tire. Katy and I were several yards away, along the side of the road where the tree line began.

The shadow kept moving, slowly but surefooted, with their back to us. It was like they knew their way. Suddenly, the silhouette started waving at someone in front of them.

I jumped over the ditch and stepped up to Katy.

"Hey," I whispered, pulling on her shoulder. "Do you see that?"

She didn't look up, her fingers trying to zoom in on the image.

I shook her lightly. She swiveled her head around to give me an annoyed look.

"What?"

"There's someone in the woods," I whispered.

"What?"

I looked up, but the shadow had disappeared.

"I swear I saw someone about fifty feet from us."

"Are you sure?"

I peered through the trees, wondering if the twilight was playing with my eyesight. I was about to shrug and return to the car, when the shadow appeared again, farther away.

This time, there were two silhouettes.

"Oh, my goodness," whispered Katy as she spotted them, too.

The shadows were standing in a small clearing in the woods. One was small, a woman with her hair tied back into a long ponytail. The second was tall and gangly, and slightly hunched, possibly an older male.

We watched in silence.

"What are they doing out here in the middle of nowhere?" whispered Katy.

The two silhouettes were so absorbed in their conversation, they didn't notice us watching from afar. One jabbed a finger at the other. The other leaned in and said something. It didn't look like a cheerful conversation.

Snippets of their heated voices faded in and out with the wind, but we couldn't make out the words.

"Looks like a fight," said Katy.

Without any warning, the smaller figure pulled something from their pocket and pointed it at the bigger figure. The man jumped back.

Katy clutched my arm. "Is that a knife?"

We watched in shock as the small figure jabbed the pointy thing at the bigger person, who threw his arms up to protect his face. He looked like he was imploring her to stop.

I spun around to see where Tetyana was. She was now on her back, checking something under the car.

I turned back to the sparring couple in the woods. If that was a knife, this would not end well.

I had to do something. I couldn't just watch in silence.

At only five feet with my heels on and with my petite Asian frame, most people underestimated me. But after ten years of Krav Maga, I'd finally got my black belt. David and Tetyana had trained us well.

Even if I didn't have my trusty Glock on me, I knew how to fight a good fight.

But before I could do anything, the smaller figure jumped forward and stabbed the man in the face. The man let out a surprised yell and covered his cheek.

My instincts propelled me forward without me even realizing it.

"Hey!" I shouted, leaping over a dead branch and rushing toward them. "Stop that!"

The two figures jumped back, startled to hear my yell.

As I ran through the woods, they whirled around and dashed off in opposite directions, crashing through the underbrush.

"Hey!" I yelled. "Get back here!"

"Asha!"

I stopped and spun around to see Katy running after me, dodging around the trees. "What are you doing?" she called out.

I turned to the clearing where the figures had been standing only seconds before. They'd disappeared into the thicket now. It was no use running after them.

I waited for Katy to catch up.

"There's something weird about this place," I said to my friend, gesturing for her to stay back. "I'm going to check it out."

"Be careful," she said.

"Watch my back, okay?"

I stepped up to the clearing, keeping my eyes and ears open for any peculiar sights or sounds. But there wasn't much to see now.

It was a small, natural opening that had formed among the densely populated trees. The ground was uneven and covered by fallen foliage. I stared at the tall pine trees huddled around the clearing. They stood silent and stiff, like they were hiding a secret from me.

A rustle in the nearby bushes made me swivel around.

"Hello?" I called out. "Is anyone there?"

Another rustle.

"We can help you if you're hurt."

It was coming from my left. As soon as I took a step toward the tree line, I heard someone running, crashing through the woods.

"Hey!" I hollered. "Stop!"

I was about to dive after them when a familiar yell in the distance made me stop.

I whirled around.

"Tetyana!" said Katy.

"Over here," I shouted, waving. But she'd already seen us and was stomping toward the clearing.

Tetyana walked up, her gun in one hand, and an annoyed scowl on her face.

"What the heck do you guys think you're doing, taking off like that?"

I liked to think that when I hit thirty, I became older and wiser. But there were still days when, in the heat of the moment, I ran into the fire, rather than away from it.

"Hey, sorry," I said sheepishly, "didn't mean to alarm you."

"We saw two people arguing here," I explained. "One had a knife and I'm sure she stabbed the other guy."

Tetyana swiveled her head, scrutinizing the clearing.

"Where are they now?"

"Bolted like rabbits."

Katy jabbed me in the waist.

"Oh, my goodness, guys, do you see that?" she said.

"What?" Tetyana and I asked at the same time.

"Look over there," she said, pointing at something in the distance beyond the trees.

I followed Katy's finger to see what got her so excited.

"Wow," I said, as I spotted the white colonial mansion set on the mountain slope.

"It's beautiful," said Katy in awe.

"That must be Cedar Cottage," I said.

"*That's* Cedar Cottage?"

"It's the only house for miles around here," I said. "We could hike from here. Guess the road winds through the mountain pass, so it takes longer."

"That's no cottage," said Tetyana. "Someone was smoking when they named that place."

"It's so romantic," said Katy, "like a lost castle in the forest."

A strange sensation came over me as I stared at it. Something told me things weren't right there.

"It's an old-fashioned manor," I said, thinking it looked more creepy than dreamy, but I didn't want to burst Katy's vision.

"Now *that's* what I'd call a cottage."

I turned around to see Tetyana had stepped a few feet away and was peering through the tree branches at something else. Katy and I joined her.

A hundred yards from us, and nestled in between the trees, was a small blue shack. A deep gully separated us from the structure. It was the river I'd heard from the road.

"A hiker's cabin," I said, staring at it.

"It looks so lonely," whispered Katy.

Below us, the river rushed through the gully. My eyes followed it as it meandered its way through the woods, like a giant moat defending the mansion on the mountains from outsiders.

Thunder rumbled from far away. A storm was on its way. As we watched, the sky lit up with a brilliant flash of lightning.

We were going to get cold and wet, or dead at worst, if we didn't get back to our car soon.

Chapter Four

I took a step closer to get a better look when a warning hand came on my shoulder.

"The bank isn't stable," said Tetyana. "The mud is crumbling. A bad storm came this way recently."

I looked over at the cabin. "I was sure the man took off that way."

"How did he get across the gully?" asked Katy.

I swept my eyes around the riverbank. "There must be a bridge to the cabin, somewhere."

"This place is spooky," said Katy. "I prefer the big house on the mountain."

"I don't like the idea of a knife fight in the woods," said Tetyana. "Who knows what else they're armed with?"

"This isn't the Russian militia," I said. "They were two people having a domestic dispute or a neighborly spat of some sort. Granted, it got out of hand."

"Not our business," said Tetyana with a shake of her head. "You already have a job lined up at the house. Let's get to our destination. It's not a good idea to be running around at night without a spare—"

A loud bang from the road made us all jump.

I whirled around.

"Our car!"

"Sounded like a gunshot," said Katy, her eyes widened in shock.

"A vehicle backfiring," said Tetyana. "I locked ours up, but that doesn't sound good. Stay behind me."

Katy and I followed Tetyana as she threaded her way quietly around the trees.

I had no idea why we were being so cautious, but this place instinctively put me on guard. Even the normally logical Tetyana, it seemed, was feeling it.

When we got closer to the road, Katy and I stopped in our tracks and waited for a signal from our friend.

Tetyana stepped up to the edge of the woods, slid behind a large oak tree and peeked out. Then, to my surprise, she slipped her gun into her holster and zipped up her leather jacket.

She turned around and gestured for us to join her. Katy and I walked over, trying not to crunch the leaves under our feet.

As soon as I looked out on the road, I realized why Tetyana had been so quick to conceal her weapon.

A large black all-wheel drive was parked behind ours. Splashed on its side was a decal that read *Falcon Hills County Sheriff*. A lone police officer was standing next to our car, hands on his hips, a baffled look on his face.

There was no sign of an accident or him crashing into our parked car. It must have been his vehicle backfiring, we heard.

"What's a cop doing here?" whispered Katy.

"Routine ops?" said Tetyana, but I could hear the suspicion in her voice.

I turned to my friends.

"I'll handle this."

I stomped my feet on the spot to make walking noises before stepping out from behind the trees. The last thing I needed was to startle a local police officer.

"Hello, Officer," I said, emerging from the tree line, rustling up a smile.

He looked up and stared at me like I was an alien from another planet. From behind me, I heard Tetyana and Katy come out of the woods and flank me.

"What are you all doing out here?" he said. His hands were now on his utility belt, one dangerously close to his sidearm.

Next to me, Tetyana stiffened. I saw her hand hover near her jacket.

Tetyana was a dead ringer for Furiosa from *Mad Max* on a good day, and that could intimidate anyone. Even a cop. Especially a small-town cop.

In contrast, most people let their guard down around me. I hoped Tetyana knew this was the time for her to step back and let me do the talking.

"Got a flat tire," I said, walking up to our car. "It's the back one on the right. I think I hit the edge of a pothole a few yards back. They really need to fix this road."

The man took his cap off, scratched his head and put it back on again. With another suspicious glance my way, he bent down to examine the tire.

I stepped closer. The name tag on his jacket read *Jensen*.

I'm the type of person who brakes hard whenever I hear a siren in the distance, even when I'd been cruising at the speed limit. And right now, the scowl on his face said he wasn't about to entertain strangers.

"We just got the spare on, a few minutes ago," I said.

The man's frown deepened.

He was in his mid-twenties, at the most. If I had to guess, he was a rookie cop sent to police a small town in the middle of nowhere. He was possibly the only law enforcement for miles around.

But we had to be careful.

Though we were naturalized citizens now, our pasts would always cling to us like a bad smell. Between the three of us, we'd blown up buildings, killed thugs, and taken their money. But our actions had always been in self-defense, to save a life, to stop a rape, to rescue a child, or to set up an orphanage for the children they'd trafficked.

But that was a decade ago.

We were normal people now, living normal lives. Except that Madame Bouchard had sent us on a goose chase through the mountains of New Hampshire to solve a mystery we couldn't yet explain.

"What were you all doing in the woods?" the officer asked, squinting at me.

I hated lying to law enforcement unless absolutely necessary, but something about his face told me it would be best to stay quiet about what we saw in the woods.

I glanced back at Katy, who still had her phone in her hand. I smiled at her, hoping she'd catch my drift.

"My friend wanted to take pictures of those red maple leaves for Instagram. We thought we'd snap a few before it got too dark. This area isn't restricted or anything, is it? There weren't any signs, so we didn't think it was a problem."

The officer turned and squinted at Katy. She gave a start as she realized his attention was on her now, then promptly turned on her megawatt smile that could charm even the hardest of hearts.

"Would you like to see my pictures?" she said smiling and walking toward him, her phone held out.

She swiped through the photographs.

"Aren't these beautiful? Everyone's going to love them."

The cop peeked over her shoulder as she gushed over her own work.

While Katy kept the officer occupied, Tetyana took a few steps toward his squad car and peeked inside. I turned and peered into the woods to see if I could spot anyone among the trees again, but there was no one.

"See this one?" Katy was saying. "It's a real beauty, isn't it? Didn't know they could get blood red like this. Look at this gold color...."

The man's hands had dropped from his hips, his shoulders were relaxed, and his face had softened.

I sighed in relief.

"Where are you ladies from?" he asked.

I noticed the officer's tone was almost friendly now.

"New York," I replied. "We took a break from work to get some fresh mountain air. This is a mini vacation for us."

"Most people come to hike in the summer."

I looked at Katy and gave what I hoped was a rueful smile.

"One of us just went through a separation, so we thought some time away from the city would do us good."

"How do you ladies all know each other?"

"Best friends since college," I said. After what we'd gone through, we were more than friends. We were family—family who'd take a bullet for one another. But I didn't tell him that. "They work with me now."

"What do you do in the big city, ma'am?"

"I own a shop in Harlem. The Red Heeled Rebels bakery. We make wedding and birthday cakes and such."

He gave me an appreciative nod.

"I'm afraid there's not much for city ladies like you up this road though," he replied, taking his cap off and scratching his head again. "You must have taken a wrong turn."

"We're actually heading up that way."

"But it's just woods and an old house. Town's the other way. You want to turn around and head back."

"We just came from Falcon Hills, Officer. We're on our way to Cedar Cottage."

He jerked up, startled.

Something changed in his face. Was it a flash of fear or a flicker of surprise? Either way, he no longer looked friendly.

Chapter Five

"**F**rom what I know," said the officer, that hostile squint coming back on, "visitors aren't welcome at Cedar Cottage."

"We were invited," I said, keeping my smile intact. "They asked us to come over and stay a few days."

That was the truth. At least part of it.

I wondered if Mrs. Robinson had informed the police of her letters. She had asked me for complete discretion over the phone. Her tone of voice suggested I was the first and only person she'd shared this news with.

"Oh, yeah?" said the officer. "Strange that. These folks aren't much for visitors. Especially from out of town."

He glanced at each one of us, a frown on his face, his eyes settling on Tetyana for a second longer than on Katy and me. Then he looked up and sniffed the air thoughtfully.

"A nasty storm's coming this way. These roads aren't in great condition, as you've already found out. Not good to be out here at night. My recommendation is for you ladies to head back to town."

Why is he so keen for us not to go to the house?

There was a woman up there who called me for help. When I made a promise, I kept it. I would not abandon her now.

"There's a small motel in town," the officer was saying, "it's not that full this time of the year. Happy to escort you over there, if you'd like."

"We're big girls," said Katy in her sweetest voice, "we can take care of ourselves. Besides, Mrs. Robinson said she was going to make a lovely supper for us tonight."

The last bit wasn't true, but I kept my face straight.

"We even brought an apple pie from the bakery for dinner," she added.

With a defeatist shrug, the officer turned back to his car.

"Thanks for stopping by," I called out, "maybe we'll see you tomorrow when we come to town?"

With another shrug for an answer, the officer got in his car and turned around, and drove back the way he came, leaving us in a cloud of dust.

The three of us stared at each other.

"Okay," said Katy finally, "this place is so strange, even the cops are weird."

"Do you guys want to know what I saw?" said Tetyana in a low voice, looking more serious than she usually did.

"What?" asked Katy.

"He had a professional-grade spike belt kit sitting on his passenger seat."

"A professional-grade what?" I asked.

"Retractable spike belt. Works automatically with a touch of a button."

"What does it do?"

"Slashes tires fast and efficiently."

We stared at her.

"Easy to use," she explained. "Conceal yourself on the side of the road, push a button just as the vehicle rolls by, and bingo. The spikes do their job and retract to the box. Happens in seconds, you never know what hit you."

"You're not serious," I said, feeling my stomach sink.

"If that was deployed as it should have, all four tires would have got busted." Tetyana paused, frowning. "If, and it's a big if, he used it on us, it malfunctioned and retracted too soon. Or he jammed it real fast once he realized who we were."

"But I didn't see his car anywhere," said Katy. "Wouldn't we have noticed it on the road?"

Tetyana glanced around her.

"With an all-wheel drive, he could get over that ditch easily. This place is new to me, but I'm sure I'd be able to stake out a few good hiding spots for a car here."

"Why would a *police officer* do that?" I said. "Or do you think he wasn't a real cop?"

Tetyana didn't answer for a while. If anyone could spot a fake cop anywhere in the world, it had to be her.

"No," she said finally, "he was the real deal. If he wanted to use that on us, he was trying to dissuade us from going up to the house."

"That's a little drastic, isn't it?" said Katy. "Is it even legal?"

"Police departments use them all the time to catch fugitives on the run. It's a good way to stop terrorists too. David showed me how he used one in the Mossad once."

"Maybe he was out to catch speedsters?" said Katy.

"On this potholed, backcountry private road?" said Tetyana, raising an eyebrow.

"Wait," I said. "I was only ten over the limit. Besides, if I was speeding, why didn't he just stop me with his lights and siren, like a normal cop?"

"He didn't have to slash our tire." Katy nodded. "He could have asked us nicely."

"He did," said Tetyana, "repeatedly. But we didn't listen."

It was turning out to be a strange day. I looked down the road where the dust was still settling from the officer's car.

"This is all speculation," said Tetyana. "We could have rolled over a few bad nails. Highly unlikely, but I can check the tire more closely once we get to the house."

"Maybe he was truly worried about us getting stuck on this road with this dinky car," I said.

"I don't think so," said Katy. "I think there's some juicy stuff going on at Cedar Cottage, and this only makes me want to go there even more."

I couldn't agree more.

I just hoped the "juicy stuff" wasn't going to kill us.

Tetyana patted the telltale bulge under her leather jacket. "Ladies, let's all keep a sharp eye out from now on, shall we?"

We got inside the car, my mind still buzzing over what had happened. I turned the key. It was a relief to hear the engine purr. I double-checked the gas gauge to confirm what I knew already. We'd filled up in town, so we had plenty of fuel. Thank goodness for that.

It was almost completely dark now. The pine trees huddled along the sides of the road, looked like angry giant shadows. Scattered water droplets on my windshield told me the storm was on its way.

I turned on my high beams and rolled the car onto the road.

My GPS said Cedar Cottage was now only twelve minutes away.

I couldn't wait to get off this gloomy, desolate road.

29

Chapter Six

My GPS was wrong.

It took us half an hour to reach Cedar Cottage.

Maybe the satellites couldn't accurately pinpoint us among the mountains. Maybe it was the gusty thunderstorm brewing in the air that disturbed the data signals.

Either way, my driving slowed down considerably.

We were in unfamiliar territory in the dark, with one tire blown. We all kept a sharp eye out for potholes, potential roadkill, and suspicious debris. We weren't sure if anyone else was hidden along the roadside with another spike belt or worse.

"You'd think anyone who owns that big house could afford to fix this road," I said, as I swerved to avoid another rut on the gravel.

"Unless," said Katy, "like the cop said, they don't want too many people coming this way."

"We'll be arriving at a bridge in a few minutes," said Tetyana, consulting her phone's GPS. "That will take us to the estate's driveway. Hopefully, they paved that."

We drove on silently.

The road narrowed the closer we got to the house until there was space for only one vehicle on the path. I hoped to goodness no one would come barreling from the opposite direction. That would be a disaster.

There was something unusual up front. I slowed down even more.

"What is that?" asked Katy, pointing a finger through the seats.

I brought the car to a complete stop and peered through the darkness.

"The bridge," said Tetyana.

She was right.

Twenty feet in front of us was a dilapidated wooden structure that looked like it would be risky to walk on, let alone drive on.

Beyond the bridge was a paved driveway, and about two hundred yards farther down was the big white house we'd spotted from the woods.

"I've seen better goat crossings in Ukraine," said Tetyana.

"Is it going to hold us?" I wondered out loud.

"If we sink, we swim," said Tetyana.

"Oh, gosh," said Katy from behind us.

I pulled my window down and stuck my face out. A blustery wind blew my hair, making me shiver.

"Close the window," said Katy.

I pushed myself up to get a better look. "The river's rushing really fast," I said, plopping back in my seat. "The storm's almost here. It'll be nasty tonight."

Tetyana opened her door and got out. With our car's headlights to guide her, she walked over and examined the wooden bridge. Two minutes later, she turned and gave me a thumbs up.

"Looks worse than it is," she said, getting in and buckling up.

"There's a truck parked up there," she said, pointing at the house. "If that vehicle navigated over this, we should be fine."

Taking a deep breath in, I took my foot off the brake. Unsure if this would be the biggest mistake I made that day, I rolled forward.

"Please don't break," I heard Katy pray from behind me.

Cringing at every thud the tires made on the wooden ridges of the bridge, I pushed on. The sixty seconds it took us to cross the small structure felt like an eternity.

I didn't realize I'd been holding my breath until I heard the last frightening thud from the back tires, followed by the smooth paved driveway underneath us.

"We made it!" said Katy.

"Oh, come on," said Tetyana, blowing a raspberry. "A cold swim wouldn't have killed us."

"Would have totaled the car," I said.

"Then we'd find a more sensible truck to drive around in."

The driveway up to the house was long and wide and lit by a row of cast-iron streetlights. It felt like we were time traveling to the past.

"What a place to build a home," said Katy, her nose stuck to the window.

Mrs. Robinson had been very cryptic over the phone.

"Come to the end of the dirt road, cross the bridge and you'll see the house. Only house for miles around. You can't miss it."

She hadn't lied. But this wasn't just any house.

It was a massive three-story piece of architecture with green gable shutters and ivy-covered white walls. Four striking pillars stood on guard on the high porch. Two chimneys and a cupola rose proudly from the tiled roof, complete with a rooster weathervane.

Almost all the windows were dark, but a pale yellow light was coming from the first-floor windows.

I drove up the driveway and parked next to the flatbed pickup truck. Beside it was a rusty white van and an ancient pale blue Mercedes sedan. Whoever lived here had little taste for cars, I gathered.

I turned off the engine.

"Looks like we've walked into a period drama," said Katy in a hushed voice as we stared at the imposing building in front of us. "An American *Downton Abbey.*"

"It's so isolated," I said, "I'm sure it gets lonely up here."

Other than the wind blasting through the grounds, it was quiet. There was nobody outside. At least, that's what I thought at first.

I wished we had come earlier in the day so we could have seen the house and the mountain views behind it properly. With only the external security lights on the building and the cast-iron lampposts along the driveway, it was hard to make out much.

"Who lives here, other than this Mrs. Robinson?" asked Katy.

"When I called back for details, she said to come down and see for ourselves. Said she didn't want us to prejudge anyone." I paused. "You realize, she thinks she's hired a private investigator team?"

"But aren't we?" said Katy. "We've been solving cases for years now."

"I wouldn't call what we tackled *cases*," said Tetyana, her voice somber. "We fought those men, rescued those kids. We taught those bastards a good lesson. It was war."

Katy and I were silent for a moment. It was hard to hear our former life summarized in such brutal words. But she was telling the truth.

"Those days are over, girls," I said, patting the dashboard. "Everyone's safe in America and we've found normal lives."

"But you're getting restless," piped Katy from the backseat, "aren't you?"

I turned to look at my friend.

"What do you mean?"

"Admit it. You can bake for snotty rich folks for only so long before you go batty. You wanted to come on this adventure. That's why you agreed to Madame Bouchard's bizarro death wish in the first place."

I stared at her, letting those words wash over me. She was right, but did I want to admit it to myself?

Madame Bouchard didn't play simple games. The consequences of her actions were severe, at times a matter of life and death. I couldn't take her deathbed request lightly. It was both a morbid curiosity and the drive to honor my promise that had brought me here.

"You too, Tetyana," said Katy, turning to her next. "Don't deny it. I've known you two for too long for you to lie to me. We're here because you want action again."

Tetyana looked away.

But Katy wasn't done.

"Asha, this is exactly why you keep putting off your wedding. David wants nothing more than to get married, but you keep avoiding the topic."

Those words stung, but I knew they hurt because she was right. My best friend Katy knew me better than I did myself.

"Thanks for reminding me," I stammered, pulling my phone out. "I have to call him or he'll start getting worried."

While I texted David to let him know we got to our destination, Katy called her eight-year-old daughter who was spending the week with her father, Peace.

I'd just hit send when Tetyana pointed to something on the far end of the grounds.

"I thought I saw someone over there."

We peered out the window. There was a wooden structure a few yards away from the main house. In the distance, I thought I heard a horse neigh. The noise was muffled, like it came from inside the building.

"What is that? A barn?" I asked.

A light came on in the house. We all turned our attention back to it.

A woman's profile showed up against a window on the third floor. She pulled back the sheers, looked out for a moment and let the curtains fall back in place again, before withdrawing. Just as it had turned on, the light turned off.

Mrs. Robinson?

I had no idea what she even looked like.

Something told me it wasn't her, but then, who would it be?

"All right everyone," said Tetyana, her hand going to her door. "Are we going to sit here and ruminate all night or go in and talk to these people?"

I opened my door, gripping the handle tightly so the wind wouldn't slam it back on me.

"Just remember," said Tetyana before I got out. "I need to know where you are at all times. I'll be right behind you when you need me, okay?"

"Roger that," said Katy and I at the same time.

The sound of wind chimes clanging wildly came from somewhere. I wrapped my arms around myself as the icy wind swirled around me, nipping at my face.

There was a massive wooden double door at the front of the mansion. But on the east end of the house was a smaller single door. The windows near it were all lit up.

Someone was in there. I was sure of it.

Even from here, I could make out the copper pots hanging from the high ceiling.

The kitchen.

"This way," I said as I walked toward the side entrance.

The loose gravel under our feet crunched as we walked toward the door while the wind whipped the wind chimes into a frenzy. They clanged louder and louder, sounding like warning bells, telling us to get back in the car and head home.

I shook my head to clear it. I had a job to do.

Katy grabbed my arm as something small and furry scurried in front of us.

"What was that?" she gasped.

"A rodent," said Tetyana. "A big one."

"That was a cat," I said, eying the mangy stray animal scampering behind the truck to hide. "Looks sick. Poor thing."

We were at the kitchen door now.

The side door was discolored from being exposed to the elements and barely hung on its hinges. From up close, I could now see the house was badly in need of repair.

I looked up at the other floors, wondering what this place looked like in daylight. It appeared imposing in the dark and from afar, but maybe it wasn't in as good condition as I thought.

Katy pushed me aside.

"Let me," she whispered.

She lifted her hand to knock.

Her knuckles barely touched the wood when the door flew open.

Katy sprang back with a shriek, trampling on my feet and almost bowling me over.

Chapter Seven

A woman in her sixties stood on the threshold.

She was dressed in a shin-length skirt, a mauve shirt, and a small pearl necklace. Perched on her head was a pair of eyeglasses linked to a silver chain.

"Right on time," she said with a friendly smile.

I recognized that deep voice from the phone call.

Katy blushed. "I'm so sorry I screamed. I hadn't even knocked when the door...."

The woman waved dismissively.

"Come inside, girls," she said. "It's brisk outside tonight."

We trooped inside after her.

It was an open kitchen with high ceilings we'd walked into, one built decades ago, but that had never been renovated.

The vintage stove and curvy refrigerator were throwbacks from the sixties. The apple-green cabinets were peeling and the cherry-red kitchen stools were something I'd have expected at a retro diner, not in this massive mansion.

The only modern item in the kitchen was a designer knife block which sat on the counter near the sink. The distinctive blood-red-handled knives would stand out in any kitchen. I could swear I'd seen them in a late-night TV infomercial once. I'd even considered buying them for my bakery.

Now that we were inside the house, I could see this place needed work. A lot of work.

"How quaint," whispered Katy as we walked past the old Formica counter. Katy had spent twenty-five thousand dollars upgrading her New York apartment kitchen with the latest stainless-steel appliances and granite counters, so I knew that wasn't a compliment.

But I liked this place.

Though that sense of foreboding I'd felt when I first spotted this house from the woods below hadn't left me, this kitchen was comforting. It was like returning to a childhood home to meet family and have apple pie and tea.

An old wooden rocking chair sat in the corner next to a fireplace. I could imagine Mrs. Robinson sitting there, knitting a warm woolen scarf.

A large pot of stew was simmering on the stove, and the smell of a pie baking came from the antique oven. I loved food, and I loved cooking even more, so the sights and smells here instantly lifted my mood.

I looked at the woman leaning against the counter, regarding us curiously. Her face was kind and her eyes were sincere.

"Mrs. Robinson, I presume?" I asked with a smile.

"You must be Asha Kade," she replied, her wrinkled eyes looking intensely at me. "I knew you'd come. Madame Bouchard told me you always came when someone called for help."

"Madame Bouchard?" I resisted the urge to look at my friends. "You knew her?"

The woman's eyes wrinkled some more.

"Only too well, my dear."

"How?" I said, unable to hide my curiosity.

Mrs. Robinson raised an eyebrow.

"I thought you knew."

"Knew what?" The words flew out of my mouth before I could stop myself.

This was our first client. Our first case, which, if we solved it to Madame Bouchard's lawyer's satisfaction, would allow us to build another nursery at our children's shelter and foster home in New Orleans. I couldn't mess up our chance now.

I cleared my throat.

"My team has worked with Madame Bouchard for years and she has always been satisfied with our service." I hesitated, gauging how much I could share with this stranger.

"I wish she'd have given us more information, but as you know, she is no longer with us…" I let my sentence trail off, hoping she'd understand.

Mrs. Robinson nodded somberly.

"I was so sad to hear of her passing."

She glanced out the window, a faraway look coming over her face.

"I knew her since I was a teen. I looked up to her. She was like this beautiful princess who lived in this castle. I wanted to be like her. It broke my heart when she started traveling after she got married. She was hardly home anymore after that."

"Home?" I asked, unsure if I'd heard right. "Are you saying Madame Bouchard used to live here?"

Mrs. Robinson turned to me, as if she'd just realized we were standing in her kitchen.

"Yes, my dear. This is Madame Bouchard's childhood home."

It took a while before any of us could speak.

"Are you kidding me?" said Katy finally. "This is her *home*?"

Mrs. Robinson gave Katy a quizzical look, like she was sizing her up. Then she turned back to me.

"I see you didn't come alone."

"Sorry, these are my colleagues, Katy McCafferty and Tetyana Shevchenko."

She didn't move to shake their hands, but regarded them politely.

"Madame Bouchard was familiar with all my team members," I said. "We each bring unique skills to the job and we're looking forward to helping you out. I'm sorry if I didn't mention this earlier."

"It's so nice to meet you," said Katy with a bright smile. Tetyana gave her a grave nod.

Mrs. Robinson stared at Tetyana for a second longer than would be considered polite.

"Are you a cop?"

Her tone was accusatory, but Tetyana merely shook her head.

"Never have been and never will be. I'm just here to help Asha."

That seemed to satisfy Mrs. Robinson. Katy flashed her another one of her million-dollar smiles.

"Mrs. Robinson, I can't wait to solve these mystery letters you've—"

"Hush!"

"Sorry," said Katy, giving her a sheepish look.

Mrs. Robinson stirred and straightened up.

"No, I'm sorry," she said, "I'm usually a better hostess than this, but this affair... it has made me all jittery." She sighed. "You all must have had a long trip. Would you like some ice tea with a slice of pumpkin pie? I just baked it."

I turned to my friends. Mrs. Robinson didn't realize what a bombshell she'd dropped on us when she told us we were standing in Madame Bouchard's childhood home. I knew Katy and Tetyana were burning with curiosity as much as I was.

"Actually, we'd like to ask you a few questions if this is a good time," I said. "Would that be all right?"

Mrs. Robinson glanced behind her and turned to us with a worried expression on her face.

"Not here. Come with me."

With another apprehensive glance behind her, she took me by the elbow and steered me through the kitchen, with my friends coming behind me.

A cold gust of air hit us as we stepped out of the kitchen through a side door and entered an empty hallway.

It was like we'd stepped back in time to the nineteenth century.

The passageway floor was made of stone and ancient wooden beams crisscrossed the ceiling. There were small wooden doors along the hallway, and I wouldn't have been surprised if a woman in a white bonnet and a long crinoline gown had stepped out with a candlestick in her hands.

"Is anyone else home?" I asked as we walked through the passageway, going deeper into the belly of this mansion.

"Everyone's home," replied Mrs. Robinson. "They always are. No one ever leaves this place."

No one ever leaves this place?

"Madame Bouchard traveled a lot with her diplomatic husband," I said. "She had apartments in New York, Paris, and London. I didn't realize she owned a home in New Hampshire."

"Ah, that one was different from everyone else. She enjoyed the high life. Didn't think much of us."

"But she wanted me to help you with your, er, problem."

"Guilt."

"Guilt?"

She stopped so suddenly, I jerked back. She put a hand on my arm and leaned in close, her dark brown eyes boring into mine.

"As much as I admired that woman, I can guarantee you she died with many regrets in that stony heart of hers. Do you know how much she neglected her own flesh and blood?"

I shook my head, feeling a chill at those words.

Without explaining herself any further, she let go of my arm and started walking again.

After throwing a surprised glance at my friends, I turned around and caught up to Mrs. Robinson. We kept walking through the hallway, not speaking.

"Are we the only guests here tonight?" asked Katy hesitantly, after a while.

"The pastor's staying overnight. He comes every weekend."

"Who else lives here?" I asked.

"You'll see soon."

"Does everyone know we're coming?"

"Not a soul. I want them to be surprised."

With that, she opened the door at the bottom of the corridor and ushered us into a spacious but cold room.

"Come in and close that door. We can talk in here."

I looked around.

An old-fashioned brass bed had been placed in the middle of the room, surrounded by neatly arranged vintage furniture. A bookshelf lined one wall. Displayed in it were trinkets from a bygone era between old tomes. Everything here was spotless. Not one speck of dust had escaped Mrs. Robinson's keen eyes.

As soon as Tetyana closed the door behind her, Mrs. Robinson clutched at her chest and started wheezing.

I stepped forward.

"Are you okay, Mrs. Robinson?"

She stood in place for a minute, gasping for breath. Then she straightened up and gave us a rueful smile.

"This is what happens when you become a senior citizen. Aches and pains everywhere."

"Would you like some water?" I ventured, seeing how pale her face had become.

She shook her head.

"I got another letter last night," she whispered hoarsely. "Do you want to see it?"

"Please."

She reached into a pocket in her skirts and brought out a small beige envelope.

I stared at this thing that had terrified this woman for weeks. This thing that had brought us up here.

"Why didn't you share this with the police?" I asked what had been troubling me all along. "They could have searched for fingerprints and done something about it."

"They won't believe an old woman like me."

She paused.

"Besides, I can't trust anyone anymore."

Chapter Eight

I dug out a pair of gloves from my purse, put them on, and took the envelope from Mrs. Robinson.

Katy was peering over my shoulder while Tetyana was standing by the door, on guard.

I opened the envelope. Inside was a thin beige piece of paper, the kind you'd find at a high-end stationery store.

"Mrs. Robinson, do you know anyone in this house who uses paper like this?"

She shook her head.

"I've been cleaning this house for many years, so I pretty much know what everyone has in their drawers and cupboards. It's hard to hide anything from me, but whoever sent this is doing a good job."

I opened the letter gently, trying not to crease the paper, and stared at the words inked in blood red.

If you tell anyone what you saw that day, I will cut your throat while you're sleeping and leave you to bleed to death. Don't ever think I can't do it.

A chill went down my spine as I read it.

"That's horrible," said Katy. "So nasty."

I peered at the letter. Even in the dim light, I could see the specks of powder on the paper.

"What's this?" I said, shaking the letter. A few flecks of white powder fell on the floor.

Mrs. Robinson shrugged.

"A sick joke," she said. "They put baby powder inside."

Tetyana shifted at her station.

"Put it away," she said, a note of warning in her voice. "Don't touch it."

I folded the letter and slipped it back into its envelope. I was about to put it in my purse when Mrs. Robinson reached over and yanked it from my hand.

"We could get it tested for you," I said.

"I'll keep it for now," she said, sticking the envelope back in her pocket. "Don't want these things floating around. That's how vicious rumors start. It's bad enough getting these letters."

I stared at her, but her face said she'd made up her mind. I had to change tactic.

"When did you get this letter?" I asked.

"Three nights ago."

"Where did you find it?"

"Where I always do. Under my bedroom door. They come between two and four in the morning. On different days, so I never know when."

I glanced over at the sturdy wooden door where Tetyana was standing.

"Do you have a video, intercom, or a peephole to see who's on the other side?"

Mrs. Robinson gave me a look.

"This house was built a hundred years ago, my dear. There weren't no intercoms and such back then."

"Who do you suspect it is?" asked Katy.

"It could be anyone."

I raised an eyebrow.

"Anyone?"

Mrs. Robinson was the type of grandmother anyone would want to have, the one who loved to feed strangers pumpkin pie with ice tea. Then again, looks could be deceiving. I'd seen my share of evil on earth, and sometimes it was those I least suspected who surprised me.

"Does anyone in this house have a vendetta against you?" I said, softening my voice. "Was there anything you did in the past that made someone angry at you?"

She looked away.

We waited.

I wondered what was going through her mind. Was it fear that was stopping her, or was she too embarrassed about something she'd rather not share?

Near the door, Tetyana shifted impatiently.

Tetyana was a woman of action and hated these long, drawn-out conversations. If she had her way, she'd line up everyone in the house against the wall, put a gun against their heads, and ask them point-blank if they were harassing their caretaker.

I was glad I was in charge.

It took a while for Mrs. Robinson to talk again. When she did, it was in such a low voice, I had to lean in to hear.

"This house has many secrets."

"Like what?" I asked.

"Ever since I came here, I knew no one was who they said they were."

"Can you tell us who lives here?"

She raised her head and gave me a surprised look.

"Why, Madame Bouchard's family, of course."

I wanted to shake her by the shoulders for speaking in riddles, but I knew better than to rush her.

"Yes, but exactly who?" said Katy, a hint of irritation in her voice. "Her children? Siblings? Cousins?"

"I thought you knew her well."

Katy and I exchanged a glance.

I'd never seen Madame Bouchard without her pristine white Chanel suit, shiny pearls, and gray hair swirled on the top of her head. I always thought of her as a septuagenarian supermodel.

That woman had power, and she knew how to wield it.

Her friendship circle included the most prominent people in the world. From royalty to celebrities, from politicians to business moguls, she had them all in her pocket. She'd been the matriarch of the international diplomatic community.

But no one had known about her family.

"I don't think anyone knew Madame Bouchard well," said Katy. "She liked to keep her private life private."

"I always thought she was Canadian," I said, remembering my first encounter with her in Toronto.

"She is," said Mrs. Robinson. "Through her husband. But her own family is from New Hampshire."

"Okay, let's start with her children," I said, recalling Madame Bouchard's last words at her deathbed.

Find my children and tell them I did it because I loved them.

I was getting a funny feeling about this case. It wasn't just Mrs. Robinson asking for our help. This had Madame Bouchard's name written all over it.

"How many children did she have?" I asked.

"One son and one daughter."

"They must be middle-aged now?"

"Barry, the son, is forty-three this year and Lisa is forty-six. I grew up with them. My mama was the caretaker of this house before me. They treated us well, so when she passed away, I took over."

"Did you work closely with Madame Bouchard?" I asked.

"She took off to college at nineteen. That's where she met her husband from Canada. After that, she only came home to have her babies."

"She never lived here after she got married?" asked Katy.

"Madame Bouchard was relieved when my mother and I took over the housekeeping and childcare. She wanted nothing to do with household stuff."

"And Mister Bouchard? What was he like?" I asked.

"He hardly came here. I think he hated it here. Always traveling. At fancy parties in Europe and Washington DC. He only came here for a few Christmases." She paused. "Poor man. He was only thirty-six when he died."

I nodded. I'd seen the old news clippings of the promising young diplomat dying of a heart attack. It had been a shock to the diplomatic community then.

"What are they like, their son and daughter?" I asked.

Mrs. Robinson looked out the window, her face pensive.

"When you grow up in a faraway place like this with only the mountains for company, it's hard to grow up normal." She turned to give me a piercing look. "Do you know what I mean?"

I shook my head.

"School was a private tutor and a brown paper envelope that came via mail once a week," she continued. "They never had other kids to play with. That makes you... a different kind of child."

"Different? How?"

"You'll find out when you see them tonight."

I raised my eyebrows and exchanged a quick glance with Katy. I guessed we were in for an interesting evening.

"Does the rest of the family sleep on this floor?" I asked.

"They all have rooms on the third floor."

"But you sleep down here?"

She shrugged. "I like it here. This has always been my room ever since I was a girl. I grew up here."

"How long have you lived in this house?"

"Most of my life. So many years I've lost count."

"How did you come about staying here?"

Mrs. Robinson let out a sigh and looked down at her feet.

"My mother brought me here when I was fifteen. Her boyfriend... my father... treated her badly. He liked to rough her up. I remember those days."

She shivered as if she could still feel the pain.

"It got so bad one day, she bundled me in the car and said 'baby, we're going somewhere safe.' Then, we drove north. That's all I knew. Just the two of us, like Thelma and Louise. We drove for so many days, I was sure we were going to end up in Santa Claus's house in the North Pole."

"You came to Cedar Cottage instead?" I said, keeping my voice soft.

"We slept in the car but we were running out of gas and money. There was a bad storm one night and I remember us getting lost and scared. So we drove up to this big house and asked to stay the night. I was surprised they let us in here. I mean, the only home I'd known back then was the projects...."

Mrs. Robinson paused to wipe her eyes.

"Wow," said Katy in a hushed tone. "What a story."

Mrs. Robinson looked up and smiled at her.

"It was Madame Bouchard who said my mother and I could stay. She was just a teen then, ready to go to college, but she was already bossing everyone around, you know what I mean?"

I nodded. That much I knew very well.

"So my mama and I stayed. We never left."

She looked out the window, even though everything outside was bathed in midnight black now.

"I grew up on these mountains."

She turned back to Katy and me.

"Mama's bruises disappeared, and I didn't have to wake up every night and listen to her cry anymore."

I put a hand out and touched Mrs. Robinson's arm. I had no words, but I wanted her to know she wasn't alone.

We'd all seen violence in our lives. We'd seen things worse than an abusive father, but I knew it hurt even more when it was someone who was supposed to care for you. Someone who was supposed to love you.

"I'm fine now, my dear," she said, giving me a genial smile. "I don't know why I'm telling you girls these stories from so long ago. You all have friendly faces. Maybe that's why. These letters have nothing to do with my past."

I raised an eyebrow.

Don't be too hasty to come to that conclusion.

"My mother lived a long and happy life. She worked hard, and she liked it here. Everything I know, I learned from her. Rest her soul."

"What about you, Mrs. Robinson?" asked Katy. "Did you ever marry?"

"My husband was a farmhand from town. We were together for eighteen years, but he died in an accident twenty years ago. I never could have children, so that just left me here."

"This is a beautiful place to call home," I said.

"As long as I do my work, no one complains. I get my space. I hardly see anyone except at mealtimes. Some may say it's lonely up here, but I like it quiet."

"What about that cabin in the woods?" asked Katy.

Mrs. Robinson turned to her with a start.

"The cabin?"

Chapter Nine

"The, er, shack in the woods," Katy said. "A small cottage-like building, near the river. Does it belong to this estate?"

Mrs. Robinson's face turned slightly dark.

"What were you girls doing out in the woods?"

There was something about that cabin she didn't want us to know.

"Our tire blew on a pothole and we stopped to change it," said Katy. "I slipped into the woods to take some pictures of the leaves when I saw it...."

"Saw what?"

Mrs. Robinson's change in tone was so sharp, Tetyana glared.

"We didn't go in," said Katy, putting her hands up defensively, "but it looked like a cute little place. I just wondered who lives there."

"No one," snapped Mrs. Robinson. "It's for lost hikers."

"Is anyone staying there right now?" I asked.

"No."

Mrs. Robinson's sudden shift in demeanor was a surprise. I had started to warm up to her, but the more we spoke, the more I felt she was hiding something from us. Something big.

"Mrs. Robinson," I said, "if you want our help, you have to tell us everything."

"I'm telling you everything I know." But she wasn't making eye contact anymore.

"Is there anyone else who lives here, other than the son and the daughter?"

"Lisa hired a new couple last year because Sally and John left so suddenly. They have rooms on the third floor as well."

"Who are Sally and John?"

"They worked with me for years."

Mrs. Robinson looked up. She was back to her normal self again.

"Sally cooked and John took care of the grounds. Such a delightful couple. They were part of my housekeeping team. Then, suddenly, without saying goodbye, they got up and left. When I went up to see their room, it was cleaned out."

"Wow," said Katy. "Why would they leave like that?"

"I have no idea. It broke my heart. I thought of them as family."

"Did you know them well?"

Mrs. Robinson wiped her face. She looked tired.

"You think you know someone, until you don't, right?" she said.

You can say that again.

"And this new couple?" I asked. "Who are they?"

"It was the pastor who suggested Jim and Nancy come and help me with the house. I'm getting old and my bones have started to creak, so I was happy to have them. They seem nice enough, but they keep to themselves."

"How long have they been here?"

"Since July."

"You mentioned this pastor stays here every weekend," I said. "Doesn't he have his own home in Falcon Hills?"

"He does. He used to come all the time when Lisa and Barry were young. He was their private tutor, you see. He was just starting to teach back then. But recently, he started coming every weekend." She paused for a moment. "Since Jim and Nancy moved in, come to think of it. He calls this place his retreat. Says he can think more clearly up in the mountains. Lisa and Barry don't seem to mind."

"A bit unusual, don't you think?"

"The pastor's been close to this family for years. He comes from a very prominent family in the area. They've been in this town for generations. Falcon Hill's blue blood, you know. Everyone respects them."

"What's Barry like?" I said, more curious about Madame Bouchard's children than the others.

Mrs. Robinson's eyes screwed tight.

"You best stay steer clear of him, girls. I've never met a meaner man in my life. Stay away, especially after he's had a drink or two in him."

"Have you had any run-ins with him?" asked Katy.

"Everyone has had a run-in with that man. I make it a point to say 'yes Barry' and get out of his way quickly every time."

"He sounds horrible," said Katy.

"If I were him, I'd probably drink every day too." Mrs. Robinson paused for a moment. "I feel sorry for him, if you ask me."

"Has he ever threatened you in the past?" I asked, wondering how someone like Barry could arouse sympathy in anyone. But I kept that thought to myself.

"Tried to clip me in the ear once for taking a half-eaten plate from his room by mistake. This was a long time ago. I had just arrived here, and he was just a kid. He only tried that once though. I told him to never lay a finger on me and he never did."

I looked over at Tetyana.

She was listening intently, but her eyes regularly darted across the room, scanning the windows and listening to any noise from the outside.

She raised an eyebrow when she saw me look her way.

Barry struck as being a man who'd happily write a death threat letter to his own caretaker lady, even if she was someone who'd lived with his family for decades.

"Did Madame Bouchard's children ever marry?" asked Katy. "Do Lisa and Barry have spouses? Kids?"

Mrs. Robinson turned to Katy with a sad look.

"There was just one little girl."

"Whose was she?" asked Katy.

"Lisa's. She got pregnant at sixteen."

Sixteen.

"Who was the father?" I asked.

Mrs. Robinson turned away.

"A kid that came from town to help John with the fencing, I think. He was here for a month and Lisa started showing five months later. Mister and Madame Bouchard got hysterical."

"I can imagine," I said.

"Their reputation was more important than anything else. Any scandal that would threaten their careers was dealt with harshly. Mister Bouchard said he'd send Lisa and the baby to someplace no one would find them, but I knew it was just raging words."

"Were the parents here at that time?"

"They were in Paris. They never saw the baby or Lisa. They only knew about it because I called them. They were livid."

"Did Lisa resent you for telling her parents about her teen pregnancy?"

"I helped her out, you see. Someone had to take care of the little girl." Mrs. Robinson's face crumpled like she was going to cry. "But then, they sent her away."

"Sent who away?" asked Katy.

"The little girl."

"Lisa's daughter?" I asked gently.

"They committed Victoria to a mental institution. They said she wasn't right. I always thought she was a smart girl, saner than anyone else in this house, but doctors know best, I guess."

What a peculiar story.

"That girl must be twenty now? Thirty? Does she live here?"

"Twenty-nine. Victoria was only nine years old when they took her. No one talks about her anymore. No one even visits her at the asylum. It's like she doesn't exist."

What a tragic family Madame Bouchard had. And we'd never known.

"This Barry guy," said Katy, "did he ever marry?"

"Barry's a loner. Always has been. Ever since he could, he took to the woods by his lone self and was always bringing in wounded stray animals. He was wild. Never got along with anyone or talked that much."

"Did he have any friends?"

"None that I know of. There's no love lost between that sister and brother, I can tell you that. They were always fighting and screaming at each other, and there was no parent to tell them to behave. Barry started drinking when he was fourteen. I saw him sneak out whiskey bottles from the drink cabinet. I don't think he's stopped drinking since then."

"The parents never cared to ask about them?"

"They were hardly home, let alone in the country," she replied. A grave look overcame her face. "I suspect they thought of their children as mistakes. They left them money and people to take care of them, but Lisa and Barry grew up like orphans."

"You never know, right?" said Katy, turning to me. "I thought Madame Bouchard's kids were spoiled, high-society brats who drove fast cars and flew to parties in LA every weekend."

"Those two hated their parents," said Mrs. Robinson. "While Mister and Madame Bouchard were having dinner parties with presidents, their kids were swimming in the streams, hunting in the woods and running around like feral children. They never listened to us, no, sir. We were just *help*."

I bit my tongue.

"Who do you think is sending you these anonymous letters?" I asked, steering the conversation back to this decade.

Mrs. Robinson shook her head and wiped her eyes.

"Could be anyone. I don't know why they'd do something like this. I've been a good worker. I've taken care of everyone in this house. I'm a God-fearing Christian woman and I've hurt no one in my life."

She looked up at me, her eyes pleading.

"Just make them stop. My old heart can't take these nasty games no more."

I reached out and put a hand on her arm to reassure her.

"I'm sorry this is happening to you, Mrs. Robinson. It's unsettling and scary." I paused. "But you need to tell us everything so we can find out who they are."

"And stop them," said Tetyana in a gruff voice. We turned to her.

"We didn't come here to just learn who they are," she said, "we came here to stop them from doing this."

I nodded and turned back to Mrs. Robinson. "You said this house is full of secrets. What did you—"

A thundering roar reverberated throughout the house, stopping me in mid-sentence.

Katy jumped with a loud gasp.

Tetyana whipped around and stepped toward the door, her gun in her hand.

Chapter Ten

"**W**ho the hell are you?"

I stared at the bulbous-nosed, red-faced man in the kitchen. He reminded me of some goons I'd met in my previous life.

I liked to think of myself as a strong-minded, independent, professional businesswoman. But for a brief moment, I felt like a scared lost girl again. Pangs of fear went through me as I watched this strange man rampage around Mrs. Robinson's kitchen.

It was Barry all right.

He was in a foul mood. Three strangers rushing over and bursting into the kitchen, ignoring Mrs. Robinson's calls for us to stop, hadn't helped.

Barry fit the description of a lone, alcoholic, middle-aged bachelor with a nonexistent social life to a T.

His skin was pasty yellow, and his hair was prematurely turning gray. A thick bushy unibrow covered his eyes, so I wondered how he could see. A large beer belly protruded over his pants, which were kept up by a pair of red suspenders.

Barry stepped toward Mrs. Robinson, shaking a thick finger in her face.

"What the hell do you think you are doing, stupid woman?"

"I was only trying to help these girls out with their car trouble," replied Mrs. Robinson, composed despite the man raging at her.

Our tire incident in the woods, however that had happened, was coming in handy now and I was happy to milk it for what it was worth. If it had been someone from this household who'd tried to stop us, they'd unknowingly given us a good excuse.

Barry stepped up to Mrs. Robinson with a nasty scowl. He leaned so close, his nose was inches away from hers.

What a bully.

The man's eyes were bloodshot, and his pupils were small and pointy. I wondered how long he'd been drinking that day. If I had to guess, I'd have said he'd been drunk since he woke up.

That scared little girl inside of me wilted, and I felt my blood heating up.

"Didn't I tell you the last time you let that lot of stinking lost hikers stay over?" he shouted, his spittle falling on Mrs. Robinson's face. She didn't even flinch. "I don't want these street trash in my house!"

Katy put on her charming smile. "If it puts your mind at ease, we manage a bakery in New York. We're here on holiday. We're not street tra—"

"Was I talking to you?" roared Barry, snapping his head my friend's way. "If I wanted to chat with a floozy, I'd talk to you. But I didn't, did I?"

Floozy?

Katy stepped back, stunned.

Barry turned back to Mrs. Robinson. He glared at her.

"I don't know why we keep you, you old hag," he said, his face contorted into a scowl. With an angry snarl, he raised his hand as if to hit her.

"Hey," I said, stepping up and getting in between them. "Don't you dare!"

Barry turned to me, his eyes bulging.

"*You!* If I had my way, I'd... I'd..."

"You'd do what, Mr. Bouchard?" said Tetyana. Her voice was calm, but there was a dangerous undercurrent in it.

He glowered at her, but I could see the hesitation in his eyes. He was a coward, and a coward chose their victims well.

"Mr. Bouchard," I said, wrestling the fury bubbling inside of me. "There's no need to shout at Mrs. Robinson. She's only trying to help us. We're running on an old spare tire which could give way on the road to town. This is an emergency, as you can see."

"This is my house!" yelled Barry, poking a finger at me.

"It's just for one night, Mr. Bouchard," I said, crossing my fingers behind me. I needed time to solve the mystery of the poison pen letters. If twenty-four hours was all I had, I'd have to make do. "We'll find a way to reciprocate to you."

"It's the Christian thing to do, Barry," said Mrs. Robinson.

He whipped around to her.

"These stupid city folk come here and trample all over my mountain."

"What do you think Pastor Graham would say if he found out we turned these girls back out into the woods tonight, with a storm coming and all?"

Barry pulled away at those words, glaring at her.

"The pastor would never say no, would he, now?" said Mrs. Robinson, her voice slightly smug.

The pastor, it seemed, had some power over Barry. After shooting another angry glare our way, Barry stomped out, grouching about "floozies and tramps."

We stood wordlessly for a minute, waiting for the unpleasant taste that man had left in the room to dissipate.

"Goodness me, what a crazy man," said Katy finally, letting out her breath.

"Now there's a good suspect for the letter writer," said Tetyana, turning to Mrs. Robinson. "You want me to make him confess?"

Mrs. Robinson shook her head.

"That man talks a big talk. Always shouting, always threatening. But that's more bark than bite."

"You don't seem fazed by him," I said.

"Give him another five minutes and you'll find him snoring in the television room and he'll have forgotten he even saw you."

She turned to us, a determined look on her face.

"Stay the night, please. I have prepared a room for you upstairs. I want you to meet everyone tonight."

"Is anyone else going to object to us staying here?" I asked.

"Lisa likes her privacy and doesn't like strangers, but I doubt she'll say anything. She's a bright one, that one, but she keeps her thoughts to herself." She paused and looked up thoughtfully. "Sometimes I don't know which is worse, the one who's always raging or the quiet one, right?"

"And this pastor?" I asked. "What's he like?"

"Pastor Graham's a guest here, so he won't say anything. He's always nice and polite, and everyone here has a lot of respect for him. Even Barry's eager to please him."

"What about the other staff? Won't they get suspicious at us showing up?" asked Tetyana.

"They're the least of my worries. They're supposed to be working for me, but they take their instructions from Pastor Graham."

"Pastor Graham?" I said. "I thought he was a guest."

"I'm fine with that. They know their chores."

"Where are they now?" asked Katy. "I'd expect to find your staff in the kitchen at this time of day."

"Nancy's taking a nap. Said she had a migraine and wanted to rest before supper. Her husband, Jim, went to the barn to check on the horses."

Just as she said those words, the side door from the staff quarters creaked open. We all turned. A woman's face poked through the door.

It was a younger woman, in her late twenties or early thirties. She was wearing blue pants, a white T-shirt, and a red turban with tassels tied over her hair.

She looked startled to see us.

"Come on in, Nancy," said Mrs. Robinson, gesturing to her. "Hope you're feeling better."

The woman didn't answer but kept staring at us. I wondered if she could speak.

"We have some lost visitors with car trouble," continued Mrs. Robinson. "I think we have enough supper for three more mouths tonight, don't we?"

Nancy entered the kitchen and walked toward the counter, her face a picture of suspicion. She didn't return our hellos or come over to shake our hands, but regarded us unsmilingly from across the kitchen counter.

"How did you get here?" she asked.

"By the road," I answered, wondering how else anyone would get up here. We weren't dressed in hiking gear, so we obviously couldn't have come through any mountain trail. Not at this time of night, anyway.

Her eyes narrowed. "So, you aren't really lost then, are you?"

"We got a flat tire on our way to town. It was getting late and our spare isn't great. Also, a severe storm is coming this way. Thought it best to drive to the nearest place we could find using our GPS."

It wasn't the whole truth, but it would have to do.

"Where are you from?"

Her voice was low and her words came out staccato fashion, like machine-gun fire.

"New York," I said.

"What are you doing here?"

"The mountain air is fresh and so healthy," said Katy, with a friendly smile. "Not like the Big Apple." She let out a small laugh. "We just didn't expect an adventure like this when we left the city."

Nancy merely stared at her.

Katy switched on her charm to her full wattage.

"What a fantastic discovery, though. What a magnificent home this is. So, how long have you been living in this gorgeous place?"

I thought I saw Nancy swallow and wondered why she looked so uncomfortable. There was something more in her than the usual small-town distrust of out-of-towners.

"Just a few months," she replied guardedly.

"Where are you from? Around hereabouts, then?" asked Katy, leaning across the counter.

Nancy leaned away.

"Iowa," she said, turning her back toward us and opening a cupboard.

Tetyana and I exchanged a quick glance.

It was Nancy who was lying now.

Chapter Eleven

"It's getting late," said Mrs. Robinson bustling around the kitchen, pointedly ignoring Nancy's surly face. "We need to serve supper soon."

"I'll give you a hand," I said, stepping up, making Nancy scowl even more.

Did that woman ever smile?

Tetyana and Katy chipped in and within half an hour, we'd set the table in the dining room on the second floor.

Connected to the dining room was an expansive living area. Someone had started a fire in the rustic fireplace in the corner, and it was sending a warm glow our way. Outside, a northwesterly wind was beating against the windows and a heavy rain had begun to fall.

After doing her part, Nancy disappeared to her room temporarily. So, Tetyana, Katy and I waited with Mrs. Robinson for the rest of the family to join us. Hearing the stormy winds howl outside, I was glad we were in here, and not stuck in the middle of the darkened, wet and lonely woods.

The roast now sat on the table with a carving knife next to it. The pot of stew was on the sideboard, ready to be served with home-baked bread and garlic butter.

If I ignored the peeling paint and worn features, this room could be the perfect showroom for an old-fashioned manor.

Above the table hung a light fixture made of deer antlers. The rustic wooden furniture and the retro dishes and cutlery added to the whimsical decor of the room.

I remembered the champagne-fueled, celebrity-studded parties Madame Bouchard attended in Paris and New York. These were the high-society functions my bakery catered for. The difference between her jet-setting lifestyle and that of her children in the mountains of New Hampshire couldn't have been more striking.

Didn't Madame Bouchard care for her own flesh and blood?

I wondered if she'd left anything to her family. Madame Bouchard had been a very wealthy woman. I'd assumed the million-dollar payouts she'd promised us for solving problems for her friends were a small allotment of her full estate.

I looked around the immense dining and living area.

This house would have a massive sales tag if it were to be sold. With possibly more than two dozen bedrooms, mostly shuttered and locked up now, it could be easily converted into a boutique hotel for hikers and skiers.

This estate was a significant inheritance, I thought, making a mental note to call Peace, my friend and lawyer, to confirm details after dinner.

"Who do we have here now?"

As soon as I heard the voice, I knew instantly it had to be Pastor Graham.

"Hi there," said Katy, getting up from her chair with a wide smile.

"Three lovely ladies from the Big Apple," boomed Pastor Graham, giving Katy a low bow and a genial smile back.

"We had our GPS and everything," said Katy, offering her hand to the pastor, "you'd think we'd be prepared, but these mountains are so confusing."

"Your fancy GPS won't work around here," replied the pastor. "I'm afraid the mountains and the woods don't help, especially during weather like this. We've had to pluck out more than one hiker from the mountains and they usually had all the fancy equipment in the world, but they had still got disoriented."

"It's a beautiful place to get stranded in, as long as you don't get frostbite or run out of food," prattled Katy, "and you, Pastor, do you live in the village?"

"I'm down there all week, busy with my congregation. But it's nice to get away on the weekends. Lisa and Barry are good to me."

He turned and smiled at Mrs. Robinson, who was serving the stew into bowls.

"Mrs. Robinson always has a place for me at the table. She's an absolute angel."

"If it wasn't for her, we'd be frozen out in the woods," I said. "We can't thank her enough."

The man tilted his head slightly.

"Most people come to this part of the world in the summer when it's nice and warm. Why would you ladies come here at this time?"

Katy let out a dramatic sigh. She was an excellent actor. I was glad she'd decided to come with us.

"I'm going through a separation right now," she said, looking forlorn. That was true. She didn't have to act any more now. "My friends thought it would be good to get me out of the city for a little while and get some fresh air in the countryside."

The pastor nodded sympathetically.

"That's not such a bad idea. Come to think of it, there are fewer crowds on the trails and you get to have the entire mountain for yourself. I suppose you'll be climbing Mount Washington this weekend?"

"Can't wait," said Katy, her face brightening. "We've been preparing for weeks at the gym. Not everyone can say they hiked up the tallest mountain on the East Coast, can they?"

"Go early, take lots of water, and take your time going up. You should be fine." He paused. "How long do you plan on staying in town?"

"Just a few—"

The sound of a door opening made us all turn.

"Ah, Jim, my boy, come right in," said the pastor, as if he was the host of the house, "we have some lovely visitors from the big city. Three beautiful young women who got lost on their way to Falcon Hills and drove straight into the arms of Cedar Cottage. Hahaha."

It was a good-looking man in his twenties who stepped in, carrying a pile of firewood in his arms. He walked with the confident swagger of a star college footballer who knew his charm. He dropped the wood near the fireplace and turned to us with a pearly smile that could have beaten Katy's in the charisma Richter scale.

Katy didn't miss a beat.

She stepped up to him, shook his hand and introduced Tetyana and me.

While Jim's smile was high on wattage, I noticed it didn't go all the way to his eyes. His eyes were glassy, like they were looking through me, not at me. I shook his hand, feeling like this extrovert bluster was all a show.

A show for whom? For us?

I noticed Jim wink at Katy as he took her hand. Nancy, who'd been lighting the candles on the table, turned away. Her face had turned dark.

I stepped up to her to give her a hand so she wouldn't feel left out, when I realized another stranger had slipped into the room, and I hadn't even noticed.

It was a mousy-looking woman with thinning brown hair and wearing an old-fashioned shapeless dress. She was hovering at the far end of the table, as if unsure what to do. She was the type of person who could be in a room for hours and no one would ever acknowledge her presence.

Who is this? How did I not see her enter the room?

Mrs. Robinson stepped up and pulled a chair for her.

"I made your favorite stew today, Lisa," said Mrs. Robinson.

Lisa?

The woman didn't make eye contact or say hello. I tried not to stare, but it was hard not to. I couldn't see any of the intelligence Mrs. Robinson talked about.

"Storm outside...." I heard Mrs. Robinson speak to her in a low voice. "... three lost girls... car trouble... just for the night..."

Lisa kept her eyes on the table as Mrs. Robinson spoke.

I couldn't believe this was the daughter of the elegant, illustrious, and demanding Madame Bouchard who twirled foreign diplomats and celebrities around her finger. Then again, getting abandoned in a rambling old mansion among the lonely mountains and being treated like you were a mistake probably did strange things to you.

Mrs. Robinson placed a bowl of stew in front of Lisa. Without looking up or waiting for the rest of us, Lisa began to eat.

She was a quiet one, all right. Though she looked mousy, those intense blue eyes, and those lips set in a thin red line told me you wouldn't want to cross her. They say still waters run deep. Lisa was a bottomless, subterranean well.

"Please, please, take a seat," said Pastor Graham, pulling a chair out for Katy.

One by one, we took our places, even Nancy, though her scowl never left her face.

The chair at the head of the table remained empty. I guessed that was where Barry usually sat. He was, I was sure, roaming somewhere in this immense house, lost in a drunken stupor.

Something Mrs. Robinson had said earlier was bothering me. *If I were him, I'd probably drink every day too.* What did she mean by that? I wondered.

Lisa and Barry may have been emotionally and physically abandoned by their parents, but their everyday needs had been taken care of. They'd had a roof over their heads, food on their plates, staff who'd tried their best to take care of their needs, and a vast outdoor playground without restrictions.

My own found-family of lost orphans had suffered much worse at the hands of traffickers, but none of us had turned into feckless drunks. There was more to Barry's story, I was sure.

Pastor Graham reached over and took Katy's hand, then turned to Jim and took his. He glanced around the table.

"Shall we say grace now?"

I took the hands of Mrs. Robinson and of Lisa and bowed my head.

"Let us give thanks to the Lord—"

"You dumb cretin!"

We all snapped our heads up.

Chapter Twelve

It was Barry.

He came crashing through the doorway, a tumbler of whiskey swaying dangerously in one hand, his face a deep shade of purple.

"You forgot to call me!" he bawled at Mrs. Robinson.

"I knew you'd come down soon," she replied in a quiet voice. I marveled at her patience. I wanted nothing more than to punch this man's nose and tell him to behave.

Instead of walking up to his chair, Barry staggered over to the liquor cabinet next to the dining table. With an angry grunt, he opened the door, pulled down a whiskey decanter and filled his glass to the brim.

He turned back to the table and gave a start as he spotted me sitting in his direct line of sight. He pointed a shaky finger my way.

"What the hell are these wenches still doing here?"

"Now, Barry," said Pastor Graham. "Is that any way to—"

"I thought I told you to get rid of 'em!"

"Please take your seat, Barry. The food will get cold," I heard Mrs. Robinson say.

But Barry was advancing my way, his finger pointed at me, like the muzzle of a gun readying for its target.

I stared at the madman, my heart hammering. He'd gathered I was a leader of my pack and hadn't taken a liking to me. I knew he was brash and mean, but I wasn't sure if he was violent.

I braced myself.

"Get out of my house!" he roared, his arm held high in the air now. "You little witch!"

I got up from my chair, ready to parry or duck.

"Barry, please sit down," said Mrs. Robinson.

Barry slammed his fist toward me, but I blocked him just in time. Tetyana sprang from her chair and pulled him away, twisting his arms behind him and propelling him away from the table.

Suddenly the entire room was on their feet.

Pastor Graham and Jim surrounded Barry. I could hear them talking to him in low voices. Barry was muttering under his breath, but he seemed to be calming down.

"My goodness, I'm so sorry," said Mrs. Robinson, giving me a napkin to wipe the whiskey that had splashed on my shirt. Her face was red with shock. "I had no idea—"

"It's fine," I said and smiled. I lowered my voice. "All part of the job."

She gave me a frazzled look but didn't reply.

I settled back in my seat, feeling rather unhinged.

It was never fun to be hit by the host. I'd have gladly hit him right back, but I had to make sure we could stay here at least another twenty-four hours. I couldn't afford to get us kicked out so soon.

"You okay?" whispered Katy.

I nodded, ignoring the searing pain in my forearm. If Barry had been sober and fit, this would have hurt much more.

I turned to Lisa who'd been staring at the altercation, her lips set in an even more austere line. It was clear she didn't approve of her brother's behavior.

"Would you pass me some water, please?" I asked.

She turned around and looked for the decanter. "He's not well...." she mumbled.

"Don't mention it," I said. "I understand."

Jim helped Barry to his seat. Then, as if he'd forgotten the incident already, he picked up his spoon and started on his stew, pointedly ignoring everyone. I was glad I was sitting as far away from Barry as I could.

"I do sincerely apologize. This is highly unusual," said the pastor, taking his seat, looking aghast. He pointed at the reddened skin on my forearm. "Would you like me to look at that? Maybe get some ointment?"

"I'm good," I said, rustling up a smile. "I train every day, so this is par for the course."

"Train?"

"In Krav Maga."

He raised an eyebrow.

"Tactical mixed martial arts."

His smile disappeared instantly at those words. Then, without another word, he turned to his stew.

Next to me, Lisa hunkered down in her chair.

She picked up the spoon she'd dropped when Barry had rumbled in like an errant steam train. Ignoring the splatter on her placemat, she lowered her spoon into the bowl, scooped up some stew and placed it in her mouth, her attention seemingly fully on her food. But I noticed the slight tremble in her hand.

For the next ten minutes, all we could hear around the table, other than Barry's loud slurping, was the ting of the spoons against the retro china.

It's time to ask my question.

I wiped my mouth with my napkin and looked around the table.

"I read in a magazine at the airport that a famous Madame Bouchard owned this beautiful house at one point."

I paused to watch for their reaction. I noticed Tetyana and Katy were discreetly glancing around the table too.

Lisa stopped her spoon halfway to her mouth and the pastor's face turned a shade paler. Barry looked up, squinted at me as if he'd forgotten who I was or why I was talking. Then, with a loud and dismissive grunt, he turned his attention back to his food.

Nancy and Jim seemed the least affected by my words. The others' reactions didn't appear to even register with them as they kept eating.

"She's no longer alive, I gather?" I asked, hoping it sounded like an innocent question from an ignorant guest.

The pastor cleared his throat. "Lots of history in this place," he said. "Is this the first time you've been in this region?"

"It is."

"The views from up here are spectacular. You'll see the mountains in all their glory tomorrow morning. Don't forget to snap a few pictures before you leave."

He was changing the topic.

Why is everyone so cagey?

Soon Katy started small talk with Jim. With the pastor adding an anecdote here and there, a semblance of normal conversation hummed around the table.

Nancy ate silently, glancing up once in a while to throw an ugly look Katy's way. I didn't know if Katy noticed her and ignored her, but she kept the chatter going.

Something told me Jim and Nancy had a row recently. They'd hardly acknowledged each other that evening, kept their distance and never made eye contact.

Though Mrs. Robinson was doing her best to play hostess, she looked pale and tired. She wheezed and coughed a few times, clutching her chest like she was in pain. She's sick, I thought as I watched her. I wondered what was wrong with her.

Across from me, Tetyana's eyes swept the room regularly. She was, as always, on full alert.

Outside, it was raining hard. The sound of heavy raindrops thrashing against the window made me feel glad to be in here, even in these extraordinary surroundings with a host who clearly resented us.

I wondered why nobody wanted to acknowledge Madame Bouchard, the matriarch of this family. I'd expected someone to at least say, "Oh, it's a sad thing. She was part of the family."

I leaned over to Lisa.

"Thank you so much for letting us stay here tonight," I said.

She looked up and gave me a suspicious look from under her eyelashes. I thought she looked disquieted, but it was hard to say. The flicker from the candlelight could have played with my eyes.

Thank goodness she's not as hostile as her brother, I thought.

I tried again. "I hate to intrude on your home like this, but I want you to know we really appreciate it."

She gave an imperceptible nod.

"It was scary when we got stuck on the road, near the woods with the lightning and all."

"It's bad tonight," she finally replied.

I had no idea what it must have been like to have your first child taken away to a mental asylum so young. I also didn't know what it was like to have cold and callous parents.

Lisa looked more like the new girl at the school cafeteria, than the owner or part owner of this multi-million-dollar mansion. I felt sorry for her.

"It's a beautiful spot you have here."

She gave another nod.

"I hear the trails through the woods are spectacular, especially at this time of the year with the fall colors. I'm so glad we brought our big camera."

"Don't go to the woods."

"Excuse me?" I said, unsure I heard her right.

A strange look crossed Lisa's face.

"Go home," she said. "It's not safe here."

I leaned in.

"Sorry?"

But Lisa had turned back to her bowl, her full attention on the food now.

Chapter Thirteen

I was glad when dinner was over.

Lisa had stopped speaking to me after that.

She'd finished her meal and got up from the table like she couldn't get away fast enough. She'd stumbled out of the door without saying good night.

Barry had already fallen asleep on his placemat after eating, so he hadn't even noticed his sister's hasty departure.

The pastor had looked embarrassed for his hosts' behavior and had tried to make up with his small talk and cordial smiles. But something about his demeanor came across as fake to me.

I wondered why any sane person from town would come up to this gloomy, unsociable house every weekend. It had been torture to sit at dinner that evening.

The pastor must have another reason for coming up here. Maybe I was getting paranoid, but I started suspecting everyone around the table.

Mrs. Robinson seemed grateful for our presence, and that made up for all the bizarre vibes we were getting that evening.

We stayed behind to help her clean up.

When everything had been put away, she took us to the third-floor rooms using the fire escape stairway that opened out to the kitchen. I wasn't sure if it was because she didn't want anyone to see us going up or because it was the route she usually took to the top floor.

Everyone else, apart from her, slept on the west wing on the third floor. Mrs. Robinson opened a door to a small room in the east wing of the third floor. We had this wing all to ourselves.

Mrs. Robinson pointedly refused Tetyana's offer to guard her door overnight.

"It's been four weeks and they haven't got me yet, have they?" she'd said. "Besides, I always lock my door and put a chair next to it."

"What about your window?" Tetyana said.

"I lock them too." She smiled. "I'll sleep better tonight knowing you all are here in the house. Now you've come, I feel a bit silly for raising such a fuss."

"It's not a fuss, Mrs. Robinson," said Katy, putting an arm around her shoulder, "that letter you showed us was real and it was nasty. You need to be careful."

"I'll be fine. I'm happy you came to see me. You all try to get some rest now. We'll talk tomorrow."

She closed the door behind her and left us with a friendly good night.

We turned to examine the room she'd given us.

"With so many empty rooms in this house, she put us in this tiny closet?" said Katy with a disappointed look.

"It's a kid's room," I said, looking around.

"Who wants dibs on that cot?" asked Katy, pointing at the makeshift bed in the corner of the room.

I sighed.

"I'm the only one who'll fit."

The main bed was a child-sized one. Tetyana and Katy would fit in it if they snuggled tight, I thought, happy to have the cot to myself.

We stood in a circle, taking in the space.

The walls were painted a pastel pink. A small door led to a closet-sized bathroom, complete with a toilet, sink and shower.

The lone bookshelf contained a mix of children's cartoon magazines and oversized picture books. A collection of young adult novels with yellowed pages and faded bookmarks filled the top shelf.

A cheap Mickey Mouse alarm clock sat on the bedside table and assorted plush toys had been piled on the floor next to the bed. Katy bent down and picked one up.

"A Care Bear. I used to have one. Didn't they stop making these ages ago?"

Tetyana and I looked at each other and shrugged. Neither of us had grown up in North America. Instead of teddy bears, I'd been surrounded by soot-encrusted pots and pans, and Tetyana had slept next to stacks of guns and grenades.

"This is that little girl's room," Katy was saying, twirling around in place. "The one they put in the insane asylum."

"There's a reason Mrs. Robinson gave us this room," I said. "My gut says there's something in here she wants us to see."

"She could also want us to hear something on this floor during the night," said Tetyana. "Whoever delivers those letters has to start here."

"That sounds creepy," said Katy. "Couldn't it be someone from town?"

"There's no evidence of anyone breaking into the house to deliver these letters."

"But Mrs. Robinson's hiding something," I said. "She's got secrets she doesn't want to share."

"Aw, come on," said Katy, "she's like the nicest person on earth."

"Everyone has secrets," I said.

"Even nice old ladies," said Tetyana. *"Especially*, nice old ladies."

"What a day," I said, moving to the windows to open them. "We need some fresh air. It feels so cooped up in here."

I opened the windows and looked down at our car. It was still in its spot where I had parked, and so far all four tires seemed to still be in good condition.

I took a deep breath of the cool, fresh air in. It had stopped raining outside, but I could still hear the thunder rumbling from far away.

The night was dark, and the moon was hiding behind gray clouds. I wondered what the view must be like from this room on a beautiful day.

"So," I said, turning around to my friends. "Who do you think it is?"

"Jim's the most normal out of the lot, but that just makes me more suspicious," said Tetyana.

"Can't say his wife is normal," said Katy. "She doesn't like me."

"She's jealous because Jim was paying attention to you all night," I said.

"But, I didn't mean—"

"If it makes you feel better, she didn't seem fond of us either," said Tetyana.

"We can't rule anyone out," I said, "it could even be Mrs. Robinson sending these letters to herself."

"Whatever for?" said Katy.

"For sympathy?" I ventured. "Maybe it's a desperate attempt to get everyone's attention? Perhaps in some strange way, she thinks it will bring everyone together and make them care for each other and her?"

"She could also be mentally unwell and did it on an impulse," said Tetyana. "Or maybe...." She paused and gave us a strange look. "Maybe it's an excuse to bring us down here."

"What?" said Katy. "*Why?*"

A shiver went down my back. I'd been feeling that too. I just hadn't wanted to articulate it in front of my friends before I had some proof.

Katy turned to me. "Do you think this has anything to do with Madame Bouchard's will?"

"Well, technically she left us money," I replied. "It's conditional on our results and we may never see a dime in the end, but it's money that belongs to this family."

"If that's true," said Tetyana, her face glum, "this game just leveled up."

I nodded.

"Peace said no one knows about Madame Bouchard's instructions to us, but what if someone found out?"

"You guys really think this could be bigger than kooky Lisa or crazy Barry?" said Katy with a grimace. "Or that creep?"

Tetyana and I both looked at her.

"What creep?" said Tetyana.

"Katy, did Jim—" I started.

"Not Jim," she replied, shaking her head. "It was the pastor. He put his hand on my thigh under the table and squeezed. Ugh."

"*What?*" said Tetyana.

I suddenly remembered how Katy had gone unusually quiet toward the end of dinner, letting Jim and the pastor do most of the chitchatting.

"Oh, no," I said, feeling sick to my stomach. "I'm so sorry, Katy. That shouldn't have happened."

She looked away, her face turning pink. "I pushed his hand off me and that was that."

Tetyana swore.

"If I'd known, I'd have slammed the bastard right in the face."

"I'm having a word with him tomorrow," I said, straightening up. "If you think he's going to get away—"

"No!" said Katy. "Don't make this bigger than it is. Besides, we've got to focus on our mission. Can't jeopardize that."

"But we can't let him—"

"You know what this means, don't you?" said Katy. "He's got something to hide too."

"That or he's just another fake padre preying on good people," said Tetyana, a dark look on her face. "It's not like there aren't many of those around." She glared at Katy. "If that man comes within three feet of you, I'm throttling him."

"I'm not keeping quiet," I said. "We need to let him know we're on to him."

"Ladies," said Tetyana, pulling out her sidearm. "I don't care what Mrs. Robinson said, I'm patrolling the house tonight." She looked up, her eyes like steel. "I suspect everyone in this damned house, and I'm going to keep a close eye on all of them."

I stared at Tetyana's weapon as she checked the chamber and racked the slide. She walked over to her bag to fish out the extra magazine she'd brought with her and slid it into her vest.

We were out of our state and didn't have a license to carry in New Hampshire. But now, I wished I'd brought my Glock too.

A strange thing happens when you put a gun to a man's head and pull the trigger. I'd done it once to the man who'd assassinated my parents. I'd done it again to the man who'd held my cousin by the neck, threatening to choke her to death.

Once you kill, your life changes.

I rarely slept well, as the images of those men's dying faces haunted me every night. But I knew if I faced another murderer or rapist, I would not hesitate to do what I had before.

Tetyana's words on our ride up flashed into my mind.

I have a curious feeling this job of yours is bigger than you think.

My gut said she was right.

"For you."

I looked up. It was Tetyana extending an arm my way. In her hand was a gleaming black gun.

"I brought an extra sub compact," she said, "just in case."

Chapter Fourteen

My phone rang, startling me.

I turned it on and held it against my ear.

"Everyone okay?"

It was my resident lawyer, my childhood friend, and Katy's estranged partner. Peace's friendly voice sounded far away, though he was calling from only two states away.

"Had a little tire trouble, but we got here okay."

I felt a jab on my arm and turned to see Katy mouthing at me.

"Um, Peace? Katy wants to know if Chantelle did her homework."

"All done. Just put her to bed," said Peace, his voice strained at the mention of my friend. "She asked when Mom's coming back. Can you tell Katy I have the same question?"

With a sigh, I looked over at Katy who was sitting on the bed, clutching the Care Bear on her lap, a stubborn look on her face.

"Hey, Katy, Chantelle's sleeping but she wanted to know when you're coming home. Peace is also wondering the same thing…"

Katy looked away.

She's still angry.

"Tell him I'll come home when he puts me and Chantelle over his precious job," she snapped.

Chantelle's beautiful little face came into my thoughts. My heart ached for her as she was now probably bearing the brunt of this dispute.

I turned back to my phone with a sigh.

"All well here," I lied, stepping away from the bed so Katy couldn't jab me again. "Except we all want you two to stop fighting. We love you both."

Peace let out a weary sigh. "Tell her I love her, would you? I love her as much as I did when I first met her."

I turned to Katy. "Peace says he loves you just like he did the first day he met you."

Katy scowled back.

"So, I got your text," said Peace, moving on, as if he knew exactly how his wife felt about him right then.

"Madame Bouchard's lawyer made a request to the probate judge to seal the court records to prevent anyone seeing her will. The request was granted, given her public status. This means unless someone starts a fight in court, the documents will be kept confidential just as she had wanted."

Tetyana raised an eyebrow. I mouthed "sorry" and fumbled to turn the speakerphone on.

"Has anyone started a fight in the courts?" I asked, putting the phone on the bedside table and turning the speaker toward my friends so they could hear as well.

"So far, no," said Peace. "We can be confident no one in the family knows of her unusual endowment to you. You can strike that worry off, for now."

"How much do you trust her lawyer?"

"If he did anything nefarious, he'd be risking his name, his practice, his finances, and his career. He's a big name and has some pretty public clients. I doubt he'll risk his comfortable position by doing anything stupid. You never know, but the chance is low."

I sighed in relief.

"Do you think Madame Bouchard had anything to do with Mrs. Robinson's letters?"

"I can't confirm that, but I wouldn't put it past her."

"She's playing with lives here," I said, silently cursing the day I met that woman. "What about the money? Have you learned anything more about how it all works?"

"Just had another conversation this morning with her lawyer to sort this out. Here's what we know so far. Madame Bouchard's given out your bakery number to a select group of people. She has supposedly told them to call you for help when the matter is too discreet to share outside the family circle or when the authorities can't solve their problems."

"Cold cases and such? From her friends and family?"

"Mrs. Robinson was the first person to call you. I don't know who the others are yet, but her lawyer promised to dig into his files to see if he can find any clues. He's being co-operative given the, er, unusual nature of this legacy."

"So there's real money here? She's not playing us?"

"That I can confirm. I looked over the financial records yesterday. She had asked her lawyer to open a separate investment account twelve months before she died. She's been scheming for a while."

"Why didn't she just donate it all to charity? Any orphanage would have done. It didn't need to be ours. Why complicate matters?"

"She loved these elaborate cloak and dagger games, remember? It's in her blood, and this was probably her last hurrah of sorts."

"A crazy hurrah, but we'll take it."

"We're also seeing a trend now with more people bequeathing to charity and do-gooders because they just can't stomach their spoiled brats wasting their hard-earned money at Ibiza or LA."

"So, Madame Bouchard's will is legit, then? If we solve these problems for these people—"

"A million US dollars get transferred to anywhere in the world we have a government registered orphanage for trafficked children. As soon as her lawyer gets confirmation that the case has been solved, he will wire the money." He paused. "I'd say she has enough for about twenty-five such, er, projects."

Tetyana raised an eyebrow.

"*Twenty-five million dollars,*" I heard Katy whisper in shock.

"Wow," I said. "Didn't realize it was that much."

"It's in an investment account, which means it can fluctuate. But it's all solid blue chip dividend funds, so it could grow over time. Expect an industry average of six to eight percent over a decade, if you're lucky. Then again, if you solve these things fast enough, a sizeable amount will be withdrawn each time, diminishing the pot."

"That's the whole point," I said. "We want the orphanages to get these resources, so they can take care of more kids. But how will her lawyer know when we've solved a case?"

"We're still trying to figure this out ourselves. According to the will, she left instructions with her contacts to call him and confirm. It was all prearranged." He paused. "I think this first case should clear most of these questions for us."

Tetyana and Katy were listening intently. Both raised their eyebrows when they saw me look. I knew what was going through their minds. We'd had bizarre clients in the past, but this had to cap it all.

"Thanks, Peace," I said, turning to the phone. "Don't know what we'd do without you."

"Hey, you're family," he said, "I'm meeting with the other lawyer in three days to see if there's anything we've missed. Chat then."

"Sounds great."

"Asha?" He paused. I could feel the tension coming back to his voice. "Be careful out there, okay? David's worried and wondering if he should have closed the dojo and come with you."

"Hey, this is a girls' getaway," called out Katy from the bed.

"We can take care of ourselves," I said, looking at Tetyana who had her Japanese Tanto knife out now and was wiping it with a leather cloth. "Besides, Tetyana can single-handedly take on an army, if need be."

"Just come home safely and bring Katy back in one piece. Watch her for me, would you?"

"I always do," I said with a smile at her. Katy's face relaxed and her pout vanished.

"I know this isn't a big mission," Peace was saying, "like the others we used to do, but..."

"But what?" I asked.

"Small-town secrets can be deadly."

"Not as deadly as Saudi human traffickers."

"Just don't trust everyone you meet."

He hung up after telling me to convince Katy to call back soon.

"Boy, what an exhausting day," said Katy, as she flung herself on her back on the bed. "Ouch!"

She pulled away like something had stung her.

"What is it?" said Tetyana and me at the same time.

Katy flipped around, pulled the comforter away and peered into the bed. Tetyana and I stepped up to her.

"You okay?" I asked.

"It's a book," she said, pulling something out from in between the sheets. She picked it up and felt the edges.

"This jabbed my shoulder."

"A kid's coloring book," I said, staring at the faded and fraying cover.

Katy opened it.

"Victoria," she whispered as she followed the childish handwriting on the first page with her fingers.

"Wait," I said, "where did we hear that name before?"

"Didn't Mrs. Robinson say it was the girl's name?" Tetyana asked, scrunching her forehead.

"The nine-year-old," said Katy, nodding. "The kid they sent off packing to the insane asylum."

She turned the pages, flipping through colored drawings and collages of animals, people, and planets. It was an activity workbook, a scrapbook of sorts.

"Mrs. Robinson wanted us to see it," I said. "That's why she put us in here—"

"Oh, my gosh!" cried Katy, her hand flying to her mouth.

I peered at the page she'd flipped open to.

We'd passed the printed pages and were now on the blank ones with space to create your own drawings.

"What the frigging hell?" said Tetyana, as she peered over her shoulder.

It was a crudely drawn picture of a stick woman. She was lying prone on the ground. Her mouth was upside down and a liquid, drawn in red ink, was seeping from her neck.

Above her body, floating in the air, was an oversized knife dripping with blood.

91

Chapter Fifteen

I t was a child's drawing, but it was clearly a murder scene.

Katy flipped the page.

We stared at the next diagram. It was a picture of a female stick figure hanging from a tree.

"Sickening," said Katy as she turned the page.

This time it was a female decapitated body. As in the first drawing, a knife floated over the girl or woman, hanging ominously above the headless body, bleeding into the paper.

"Disturbing," I said, trying to imagine what would make a nine-year-old create such monstrosities.

"Is this why they locked her up?" whispered Katy as she flipped to another page.

"Oh, my goodness," she said.

Instead of another hideous drawing, the page was filled with messy, childlike handwriting. The words, "I hate this place," were written over and over, line after line, covering the entire blank page.

"A call for help," said Tetyana, shaking her head.

Katy snapped the book shut and leaned back against the headboard with a grimace.

"This is so sick."

I sat on the bed next to her and put my chin in my hands. I'd seen a lot in my life, but this was difficult to swallow.

"Kids aren't born this way," I said. "Something must have happened to her."

"Something in this house," said Katy, looking up at the ceiling as if it would have the answers she was looking for. "You know how I thought this house looked so romantic?"

I nodded.

"I've changed my mind. This place gives me the heebie-jeebies."

"Me too," I said, shifting on the bed to lean against the headboard.

"Oh!" I said, feeling something lumpy under the sheets. I moved to the side, bumping into Katy. "Hey, I think there's another book under here."

"Out, you two," said Tetyana, snapping her fingers.

Katy and I scrambled out of the bed just as she whipped the comforter away. Nothing. She ripped off the top sheet, making the pillows fall to the floor. Still nothing. Finally, she pulled out the fitted bottom sheet.

We stared at the large brown envelope sitting snugly on the mattress.

"Mrs. Robinson sent us on a scavenger hunt," said Katy.

I leaned over to pick it up, opened the envelope and felt inside.

"Papers," I said, pulling out a stack of neatly folded sheets of paper. I threw the envelope on the mattress and unfolded the stack.

It was regular printer paper and someone had used them to photocopy letters.

Mrs. Robinson's hate mail.

"Whoa," said Katy, swiping the top sheet from my hand. "This is exactly like the one she showed us. Look. Same handwriting in all caps."

"These were copied recently," I said, feeling the crisp paper.

"She could have told us about these," said Tetyana, frowning.

"Barry interrupted us, remember?" I said. "After that, there was always someone else around so she couldn't speak freely. She put them here for us to find them."

"Why didn't she point them out to us when she brought us here?" said Tetyana. "She had ample time to talk to us and there was no one around." Her trained eyes swept the room. "Unless someone's installed wiretaps here, and that was what silenced her."

"Don't you think that's a bit much?" I said. "This is the stuff of Agatha Christie, not Robert Ludlum."

"Guys," said Katy, who'd been staring at the paper in her hand. "You have to see this."

I peered over my friend's shoulder.

Katy read the letter out aloud.

"You won't be alive for too long, old woman. I'm going to get you soon. I'm going to cut your throat, like I told you I would."

Just like the horrid picture in the child's book, I thought, feeling nauseous.

Katy took the second paper from my hands and read it out loud.

"I thought you were my friend. I thought you were family. But you're just another nasty old hag who has betrayed me. If I could, I'd hang you."

Whoever sent these letters must have read the diary.

Katy shot me a horrified look before unfolding the third paper and reading it out loud.

"I hate your guts. But I guess you knew that. Just wanted to let you know I'll be the one who'll send you to your grave with your head cut off. Sleep tight. Nighty night."

"Gosh," I said. "They're ugly."

Katy threw the papers on the bed with a disgusted look on her face.

"That's the lot. Plus the one she had on her today," she said. "Someone really mean lives in this house."

"Mean?" said Tetyana. "Psychotic."

"And criminal," I added.

"Poor Mrs. Robinson," said Katy.

"Anyone in the house could have sent these," said Tetyana, thoughtfully. She turned to me. "Are you sure you saw a white dust in the envelope?"

"Some was caked on the paper." I turned to Katy. "Didn't you notice it too?"

"I was too busy thinking of the nasty message. You were the one holding the letter, remember?"

"Any idea what it could be?" I asked, turning to Tetyana.

"I can think of a few possibilities," she replied. "Russian intel agencies use ricin in letters to enemies. Remember the Anthrax letters after 9/11. That would work. If you really want to get someone, even regular ant poison powder would do the trick, if administered over time."

We stood speechlessly around the stripped-down bed, trying to grasp what we'd discovered.

"Do you guys think this has anything to do with the daughter in the asylum?" asked Katy finally.

"If the girl hadn't been locked up, I'd have suspected her first," I said. "The drawings are eerily similar to the threats in these letters."

"Why would she send these to Mrs. Robinson, though?" asked Katy.

"Your hunch is as good as mine." I paused. "Did Mrs. Robinson say if that girl got out of the hospital?"

Tetyana shook her head.

"Didn't mention it, but she could have got out or escaped."

Katy gave her a wide-eyed look.

"You think the girl's in the house?"

Tetyana shrugged.

"Lots of hiding spots in this old place."

A sudden creak somewhere made Katy and me jump. Tetyana stiffened, her hand immediately going toward her holster.

We stood silently, listening.

But the house had gone quiet again.

"Was someone listening in, you think?" I whispered, pointing at the door.

Tetyana stepped over to the door and examined the wood.

"Solid oak. Made when they used to build them right. Not the thin plastic things they put in apartment complexes."

She pulled her gun from her holster and turned to me.

"Back me up."

I walked over and positioned myself behind her. I pulled the gun she'd given me and aimed it at the door.

"Ready," I said.

In one swift movement, Tetyana unlocked the door and pulled it open, her side arm aimed forward.

I peeked out.

There was no one.

After checking the corridor, Tetyana closed the door and bolted it.

"Probably a wall panel or a floorboard contracting," she said, holstering her weapon. "It's getting cold in here."

"That was weird though," said Katy.

I looked at my friends, suddenly realizing who we'd overlooked. "Nancy!"

"What about her?" asked Katy.

"She's the only one close to the girl's age now. She came here with Jim a few months ago and I'm sure she was lying about coming from Iowa."

"Very fishy," said Katy, nodding. "She could have come back to take revenge for something that happened to her when she was a kid."

"Or she could be truly mentally ill," I said, gesturing at the book lying on the mattress. "That would mean there would be no rational reason for her actions other than whatever demons are plaguing her."

"Whoever it is," said Tetyana, "we have to stop them."

Katy and I turned to our friend.

"We can't rule out the option that this girl is *not* Nancy," she said.

"Someone else we haven't met yet?" I asked, feeling a tinge of fear.

"Potentially hiding in the house," said Tetyana.

Chapter Sixteen

"F reaky," said Katy with a visible shudder.

"There's only one way to find out for sure," said Tetyana. "We check all the rooms tonight, one by one."

Katy's eyes widened.

"You want to go barging into a room that might or might not have a death-threat-letter-writing crazy person inside?"

"I survived a Russian torture camp before I turned eighteen," replied Tetyana in a deadpan voice. "Besides, didn't we go after those gangsters and make them pay? We survived, didn't we?"

"That was a long time ago. We were young. We didn't have a choice."

"You're getting soft," said Tetyana with a friendly jab at Katy's arm, "you've become a suburban housewife."

"Nothing wrong with suburban housewives," grumbled Katy. "I like my safety and I'm a mom, not like you two. I have to think of Chantelle."

I shot a look at Tetyana that said, *Don't argue.*

"I'm not asking you to come with me, Katy," said Tetyana. "I'd prefer you sit tight, right here in this room with the bolt on."

Katy grimaced.

"Then we sit up all night, biting our nails, worrying about you."

"It'll be just you this time. Asha's coming with me. I'll need backup."

I sat up.

"Count me in."

"So now I'll be sitting here all alone, worried sick about *both* of you?" wailed Katy.

"For frigging sake," said Tetyana, "we'll be scouting for a mentally unstable young woman, not an Islamist fundamentalist terrorist group."

"You'll be safe here," I said to my friend. "And we'll be fine. We've been on more dangerous missions."

Katy shook her head, unconvinced.

"Those gangs were organized and we could predict their actions. But this girl..." She looked down at the open book. "She's kooky as heck. And that mother of hers? She's quiet, but there's something sinister about her. I'd swear, there's a lot wrong with this entire family. It's like a bad horror story waiting to happen."

"That poor woman is probably more lost and muddled than anything else," I said. "It's sad any way you look at it."

"I can't shake this feeling someone's out there to get us," said Katy, gloomily. "Maybe someone in this house knows who we are."

"Peace said they don't know about the will," I said. "This has the feel of an internal family affair. A secret haunting them from the past."

"When are you two planning on starting your jaunt?" asked Katy.

"In one hour," said Tetyana. "Once everyone settles in for the night, we'll check all the rooms."

"They could have locked their doors," I said.

"A lock has never stopped me."

"Barry's going to make a ruckus if he's up and about," I said, wondering if Katy was right. I was beginning to feel this excursion was getting away from me. "We need to be careful, Tetyana."

She nodded.

"We'll take the fire escape to the kitchen and check out the rooms near Mrs. Robinson's first. From there, we'll move from the east wing to the west, floor by floor. They'll all be sound asleep by then."

"What if they wake up and find us in their rooms?" I asked. "We'll have to have a darn good story."

"I'll zap them with my memory-erase laser stick."

"You have one of those?" said Katy with a shocked gasp.

Tetyana smiled.

"I wish. The only people who'd invent it would be the CIA or the Mossad. If they have, maybe I can convince David to wrangle one from them." She turned to me. "We'll cross that bridge when we get there."

Great.

She paused and threw a critical eye over the pant suit I'd been wearing all day.

"Might want to get your gear on. You'll be able to make a faster getaway if needed."

Double great.

I trod over to my suitcase on the floor of the closet and pulled out the small plastic packet from the back. Normal people threw their swimsuits into their luggage in case there was a pool at their destination. In the same way, I threw in my mission clothes regardless of where I was going, a habit from years ago.

"While you two are roaming around, I might as well check this room," said Katy, making the bed again. "Who knows what else we'll find here."

I pulled out my black yoga tights, unmarked black T-shirt, black boots, and a thin Kevlar vest, which looked like a harmless hiking jacket you'd get from any department store.

Tetyana had got us tailor-made Kevlar vests the first month we'd arrived in New York. Though we'd escaped our captors and were safe in this new country, we knew we had to be prepared for the unexpected.

All fugitives do.

I hadn't realized I'd need to use my vest again.

I changed and slipped the gun into a compartment in my vest. A surge of adrenaline went through me as I felt the bulge of the weapon next to my ribs.

I smiled to myself.

Maybe Madame Bouchard knew me more than I knew myself. Maybe she had concocted this game *for* us.

I had no desire to return to a life of fear. I didn't want to wake up in the middle of the night drenched in sweat again. I hated running from city to city, country to country, wondering when we'd get caught or assassinated. And I never wanted to fear my loved ones getting hurt, kidnapped, or murdered anymore.

But a secret part of me yearned to feel that wild rush again. That fired-up, red-blooded feeling of being *alive*, despite every danger.

Katy was right.

We'd become comfortable. Too comfortable. I was ready to get back into action.

I swaggered over in my mission gear to help Katy, who was now going through the bookshelf.

While Tetyana checked the bathroom, the walls, the carpet and even the ceiling for anything suspicious, Katy and I pulled the books down, one by one. We flipped through the pages to see if we'd find more letters, drawings, or other clues.

An hour later, Katy and I stared at the children's books jumbled in a pile on the ground, disappointed by the wasted effort of our search.

Tetyana had also found nothing and was now scanning the grounds through the open window, getting a lay of the land.

I walked over to join her.

The girl's bedroom was at the end of the east wing and had windows on both the front and the side. The window looking toward the front of the house was shut and curtained. But the side window was angled so that if we leaned out, we could see part of the grounds. That was where we were.

I placed my arms on the windowsill and looked out. It was almost one in the morning and a frosty chill had settled around the house. It was eerily quiet outside.

The exhaustion of the day was slowly catching up to me. If we were going to check the house that night, I'd have to be fully alert. I gave my arms and legs a good shake, stretched, then leaned outside to take a deep breath of that cool mountain air, when Tetyana pulled me back roughly.

"Duck!" she hissed.

I dropped to the floor, startled.

"What is it?" whispered Katy. She'd been sitting on the bed, cross-legged, flipping through the child's activity book.

Tetyana leaned toward the window to peek out again. Burning with curiosity, I rose from my corner and joined her.

Silhouetted against a lamppost in the driveway was a lone dark figure. It reminded me of the shadow I saw in the woods and I let out an involuntary shudder.

"Did they see us?" I whispered.

"Negative," said Tetyana, "they're facing the other direction."

"Who is it?" whispered Katy urgently.

"There's someone out there," I whispered to my friend.

"*Who?*"

"Could be anyone. Looks like a man."

Tetyana peeked out from her side of the window again.

"He's on the move. Near the barn now."

Her eyes widened. Tetyana was never one to get surprised.

"They waved," she whispered.

"Oh, my goodness," said Katy, a hand flying to her mouth. "At you?"

"Negative," said Tetyana, "there's someone else on the grounds."

I rose slowly again and peered through the darkness.

The shadow had disappeared.

It was pitch black near the barn. The structure was placed well away from the grounds, almost at the tree line where the mountain slope turned upward. On one side of the barn was a fenced paddock, and on the other was a pile of lumber, stacked up to almost six feet high.

"Wouldn't they have seen our light on?"

Tetyana nodded. "Probably."

"That means they saw us."

"Not necessarily. They'd know we're up, but they wouldn't have noticed us looking. You didn't stick your head out, did you?"

"You pulled me back, remember?"

"They didn't look like they were in stealth mode. I'd say they weren't expecting anyone to be watching at this time."

I thought I saw a movement near the lumber stack, and half wondered if my eyes were now playing tricks on me.

"At ten o'clock," said Tetyana urgently.

I focused my eyes to the left of the barn.

"Whoever it is, knows their way around the grounds," said Tetyana.

As we watched, a light turned on inside the barn and a man's shape was silhouetted against the open doorway. But only for a second.

The door opened wider, spilling the light onto the ground. As we watched, a second figure followed the first person inside.

Then, just as swiftly, the door closed behind them. In seconds, the light inside the barn turned off and the surrounding area plunged into darkness.

"Wow," I said, pulling back. "I'd love to know what the heck is going on in there."

Tetyana turned to me.

"Sounds like our recon exercise will start outside now. You ready?"

Chapter Seventeen

I pulled my weapon out.

"Katy, shut the windows, lock the door and don't open anything till we return," said Tetyana as she marched toward the door, her gun drawn.

She put her hand on the ancient doorknob and turned it slowly. I stayed in position behind her, ready for anything, but the passageway was empty.

We stood by the open door for a minute, listening carefully.

A muted, muffled sound was coming from somewhere inside the house.

"There's someone downstairs," whispered Tetyana. "Let's go."

We stepped out and closed the door. It was a relief to hear the click behind us as Katy locked herself inside.

"Where is it coming from?" I whispered.

"First or second floor," said Tetyana. "Let's check the kitchen first."

We had walked half the length of the corridor when a screeching yell came from downstairs. I sprang back in shock, banging into the wall.

"Mrs. Robinson!" I said, my heart racing. "They got her!"

"That wasn't her," said Tetyana, putting a hand out to stop me from rushing down. "I'm sure of it."

"That was an angry screech," I said, my heart still pounding. "A pissed-off I've-had-enough-screech."

"Move quietly," said Tetyana.

She darted toward the stairwell door. Though Tetyana was two years older than me, she was moving with the grace of a young panther stalking her prey.

I scampered after her, mimicking her quiet, fast moves as best as I could. It had been a while since I'd been on a covert mission. While I trained at the dojo with David every night, I hadn't been prepared for this. I cursed myself for not taking my workouts more seriously.

It took us ten seconds to run down to the first floor. At the bottom, the stairwell opened to a small alcove that led to the fire entrance, which, in turn, led to the grounds. This was the main door everyone would run out of, if there was ever a fire in the kitchen.

We stopped in the alcove and listened in. The side door to the kitchen was jarred open a few inches and a yellow light streamed out.

Someone was inside.

The muffled sound we'd heard earlier came clearly now. It was the sound of somebody crying.

Tetyana glanced through the opening and pulled back immediately. She slipped her weapon in her holster and turned to me with a look I was familiar with by now. It was the *you-take-care-of-this* look.

She stepped forward and opened the door wide for me.

I peeked inside.

It was Nancy.

She was sobbing on the kitchen counter and beating her fists on the hard surface, like she was ready to break it into pieces.

Taking a deep breath, I stepped inside and walked toward her, hoping I didn't look or sound too threatening with my all-black gear.

At barely five foot and ninety pounds, I sometimes got mistaken for a teenager, but whenever I donned my mission uniform, I felt like that kitten looking in the mirror and seeing a lion look back. But I knew this situation called for more house cat than lion.

I stopped halfway.

"Hey, Nancy?" I called out in a soft voice. "Are you all right?"

She didn't hear me. Her sobs got louder.

"Nancy? You okay?"

She raised her tear-stained face my way and blinked rapidly.

"What happened?" I asked, getting closer.

She wiped her face quickly, but her chest was heaving, and she looked incapable of speech.

I felt Tetyana sidle up to me. Dealing with emotional folk wasn't her bailiwick. I was sure she regretted running down in a mad scamper now.

I tried again. "Was it you who just screamed?"

Without answering, Nancy put her head on the counter and turned her body away from us.

This time, I felt Nancy was not crying as much as trying to evade any more questions from us.

What now?

The side door to the kitchen opened. Tetyana and I jumped forward, training our weapons at the door.

"Put those things away!"

It was Mrs. Robinson walking in, in an old-fashioned nightgown.

We holstered our weapons and stepped back.

"Sorry, thought it was someone else," I said, feeling my neck going warm. "We heard Nancy crying, so we came down...."

Throwing us a confused look, Mrs. Robinson walked toward the sobbing Nancy.

"What's going on, my child?" she said, putting an arm around the younger woman's shoulders.

Nancy lifted her head.

"It was an awful dream."

"What a terrible thing," replied Mrs. Robinson.

"A horrible nightmare," said Nancy, wiping her eyes. "I can't sleep in this house. Haven't been sleeping for weeks now."

"There, there, now," said Mrs. Robinson, rubbing Nancy's back. "All that traveling and moving does funny things to your sleep. It can stress anyone out. But you're here now. You'll settle in soon."

I exchanged a quick glance with Tetyana.

I didn't know any normal adult who'd break into sobs from a mere nightmare. I couldn't help feeling like Nancy was lying again.

That angry screech and that banging on the counter with her fists told me she had been mad at something. Or someone. What did she see that made her so angry?

"Let me make you a nice cup of tea now," said Mrs. Robinson, stepping toward the kettle. She glanced at us and smiled genially. "Sounds like she woke you two up too. Tea for everyone then."

I forced a smile back.

Part of me felt silly for having turned our weapons on her. We'd worked ourselves up to a lather and had overreacted. Then again, there was something wrong with this picture, and Mrs. Robinson was refusing to see it or simply not seeing it.

Nancy was wearing the same clothes she'd worn at dinner. Unless she went to sleep in jeans and T-shirt, she wasn't telling the truth.

"Is your room on the third floor too, Nancy?" I said walking up to the counter, keeping my voice friendly. "Did you come down here after you woke up?"

Nancy stared at me.

"I, er, fell asleep in the rocking chair," she said, pointing to the corner of the kitchen where the fireplace was.

"What about Jim?" I said. "He wasn't with you?"

She shot me a strange look.

"He's in our room, I guess. I mean, of course, he's in our room upstairs."

Jim must be a pretty sound sleeper for him to not hear his wife's screeches. She had been loud enough, I was sure we'd have heard it even with our door closed.

As if reading my mind, Nancy turned away with a scowl. She'd stopped crying, but she clearly didn't want to talk anymore.

"We've all had bad nights," said Mrs. Robinson, taking a couple of mugs from a cupboard. "We'll have you warmed up with a hot cup of chamomile and you'll be out till the morning like Sleeping Beauty."

She glanced at us.

"Take a seat, you two. I think we could all do with a cup of tea."

I pulled out a stool and sat down. Tetyana stood beside me, strategically positioned with a view to the window.

The rain had stopped, but the windowpanes were still wet, giving us a ghostly view to the driveway out in front.

"Here you go, my girl," said Mrs. Robinson, handing Nancy a mug. She poured two more mugs of tea, brought them over and set them in front of us.

She settled on a stool next to Nancy with her own cup and looked at Tetyana and me across the counter.

"Are you comfortable in your room, my dears?"

"Very," I said with a slight bow of the head, "thank you for putting us up."

"You found everything you need?"

That was a loaded question, if there was one. I hesitated to bring up the photocopied letters and the children's book in front of Nancy.

"We have, Mrs. Robinson," I said, picking up my mug. "Katy's upstairs in bed, reading a good children's book, the one you left for us."

I watched her closely for a reaction, but there was no flinching, no recognition, nothing to give her thoughts away.

"Feel free to borrow any of them," she replied with a nod, "there are some good storybooks on the bookshelf."

I turned to Nancy and forced another smile.

"So Jim must sleep like a log, eh?"

A red flush crept up her neck. Her eyes flitted to the window and back, and her hand holding the cup trembled slightly.

"Dead to the world," she said in a low voice.

She appeared more angry than scared.

"I could be yelling in his ear and he'd never hear me."

Nancy was a liar and a bad one at that.

I looked at Mrs. Robinson, who was sipping her tea, oblivious to what was going on in front of her.

Next to me, Tetyana stirred.

She put her mug down, wiped her mouth with the back of her hand, and turned to me.

"I need some fresh air," she said, "I'm going for a short walk. Wanna join me?"

"Right now?" said Mrs. Robinson in surprise. "It's dark outside."

"Just a short stroll around the house," said Tetyana, stretching. "We've been cramped in our car for hours. It will be nice to stretch my legs a bit."

I nodded and added a yawn.

"Me too. A walk will do me good. Otherwise, I'll wake up tomorrow all stiff and sore."

Tetyana rolled her shoulders for effect.

"Be careful," said Mrs. Robinson.

"Careful?" said Tetyana, turning around. "Out here?"

Mrs. Robinson looked at her, concern in her eyes. Or was it a warning?

"Sure, this isn't the Big Apple, my dear. No one's going to jump out from behind a tree and stab you or anything...."

We stared at her.

"Just watch your backs."

Chapter Eighteen

Watch your backs?

I wondered what she was trying to get at.

I also wondered if she knew about the two people who'd just walked into the barn. I had so many questions, but with Nancy here, sipping her tea, her dour eyes on us, I had to choose my words prudently.

I rustled up a smile.

"But Mrs. Robinson, what on earth would we bump into at this time?"

She blinked and looked down at her mug.

"Moose."

"Moose?"

"You gals haven't seen one up close," she said to her cup. "Just be careful."

Tetyana put her hand on the doorknob.

"Don't you worry. I can handle a moose or two." She pulled the door open. "Don't lock us out," she said before stepping out.

"Thanks for the warning," I said with a wave at Mrs. Robinson. "We won't be out for long."

I walked out into the cool night air after my friend and closed the door behind me.

"Watch your backs?" I said as we walked away from the house. "She was warning us."

"I would too, if I'd been getting death threat letters."

"She's hiding things. Why would she do that if she wants us to help?"

"Beats me," said Tetyana with a shrug. "One thing I know is this place is stifling. I'd kill myself if I had to live here."

"Whoa," I said as I stumbled over a dead branch. "What happened here?"

"Storm was worse than I thought," said Tetyana.

That was when I noticed the tree debris scattered all across the grounds.

"We'll need to clean up the driveway before we can get our car out of this mess," said Tetyana, marching down the driveway like she had to be some place important.

This wasn't a late evening stroll.

"You saw something, didn't you?" I said, hurrying to keep up with her long strides.

"The barn. Thought I caught a silhouette near the window. Let's check it out."

Keeping to the shadows, we hurried along the driveway. The only light illuminating our path was the line of old lampposts and the pale moon peeking from behind a dark cloud up above.

"Hey," said Tetyana, halting just as we passed our car. She took a few steps backward, her eyes on our vehicle.

"What is it?"

Our rental car was in the same place I'd parked it earlier. I glanced at the tires anxiously, half-wondering if someone had slashed the remaining tires. But, other than the grime and dust from our long drive, nothing seemed out of the ordinary.

"You don't see it?"

"What are you talking about?"

Tetyana walked to the back of the car and pointed at something. I stepped up and peered at what she was looking at.

A chill went down my back.

Someone had carved two words into the back panel of the car.

"Go home," I read out aloud.

"I'm a hundred percent sure that wasn't there when we rented it," said Tetyana.

I shook my head mutely, shocked anyone would so brazenly damage our vehicle like this.

"They used a sharp knife," said Tetyana, examining the slashes. "Nicely done, neat cuts."

"But the alarm never went off."

"They were careful to not rock the car. Whoever did it was precise and patient."

I glanced at the house. If the person who did this was watching us now, they'd know we'd got their message.

Our bedroom light was on. Katy was still up, possibly combing through the girl's possessions to find more clues. I felt bad for leaving her alone, but I was glad our door and windows were all locked.

The light in the kitchen was on too. I imagined Mrs. Robinson and Nancy having a heart-to-heart, though I wasn't sure if Nancy was capable of soul-searching conversations. She seemed like an angry young woman who thought the world hated her, the type to find any excuse to get furious.

It was a bizarre house. I couldn't wait for the morning, so I could see this entire place and the people here in daylight.

Tetyana took my keys and opened the passenger door. She fished out a torchlight from the cubbyhole, then crouching on the front seats, examined the inside of the car.

I paced up and down next to our vehicle, trying to think.

Barry had been too drunk to find his way to the dining room in time, let alone deface a vehicle with precision like this.

Mrs. Robinson had invited us here. If she hadn't wanted us around, her invitation made little sense. It couldn't have been her.

Pastor Graham had shown his true colors when he touched Katy inappropriately. He was a pervert all right, but that didn't mean he'd vandalized our car or left threatening messages.

The most welcoming person so far had been Jim, but I knew not to take him at face value. I'd been around the world and back and knew that sometimes it was the friendliest people we had to be wary about.

"Nancy," I said out loud, more to my myself.

Tetyana pulled her head out of the car and walked over to the front.

"She's the most likely one," I said. "She doesn't want us here."

Tetyana shook her head.

"She'd have smashed the windows and gone bat crazy. I can't see her standing patiently here, making fine knife art on our paint."

She pulled up the hood and shone her torch inside.

"Could have been Jim," I said, "he was the last to arrive at dinner and was outside just before that."

Tetyana turned to me and nodded.

"I'd keep an open mind on him. He's all show. There's something going on there." She paused. "He's a druggie, if I'm guessing right."

"Jim?" I said in shock. "But he looks so healthy and solid—"

"I've seen druggies in better shape than him," said Tetyana. "He's not a regular, but I'd bet my Glock the man gets high once in a while."

"What about Lisa?" I asked. "She snuck in pretty quietly to the dining room, didn't she?"

"Crept alongside the wall like a stealthy cat, like she didn't want anyone to notice her. She was in her seat long before you saw her."

I stared at Tetyana, as I recalled the peculiar conversation I'd had with Lisa.

"Do you know what she said to me at dinner?" I pointed at the car. "These exact same words."

"Go home?"

I nodded.

"She said something about staying away from the woods. Something about it not being safe." I paused and shook my head. "It's hard to imagine her doing something like this, though. This is too bold and we're practically parked in front of the house."

"I can't believe I missed it," said Tetyana in frustration. "I had my eyes out every time we were in the kitchen and when you were setting up in the dining room."

"Maybe it was when we were in Mrs. Robinson's room. We were occupied and didn't have a good view of the driveway."

Tetyana lowered the hood and pushed it down to lock it. Then she turned her torch off.

"All clear."

"What were you looking for? A bomb?"

She looked out into the grounds. "Out here, I'd expect someone to mess with our brakes or something similar."

A shiver went down my back.

"Maybe Katy is right," I said. "Someone here knows who we are."

With a shrug, Tetyana slipped the torch into her vest and took out her Glock. She was the practical kind. She'd need hard evidence before coming to conclusions. It was Katy and I who had runaway imaginations.

I glanced at the house again. The kitchen light had gone off. The tea party was over. I imagined Mrs. Robinson had gone off to bed, but wondered about Nancy.

"Don't you think it strange," I said, "that no one else came down when Nancy screeched?"

Tetyana nodded. "Been thinking about that. Maybe she's done this before. Waking up screaming from a nightmare."

"I don't believe Jim cares for her much either. Those two don't get along."

"Maybe he's having an affair with Lisa?"

I looked at my friend to see if she was joking.

"Impossible," I said. "They're night and day."

"Never make assumptions about your enemies," said Tetyana. "That's how you end up dead."

Chapter Nineteen

"Wouldn't you expect dogs to be running around in an estate this size?" I said, looking around.

"Unusual, that," said Tetyana.

She locked the car and threw the keys back at me.

"Let's find out what's so special about this barn."

I took out my weapon and followed her in the barn's direction.

It wasn't moose we had to be careful about here, I thought, as we crisscrossed the grounds. It was the people in this house.

We took the long way, slipping across the driveway and moving to the nearest tree, then to the next, staying in the shadows.

So far, I'd been cursing the clouds, wishing they'd move aside to give us more moonlight. But now, I wished a cloud would cover the moon fast, so we wouldn't be so exposed.

When we got to within three yards of the barn, Tetyana stopped and put her right arm out.

I halted.

A small animal ran in front of us, startling us. It was the feral cat we saw when we arrived at the house.

"Shh…" said Tetyana. I wasn't sure if she was speaking to me or the cat. Hearing her, the animal skedaddled behind the stack of lumber.

I looked at the barn, wondering what we'd find inside. The lights were off and there was not a sound to hear. I hoped they didn't have dogs in there. We'd rouse the entire house if they started barking.

"Perimeter check," whispered Tetyana. "West to east. Keep close to the side."

With a chill, I realized something.

If we'd spotted the two people from our window on the third floor, anyone looking out could easily see our silhouettes too. I looked back at the house, trying to suppress a panic attack, but all the lights were off. It seemed even Katy had gone to sleep.

Tetyana and I walked the length of the barn, peeking in through the windows and trying the locks and latches.

The place was latched down tight, and it was so dark inside, it was impossible to see anything. I wondered how Tetyana had seen a shadow in the windows all the way from the kitchen.

Either she had imagined it or her training had kicked in.

I followed her, keeping my eyes and ears open.

The smell of horses came to us as we got closer to the paddock area. A horsey snort confirmed our findings. I hoped we hadn't woken the animals up. If they began to get restless, we'd give away our presence.

We stepped away from the barn and slipped behind an oak tree near the stack of lumber. I hoped the snorting horse would drift back to sleep soon.

"How long do we survey the barn?" I whispered.

"Until we find out who walked in an hour ago."

I zipped my vest all the way to my neck. This could be an all-nighter, and the air seemed to be getting chillier by the minute.

After half an hour, I rubbed my hands to keep warm and tried not to let my teeth chatter. Next to me, Tetyana was standing stock still, as if she was at a road crossing in New York, waiting for the light to turn. Impatient, but still.

"Hey," I said in a low voice, "if Nancy is the institutionalized daughter, wouldn't someone recognize her? Especially her own mother?"

"It's a sizeable gap between nine and twenty-nine."

"Still. There would be clues."

"Maybe she's wearing a disguise?"

"She could have hooked up with this Jim guy, found a way out of the asylum, and convinced the pastor to get them jobs here."

Tetyana said nothing, her gaze fixed on something distant, away from the barn.

I pressed on, working on my theory.

"Now she's back, and possibly sending threatening letters to everyone, including Mrs. Robinson. Perhaps it's her way to take revenge on a family that abandoned her. What do you—"

"Did you see that?" said Tetyana in a warning voice, interrupting me.

I squinted in the direction she was looking.

"What is it?"

"Wait for it," she whispered.

I scanned the woods, wondering what I'd be waiting for. The grounds looked dead to the world. Unless a pre-hibernating bear or a moose had ventured too close to the house, I couldn't imagine what we'd be seeing.

Tetyana clamped a hand on my arm.

"There."

That was when I noticed the faint flicker of light coming through the trees.

"Someone's out in the woods?" I said.

"Yes, but do you know what's over there?"

"The cabin!"

Tetyana nodded.

"It's closer to the house than I thought."

"The road we came on winds around the mountain. That skewed our sense of distance."

"I thought Mrs. Robinson said nobody lives there."

Tetyana didn't reply, her eyes peeled on the light which was flickering back and forth, like a wind was blowing a candle flame.

I wondered who'd want to spend the night in that cold ramshackle of a place at a time of year when storms were frequent and there was frost on the ground.

"A candle in that place is a fire hazard," I said. "Come to think of it, the entire shack is a fire hazard."

"It's also a good hiding spot," said Tetyana.

I shook my head.

"I'm sure everyone in the house knows of that cabin. It can't be a—"

A scraping noise from the direction of the barn silenced me.

We turned to see the barn door opening slowly. We pulled back into the shadows.

A man's frame silhouetted the lit doorway. He turned around and looked back inside, as if to check on something. Then he turned off the lights and shut the door.

We followed the shadow with our eyes as he slunk through the grounds. The old lampposts along the driveway illuminated his figure as he got closer to the house.

"It's not Barry," I said, "too surefooted."

Tetyana nodded.

"Pastor Graham?" I whispered.

"Hard to say," Tetyana whispered back.

I looked at the figure again. He was wearing a coat which made it difficult to distinguish him.

He got to the side door and fumbled. It took a while, like he was having a hard time opening the door. I hoped Mrs. Robinson hadn't locked us out.

"Maybe it *is* Barry," I whispered.

"When he turns the lights on in his room, it'll give us a clue who he is."

The man finally got in, but didn't turn on any lights.

"Could be Jim too," said Tetyana. "He didn't hear Nancy scream because he wasn't in the house."

I looked back at the barn. "If I'm not mistaken, there's a second person still inside."

We waited quietly, our eyes on the house, waiting for a light to turn on and give us a clue.

Next to us, the barn was silent. Even the horses had settled down.

"Frigging hell," said Tetyana after ten minutes, "let's check the barn."

We'd just got to the barn door, when a blood-curdling scream echoed through the grounds.

Chapter Twenty

Tetyana and I spun around and dashed toward the house.

A light went on the first floor in the staff quarters.

"Mrs. Robinson?" I called out when we got close to the side door.

Tetyana fumbled at the door.

"Wasn't her. That was Nancy. Again."

"Are you sure?" I asked, but Tetyana was too busy tackling the door.

My mind whirled. The scream sounded genuinely in distress this time. It wasn't Nancy's enraged shriek we'd heard earlier.

Maybe Tetyana was right. My mind had been so busy with Mrs. Robinson's death threat letters, I had automatically associated all danger with her.

"Did that idiot lock the door on us?" said Tetyana, banging on the door. "Darn thing's jammed," she grumbled as she rattled and pulled.

I looked up at the house.

Other than the light on the first floor, our bedroom was the only one with a light on now. I wondered if Katy had heard the scream and had already come rushing down.

For the second time that evening, I was surprised how everyone in this house seemed to sleep through all this noise. Granted, it was a vast house, but still.

Did everyone become deaf at night? Or did they just not care?

"Stand back," said Tetyana, taking a few steps away from the door.

I jumped back.

Tetyana gave a swift kick, and the door flung open.

We ran into the kitchen. I turned on the light just as Nancy crashed through the side door that opened to the staff quarters.

She halted when she saw us. I noticed her face was contorted into a ghastly expression. She wasn't acting now.

"What happened?" I asked, running toward her.

She opened her mouth to speak, then closed it again. I noticed her whole body was shaking.

"Nancy? You okay?"

She gave me a wide-eyed look.

"For goodness's sake, talk to us."

Her mouth opened, but nothing came out. She seemed to have gone mute.

Tetyana stepped up to her, took her by the shoulders and shook her roughly, until her head bobbed back and forth. That seemed to do it. Nancy looked at Tetyana in surprise and collapsed into her arms, sobbing.

Tetyana stood stiffly while Nancy bawled her eyes out on her shoulder. Tetyana shot me an awkward look, as she held her gun limply with one hand, and reluctantly patted Nancy on the back with the other.

"Nancy," I said. "You can talk to us. What's going on?"

She lifted her head from Tetyana's shoulder and turned her tear-stained face to me.

"Mrs. Robinson..."

She swallowed like she couldn't finish her sentence.

A frisson of fear went through me. I stepped up to her.

"Mrs. Robinson? Is she okay?"

"What the frigging heck happened?" snapped Tetyana, pushing the woman away and glaring at her.

"She's... she's... in her room," said Nancy, pointing a trembling finger at the door she'd just burst through.

Pushing her away roughly, Tetyana dashed toward the door.

I raced after my friend.

Where is everyone?

Tetyana was already at Mrs. Robinson's room.

"Mrs. Robinson?" she hollered, banging on the door.

Nothing.

"Please let her be okay," I prayed under my breath as I darted toward her, scarcely registering Nancy running at my heels.

Tetyana yanked the door open and dashed in. I rushed inside after her.

We screeched to a halt near Mrs. Robinson's prone body on the floor.

"Oh, no!"

I fell on my knees next to her. Tetyana was already checking her pulse.

"Mrs. Robinson?" I said, shaking her by the shoulders. "Mrs. Robinson?"

"Faint but still beating," said Tetyana, looking up.

Mrs. Robinson's eyelids were half-closed, but I could see her eyes darting back and forth underneath. She was breathing harsh, shallow breaths, like it took every ounce of energy to carry out this simple action.

At least she was conscious.

"Mrs. Robinson," I said, trying to calm the panic rising inside of me. "Stay with me, okay?"

She tried to move her mouth, but her face was frozen. I let go of her shoulders and felt her limbs. There was no blood anywhere, just stiff muscle.

"Could be a stroke," I said, looking up at Tetyana, "or a heart attack."

"Call 911!" Tetyana barked at Nancy, who was nervously twitching next to us. "Now!"

While I held Mrs. Robinson by the shoulders and talked to her, Tetyana loosened her top buttons.

"Did you take anything tonight?" I asked. "Any medication?"

She didn't respond, as if she was focusing every effort on staying alive.

"Blink once if you took something," I said, "just once."

Mrs. Robinson's face didn't change.

Tetyana lowered her head to check her breathing.

"She needs a doctor fast."

She looked up at Nancy, who was standing in the same position as she'd come into the room.

"Did you call 911?"

Nancy gave Tetyana a frozen look. She had gone mute again. And deaf.

"What the hell!" shouted Tetyana, springing to her feet. She pulled out her mobile and punched in the numbers.

Mrs. Robinson stirred in my arms and mumbled something.

I leaned in closer.

"We're here, Mrs. Robinson," I said, wishing I knew her first name. "We're not leaving you. We're getting you help."

Her lips moved, but no sound came out. I draped one arm around her shoulders and squeezed her tightly.

She blinked and swallowed. She was desperately trying to tell me something, but the words weren't coming out.

"You're going to be fine," I said. "Do one thing for me, okay? Can you move your arm?"

I could see her trying, but her arm barely moved a half inch off her body.

"That's great. Now, what about your hand? Can you wiggle a finger for me?"

Nothing.

She fell back in my arms, like she was too exhausted to try.

"That's perfect. You're doing just fine. Just focus on breathing, okay? We're going to take care of you. Don't you worry."

I babbled on, knowing the only thing I could do was to keep her conscious until qualified help arrived.

An angry cuss from Tetyana made me look up.

"What the...? The darn connection's gone!"

She punched the screen so hard, I was sure it would shatter into pieces.

"Th... there... there's a phone...," stuttered Nancy, coming to life.

"Where?" barked Tetyana, spinning around to face her. "Where's the phone?"

"In... in... in the... kitchen," stammered Nancy, her face white.

Tetyana turned around and bolted out of the room at the same time someone came barreling inside.

They both sprang back in alarm.

"What in good God's name is going on here?" said the pastor, rubbing his forehead where Tetyana had banged into him. He was in striped pajamas, like he'd just jumped out of bed.

"Do you have a working phone?" shouted Tetyana, making him take another startled step back.

"Mrs. Robinson needs help!" I cried.

That was when he spotted her lying on the floor.

His eyes widened.

"We need medics here ASAP!" shouted Tetyana in his face.

With shaking hands, he pulled his mobile phone from his pocket.

"Doctor Fulton," he whispered as he dialed. "Doctor Fulton, Doctor Fulton," he repeated as if that would conjure up the physician.

Tetyana hopped from one foot to the other, like she was trying her darnedest to stop herself from grabbing the pastor's phone and dialing faster. I held on to Mrs. Robinson, rubbing her arm, hoping and praying she'd recover from whatever was happening to her.

"Stay with me, Mrs. Robinson," I said. "We're going to get you help."

"What in God's name?" squawked the pastor, shaking his phone in the air. "There's no reception!"

With an exasperated grunt, Tetyana pushed him out of the way and dashed out to the corridor.

"Where's the frigging landline in this house?" I heard her shout in the passageway.

With another frightened look at Mrs. Robinson, the pastor ran after Tetyana.

Chapter Twenty-one

Mrs. Robinson's breaths were coming faster and more shallow.

Her skin was cold to the touch. I clutched her hand tightly to let her know she wasn't alone.

From somewhere in the depths of the house, people were hollering. I heard someone shouting something about a first-aid kit.

Nancy stepped up to Mrs. Robinson and kneeled on the other side. She was no longer the sullen, angry woman we'd met earlier. She looked concerned.

And stunned.

She took Mrs. Robinson's other hand.

"Is... she... she going to be okay?"

Nancy had that same deer-in-headlights look she'd had earlier in the kitchen.

"She'll be all right," I said, unsure of my own words.

"Please be okay," whispered Nancy, rubbing her arm. "Please get better."

"Stay awake," I said, desperately trying to recall my first aid lessons. "Help will be here real soon."

I did another quick check of her body.

Mrs. Robinson didn't have any visible cuts or bruises, or any bullet holes. She wasn't bleeding from anywhere.

I had thought this was a stroke or heart attack, but I now wondered if it was something else altogether. She'd been wheezing and clutching her chest a few times that evening.

I scanned the room.

There were no guns, or upturned pill bottles, or even a bloodied knife. The windows were shut, and the room looked exactly in the same condition we'd seen it before. Except for the bed.

Mrs. Robinson had been asleep when this... whatever it was... had afflicted her. Either she had tumbled from her bed or had got up in a hurry and keeled over.

I glanced at Nancy across from me.

"Was it you who screamed just now?"

Nancy nodded, without looking up.

"How did you find her?"

"I... I came down and knocked on her door. When she didn't open, I thought she was sleeping, so I turned around...."

She paused as if she wasn't sure what to say next.

"What happened then?" I said, hearing my voice harden. "And don't lie."

She looked up and shot me a dismayed look.

"I'm not lying," she said. "When I turned to go back to my room, I heard her door unlock, so I turned back. And she... she..."

"Mrs. Robinson?"

A nod.

"What did you see?"

"She was standing there..." Nancy stopped to swallow hard. "She was standing at the door and swaying. Like she was going to fall, like, she was going to faint..."

"Did you see anyone else?"

She shook her head.

"What happened then?"

"She tried to tell me something, but... it was like something got stuck in her throat. She gurgled..."

"Gurgled?"

"She clutched her chest, you know, like she always does when she coughs."

"Why didn't you call for help?"

"I... I don't know. I didn't think... I didn't know what to do." Nancy swallowed again and gave me that wide-eyed look again. She looked like she was about to burst into tears.

"Then, she fell down. One second she was standing up, and the next second she was on the floor like this."

Nancy looked down at Mrs. Robinson as if she still couldn't believe her eyes.

"That's when I screamed."

She looked as shocked as I felt. Unless she was a fantastic actress, she was telling the truth. Something told me I could trust her words. This time, at least.

"Nancy," I said, "what were you doing down here at this time of night?"

She shot me a fearful look from under her eyelids.

I leaned over and felt my voice harden again.

"You need to tell me."

She looked away. "I came down because I wanted to—"

A loud commotion in the corridor made us both turn. It was Tetyana and the pastor rushing back.

"Doctor Fulton's on his way," said the pastor, panting. He hurried over and kneeled next to me. Then he glanced up at Tetyana.

"I still think we should take her to him."

"That's dangerous," snapped Tetyana, "If she's having a stroke, she can't be moved."

With a desperate sigh, the pastor took Mrs. Robinson's hand from me. He bowed his head and said a prayer under his breath while we watched.

I gripped Mrs. Robinson's shoulders and rubbed her arm, praying silently in my own way.

Please, please stay with us, Mrs. Robinson. Please.

Tetyana started pacing the room. I saw her impatiently check the window to see if it was locked. Then, she stepped over to the bedside table to check the contents on it.

Mrs. Robinson's breaths were coming louder and raspier.

"Keep breathing," I said, my voice cracking. "Please keep breathing."

Pastor Graham's head bowed even lower over her hand, and his prayers came faster.

I'd just met this woman lying in my arms. I hardly knew her. But at that moment, all I wanted, more than anything in the world, was for her to take another breath.

"Please, Mrs. Robinson," I pleaded, hearing my voice rise in pitch, "keep breathing. That's it. Stay with me."

Pastor Graham's prayers got louder and louder as he invoked all sorts of saints. Across from us, Nancy started to cry silently.

Suddenly, Mrs. Robinson shuddered like something hit her. Her eyes rolled back and a strange gurgling sound escaped from her lips. Then her body convulsed.

"Oh, no," I said, panic rising inside me.

What do I do? What do I do?

Then, with one horrific shudder, Mrs. Robinson's face fell to the side, her eyes partly open.

"No!" I cried, clutching her shoulder. "Wake up. Stay with me!"

Nancy started wailing.

"CPR!" hollered Tetyana from across the room. "Give her CPR!"

I was already on my knees, leaning over Mrs. Robinson's chest.

I put my hand on her nose and reached for her mouth. For the next few minutes, I scarcely registered what was going on around me. All I knew was I had to make her breathe again.

I hazily recalled the pastor shouting and Nancy screaming. Tetyana sat across from me, holding Mrs. Robinson's wrist, taking her pulse. I thought I heard Katy's voice too, but I didn't have time to look up.

I alternated between chest compressions and rescue breathing. I was on autopilot. After a while, someone tried to pull me away, but I didn't break. I couldn't. I wanted this woman to live.

I didn't realize how long I'd been going on until a firm hand rested on my shoulder.

"It's okay," said the voice next to my ear. "You can stop now."

It was Tetyana.

"No," I said, shaking my head.

"You've been at it for more than half an hour," whispered Tetyana, pulling me away with a firm hand.

I wiped my face and stared numbly at the lifeless body in front of me. I barely registered the sweat streaming down my back and face.

My body was shaking uncontrollably from exhaustion and the horrible, sinking feeling I had failed.

I reached over and touched Mrs. Robinson's hand. She was still warm, but she had stopped breathing for good.

Chapter Twenty-two

Mrs. Robinson's room was crowded.

Almost everyone in the house was there.

Lisa, Nancy, Katy, and Pastor Graham were standing bunched together by the doorway with shocked expressions on their faces.

I presumed Barry was sleeping in a drunken coma somewhere on the third floor. And Jim, I knew, had rushed out in his truck to pick up the only doctor in town.

The only emergency services nearby were the police officer we'd met on our way here, but he couldn't have done any more than we had.

What Mrs. Robinson had needed was prompt and proper medical attention, but the nearest clinic was an hour away.

All that was futile now.

I collapsed backward and leaned against the wall, unsure whether to scream or cry.

Pastor Graham walked over to the bed, picked up a pillow and placed it under Mrs. Robinson's head. Not that she felt discomfort anymore, but it was a kind gesture. Then he took a sheet from the bed and covered her body, leaving only her face in the open.

Tetyana had closed Mrs. Robinson's eyes, but her mouth was slightly open. She looked peaceful, as if she'd decided to sleep on the floor instead of on her bed that night.

An angry yell made us all turn.

"What the hell is all this? How come no one woke me!"

It was Barry.

He pushed in between Lisa and Nancy and staggered into the room. He stared at the body on the floor, his hair standing up like he'd been electrocuted.

"What the dickens is this? Why didn't anyone tell me what's going on? How come I'm the last to hear anything in my house?"

He swayed like a massive pine tree in the wind. I sat up and moved away, afraid he was going to fall flat on top of Mrs. Robinson and me.

He swayed again. I watched him in shock, too exhausted to do anything, but Tetyana lurched toward him, and caught him just in time.

Barry pushed her aside, staggered back and clutched onto Lisa's arm. Lisa's face turned dark. I wasn't sure if she was disgusted or incensed by her brother, but she reached over and wrenched his hand from her arm and pushed him away.

That didn't seem to faze Barry.

He turned to the pastor.

"What the hell is wrong with her?"

The pastor crossed himself. "It's a very sad day for—"

"She's gone!" wailed Nancy, interrupting him from behind. "She's gone for good!"

"What the hell do you mean she's gone?" said Barry, snapping at Nancy.

I caught a flash of fury cross her face. Her eyes fired up, and she pointed an angry finger his way.

"You *killed* her, you big brute. You drove her to her death. It was you!"

Katy and I locked eyes.

Did I hear that correctly?

Those words had a strange effect on Barry.

With a howl, he stomped through the room, pulling at his hair, beating his chest and roaring like a mad bull.

I scooted to the side to avoid getting stepped on. Tetyana put an arm up to stop the man from trampling over Mrs. Robinson.

But Barry was out of control.

A flailing arm hit a glass of water on the bedside table which came crashing down, breaking into smithereens on the floor.

Nancy gasped.

Lisa shot him a furious look.

The pastor took a step toward Barry.

Yelling at the pastor to get off him, Barry swept everything on Mrs. Robinson's table to the floor. It was like watching a child throw a tantrum.

Mrs. Robinson deserved better than this.

"This house is cursed!" he bawled. "It's a sick place!" He reached for the bedside lamp and jerked it out of the outlet, making electric sparks fly.

I wanted to do something, but this wasn't our home. This wasn't our family.

Tetyana was standing next to me, glaring at the crazed man. Though we both had our weapons on us, we couldn't just tackle our deranged host and pin him to the ground, like we'd do with a criminal.

Lisa hadn't said a word since her arrival, but her face said she was beyond angry. Nancy was sobbing next to her, too hysterical to speak.

"Calm down, for heaven's sake," said the pastor, pulling on Barry's elbow. "Stop this madness!"

But Barry was a big man. I didn't think he could control himself now, even if he had wanted to. It was like watching a wild buffalo rampaging in the midst of a funeral.

Barry looked at the lamp, like he'd just noticed it in his hands. With a roar, he smashed it against the wall, breaking the light bulb.

I jumped up.

"Control yourself!" I shouted before my brain could kick in. "Show some decency for goodness's sake."

Barry turned and stared at me, the broken lamp handle still in his hand.

"What did you say?" he asked in a low, dangerous voice.

"Show some respect for Mrs. Robinson," I replied with gritted teeth. "Her body's not even cold yet, and you're running around like a mad dog around her."

Something flickered in his eyes.

"Mad dog?" howled Barry. "How dare you! Who the hell are you to call me mad?"

He advanced on me, his eyes burning fire, the lamp handle held high.

I ducked.

Tetyana pushed me behind her and faced Barry, her face five inches from his.

"You touch one hair on her and you're a dead man," she snarled.

Barry stopped in his tracks.

The pastor stepped up and pried the lamp from Barry's hand.

"For God's sake, settle down," he said.

He glanced over to Nancy and let out an exasperated sigh.

"No one's accusing anyone of anything. I know we're all a little rattled, but Mrs. Robinson most probably died of a heart attack."

To my surprise, Barry slipped to the floor next to Mrs. Robinson and sobbed.

I shook my head.

The man was wasted. He acted more like a child than an adult. No wonder Lisa was disgusted by her own brother.

The pastor took control of the room.

"Mrs. Robinson's been sick for a while now. We all did the best we could do. Now, can we show some respect by staying calm, please? Jim's gone to bring Doctor Fulton over soon. We'll figure out what we have to do next."

I looked at Mrs. Robinson's helpless body on the floor. I felt responsible for her death. She had called us for help, and we had done nothing to stop this.

I swallowed hard.

Nancy was right. Or half right, at least.

Someone had driven Mrs. Robinson to her death. Someone had made her life hell in her last few weeks on earth.

This wasn't an accidental death.

The letter writer had got their wish. It could have been anyone in this room. My task now was to find out who did this.

I looked at my friends. Tetyana was standing next to me, leaning against the wall, her expression taut. Katy was standing on the threshold of the room, her face pale, a sad look in her eyes.

The pastor cleared his throat and looked at Tetyana and me in the corner.

"I think the family would like to be alone with Mrs. Robinson for the moment."

I nodded.

I had already begun to feel like we were intruding on a private affair. It was admittedly a strange family, but we were the outsiders here.

With one last look at Mrs. Robinson, I stepped away from the wall.

I walked past Lisa on my way out.

"I'm sorry for your loss," I said, but she said nothing back.

Katy had already stepped out of the room and was standing in the corridor, her arms wrapped around her, like she was cold. I reached out to her for a much-needed hug.

Tetyana came up from behind us.

"Let's go to the kitchen," she whispered, "I found something you need to see."

Chapter Twenty-three

We trooped into the kitchen.

It felt much colder here now.

One look out the window told me Jim's black pickup truck was gone.

I wondered what was taking him so long. I hated to think of Mrs. Robinson lying on the cold floor. I wished we could have moved her somewhere more dignified, but I knew we couldn't move her before the doctor examined her.

My mind was in a haze, trying to come to grips with Mrs. Robinson's sudden death.

I poured myself a glass of water and joined Tetyana and Katy huddled around the kitchen counter on the same stools we'd sat on only an hour ago with Mrs. Robinson and Nancy.

"It's horrible," said Katy, wiping her eyes. "I know we just met her, but she was a good soul. I knew it in my bones."

Tetyana merely nodded, eyes cast down.

I took a deep breath in to settle my frayed nerves. Mrs. Robinson's death had rattled me more than I'd expected. Part of me wanted to cry, but we had work to do.

Work we'd promised Mrs. Robinson we'd do.

"I wish we could get everyone out of that room and lock it," I said, lowering my voice. "Barry's destroyed a bunch of evidence in there already."

"Under any other circumstances, I'd have told the gang to get the hell out," said Tetyana, shaking her head. "But we're guests here, strangers they hardly welcomed. It's not our place to tell them what to do."

"Even if it's a murder?" whispered Katy.

"We don't have any evidence of that," I said and paused. "Yet."

"But Nancy said so."

"We can't be sure if she meant that literally or if she was referring to how Barry's obnoxious behavior drove her to death," I said.

"I'd like to know what Nancy was doing down here," said Tetyana. "Quite convenient she showed up just as Mrs. Robinson fell to the floor, isn't it?"

"Suspicious as heck," said Katy. "There's something odd about her and Jim appearing out of nowhere to work here."

"The strange thing," I said, leaning in, "is how she reacted to Mrs. Robinson's death. She seemed genuinely frightened and shocked."

"Crocodile tears," said Tetyana.

"Could be. But I felt her sadness, then her horror when Mrs. Robinson died."

We sat silently for a while, collecting our thoughts.

"It's maddening," said Katy, thumping a fist on the counter, "if we tell them about the letters, we'll be alerting the murderer."

"Maybe the doctor will help us," I said. "The way Mrs. Robinson was coughing and wheezing all night, makes me think this could be a case of poisoning. I'll be interested to hear what he finds."

I turned to Tetyana.

"Do you think we could have saved her if we got help faster?"

"Hard to say," she replied, pulling her mobile phone out and tapping the screen. "How do the darn cellphone towers suddenly stop working at the same time?"

I took my phone out. The signal bars were green and full, but the phone line wasn't connecting. I reset my settings and double-checked, but it refused to work.

"Mine's stopped too," said Katy. "I was looking up the history of this house online when suddenly the Internet went out. I was about to text you and find out what you were up to. That's when I realized my phone had conked out."

"There's no cellular reception in this house anymore," said Tetyana, a worried expression on her face.

"Was it the storm?" I asked.

"A storm can take a tower out," said Tetyana, "but the bars are still green, which is strange."

She stood up and scanned the room. "Unless...."

"Unless what?"

"Someone jammed the signal."

"That's crazy," said Katy, "that only happens in espionage films or murder movies...." She trailed off.

I turned to Tetyana, remembering what she'd said to us outside Mrs. Robinson's room.

"Didn't you say you found something you wanted to show us?"

Tetyana reached into her vest and pulled out a long white envelope.

"Saw this on Mrs. Robinson's bedside table, just now. Thought it was one of those letters, but it's not."

She placed the envelope on the counter in between us. It was sealed and had an airmail stamp with a postal watermark on it. This meant it had come here by mail.

Katy and I peered at the typeface on the face of the envelope. The letter had been addressed to Mrs. Robinson, but it was the address under the FROM line that sent a chill down my spine.

"Madame Bouchard?" said Katy in a shocked whisper. "How did she send this from her grave?"

"Maybe she mailed it before she died and it got lost." I picked up the letter to examine it. "Wait, this was stamped four days ago."

"The day after her death," said Tetyana. "Stranger and stranger."

"Could have been the lawyer," I said. "Maybe this letter was part of her last will and testament and he was merely following instructions. We must let Peace know."

"This hasn't been opened," said Katy. "Mrs. Robinson must have just got it."

I looked at my friends. They looked back at me.

I knew what we had to do.

"You know it's illegal to open someone's letters, right?" said Katy, reading my mind.

"She's dead, Katy," said Tetyana.

"I don't care about the million-dollar payout anymore," I said, "I just want to find out who hounded Mrs. Robinson. And I want to expose them."

"Expose them?" said Tetyana, her mouth set in a stern line. "I want to make the bastards pay."

Katy gave a determined nod. "I'll do whatever we have to do."

She got up and walked over to the cutlery drawer. She rummaged around until she found what she was looking for and came back to the counter with a small steak knife in her hand.

She took the letter from me and slit it open.

I glanced at the door. Barry's shouting had died down, and it seemed like the pastor was keeping everyone calm as they kept vigil over Mrs. Robinson's body.

"I'm keeping an eye," said Tetyana as she saw me look. "We're good."

"It's a will," said Katy, unfolding the letter. "A handwritten will." She placed the single piece of paper on the counter and smoothed the creases.

Tetyana and I leaned over the counter.

"It's a codicil," I said, "an addendum to Madame Bouchard's will."

"Looks exactly like the one Peace showed us," said Katy, "same lawyer's insignia on top and everything."

She was right. Madame Bouchard's formal will was fifty pages long, chock full of legalese that Peace said was standard wording. This letter was in the same format, but it had only two paragraphs.

The first explained who she was, and that this was an addendum to her last will and testament dated a week before she died.

The second paragraph had only four sentences.

Katy read it out in a low voice while Tetyana and I leaned in to hear.

"I bequeath my New Hampshire home and all its possessions to the Red Heeled Rebels for their use as an orphanage for the lost and abandoned children of America. My offspring made their beds a long time ago. They can lie on them now. Only God can help them for the sins they have committed."

Chapter Twenty-four

We stared at the paper for what must have been a full minute.

I rubbed my eyes and read the paragraph again. Then I looked up at my friends. Their faces told me they were as shocked as I was.

"Madame Bouchard left this house to *us*?" said Katy.

"A mother's true love, eh?" said Tetyana, taking the paper to scrutinize it. "She's playing everyone from her grave."

"A sick joke, maybe?" I said.

"I think this is the real deal," said Tetyana.

Katy leaned in. "Barry and Lisa aren't the most charming people, but what do you have to do to get disinherited like this?"

Tetyana and I shook our heads. Mrs. Robinson had been right. This house held too many secrets, and we were just scratching the surface.

"We need to talk to Peace," I said, rubbing my tired forehead. "He can tell us where it came from and who wrote it and if it's real."

"Looks pretty legit to me," said Tetyana. "Sure, this could be forged, but why would anyone do that? Unless it was one of us, and I'm sure none of us did this."

I felt the raised logo with the tip of my finger. It felt real, but I'd seen cleverly forged passports that had fooled even the US immigration department.

Anything was possible.

"The thing is Mrs. Robinson died without knowing what was in this letter," I said. "Why didn't she open it? Whenever I get snail mail, I rip the envelope to see what's in it while I'm still standing at the postbox."

"Me too," said Katy. "I never get real mail anymore."

"Did someone plant this at her bedside table then?" said Tetyana.

"Maybe the same person who sent the hate letters?" I suggested.

"The same person who killed poor Mrs. Robinson?" said Katy.

"But why would they do that?" said Tetyana.

"To frame us?" I said and immediately shook my head. "No, that makes little sense."

Katy looked around the kitchen and then at us. "If this letter isn't a dud," she whispered with a glint in her eye, "does this mean we *own* this mansion now?"

I stared at my friend, letting her words sink in.

We fell silent after that, trying to come to terms with our discovery.

The sound of a vehicle's engine made us all swivel around on our stools. The headlights of a car cut across the window.

Jim's truck was coming up the driveway. The truck stopped halfway toward the house and Jim's head popped out of the window.

We watched as he maneuvered his vehicle around a dead branch and park a few spots away from where he'd parked earlier.

Jim and a stranger stepped out of the truck, slammed the doors shut, and hurried across the driveway toward the side door.

"They're coming!" said Katy, grabbing the codicil from the counter and stuffing it into her pocket. Tetyana picked up the envelope, folded it and slipped it into her vest.

With a quick twist of the doorknob, Jim opened the door and held it wide for the doctor to enter.

The man we'd all been waiting for stepped inside with his doctor's bag.

It was a man in his mid to late sixties. Tall, thin and pale, and with a nasty cut on his nose, Doctor Fulton looked like someone in need of a medic himself.

I wondered how he'd got that fresh facial injury. He didn't look the sort of man to get into a bar brawl. It triggered a memory in the back of my brain, but for the life of me, I couldn't make sense of it.

"Ladies," he said with a slight nod, seeing us.

He spoke with a slightly nasal tone. I wondered if it was the damage to his nose or if he always spoke like that.

"Doctor Fulton?" I said.

"Where is she?"

"In her room." I pushed my stool away and stepped toward him. "I'm afraid we have bad news. Mrs. Robinson expired several minutes ago."

His shoulders drooped, and he stared at me as if he didn't want to believe it. Jim was staring at me too, from behind him.

"She's gone?" he whispered.

"I'm sorry."

The doctor shook his head, his brow deeply furrowed. "But she was in such good health. Fit for her age. I can't imagine how—"

A yell in the corridor made us all turn.

"I told you already! Leave me the hell alone!"

I'd recognize that voice anywhere now.

Barry stomped in, arms swinging, and spittle trickling down his chin.

The man's deranged, I thought. Completely and utterly unhinged.

I remembered the scrapbook Katy had discovered in our room. Suddenly, instead of feeling disgust, I felt pity. Maybe he wasn't just a common, middle-aged ass of a drunkard. Maybe he was in serious need of psychiatric help.

Do mental health issues run in the family?

"You!" he roared as he spotted us three at the kitchen counter. "I want you all out!"

We stared at him in shock.

Ignoring Jim and the doctor, Barry strode toward us.

"Interfering busybodies! You city folk come in here and look what happened? Don't need no squatters in this house. You hear me!"

He's kicking us out?

Pastor Graham came up from behind Barry and put an arm on the man's shoulder. Barry jerked his hand off.

"Leave me alone, you old fool!"

"Calm down. There's no need for—"

"Who invited you people to trespass and hang around here, huh?" said Barry, his eyes dark and flashing in fury. "I want you lot out of my home!"

Was Barry on any medication? I wondered if he was truly upset at us or if he was reacting to Mrs. Robinson's sudden death the only way he knew how—lashing out at anything and everything.

He took one step closer to us.

Tetyana moved forward.

"Barry—" I heard the pastor say.

Within seconds, Barry swiped at Katy's head and yanked her hair back.

"Let me go!" shrieked Katy as she fell off her stool.

Chapter Twenty-five

Katy struggled, but Barry kept his stubborn grip on her hair.

He whirled her around the room, like they were taking part in a strange and cruel dance.

I jumped in.

"Let her go!" I shouted, pulling at his hand. Katy shrieked and tried to push him away, but that only made Barry hold on tighter.

"Hey!" I heard Tetyana shout.

She was behind Barry, her hands clamped down on his shoulder. He buckled under her grip, yelling in pain. Within seconds, she pulled him off Katy, twisted him around, and pinned his arms to his back.

Barry bawled, his spittle flying everywhere, but Tetyana held on. For an obese drunkard, he had strength.

"Settle down!" she yelled.

But he writhed even more. As if she'd had enough, Tetyana slammed him against the kitchen wall.

"Stop it!" exclaimed the pastor, rushing over.

I pulled a trembling Katy away from the melee.

"You okay?"

She gave me a petrified look, too shocked to answer.

"Lemme go, you fool!" screamed Barry.

The pastor raised his voice. "For God's sake, behave yourself! For your dead mother's sake!"

That seemed to do it. Barry stopped struggling. He turned and stared at the pastor like he was seeing him for the first time.

"Settle down, my good man," said the pastor, his voice softened.

Barry opened his mouth to reply, but nothing came out. Tetyana released the man and stepped away.

"Relax," said the pastor in a calm and soothing voice. "Everything's going to be okay. You'll be fine."

I noticed tears running down Barry's face. Was it the mention of his mother's name that brought the tears?

The pastor took Barry by his arm and ushered him to the rocking chair in the corner.

"We can't go attacking people like that," I heard him say in a quiet voice, like he was speaking to a child. "Whether or not they're strangers. You need to watch yourself, my man. Didn't we talk about this?"

Barry didn't reply. He shot a wretched look at the pastor and collapsed into the chair. Then, he dropped his head into his hands and started moaning.

The doctor who'd been crouching on the threshold, ready to bolt outside if Barry came too close, stirred.

He shot us a wild-eyed look.

"I need to see Mrs. Robinson," he said, nervously glancing around him, like he didn't know where he was anymore.

Jim, who'd been slinking into a safe corner of the kitchen turned around to us, his face slightly red. I noticed those glassy eyes again.

It was like he wasn't fully there. Maybe Tetyana was right, and he was on drugs.

He gave Tetyana an apologetic shrug, like it embarrassed him that he hadn't been the one to stop Barry.

"I, er…," he stammered, "don't think he had his meds tonight."

"Mrs. Robinson?" repeated the doctor, in a firmer voice.

"She's in her room," I replied.

Jim turned to the doctor. "I'll take you."

Pastor Graham was pouring water into the kettle to make tea for Barry while Barry was rocked back and forth in his chair, moaning.

"What's wrong with him?" I whispered as I sidled up to the pastor. "What does he take meds for?"

"This and that," said the pastor, his eyes on the kettle.

"Was Barry close to Mrs. Robinson?"

The pastor didn't look up. "We were all close to her."

"It's a very sad day."

"She kept us all together. If I'd known she was sick…."

The pastor turned his back to me. He reached up to take a packet of tea bags and two mugs from the cabinet on top.

I had so many questions, but I didn't want to bother someone who was grieving. Then again, Pastor Graham was not really part of the family.

"The doctor just told us she was in fine health," I whispered. "He sounded surprised."

"Did he now?"

"Didn't you notice her coughing and wheezing recently?"

The pastor fiddled with his tea mugs. I wondered why he didn't turn my way. Was he concealing his expression or was he truly that absorbed in his tea making?

Tetyana was keeping one eye on Barry, ready to leap on him if he gave any more trouble. Katy sat quietly on her stool, a glass of water in front of her, recovering from the shock of being violently twirled around the room by her hair.

"Did you see how she was at dinner tonight?" I said. "Was that unusual of her?"

The pastor let out a sigh.

"I thought it was a common cold or something. You never know when these things can happen. We think we have years to go, but Providence decides when we will go and how."

He turned around, a strange expression on his face I couldn't quite make out.

"It's God's will."

He paused as if he was trying to choose his next words carefully. He turned to Tetyana and Katy, then back to me.

His eyes narrowed.

I braced myself.

"I think you all had best leave now."

An awkward silence fell in the room.

Tetyana, Katy, and I stared at the pastor. All I could hear was the kettle whistling now. Barry had stopped moaning, like he was listening in too.

In their silence was a strong message. The pastor didn't need to tell us anymore. We were strangers and no one here wanted us around.

I scrunched my forehead, trying to think of how we would convince them otherwise.

We couldn't share the codicil with the family yet. When we did, we'd have to do it without making anyone feel threatened. If Barry reacted in fury at our presence without knowing this important fact, I couldn't imagine how he'd react when he heard the news.

I sighed.

The kettle started whistling, and the pastor turned his attention back to his tea.

Tetyana stepped over to the window and gazed out.

"Crazy storm last night," she said to no one in particular. "I'll go clean the driveway so we can get our car out."

She turned to the pastor.

"There's some free kindling for the fireplace out there. Happy to pick it up for you."

The pastor gave a noncommittal nod and walked over to Barry with a mug of hot tea. He was clearly not interested in continuing the conversation with us.

Tetyana opened the side door and walked out.

Just as the door closed behind her, Lisa and Nancy entered through the door to the staff entrance. Both had red eyes.

"Water's boiled," said Pastor Graham, seeing them come in. He was kneeling in front of Barry, cajoling him to take a sip of the tea.

Lisa strode across the kitchen toward the kettle, deliberately ignoring us. Nancy followed her like she was on a leash, eyes averted. I couldn't help but think she looked like an obedient pet.

The get-out-of-our-home vibes were even stronger now. Katy and I glanced at each other. It was like we were invisible.

Normally, we'd never hang around a mourning family who wanted their privacy. But this was different.

I was sure this family didn't want us around because they were more interested in hiding their secrets than finding out how their caretaker had died.

Chapter Twenty-six

"I'm going upstairs to get our bags," said Katy, speaking loud enough to make sure everyone heard. But no one looked her way or acknowledged her.

"I'm coming with you," I said.

Katy and I didn't speak until we got back into our room. I closed the door behind me and let out a sigh.

"What a day."

"How are we going to make them let us stay?" said Katy, plopping down on the bed.

I shook my head. "No idea."

I walked over to the window to check on Tetyana. Through the light of the lamppost outside, I could see her figure below, moving around our car.

The major portion of debris had fallen about twenty yards away on the driveway, but she was pottering around our vehicle. I wondered what she had up her sleeve.

I paced the room.

Think, woman, think.

Katy squatted next to the bed and spread the photocopied letters in front of her. She stared at them, as if willing them to speak to her.

"I don't think the Internet and the phones going down was a coincidence," I said, "or that it had anything to do with the storm."

"We'll find out pretty quickly when we head back to town," said Katy.

I nodded. "I think it's time to talk to that cop. He knows something. He was warning us to stay away."

"No one's talked about murder yet though," said Katy, "except for Nancy."

"Barry's a world-class jerk, but I can't see him murdering anyone in a cold and calculated way."

"If you ask me, I don't think he's fully there," said Katy, tapping her head.

"There were no stab wounds, choke marks, or bullet holes on Mrs. Robinson. She looked like she had a stroke or a heart attack. The doctor should tell us soon enough."

I kept pacing, my eyes on the floor, my brain revving like a beat-up car, working hard but going nowhere.

"They'll suspect us, you know?" I said, giving my friend a sober look.

"Why?" said Katy.

"We're the only ones to gain here," I replied. "Maybe Mrs. Robinson's death had something to do with Madame Bouchard's will. Maybe not. But we can't deny that we got here just in time to see her die *and* we inherit the house. There'll be lots of questions."

"But we inherit the house from Madame Bouchard, not Mrs. Robinson."

I nodded. There were many threads that still needed to be unraveled, and I hated the thought of being kicked out before we figured them all out.

"We need to get through to Peace. He'll clear this codicil for us."

"What I want to know is why did Mrs. Robinson go to the trouble of copying the letters?" said Katy, picking up one photocopy. "Where are the real ones? I can't help but feel they contain the answers to her death."

I turned to my friend.

"You're right, Katy. We need to find the originals."

"How do we do that?" she said glumly "If you haven't noticed, we're being kicked out."

"We need to think of something fast."

"Would they seriously chase us out like this in the middle of the night?" Katy asked.

"They'd want us gone by the morning for sure," I said, turning back to my friend. "Unless..."

"Unless what?"

"We slash our spare tire."

"That sounds dangerous," said Katy.

"Desperate times..." I said, trying to get my foggy brain to work. "We could also pretend you're sick. Too sick to move. A bad cramp or something. Can you handle that?"

"There's a doctor in the house, remember?" said Katy. "I can pretend all right, but if he's any good, he might see right through me."

"You've done it before."

"True, but—"

"Or, one of us could disappear."

Katy frowned. "What do you mean?"

"We could pretend one of us walked into the woods and got lost. But in reality they're here, in this room. Unless someone comes barging in, no one will know."

"Are you planning to lock me inside again?" said Katy.

"It's for a good cause."

"I hate this room. It's lifeless. Full of *dead* stuff."

With a sigh, I turned to the window to look for Tetyana, but she was no longer on the driveway. I leaned out to scan the grounds.

Where did she go?

Other than a few branches that had been moved to the side, she'd hardly cleared the driveway.

"Asha?"

Katy's voice was guarded.

I whirled around.

"What?"

She was on her knees, half inside the small closet, staring at her open suitcase. Her clothes, makeup, and undies were jumbled together in a disheveled mess, like they always were.

"Someone's been through my stuff," she said.

"Are you sure?" I said, walking over. Katy wasn't the neatest person on the planet. "How do you know?"

"I *know*, okay? There's a method to my mess. I'd know if someone went through my bag, and someone has."

Katy fished out her wallet from the jumble and opened it. She pulled out the picture of her and Chantelle and pushed it into a different slot. Then she checked her money.

"Everything's mixed up, but they didn't take anything, thank goodness," she said, with a relieved sigh. She turned to me. "Do you think it's that creepy pastor?"

"I wouldn't put it past him," I said.

My own clothes were neatly tucked inside my closed suitcase. I bent down and flipped the cover open.

Katy gasped.

"Oh, no."

Someone had rifled through all my stuff and then thrown it all back in a heap.

I kneeled on the floor and rummaged through my clothes to see what was missing. My purse was still there, but there was something more important I was looking for.

There.

I grabbed the small pill bottle and clutched it against my chest.

"Your sleeping pills?" said Katy, making a face.

I nodded mutely. They were a lifesaver. It was the only way sleep came to me—the kind of sleep without nightmares.

"What about your wallet?" said Katy. "Check that."

I plucked it out and opened it. My money was still there, but my credit cards and driver's license had been pulled out and pushed back in halfway, like whoever did this had been in a hurry.

"All there?" asked Katy.

"Everything is here, but they were checking my ID."

"Same here," said Katy. "They pulled out my cards too. Nothing's in the right place anymore."

I leaned over to Tetyana's backpack and flipped the cover. Her neatness level was several echelons higher than both of ours, but now her things looked in as awful shape as Katy's.

I sat back to think.

"If it was the pastor, he didn't do this to just check out our lingerie. Whoever came in here wanted to find out who we are."

Katy turned and gave me a defiant look.

"The more they want to scare us away, the more I want to stay."

I nodded. "Me too."

We sat on the floor, staring at our bags.

I'd been so busy giving CPR to Mrs. Robinson I hadn't noticed who had come to her room or when.

"Katy," I said, turning to her. "How did you know Mrs. Robinson was dying downstairs?"

"Someone banged on our door. I thought you were in trouble. I know you said not to open, but I did. Then I heard everyone race down the main stairs, thundering like a herd of cattle. I just followed them. I thought the house was on fire, to be honest."

"Everyone raced down? No one was missing?"

Katy wrinkled her nose.

"Things were going berserk around me and I was more worried about you two... Sorry, I don't remember."

"Whoever banged on the door wanted you out so they could come in."

Katy stared at me.

"We're the only ones on this wing," I said. "Wouldn't you expect everyone to run down from the west wing as soon as they heard the news, not come all the way and knock on this door?" I paused. "Did you see who it was?"

"No one was in the corridor when I came out—"

The room lights flickered, making Katy stop in mid-sentence.

We looked up to see the ceiling light flicker intermittently, like it was about to go out.

"Didn't Jim say they have an electric generator for this place?" I said.

"If you ask me," said Katy, "this house is haunted. Look, even the Mickey Mouse clock has stopped working."

I stared at the clock, an idea slowly forming in the back of my mind. I jumped up and walked over to the door.

"Come on!"

"Where are you off to?" called out Katy.
"I know how to stop them from booting us."

Chapter Twenty-seven

"So what's your plan?" Katy whispered as she slipped our bedroom key in her pocket.

"The starter relay," I said. "David showed me how to remove it. We disabled one of the goon's cars back in Nairobi, once. It's easy, fast, and we don't even have to open the bonnet. No one will guess what we're doing."

"Why do I feel like the rental company is going to be very unhappy when we return the car?"

After a quick glance around, we slipped through the corridor toward the back stairwell. The fire exit was the fastest way down, and I didn't want to bump into any of the family members on the main stairway.

"Hard to believe Madame Bouchard owned this house," I whispered. "Lived in luxury apartments all around the world but ignored her own childhood home."

"I'm sure this place was impressive at one point," whispered Katy, eyeing the faded wallpaper along the corridor walls. "Funny how after she got married and had two babies, she scooted off like there was fire on her tail."

I shook my head. "What would make a mother abandon her own children?"

"What about that Canadian ambassador who swept Madame Bouchard off her feet? Talk about a deadbeat dad."

"He died a few years after they moved to Toronto, I think. But I don't think he cared much for this place or his kids either."

"Some dysfunctional family. No wonder Lisa and Barry are messed up."

I opened the door to the stairwell, and we climbed down, trying to keep as quiet as we could.

"What now?" whispered Katy when we got to the bottom.

I put a finger to my lips.

We were in the alcove where the fire door led to the grounds outside. To our right was the door that connected the fire stairwell to the kitchen. Next to it was the door to the staff quarters.

I stood still for a few seconds, listening in, with Katy breathing down my neck.

The loud sounds from the kitchen made me glad we had left. Barry was raging again, and this time it sounded like he was bringing the entire kitchen down with him, pots and pans and all. We could hear Lisa, the pastor, and even Nancy imploring him to calm down.

The sound of something crashing against the wall made us jump.

"Why do they tolerate that man?" said Katy with a grimace. She stepped toward the fire exit door that would take us to the grounds.

"Wait," I said as a new idea formed in my mind. "This is a good thing," I whispered, "we can look for the letters while they're preoccupied."

I motioned her to follow me.

I slipped through the small door to the staff quarters. Katy and I tiptoed through the corridor toward Mrs. Robinson's room, keeping our ears and eyes alert.

The banging, crashing and yelling from the kitchen was music to my ears. Barry's tantrum was keeping everyone away from us, and that was all that mattered.

While Katy kept watch behind me, I reached out to turn the doorknob. I felt my heart race as I realized we'd have to answer more than a few questions if Doctor Fulton was inside.

"Quick," whispered Katy. "Footsteps."

I yanked the door open, and we stumbled inside. Katy closed the door behind us hurriedly. We stood by the door, staring at each other, listening for any more sounds from the corridor.

"Must have gone to the kitchen," whispered Katy.

I looked around.

The room was empty. Someone had already removed Mrs. Robinson's body. I wondered where they had taken her.

They had also attempted to clean up the mess Barry had made earlier. They had placed the broken lamp back on the bedside table. The glass shards had been picked up and thrown in the bin. The bedsheets had been folded and placed back on the bed.

"You take the left side and I'll take the right," I whispered as I walked to the bedside table where Tetyana had found the codicil.

For the next fifteen minutes, Katy and I combed through Mrs. Robinson's room, slowly and methodically, stopping every few minutes to listen in, in case someone had heard us.

"She lived like a nun," whispered Katy after checking the wardrobe.

"Somebody could have removed some of her stuff too."

"I think she lived the minimalist lifestyle. She didn't even own one lipstick."

"Check for secret places," I said, flipping the comforter away from the bed and feeling for anything hidden between the sheets or on the mattress. "They have to be hidden somewhere here, like that book in the girl's room."

"Do you think someone found them already?" Katy whispered.

I paused to think. "I've been wondering about that barn. There's something going on in there. If we can check it before we—"

That was when I spotted the bible lying on the windowsill. I pounced on it.

"Ah!" said Katy, perking up at the sight of the book. "I'd bet you anything they're all stuffed in there. I can see her doing that."

I flipped through the pages rapidly at first, then slowly. I felt the back and front covers and the binding for any hidden pockets and shook it. But there was nothing.

I gave Katy a disappointed look.

She plopped on the bed with a sigh.

"If you were Mrs. Robinson, where would you put the originals?" I asked.

"They could be anywhere in this big house," said Katy, "It will be like looking for a—"

"The kitchen! Where she spends most of her time."

"But everyone in the house has access to the kitchen."

"Maybe she suspected someone would check her room, so she put it in a place no one would guess."

"Hidden in plain sight?"

"Exactly."

"How do we search the kitchen without anyone wondering what we're doing?" said Katy.

"We'll figure something out," I said. "But first we need to stop them from kicking us out."

I put the bible back where I'd found it. That was when I spotted it.

"Look!" I said, reaching over to the windowsill.

"The letters?"

"Keys," I said, as I pulled out a large set of keys in one giant steel ring. "Hidden behind the bible."

"What's it for?"

I held them up to examine them. The keys were in all sizes and shapes, some old, some new.

"She was the caretaker here, wasn't she? That meant she had access to the whole house. These are probably her master keys."

I turned to my friend.

"Do you know where I'd like to check next?"

Katy gave me a wary look. "The bedrooms upstairs?"

"I'd like to see where they took Mrs. Robinson's body. Remember, she put that letter back in her pocket? Maybe she still has the others on her."

"Unless the person who sent them already removed them."

"Let's find out," I said. "Ready?"

I reached over to pull open the door.

Just as my fingertips touched the handle, a loud boom reverberated throughout the house, shaking the floor beneath us.

Chapter Twenty-eight

I recoiled, pulling my hand back in alarm.

We stood frozen by the door, not breathing.

"Do they have earthquakes in New Hampshire?" whispered Katy, a horrified expression on her face.

We stood still, waiting for another tremor, an aftershock, but the grounds had turned silent again.

"We need to get out," I said, pulling the door open. "If that was an earthquake, we can't stay inside."

Katy and I scrambled through the corridor and back to the fire stairwell. I pulled at the door to the outside.

"Don't they lock any doors in this house?" I heard Katy mutter from behind me as we ran out. "If this was the Bronx..."

The door closed with a soft thud behind us.

The sky had lightened slightly, and a gray mist was swirling through the air. Dawn was on its way, finally.

I scanned the grounds. Tetyana was nowhere to be seen.

Where is she?

I ran to the edge of the wall and peeked out. Our car was still in its original position and intact. Jim's truck was where he'd parked it halfway down the driveway, when he'd brought the doctor over.

But no one else had run out of the house. Through the kitchen window, I could see they were all still inside.

Didn't they know basic earthquake safety procedures?

"Who's that?" said Katy, pointing at someone in the distance.

I peered through the mist.

Someone was near the bottom of the driveway and walking toward the house, carrying something heavy.

The side door to the kitchen banged open.

It was the pastor. He stepped out and swiveled around, a dazed look on his face.

"Come," I whispered to Katy and stepped away from the wall.

The pastor turned when he saw us appear from the side of the house.

"Did you hear that bang?" I called out. "Was it an earthquake?"

He rubbed his forehead.

At dinner the evening before, Pastor Graham had looked friendly and suave, like someone who had it all together, even acting as the host of the house. But he was clearly no longer in his element.

"Thought it was a car crash or something, but with Barry acting up and all...." He paused. "Where did it come from?"

"Outside, somewhere in the grounds," I replied.

"Tetyana!" said Katy.

We all turned toward the driveway.

She was right. The figure had come closer now, and it was unmistakably our friend hauling a pile of dead branches in her arms.

"All okay?" she called out.

"All good," I hollered back.

"What was that blast?" said the pastor when she got closer. "I felt the earth shake there for a minute."

Tetyana walked up to us and tossed the branches next to the driveway.

"Sounded like lightning struck a tree or something," she said, looking at the sky.

It was still dark and gray, but a thin light shone in the horizon, where the sun was peeking out. I was sure the storm had already passed.

Is another one on its way?

"Was about to investigate, but I wanted to make sure all was okay at the house first." She turned to the pastor. "You want me to check the grounds?"

"Oh, please do," he replied, relief washing over his face, "I have enough trouble to contend with inside."

"Hey!"

We all turned.

Someone was hollering from farther away on the grounds.

"What's going on now?" said the pastor, the worried look coming back to his face.

Somebody was yelling at the bottom of the driveway, from where Tetyana had just come. We could see a figure running toward the house now.

"Who's that?" said the pastor, peering out.

"Jim!" I said.

"Is he all right?" said Katy.

"Hey!" hollered Jim as he ran toward us, flapping and flailing his arms.

"What in God's name is going on?" said the pastor.

"The bridge!" shouted Jim, panting loudly. He stopped next to his truck and leaned against the door, hyperventilating.

"Speak, young man," said the pastor in an exasperated voice. "Did someone else die?"

Jim gave a wide-eyed look at the pastor.

"It's the bridge."

"What about it?"

"It's gone!"

"What in heaven's sake are you babbling about?"

"The storm... It swept it away."

"Are you serious?" I said.

Jim looked at me, still breathing hard. "It's in pieces, I tell you."

"My goodness," said the pastor, his face turning pale. "You really mean to say the bridge has crashed?"

"Gone," said Jim, gesturing with his arms. "The river's rushing. Must have loosened some nuts—"

"How are we going to get to town now?" said Tetyana.

Jim gave her a confused look and wiped the sweat running down his face. He shook his head.

"We're all stuck here now."

"What a nightmare," said the pastor. "What a horrible nightmare..."

An emergency siren in the distance made us all turn.

"The police!" cried Katy.

Tetyana turned to us.

"Come on," she said. "Let's go check what's going on here."

Katy, Tetyana and I turned around and marched down the driveway toward the bridge.

After a few minutes, we heard the men follow us from about twenty feet away, the pastor breathing laboriously.

The siren was getting closer and louder. And the sky was getting lighter.

I couldn't wait for morning to come. This place was creeping under my skin and burying itself there.

Chapter Twenty-nine

I glanced behind to make sure the pastor and Jim weren't within hearing distance.

The pastor had slowed down and Jim was walking at the older man's tempo to stay with him.

Good.

I turned back to my friends. "Funny how the cop heard the bridge go," I said, lowering my voice, "I thought he worked in town, half an hour away."

"Lurking around here, probably," said Tetyana.

"In the middle of a stormy night?"

"Maybe he was hanging around to help us?" said Katy, her voice sounding hopeful.

"My guess is they have one police officer for the entire town," I said. "If the power lines and cell phone towers are down, you'd think he has better things to do than drive up here to take care of a small group of people."

"I'd bet the cell phone and the Internet issue was localized to this house," said Tetyana.

"Someone tampered with them?" said Katy. "To distract us from Mrs. Robinson's death?"

"Maybe to spook us," said Tetyana. "One more way to scare us away from this place."

We took the last curve on the driveway. From here, we could see the bridge and the road that led to this house.

"Oh, my," said Katy.

"Unbelievable," I said.

Jim was right.

The bridge had disappeared.

A large part of the structure had fallen into the water, exposing rusted iron cables and rotting wood jutting from the two ends. The leftover portion was the size of a footbridge, but I doubted it was safe for anyone to walk on.

"Hey, there!" said Katy with a wave.

The same officer who'd stopped us earlier was now standing on the embankment across from us. He was staring at the broken bridge, hands on his hips.

The squad car's headlights shone across the open chasm, the halogen lights bursting through the swirling fog.

Tetyana, Katy and I walked up to the edge of the bank.

The officer didn't wave back. He didn't even smile.

The stream had become a raging river now and was gushing furiously, reaching a crescendo as it hit the rocks below. I wondered how much force it would have needed to break this bridge down.

A nagging feeling came to the back of my mind. *Was it the storm or was it a person who did this?*

"Ahoy there!" Pastor Graham shouted from behind us.

The officer turned to look at the men joining us. He didn't smile or acknowledge them either. His frown deepened.

"What happened here?" he hollered.

"Heard a bang and saw it down," shouted Jim, trying to make himself heard over the rush of the water.

"Everyone okay?"

Next to me, I heard the pastor take a deep breath in as if to calm his nerves.

"No one was here when it happened," shouted Jim.

"Oh, good," said the officer.

"But we have a death, Officer Jensen," called out the pastor.

"A what?" exclaimed the officer, putting a hand around his ear.

"Mrs. Robinson..." said the pastor, raising his voice. He paused and took another deep breath. "Heart attack, we think."

The officer's eyes widened.

"She's gone," said Jim.

"Doctor Fulton's here," continued the pastor, shouting, though his voice was cracking now.

"Mrs. Robinson *died*?" said the officer in shock.

No one said anything for a while. Everyone bowed their heads, watching the river.

It was surprising how a stream could turn into this powerful force of nature in such a short time. I wondered if I'd been wrong. Maybe this was an act of god, after all.

The storm could have easily wreaked havoc on the bridge and brought it crashing down. I remembered how terrified I'd been to drive over it only a short while ago.

I looked up at the officer who hadn't yet said much. He looked as unsure as we all were.

"Is everything okay back in town?" I yelled across the water.

He turned to me with a strange expression on his face.

"Yeah, why?"

"Internet's down here. Cellphone reception's out too. And the electricity's acting strange," I shouted back. "What about the town?"

The cop shook his head.

"Nothing that bad. Just a few branches down. I'd know if that happened." He took off his hat and scratched his head like that would help him think more clearly. "Strange that."

"We'll manage," said Jim, walking along the embankment, examining what was left over of the bridge.

"You need emergency supplies?" called out the cop.

"Have a diesel backup generator," Jim shouted back. "Already up and running. We'll be good."

"I guess we can live without a phone for a short while," I heard the pastor say in a quiet voice next to me.

"We have electricity, food, and water and a place for everyone to sleep," said Jim. "We're good for a week."

A week?

I wondered if he had counted us in there as well, not just the immediate household members.

"Best to ride the storm out then," hollered the officer, looking relieved, "I'll get some help from town to fix this thing up."

Jim gave him a wistful smile. "Hey, Jensen, if the food runs out, shuck a few hot dog packets across the water, would you?"

No one smiled, least of all the officer.

"What about a rescue team?" said the pastor, his frown deepening. He seemed more worried than any of us at the state of the bridge.

"A rescue team?" echoed the cop.

"Through the mountains," said the pastor, though his voice was unsteady now.

"In this weather?" said the officer. "Too risky to come through the mountain pass."

"There are five inches of snow up on the trails," said Jim, turning to the pastor.

"I'll call for reinforcement," said the officer. "They're all out of town, but I'm sure I can rustle something up." He stared at us for a second. "Best for you all to stay put right there."

Officer Jensen was at least twenty feet from us, across the gully. But something in his demeanor, even from this distance, told me he wasn't telling us everything. It was the way he stared and frowned, like he suspected all of us.

Does he have a connection with anyone in this house? Does he know something we don't know?

"What about Mrs. Robinson?" I asked.

Everyone turned to me.

"Where is she?" I said, turning to the pastor. "What did you do with her body?"

"The wine room," said the pastor.

"The *wine* room?"

"Behind the servants' quarters. It's not a fridge, but it has stone slabs for walls, no heating and faces north, so it stays cool. It will have to do for now."

No one spoke for a while.

I felt a pang of sadness to think Mrs. Robinson was no longer with us. We'd been talking to her only a few hours ago. She'd been an intelligent and welcoming woman who'd wanted to get to the bottom of a cruel mystery.

Something stirred in my gut. It was odd for the bridge to break down like this. It was too convenient.

I turned to Tetyana and Katy and noticed a steely look in their eyes.

One thing was for sure. Our wish had been granted. They couldn't get rid of us now.

Chapter Thirty

Tetyana spotted the two strangers first.

"Friends of yours?" she asked.

The five of us had turned back to the house and were walking abreast, immersed in our own thoughts.

Officer Jensen had promised to check on us the next day, but I felt a hard knot in my stomach to see him drive off, knowing our only route to the rest of the world had been temporarily cut off.

My mind had been whirling.

The universe had a funny way of answering our prayers. We needed to be more discerning about what we asked for, I thought.

We were halfway up the driveway when Tetyana spotted the figures.

"Who are you talking about?" said the pastor, glancing around him.

I peered into the woods through the fog. "Where?"

"At eleven o'clock," said Tetyana.

We all turned.

Katy gasped.

About a hundred yards ahead of us were two silhouettes standing under a lamppost, right next to our car. They looked uncanny, like ghosts appearing through the mist.

"Is that Nancy and Lisa?" I said, squinting to see if I could make out the resemblance, but these two were taller and skinnier.

"Negative," said Tetyana.

The pastor halted, making all of us stop too.

"Who in the good lord's name is that?" he said, frowning.

"Where in tarnation did they show up from?" said Jim.

"I take it you're as surprised as we are?" said Tetyana.

Jim and the pastor looked genuinely bewildered. This place is getting stranger by the minute, I thought with a shiver.

"Do you have other houseguests we haven't yet met?" I asked.

The pastor shook his head. "I know everyone who comes and leaves the house."

"We have no guests, other than you three," said Jim.

Katy and I exchanged a quick glance. I knew what she was thinking.

Mrs. Robinson had invited us over without telling the family. They were still under the impression that we were lost tourists. We had no idea if she had invited others too, surreptitiously.

From the corner of my eye, I saw Tetyana pull her sidearm from her holster. A quick glance at Jim and the pastor told me they hadn't noticed her movement, their eyes on the strange apparitions on their driveway.

"Well, let's go find out, shall we?" I said, putting a hand inside my vest, ready to bring my weapon out too, if I needed to.

There were five of us and two of them. Plus, two of us were armed, if it came to that.

We continued walking abreast, but at a slower pace, as we gauged the strangers with every step forward. For just one moment, we temporarily forgot our differences as we joined in solidarity against this unknown adversary.

But the two figures didn't budge. Or make any threatening movements. They just stood by our car, waiting for us.

How did they get here?

Tetyana had been hanging around in front of the house most of the night, which meant she would have noticed anyone walking up from the woods or the driveway.

The bridge had collapsed and the mountain pass behind the house had been snowed out, making it too precarious to use. There was no other way onto the grounds as far as we knew.

The fog lightened as we got closer to the house, and the strangers' profiles became clearer.

It was a couple, a young couple, in their mid to late twenties. They were wearing hiking gear and were carrying oversized backpacks.

Hikers?

From behind the house, I could see the smoky shadows of the mountains emerge like a pastel painting. The storm had passed and dawn was breaking.

The two people under the lamppost didn't move as we got closer, but I could see they were watching us as warily as we were watching them.

At twenty feet, the pastor stopped and called out.

"Hello there?"

"Hi," replied the man with a wave. He sounded younger than he looked.

"Can we help you?"

"Yeah, we got lost."

"How did you get here?" asked Jim.

"Got sidetracked up on the mountain late yesterday," replied the man. He pointed at his silent partner. "Sprained her ankle, so we thought to make it back to town, but we took the wrong way."

The man was only wearing a lumberjack shirt, not the most appropriate clothing if he'd been hiking on the range in this weather. The woman next to him was standing still, almost pouting, like a petulant teenager. She was in hiking pants and jacket and had her long brown hair in a ponytail.

"You walked all night?" asked Tetyana. "On a sprained ankle?"

The man nodded. The woman stood like a statue, without even a twitch of her face.

The most unusual thing about the woman was the tinted shades she had on, those small, round, grandma-like glasses. Most prescription eyewear with sun protection turned dark when exposed to the sun, but there was no sun at this time.

Who wears sunglasses at night?

"Must have been one heck of a hike," said Tetyana.

"Worst ever," said the man.

"In this storm, it would be," said the pastor in a quiet voice.

"We're experienced hikers. We do a trail every weekend, but the mountain sure beat us this time."

"No hypothermia?" said Tetyana.

The man showed us a small, heated lamp he was carrying.

"We have our winter gear. Got our layers on and brought our fleece too. Normally, we'd be all right. Could have camped up in the mountains for the night and come down tomorrow. But it was getting nasty with the rain, so we followed the light."

I wondered what someone who'd hiked all night through a snowed-in mountain pass, in a terrible storm, would look like.

Not like these two.

They looked too well put together. They were trying too hard.

"The light?" said Katy. "What light?"

"This place," the man said, gesturing to the mansion behind us.

"We didn't know if it was a shack or a cabin, or if someone had put up a tent, but we thought lights meant people, and people meant a way back to town, so we came through the trail real fast as soon as the storm cleared."

I looked over at the mansion.

Jim's generator was humming somewhere in the background, and the lights were still on. I wondered where Lisa and Nancy were and what they were up to.

"Sorry to disappoint you," said Jim, "but there's no way to town anymore."

The man raised his eyebrows but didn't reply.

"Our bridge is down," continued Jim. "Happened half an hour ago. No way out until we fix that."

The couple didn't respond. There were no gasps of horror or worried looks, just placid acceptance at the turn of events.

"That's too bad," replied the man in a flat voice.

"Well…" said the pastor, looking around him, flustered. "We can give you shelter and food at least, but I'm afraid we're all stuck here for the time being."

Jim nodded somberly. "There's no way in or out."

"Except for the mountain trails, apparently," said Tetyana. I detected a hint of sarcasm, but no one else seemed to notice.

Given our past, it was difficult for me to not feel paranoid. Every shadow had a double meaning. Every word came with a potential threat. It had been a strange forty-eight hours. I had to keep my emotions in check.

"Well, I'm sure we can get you cleaned up and find a place for you to sleep," said the pastor, separating from us and walking toward the house. "God knows, we will all need some rest after this," I heard him mumble as he walked away.

"I'm going to go check on the generator," said Jim, as he stepped away from us and walked toward the barn.

Tetyana, Katy, and I looked at each other. That left us in the awkward position of welcoming these two arrivals to the house, despite being unwelcome guests ourselves.

The couple turned to us, expectantly.

"The local cop is coming to check on us tomorrow," I said. "If we can get you two across the gully, I'm sure he can give you a lift to town."

I might have imagined it, but I thought the woman gave a start when I said "cop."

Chapter Thirty-one

"Hi, I'm Katy," said my friend, flashing a smile and stepping forward.

"I'm, er, Charles," said the man. "This is Caril."

Katy gave a start.

"Caril and Charles?"

Does she recognize them?

I took in the couple standing in front of us. Neither looked familiar to me. I hadn't heard those names before, but something had alerted Katy.

She recovered instantly.

"Are you from around here?" she asked, turning on her friendly smile again.

"From Maine," said the man. "We go all over the world hiking the tallest peaks. We come here every year to go up the White Mountains. It's the highest range in this part of the country."

Something about these two smelled fishy.

Charles was pale and pudgy, more like someone who spent his days in an underground bunker playing computer games than someone who hiked outdoors. The woman was scrawny and sickly looking.

I'd have expected anyone who climbs the tallest mountains in the world to have toned muscled and a ruddy complexion. Caril and Charles had the right gear, but if they were mountain climbers, Katy and I were princesses at Buckingham Palace.

"Good thing you saw the house light from up there," said Katy brightly. "If we hadn't got the generator up, you'd still be stuck on the mountains."

"We've been through worse," said Charles with a shrug. "Remember Peru?" he said, turning to his partner. She didn't respond. "Besides, the human body is resilient. We humans can survive anything."

I raised my eyebrows.

"Anything?"

"You'd be surprised."

Tetyana leaned over. "Did you see a hiker's cabin on your way down here?"

A strange look crossed the woman's face.

"Cabin?" said the man.

"The shack along the trail," said Tetyana. "Looks like it was built for hikers like you to stay the night safely."

Charles shook his head and pursed his lips. "We must have taken a different trail."

The woman reached over and took the man's hand. It was a simple gesture, but I couldn't help wondering if that was a warning to not talk too much.

"A house is so much more comfortable than a shack in the woods," said Katy with a small laugh, breaking the awkward silence. "Well? Shall we go inside then and get a warm cup of tea?"

Charles nodded.

"After you," said Katy as she swept her arm grandiosely at the manor.

As our friend ushered the couple toward the house, Tetyana and I followed them quietly. I wondered at how promptly both the pastor and Jim had left the scene. *Did they know something we didn't?*

The five of us trooped inside the kitchen.

Nancy was cutting a hunk of meat on the counter. In her hands was one of the red-handled knives I'd seen on the knife block before.

Doctor Fulton was sitting in the rocking chair in the corner, his phone in one hand, punching it, vainly trying to make it work.

Pastor Graham, Lisa, and Barry were nowhere to be seen.

Nancy raised her head as we piled in and scowled at the sight of the two strangers.

"Pastor said you were coming," she said, squinting at Charles and Caril. "If you all are looking to stay here, you'd better get to work."

With an angry sniff, she turned back to her cutting board.

"No eggs or bacon, so no breakfast," she said as she sliced the slab of meat in two with one deft chop. "Jim was supposed to go to town to get groceries but that ain't happening today, so no complaining."

I didn't blame her for being upset.

Mrs. Robinson was gone, which meant she and Jim had been left alone to take care of the household duties. On top of that, five uninvited people had shown up without notice.

I walked up to the counter.

"Hey, Nancy. Happy to help you out."

"Me too," said Katy. "And I can eat veggies and steak for breakfast any day."

Nancy gave another withering glare at Charles and Caril.

"We've got some dry food in our backpacks," said Charles, seeing her face. "You don't have to bother about us. We're good."

Nancy replied with a scowl.

"Happy to wash dishes," said Charles.

At least he was trying.

Nancy gave a nod and turned back to her cutting board.

"You can wash up first," she said, not looking up. "Toilet's just outside."

I sighed in relief to know she wasn't going to throw a Barry-like tantrum. Things were looking bleak enough without everyone in this house acting out.

With their bags still on their backs, Caril and Charles walked toward the staff entrance. I watched them stumble out of the kitchen, a strange feeling coming over my stomach. It was like a red flag just went up. Something bothered me, but I couldn't put my finger on it.

"I'll get the veggies," said Katy, walking up to the fridge and opening it.

I turned to the doctor. He'd been silent all along and had not said a word to the couple or to us.

But he was looking up now, his attention transfixed on the door through which Charles and Caril had disappeared. He touched the wound on his nose.

"Doctor Fulton," I said, making him jerk around. "Is your phone working?"

He gave me a startled look, like he just realized where he was. "My phone?"

"Yes."

He straightened in his chair and seemed to collect himself.

He shook his head.

"No, I'm afraid it isn't. Pastor Graham said nothing was working here, even the landline, but I didn't expect it to be this bad."

Tetyana walked over to me, a concerned look on her face.

"I'm going to check up on the car," she said.

I nodded. The car again. Something was up.

"Keep your eyes open," she whispered before stepping out.

"Are you going to help or not?" snapped Nancy, looking my way.

I walked up to the counter with a sigh. I felt like I was feeling my way through a constantly changing labyrinth. Every time I thought I figured something out, something new popped up.

Doctor Fulton turned in his chair when Charles and Caril returned to the kitchen. They looked casual enough, even comfortable in the house, as they put their bags down and walked up to the kitchen counter.

The doctor's eyes flickered nervously. Was it fear I saw in them? Did he know these two strangers?

He stirred and got up wordlessly. Then, he shuffled over to the side door that led to the staff quarters.

I exchanged a glance with Katy, who'd now taken up vegetable-chopping duties. Under instructions from Nancy, Charles had begun to wash the potatoes and Caril was unloading the dishwasher.

The kitchen was getting busy.

But it wasn't the buzz of an engaged and happy team. It was the silent sound of people, none of whom wanted to be here, working under duress.

I had so many questions for the doctor, the pastor, Jim, and even Katy and Tetyana. But I had to be discreet.

I put the dishcloth on the counter. "Just going to the washroom. Be back in a minute," I said to the room as I stepped toward the staff entrance.

It was time to find Doctor Fulton and ask him my burning question.

How did Mrs. Robinson die?

Chapter Thirty-two

Doctor Fulton was pacing the corridor, muttering to himself.

His back was to me, but I noticed the hand holding his phone was trembling.

"Was it a heart attack?"

He spun around and gawked. The doctor looked more sickly than when I first saw him.

I walked up to him.

"Sorry, didn't mean to startle you."

He blinked rapidly.

The man's skittish.

"I was with Mrs. Robinson in her last moments," I explained, softening my voice. "I held her till she stopped breathing."

I had his full attention now. He nodded, almost absentmindedly.

"You... you administered the CPR?" he said.

A pang of guilt went through me. I looked away.

"I didn't try hard enough."

He stared at me, silently.

"Doctor Fulton," I said, "can you tell me what Mrs. Robinson died of?"

He looked away and fixed his eyes on something on the wall behind me for almost half a minute.

I waited.

He seemed to be deciding whether to answer, and I didn't want to frighten him to silence.

"I wish I could tell," he said finally, letting out a heavy sigh.

He started pacing again, his face shrouded in worry. It was like he'd forgotten I was here.

A scraping noise came from behind me. I turned to look.

Nothing.

Maybe I imagined it.

I turned my focus back to the doctor.

"She was the epitome of good health," he was saying, more to himself than me. "I used her as a model for how one can grow older and stay active, getting none of the horrible diseases everyone else seems to have these days. Obesity, diabetes, heart disease, cancer. This is what my patients have."

He turned to me with a grave look.

"She was too young to die."

"How old was she? In her sixties?"

He nodded. "So many of my patients are decaying in mind and body, sitting on their couches, stuffing themselves with cookies and chips. She wasn't one of them. She called herself old, but she was fit as a fiddle."

He looked down at his shoes and shook his head sadly.

"It's a shock she died like that. This puzzles me."

"So, you don't think it was a heart attack, then?" I prodded gently.

He didn't answer, staring thoughtfully at the floor instead.

"Could it have been something else?"

"Like what?" he said, looking up quickly.

You're the doctor, I wanted to say, but I stopped myself just in time.

"Perhaps something she ate or drank yesterday?"

He started pacing again.

"Impossible."

"Something she ingested by mistake?" I said. "Or inhaled, perhaps?"

"That's preposterous. It would have to be strong enough to kill her. What an insinuation. She was a smart woman. She'd never do anything stupid."

"Unless...," I said, hoping this wouldn't backfire on me. I knew it wasn't smart to trust anyone in this house, but the doctor was an outsider from town, and he seemed genuinely perturbed by what had happened. I had to trust my instincts.

"Unless what?"

"Unless someone deliberately gave her something, and she didn't realize what she was taking."

Doctor Fulton stopped pacing, pulled his hands out of his pockets and gaped.

"That's madness," he said. "What an absolutely ridiculous suggestion. How could you even think of such a...?" He leaned toward me and scrutinized me.

"What makes you say that?"

"She was coughing and wheezing last night. Everyone seemed to think that was unusual of her."

The doctor raised an eyebrow.

"Mrs. Robinson coughing? But she hardly caught a cold."

"Some household members said she'd been like this for a few weeks. She clutched her chest a few times when she coughed. It was like she was in pain."

"That doesn't sound like her at all."

I paused. This was it.

"Doctor, did you know Mrs. Robinson was getting anonymous letters?"

He stared.

"Death threats delivered in envelopes that had some kind of white powder."

His face turned pale, but he didn't reply.

"She showed us one of them. She thought it was baby powder, but it could have been anything."

"Where... where is that letter?"

"She took it back and put it in her pocket." I paused. "You didn't check her pockets, did you?"

He shook his head. "It didn't even occur to me..." He paused and squinted. "What are you saying?"

"I'm saying someone may have tried to poison her using those letters."

"How did you find her tonight?"

"It was Nancy. We heard her scream and came running here to see Mrs. Robinson fainted on the floor. She was having difficulty breathing. She also had a hard time moving her fingers and arms. That's why I thought it was a stroke at first."

The doctor rubbed his face, like he was trying to get rid of his exhaustion.

"Doesn't make sense," he said. "If she had suspected something, she'd have called me. I told her to always call me if she needed help. She was the one who alerted me whenever Barry fell ill."

"She came across as someone who'd ask for help for everyone else but herself," I said.

The doctor nodded sadly.

"Aye, that she was. But she was also a responsible woman. She knew everyone depended on her. She was such a good person."

I felt guilt rise in me again. Mrs. Robinson had depended on us to save her, and we'd failed. I had failed.

We stood silently for a moment, regarding each other across the dimly lit corridor.

I felt a prickle in my neck, like someone was watching us. I twisted around, but there was no one.

I turned back to the doctor.

"Is there any way to find out if she had ingested something she shouldn't have?"

"These circumstances are too strange. There are too many unknowns..." He suddenly straightened up.

He turned to me, confidence returning to his face. "I'm going to order an autopsy. I believe it's warranted. Yes, indeed."

I nodded in relief.

"The pastor said Mrs. Robinson's body is in the wine cellar now," I said. "Where is that?"

The doctor pointed vaguely in the direction of Mrs. Robinson's bedroom. That was when I noticed the smaller steel door next to it, like the entrance to a large walk-in cooler or fridge.

"It was Lisa who suggested the wine room," said the doctor. "She and Pastor Graham helped me to take her down. Not the most dignified place, but it's the best we can do until we find a way to get out of here. It's locked so no one can go in there."

"Who has the key?"

"I never asked...," he started but stopped himself. The doctor shot me a suspicious look.

"Wait. Who are you again? You're not from town, are you?"

"No, we got here yesterday."

"What are you doing here?"

"Mrs. Robinson called us for help. She wanted us to help her with the letters." I paused. "We're a private investigator team."

The doctor sighed and shook his head.

"Why didn't she call me?" he said, vehemence in his voice.

I shrugged. "She said she couldn't trust anyone."

The doctor rubbed his face wearily again, like he was befuddled by the day's events.

"By the way," I said casually, "do you recognize those two lost hikers?"

He gave me a startled look but didn't reply.

"Have you met them before?"

It wasn't a hard question. The answer was a simple yes or no.

"Never seen them before."

"They're not from town, then?"

Doctor Fulton turned abruptly and walked toward the washrooms, like he was in a hurry now.

"Look, I need to freshen up," he said, no longer looking at me. "It's been a long day."

"Doctor Fulton," I called out as he opened the door to the toilet. "You might want to check that cut on your nose."

His hand flew to his face, as if he'd just remembered that wound.

"I er, ah, took a misstep and grazed myself on the stone wall, when we were moving Mrs. Robinson's body into the cellar."

I nodded, though I knew he was lying.

That didn't happen a few minutes ago. I'd seen it on his face when he arrived at the house.

Before I could pepper him with more questions, the doctor opened the bathroom door, walked in, and closed the door behind him.

From inside, I heard the turn of the latch and a loud and desperate groan. Then a slam, like he'd smashed his fist against the wall.

Chapter Thirty-three

I lowered my voice.

"Did you see anything?"

Katy shook her head.

"Didn't have time to check properly with nosy Nancy around, but I looked everywhere I could, even in the recipe books on the windowsill." She let out a sigh. "Maybe the letters aren't in the kitchen?"

"We can do a more thorough search tonight," said Tetyana, "when everyone, including Nancy, has gone to bed."

The three of us were huddled next to our car in the driveway. It was chilly outside, but other than our room upstairs, this was the only place we could talk without worrying about eavesdroppers.

Tetyana had the bonnet up and was checking the engine oil. In reality, she was using it as a cover to keep a sharp eye on the house and the grounds. She was also waiting for a good time to sneak into the barn to find out what was so special about it.

A neigh in the distance reminded us there were animals inside.

"Funny, they don't let them out," I said. "Wonder how many they have in there?"

"No dogs either," said Katy. "I don't trust a big house like this with no pups."

"Weird place, that's for sure," said Tetyana.

It had been a strange morning all around

Surprising everyone, Nancy had rapidly embraced her role as Mrs. Robinson's replacement. She bossed everyone around, including Jim, who kept disappearing to the barn, to avoid her sharp tongue, it seemed.

Working silently together, Charles, Caril, Katy, and I had helped Nancy out in the kitchen. It was strange that Caril was standing up and moving about the way she did, for someone with a twisted ankle.

Maybe the injury wasn't that bad, I thought. Then again, maybe they weren't telling the whole truth.

When we were done that morning, a large batch of soup sat simmering on the stove. Grilled vegetables were cooking in the oven and a turkey Nancy had dug out of the freezer was thawing on the counter.

"It will be turkey sandwiches for the rest of the week, or till they fix the bridge," she'd said with a warning note in her voice. "Be prepared for turkey for breakfast, lunch, and dinner and you all can make your own sandwiches."

She had even made sleep arrangements. Doctor Fulton and Charles and Caril now had rooms on the west wing on the third floor.

I wasn't sure if Nancy was a snob or if she just didn't like the couple. The scowls she'd given Katy the day before were now being offered to Caril and Charles. In response, they'd kept their heads down and kept to themselves.

We'd finished breakfast with the rest of the family, with Katy sitting as far away from the pastor as possible. Afterward, we'd helped Nancy clean up and left the house on the pretext the car needed fixing.

The phones and the Internet were still down, and we had no idea who the letter writer was. But the doctor was suspicious of Mrs. Robinson's death now. If he could get an autopsy approved, we'd have evidence. That was progress enough.

It wasn't even noon yet, and it had already been a rough morning.

Now that we were outside in the early morning light though, we had a better view of the house and the grounds.

Up close, we could see the decay on the roof and walls, and the broken hinges on the doors and windows. This house hadn't been repaired for years, maybe even decades.

Despite the rundown mansion, the view was breathtaking from up here. Impossibly tall pine and spruce trees covered the rugged terrain behind the house. Maple and birch trees with their multicolored foliage lined the perimeter of the grounds, and the snowcapped mountain range rose grandly on the horizon.

We were in mountain country, a part of the world many people never get to see. If Mrs. Robinson's death hadn't been weighing on my shoulders, I'd have enjoyed this view.

I turned to Tetyana, who was wiping her hands on an oily rag.

"Do you really think it was the storm that brought down the bridge?" I asked.

Tetyana leaned in to tighten the oil cap.

"Or was it Jim?" I said, lowering my voice. "He was outside when we heard the bang."

"His motive?" said Tetyana, studying the engine pensively.

"Motive?" I collected my thoughts. "Maybe he's the killer. He knows we know more than we show and doesn't want us to leave the house. Maybe we're next?"

"I don't think so," said Katy, "Jim's not a murderer. My gut says he's a good man."

"Don't make assumptions, remember?" I said to Katy.

Tetyana shrugged. "Thing is, Jim wouldn't know how to bring down a bridge even if he wanted to."

"So, what are you…" I stopped, watching my friend who was now studiously ignoring me.

There was only one person in our midst who had the training and the knowledge to blow up a bridge without getting caught.

Katy let out a gasp as she realized the same.

"It was you!" she said, jabbing Tetyana's arm.

"Why in goodness's sake would you do that?" I said. "Now we're stuck here with a murderer on the loose."

Tetyana moved away from us and tinkered at something else on the engine.

"Tetyana," I said, my voice rising. "What are you playing at?"

"I don't play."

"Fine, but you had a hand in this, didn't you?"

"Do you seriously think I'm capable of doing something like that?"

"Yes!" Katy and I chorused.

Tetyana could and would single handedly take on the entire New Hampshire Army National Guard and defeat them, if she put her mind to it.

She straightened up and looked at us from across the engine.

"Didn't you say we had to find a way to stay? These guys didn't sound like they wanted us around, so I had to think fast."

"Are you kidding me?" I spluttered. "I was going to pull the starter relay from the car and you blow up—"

"Keep your voice down."

"Did it not occur to you we had easier solutions?"

"Anyone would smell that starter trick in a minute," she replied. "Good idea, but it's amateur and temporary."

"You brought down a bridge!"

"No need to announce it to the world."

Katy gave her a wild look. "What were you thinking? We'll be stranded here for weeks!"

"Not true," said Tetyana. "There's enough lumber next to the barn. Give me a few hours and I can easily get a makeshift footbridge up and running."

"A footbridge?" I said. "How about something strong enough to take our car?"

"For that, I'll need to wrangle some extra muscle. With a few additional hands, it should take a day or two."

"A bridge in two days?" said Katy. "Impossible."

"The Russians loved to blow up our bridges, again and again. How do you think we got our armored cars over to fight them before they got away?"

I was beginning to think bringing Tetyana to this mission was like bringing an anti-tank rocket launcher to a job that needed a spanner.

"How on earth did you do it?" I asked, vacillating between wanting to shake her and feeling awed by her ingenuity and gumption.

"A pipe bomb."

"Are you out of your mind?"

"Didn't need much. I had the gunpowder. Scrounged a few scraps of pipe from near the barn and twenty minutes later, I got myself a nice little IED."

"IED?"

"Improvised Explosive Device. All I had to do then was to hide behind the pine trees till the coast was clear."

"Don't you think this was a tad overkill?" asked Katy.

"If there's one thing I've learned about this house, it's that nothing is what it seems." Tetyana paused. "The danger here is greater than we can see."

We stared at her.

"Don't you realize what we're sitting on? What this place is worth?"

Katy and I exchanged looks.

"Ten million? Six million at least?" said Katy.

"If that codicil is real, we own this property. This entire estate." Tetyana's face took on a determined look. "Do you know how hard it would be for us to rustle up the cash to fund another place for lost kids? Madame Bouchard put this in our laps, on purpose. I for one don't plan to give it up without a fight."

She was right, but I was sure there were other ways we could assert our rights. Besides, I wondered, did we really want to be burdened with this remote and crumbling place?

"I have an urgent email drafted to Peace in my outbox," I said. "As soon as the Internet turns back on, that will be on its way. Hopefully, he can clear this for us."

Tetyana nodded. "Until he does, damned if I'm going to slink away quietly while they try to wrestle this out of our hands."

"Tetyana—"

"I didn't blow that bridge up for the fun of it."

"We don't know if the codicil is legitimate."

"Yet."

"Yet."

Chapter Thirty-four

"Our family feud mystery has turned into something that might or might not implicate us now," I said, shaking my head.

"I doubt Mrs. Robinson's death was natural," said Tetyana. "Our first job is to figure that out."

Katy nodded. "I suspect everyone, even that hiking couple." She paused for a second. "Especially them."

"Never saw them come in," said Tetyana, "which means they must have been on the grounds before we got here, hiding someplace."

"Strange how fast that twisted ankle healed too," I said.

Katy nodded. "They're lying."

I turned to her. "Do you recognize them from somewhere?"

"Never seen them in my life."

"You had a funny look on your face when they told their names."

"You mean *Caril and Charles*?"

"Does that mean something to you?"

Katy shrugged.

"It's probably nothing."

"Katy," I said. "Something's bugging you. Tell us."

"Don't you guys ever watch TV?"

I shook my head. "No time."

"Got better things to do," said Tetyana.

"Why? Are they actors?" I asked. "Famous people we should know?"

"Haven't you guys heard of the *Natural Born Killers*?"

A chill went through me.

"I thought everybody knew who Caril and Charles were," said Katy.

"Are you saying we have two serial killers in the house?" I whispered hoarsely.

"The real Caril and Charles are both dead. Their killing spree happened in the fifties."

"Let me get this straight," said Tetyana, "a young couple shows up out of nowhere in this house, and they have the same first names as two serial killers from decades ago?"

Katy gave a slow nod. "Weird, isn't it?"

"Are you sure those are the *exact* same names as the *Natural Born Killers*?"

Katy nodded.

"They've got some gumption announcing themselves like that," said Tetyana, frowning. "Especially if they're planning on following in their namesakes' steps."

"Gosh, I hope not," said Katy, turning white.

We stared at each other silently, trying to digest this new piece of information.

I knew negativity bias was an innate human trait. Plus, it hadn't helped that we had all gone through hell and back many times before. I had a tendency to jump to outlandish conclusions, especially during times of crisis.

Then again, being stuck in a decaying mansion deep in a remote mountain region with a dead body in the basement and all access to civilization cut off counted as a crisis.

"Could it be coincidence?" I said, forcing myself to see the other side. "Charles is a common name."

"Caril isn't," said Katy. "The thing is, I'm sure those aren't even their actual names."

"What makes you say that?" I asked.

"I was cleaning the carrots and needed the paring knife. Caril had it next to her. I called her name three times. She was working at the counter but never looked up. Charles had to come over and nudge her. I know she's not deaf. She was talking to me before, so that was weird."

"So," I said, "they're not who they say they are."

"Looks like we've got more digging to do, girls," said Tetyana.

The labyrinth was getting even more convoluted, I thought with a sigh.

We would need all our firepower to survive this strange house.

——

Before we walked back inside, Tetyana, Katy and I had a furious debate on whether to warn the others about the mysterious hiker couple.

Tetyana was in the emphatic *no* corner, while Katy said an unequivocal *yes*. I wasn't so sure we could trust anyone just yet, just like Mrs. Robinson had felt.

My vote was to wait and see before telling anything to anyone.

Tetyana slammed the car bonnet down and locked the car, and we walked back into the house.

I felt myself bracing as we entered through the side door. For what, I didn't know. Bloodied bodies littered on the floor?

Inside the kitchen, Pastor Graham, Doctor Fulton, and Nancy were sitting around the counter, drinking coffee. The fireplace had been started, and the kitchen smelled of old-fashioned home cooking.

I felt my shoulders relax. *They're not dead*, said a small voice from the back of my head. *Not yet, anyway.*

All three turned as we walked in.

"You ladies okay?" asked the doctor. "Car's not in terrible shape, I hope."

"Seems like we drew the short end of the stick at the rental car lot," I replied, "but it should get us back to town once the bridge is fixed."

Nancy let out a sigh.

"Hope that won't take weeks. I'll run out of flour."

"Don't want to scare you, but it might take a while," said the pastor.

"How long is *a while*?" asked Nancy, screwing her eyes as she looked from the pastor to the doctor and back again.

The doctor shrugged. "Don't look at me. I'm a doctor, not a civil engineer."

Tetyana cleared her throat.

"If a few folks can give me a hand, I can get something decent up in a day or so," she said.

Everyone turned to her.

"You can do that?" said Nancy, sitting up, eyes wide.

"A temporary makeshift crossing until you find a more permanent solution."

Everyone at the kitchen counter was staring at her now.

"I'll need a few sturdy planks, some basic construction equipment, and a couple of tall ladders to throw across the banks for scaffolding."

"My goodness," said the pastor, slapping the counter. "That would be super. By the time they rustle up a construction crew from town and all that, it could take days, maybe even a week, knowing them."

"With the right equipment, it will take a day."

"Well, you're a godsend, my dear," said the doctor giving her a smile. "Have you, er, done this sort of thing before?"

"Joined the army a few years back," she said, not specifying which country. "Picked up a few essential skills."

"Impressive," said the pastor, looking at her in awe.

If only they knew, I thought.

"I'm no engineer but I can make do with the right stuff," said Tetyana. "I will need some help though."

"I'm a little too old to carry planks for you," said the doctor, "but I'd be happy to hand you the tools and make you tea."

"Used to be a strapping young man once," said the pastor, giving her a wistful look, "can lend you some muscle, if you'll take old muscle."

"I'll take help wherever I can get it."

The doctor's frown had disappeared. He let out a relieved sigh. "Seems like I got stuck here with the right folks," he said, bringing his tea mug up as a salute to Tetyana. "Thank you."

"Where's Jim?" I said. "We could do with his help too."

"Feeding the horses," said Nancy, pursing her lips. Her face turned a slight pink. "I think."

She's mad at him about something.

"What about the couple?" asked Katy, looking around the kitchen. "Where are they?"

Nancy shrugged. "In their room, I guess, keeping to themselves."

"Exhausted, probably, after that hike through the mountains all night. That must have been hellish," said the pastor, shaking his head. "Nancy didn't give them much of a break this morning either."

"How they didn't get hypothermia is a miracle," said the doctor, frowning at his tea mug.

The pastor stood up.

"Coffee?" he asked, friendly now that we had turned out to be useful.

Tetyana shook her head.

"I'd like to get a head start. I'll scope the barn for any material we can use."

The pastor's smile vanished instantly.

"The barn?"

"Is it locked?"

A dark shadow crossed his face.

"I'll get Jim to show you around."

"No need to bother him if he's busy with the horses. I can look."

"No," said the pastor, his voice so forceful, even the doctor and Nancy shot him surprised looks.

"Lots of heavy equipment in there." He paused as if he was choosing his words carefully. "It's not safe for you to go in there by yourself."

Chapter Thirty-five

Tetyana rattled the doorknob.

"What if the killer's inside?" whispered Katy from below. She was standing at the foot of the steps, refusing to come up to the door with us.

It was Tetyana's idea to check out the cabin in the woods first.

We'd told the coffee crew in the kitchen we were going to explore the woods for lumber to build the footbridge.

Though we knew a perfectly usable pile of planks were stacked next to the barn, the pastor didn't volunteer that information. He looked relieved to know we weren't going anywhere near the barn.

"If someone's squatting here illegally," said Tetyana, banging on the cabin door, "we have a darn good reason to find out who it is."

"We're not the official owners yet," I said. "Even if the codicil is legit, there'll be tons of paperwork to do. We must handle this delicately with the family too."

"Damn the family," said Tetyana, taking what looked like a penknife from her pocket and bending over to the keyhole. She stuck the pointy end inside and wiggled it.

I stepped down and signaled to Katy to follow me. "Let's go check the back." If Tetyana had decided to break into the cabin, I wasn't going to be able to stop her.

If my found-family had one common characteristic, it was that we all had an independent, stubborn streak. Once one of us had made up our minds, no amount of cajoling, pleading, reasoning or even bribing could sway us.

It had been true ten years ago when we had all met under adverse circumstances. It was still true today.

Katy and I walked around the cabin, watching our steps and keeping our eyes open for anyone or anything suspicious.

The sky was overcast, a dull gray that sucked any joy left from the day. The sun had disappeared behind the clouds again and from far away, I could hear the angry rumblings of a storm in the distance. But at least we had enough daylight to make out our surroundings in the woods.

As we toured the little structure, I realized it was in better condition than the manor. The ground was uneven in this part of the woods, so thick wooden stilts had raised part of the cabin. Whoever had constructed this had taken care to do a good job.

"Lookee here," said Katy, walking up to the biggest window and balancing on an errant log to see better. She peered inside. "It's about as big as a one-bedroom apartment in Manhattan."

"You mean there's hardly space for a dog in there?"

"Bed's not made," she said, putting her hand over her forehead to clear out the reflection. "There's a bag or something on the floor."

I stepped up next to her and peered inside, getting on my tiptoes on the log.

A cot was set against one wall, and a dorm-sized kitchenette was against the opposite wall. A roughhewn wooden table and two simple chairs were set next to a wood stove which, I was sure, doubled as a cooking and heating appliance.

There was a small door to our left that looked like it led to a closet. Through the opening I glimpsed a toilet and sink.

Plumbing. This meant this shack was self-sufficient. They had really thought things through.

"See those candles on the table?" said Katy. "That's what you saw flickering last night."

"Hey, check out the floor near the kitchen sink," I said.

Katy flattened her face against the window.

"That puddle is fresh," I said, "someone was cleaning up at the sink and spilled some water but forgot to wipe it up."

Across from us, we could see the door being rattled furiously. From around the structure, we could also hear Tetyana's curses coming through loud and clear.

"Someone's staying here, or stayed here recently," said Katy.

"Who do you think that could be?"

"Squatters maybe," said Katy. "Freeloaders looking for a place to stay for the winter. Or it could be a regular hunting cabin. Hunting season's just finished."

"Or maybe it was the lost hikers?" I said, raising an eyebrow.

The main door to the shack slammed open and Tetyana barreled inside. Katy and I sprang back instinctively.

Tetyana strode up to the window and opened it with a wide grin.

"Look at you two. Like two little match girls. You can come in the normal way now."

Katy and I jumped off the log and walked around the shack to the front.

"You didn't break the door, did you?" I asked, scrutinizing the lock.

"I know how to pick a lock like anyone else," replied Tetyana, bending down to examine the water puddle near the kitchen sink.

Katy raised an eyebrow. "Like you know how to blow up a bridge?"

Tetyana shot her an offended look.

"It's warm in here," I said, closing the door behind me and walking over to the woodstove oven. "The cinder's still glowing. Someone's definitely been staying here."

"Don't touch!" said Tetyana as Katy reached over to pick up something on the floor.

Katy hastily drew her hand back.

"It's a scarf," she said. "Who do you think it belongs to?"

"Caril?" said Tetyana.

"That means they stayed overnight here," I said, poking my face into the little bathroom. "But then they showed up at the house in the middle of the night, pretending to never have seen this place. Why would they do that?"

Using a paper towel from the counter as a makeshift glove, Tetyana opened the cupboards, one by one.

"Food cans and a can opener. There's water on tap and firewood for the stove. It's not like anyone was going to starve here."

"What does all this mean though?" said Katy, twirling around the room. "None of this makes any sense."

"They're here for something," I said. "Remember how guarded Mrs. Robinson was when we asked about this place? I get this funny feeling she knew the couple were staying here."

"Why would she protect someone with serial killer names?" said Katy.

"Hey," said Tetyana, "look at this, will you?"

Katy and I joined her at the small kitchen window.

"A path," said Katy. "The end of the mountain trail everyone's talking about."

"It's heading down toward the gully." Tetyana pointed at something farther away. "Do you recognize that spot?"

"It's the clearing," I said. "Isn't that where we were last night, where we got our tire problem?"

"You're right," said Katy, leaning across the counter. "That's where I went looking for my leaf pictures."

"It's where we saw that man and woman argue," I said, turning to my friends. "They were right here."

Chapter Thirty-six

"Curiouser and curiouser," I said, turning around and walking to the door.

Closing the door behind us, we stepped down and walked around the cabin toward the trail, our boots squelching through the wet leaves on the ground.

Tetyana checked the compass on her watch.

"That's heading east," she said, "if that trail goes straight down, it could even get us to town."

"We'll need a bridge to cross the river though," said Katy.

"I can't believe there's only one way to this house," I said, as we treaded through the path. "This estate must be several, if not hundreds of acres. There must be other points of entry."

"Other than the mountain trail?"

I nodded. "Unless the gully winds itself around the entire house like an old-fashioned moat, there has to be another way out."

We stopped talking as we got to the clearing. From here, we could see the gully was filled to its brim, the storm water thundering through the open chasm.

A small piece of earth from the bank crumbled and fell into the water as we watched.

Tetyana hadn't needed a lot of help to bring the rickety wooden bridge down. It was already rotting underneath, ready to fall any moment. I shuddered to think of how we drove over that decayed structure only a day ago.

The three of us stood by the embankment, examining our surroundings, trying to spot clues we might have missed the last time.

"Was it Charles and Caril we saw?" I said.

Katy shook her head. "The man was taller and skinnier. Not at all like Charles."

"They ran off through the trees from the other side of the bank," I said. "Where did they go off to?"

"Could have hidden among the trees until we got to the house, then snuck across the bridge and into the cabin," said Tetyana. "Or they could have walked back to the road once we left and got into their vehicles parked somewhere out there."

"We didn't see any cars on the road," said Katy.

"I wasn't looking, but if I did, I'm sure to find a few good hiding spots along the roadside." She stopped. "But that would mean effort on their part. They'd have to have an excellent reason to conceal their vehicles deliberately."

I turned to Katy.

"Did that woman's profile remind you of anyone?"

"They were far away, and it was dark," said Katy, poking a twig with the tip of her shoe, trying to remember. "I guess it could have been Caril."

"It could also have been Nancy," I said. "She's similar in size and height."

"And age too," said Tetyana.

"But Nancy was at the house when we got there," said Katy.

"She had ample time to run back to the house," I said. "We saw her about half an hour after we'd gone inside, remember?"

"Wouldn't we have seen her run along the driveway?"

"Not if she kept to the woods and took the long way round."

Tetyana stepped up to the riverbank, her eyes on the gushing water below. "Maybe there's a way to cross here," she mumbled.

I turned back to Katy. "Did you notice Doctor Fulton's face?"

"That cut on his nose?" said Katy.

I nodded. "Said he got it from a jagged edge on the wine cellar wall. He was supposedly too busy moving Mrs. Robinson to notice when it happened."

"Horse manure," said Katy. "I saw that cut when he came in."

"Me too."

"Do you think it was him out here?"

"I just can't see him darting through the woods."

"Me neither."

"Oi, detectives," called out Tetyana, "come see this."

Katy and I walked over to where she'd been strolling along the gully, away from us.

"Check that out," she said, pointing at something on the ground.

Katy bent over to look and teetered at the edge. Tetyana grabbed her by the shoulder and pulled her away from the river.

"It'll be a cold, rough swim for you, if you don't watch out."

"What are we supposed to see, Tetyana?" I asked.

"The grass is crumpled and the leaves have been disturbed."

She was right. The frost on the ground had cleared, but the grass was squashed like someone had stomped through the area.

"Could it have been the storm?"

She shook her head. "Someone went that way, and they weren't tiptoeing."

She started walking along the river, stopping every few feet to examine the ground. We followed her, our eyes on the grass.

"The leaves covered their shoe markings," said Tetyana, "pity."

In fifteen minutes, we came to the edge of the tree line. We had also moved away from the river.

Tetyana halted and put out a hand to signal us to stop. Then she stepped out of the tree line and onto a rocky graveled area.

After scanning the surroundings to make sure no one was around, she motioned us to join her.

We walked over and flanked her, trying to figure out where we were.

"Where's the river?" I said. "I can hear it. It's not too far."

Tetyana stomped her right foot.

"Under here."

"The river runs underground?" I said, looking at her in shock.

She nodded. "You missed the gully narrowing about twenty feet back. It disappeared, but I'm sure it's running under here and probably pops up again down the line."

She walked a few yards to where a handful of rocks had been scattered, like something heavy had dropped on them. She bent down to examine the muddy brown earth underneath.

"Tire tracks," I said, kneeling next to her, squinting at the faint markings. "How did you even notice them?"

"See how the rocks were thrown this way? A vehicle's wheels dug in right here."

"Maybe it was the rain that pushed the rocks away?" said Katy.

"Rain doesn't leave tire tracks."

"Wouldn't the rain have erased the tracks though?" I asked.

"It was a heavy-duty vehicle. The wheels sunk in here."

"We didn't hear a car though," said Katy.

"That's because our focus was on the cop," I said.

Tetyana bent down and traced the tire tracks with her finger. "It was an all-wheel drive. The only kind that can make it up here."

She took her phone out and snapped a picture.

"Once we get the Internet back, I can compare tire markings and see if I can identify the vehicle."

"The only person with an all-wheel drive SUV is the police officer," I said. "The other person is Jim."

"I could swear the man we saw was older and slower," said Katy. "Jim and the cop are fit and lean. It wasn't them."

"Could have been anyone from town too," said Tetyana, gazing at the gravel pit. "That man or woman you saw could have run out here, got into their truck and drove off."

I turned to Tetyana. "Are these fresh marks?"

"It's a wild hunch, but I'd say a day or two."

"What is this place?" said Katy, looking around her.

"An ancient riverbed of sorts," said Tetyana, squinting into the distance. "Someone was using this dry bed to get closer to the house without coming on the main road."

"I knew there had to be another way to town," I said. "But we're not that far from the house. I'd be surprised if no one knew about this path."

"Maybe they do, but no one wants to admit to it?" said Tetyana.

Katy pointed at the pine trees lined like a dark green wall behind us. "That's an entire forest we'll have to chop down before we can get any vehicle out here. It's not the most convenient road."

"True, but that shouldn't stop anyone walking out here and calling for someone to pick them up," said Tetyana. "Or have someone come to drop something off for the house."

"Or for the cabin," I said.

Tetyana got up and wiped her hands on her pants. "I'd swear that everyone in this house knows a lot more than they're letting on."

Chapter Thirty-seven

"Hey there," said Jim, leaning close to Katy and giving her a wink. "Are you trying to hog all the bread?"

With a friendly smile, Katy passed him the bread basket.

I glanced over at Nancy to see if she'd noticed Jim flirting, but an animated conversation between the pastor and the doctor was preoccupying her now.

Nancy seemed to take turns being unpleasant to those around her. We, especially Katy, had been her target on our first day. Then it had been the hiker couple. Now, it seemed like Pastor Graham was her next victim.

She stared at him with a scornful look, as he enthusiastically described a horse race he'd seen years ago, while the doctor listened politely. The pastor seemed oblivious to the glares coming his way.

That afternoon, while we were exploring the grounds and the cabin, Nancy had checked the pantry, rationed the food, baked bread and made preparations in case we were going to be stranded for a week. Despite her foul moods, under that sullen face lay a conscientious person who wanted to do her part for the house.

I wondered what drove her. I also wondered why she was so quick to judge and scorn others.

Late afternoon, when it got close to suppertime, Nancy had engaged Caril and Charles to sweep the dining room floor and set the table while Katy and I helped her prepare the dishes, plate the food and bring them up. Tetyana had been on cleaning duty, loading and unloading the dishes.

Jim had run off to the barn again, to check up on the generator, or so he'd said. The pastor had disappeared and there had been no sign of Barry or Lisa.

Doctor Fulton had sat nursing a beer and reading a book in the rocking chair in the kitchen, with strict instructions from Nancy to not get in the way. He refused to read alone in the living room upstairs. He didn't leave the kitchen all afternoon, saying he preferred company.

The nervous twitch on his face never eased.

I was now seated between Lisa and Doctor Fulton at the bottom end of the table. Lisa was quiet as usual, an aloof air about her, while the doctor fidgeted in his seat like he was anxious about something. I wondered if Mrs. Robinson's death was playing heavily in his mind.

Caril and Charles had joined us for dinner as well, but they kept to themselves in their corner, next to Barry. Caril still had those sunglasses on and rarely looked up from her plate.

On the surface, they looked like unassuming, grateful guests who'd been invited for a meal and a place to stay during a storm, but didn't want to make a fuss.

But beneath their quietness, I felt something simmering, something I felt in my bones would come to a boil soon.

Perhaps it was knowing what their names signified that made me paranoid. All I could notice now was how watchful they were.

How quiet and watchful they were.

I felt a cold shiver go through me.

The doctor finally wrenched himself free from the pastor and turned to Nancy.

"You saved the day, my dear," he said with a nod and a fatherly smile. "I don't know how you did it, but this is a darn good meal for a place that's cut off from everything and running on a generator."

Nancy's face lit up. She returned a shy smile at the doctor.

"Fantastic dinner. Bravo to you!" said the pastor, raising his glass at her. "I'm so glad you and Jim came to Cedar Cottage."

Nancy's smile vanished in an instant. She turned back to her plate with a scowl.

Katy and I exchanged a glance.

What was that all about?

For a moment, I felt like we'd tumbled down Alice's rabbit hole and had walked in on the Mad Hatter's tea party.

I wondered if the grief and shock everyone had shown the night before at Mrs. Robinson's death had been a show. No one brought her name up. No one murmured feelings of sadness at her passing.

It was like the caretaker who'd lived in this house for decades, cooking and cleaning and making everyone's lives comfortable, had already been forgotten.

The pastor and Jim were having a hearty conversation. Even Barry seemed in relatively good spirits, trying to make slurred talk with anyone who'd listen between slurping his soup and telling Nancy how tasty it was.

Lisa was her usual mousy self, sitting next to me with her head low. She'd come to the dining room early that day and had been the first person to sit at the table. I could see she was now listening to the conversation around the table with more alertness than the evening before.

Lisa had actually smiled when I'd walked in.

She's trying to make up for the night before, I thought, thankful our hostess was warming up. Though she said little, she was making eye contact with everyone. An impressive progression.

Katy, our self-appointed public relations representative, played the gracious guest and kept her part up. She knew how to distract others from Tetyana's constant vigilance of the room, and from my discreet observations of everyone around the table.

Almost everyone was engaged in conversations about food or racehorses. For a household in mourning and a dead body lying in the wine room, I felt this dinner party a bit obscene.

"How's the bridge repair going?"

It was Doctor Fulton.

Normally, Tetyana wasn't one for small talk, or for any talk. But she knew her role that evening.

"I'll need a chainsaw and an electric drill," she said. "I should have something up tomorrow."

"Got lots of tools in the barn," said Jim. "Got a circular saw that can cut though wet lumber."

"Great," said Tetyana, "I'll go to the barn first thing tomorrow morning."

"Jim will get it for you," said the pastor, speaking quickly. He turned to the younger man. "You'll prepare everything for her, won't you?"

Jim's face turned taut, but he gave an obedient nod. "Yes, Pastor. I'll get everything out by dawn."

I tried not to look at my friends.

What's so special about the barn?

I sat back in my chair, listening to the hum of conversation around me. Though I'd known her for only a very short while, I missed Mrs. Robinson.

She'd been central to this mystery, and she'd left without telling us everything she knew. I wondered how we were going to unravel all the threads that were coming loose in this maddening household.

We had too many unanswered questions about the barn, the cabin in the woods, the two people arguing in the clearing, the mysterious tire tracks on the old riverbed, the hiker couple who'd appeared out of nowhere, the pastor's strange hold over this family, and Mrs. Robinson's death letters.

Were all these even related?

Discovering the codicil had been our biggest shock. It blew my mind to think we could be the new owners of this manor. While Tetyana seemed to think it was a real possibility and Katy wished it would be, I wasn't sure if it was a hoax.

If it was real, what a cruel inheritance it was. Madame Bouchard's vengeful legacy to her own family.

I remembered how she had clutched my arm as she had breathed her last breaths. *Find my children and tell them I did it because I loved them,* had been her exact words.

I looked up and glanced discreetly at Lisa and Barry. Both had their heads down over their plates.

What did they do to anger their mother this much?

No, we weren't at the Mad Hatter's tea party.

We had tumbled into a more sinister place. We were in the Queen of Heart's labyrinth garden. An improbable maze with upside-down stairs, walls that move, and tunnels that go nowhere. A strange place inhabited by strange folk.

And somewhere in an upscale graveyard in New York reserved for affluent customers, the Queen of Hearts, herself, was having a good chuckle at us.

What a day, I thought as I forced myself to swallow another spoonful of soup. I needed the nourishment, but my appetite had disappeared. I was exhausted, badly in need of sleep, and time to think.

What I didn't know then, was the night was only going to get longer.

Chapter Thirty-eight

Something made me look up.

It was Caril.

She was staring at me from the other end of the table.

She kept her gaze steady while I tried to maintain a stoic face. But I was faltering. I watched her watching me, wondering what was going on behind those dark glasses.

I gave her a cordial nod.

Any normal person would have acknowledged someone looking back at them. A nod back, a smile, an embarrassed look away, but Caril's face remained motionless.

Who is this woman?

Next to me, Lisa broke a piece of bread and put it in her mouth. Then I heard the click of her spoon on her bowl.

Caril's face shifted. She was staring at Lisa now.

Across from her, Charles was having a chat with Barry, or rather listening to Barry rumble on about something. Charles was nodding politely, but I could see his attention was on everyone else.

His eyes kept sweeping across the table, as if he was expecting something to happen.

"A toast."

I looked up, startled. I'd been so engrossed in Caril and Charles, I hadn't been following the conversation around the table.

Pastor Graham pushed his chair back and stood up, a glass of wine in his hand.

"A toast?" I asked, aghast.

A celebration when someone just died?

The pastor nodded.

"Yes, a toast," he said, seeing my face. "To Mrs. Robinson."

The room fell silent.

The pastor scanned the table.

"Most of you here knew Mrs. Robinson well. She was a strong woman. A loving woman. She treated us like family. She *was* family. To all of us."

Jim raised his glass.

"Hear, hear," he said.

"She was an amazing person," continued the pastor with a sad smile, but his words sounded mechanical, hollow.

"The only comfort we can take," he continued, still standing, "is that our loving Mrs. Robinson went to the afterlife without much pain. Angels were watching over her. She had a good life with us and in the end, it was a fast and painless transition for her."

"To Mrs. Robinson," said Jim, raising his glass, but I couldn't help but feel he was parroting something he'd been told to say.

Next to me, Doctor Fulton kept his eyes on his plate. His face was pale and his lips were set in a thin line.

I wanted to nudge him and ask him if this was true. *Did Mrs. Robinson really have a painless death?*

I was there when she died.

Her transition hadn't been fast or painless. She'd struggled to breathe. She'd choked on her own saliva. She had fought to stay alive.

Her last days on earth weren't the most pleasant ones either. They'd been wracked by death threats and bad health.

Pastor Graham's tribute didn't ring true.

Maybe he was being sincere. Maybe he was just trying to make everyone feel better. Maybe he didn't know about the death threats she'd been receiving.

Doctor Fulton cleared his throat, as if he wanted to speak. But Jim scraped his chair back and stood up, glass in his hand.

"Mrs. Robinson was one of the nicest women I had ever known. She treated Nancy and me like family from day one," he said. "Here's to dear Mrs. Robinson. May her spirit live forever among us."

There was an awkward silence, as people picked up their glasses for the toast.

Next to me, I heard a quiet sob.

I turned toward my neighbor.

Lisa let out another sob, her face almost on her plate. I put my hand on her arm to comfort her. Her skin was clammy and cold. I felt my skin crawl, but I didn't want to pull away rudely.

"It's so sad," I said, trying to think of the right words for a grieving person. "But she's in a better place now. She died peacefully," I babbled on, but Lisa didn't respond. Instead, she buried her face in her napkin.

I looked around the table.

Lisa was the only person in the room who'd shown genuine grief for Mrs. Robinson's death. The others seemed like they were putting on a show.

"Mrs. Robinson..."

I turned around.

Dr. Fulton was trying to speak.

"Mrs. Robinson was…"

He stopped abruptly and clutched his throat.

"She had…"

"Doctor Fulton?" I said, leaning toward him. "Are you all right?"

He gasped and wheezed, like he was struggling to breathe. A choking sound escaped from his mouth and his face turned a beet red.

I let go of Lisa, pushed my chair back and stood up, my heart pounding.

Please, no.

My voice rose.

"Is something stuck in your throat?"

He didn't answer. He couldn't.

Around me, I vaguely heard the sounds of chairs being scraped back, of people shouting.

I threw my arms around his chest, readying for the Heimlich maneuverer when a firm hand fell on my shoulder.

It was Tetyana.

"I'll do it," she said, pulling me away and taking my position.

I jumped out of the way to give her space. She was stronger than I was, and her arms were longer to fit around the doctor's stomach.

Everyone was standing up now and staring at Doctor Fulton.

Tetyana put her fists against the doctor's rib cage and pumped.

Once.

Twice.

Three times.

But the doctor's face only turned redder and redder. Nothing came out.

She tried again.

I whipped my phone out and tried to dial nine-one-one, but the connection was still down. I saw Katy had pulled out her phone too. She shot me a horrified look.

What's happening?

Tetyana pulled her arms back and squared her shoulders to try again.

With a loud and chilling groan, Doctor Fulton fell face down on the table.

Chapter Thirty-nine

"Is he dead?"

It was Lisa. She was staring at the doctor.

She was the only person still seated, as if she was too shocked to move.

I turned my attention back to Doctor Fulton.

Tetyana gently raised his head and reached over to check the pulse on his neck.

Pastor Graham and Jim were hovering behind her, their expressions a mix of disbelief and terror. Nancy was on her feet, her napkin covering her mouth as if she was trying to stop herself from screaming.

Caril and Charles were huddled near the doorway, clutching at each other. They looked genuinely horrified.

For once, Barry had gone silent, his face white, and his mouth in a silent O.

All eyes were on Tetyana now.

She looked up, her face grim. Her expression told us everything.

"He's gone," she said as she placed his head back down on the table.

I stared at Doctor Fulton.

He was seated in his chair, his head slumped over, his chin on his chest, and his lifeless eyes closed. If I'd just walked into the room, I'd have thought he had fallen asleep in his chair.

Pastor Graham stepped up.

"Heart attack!" he yelled, waving his hands erratically.

Tetyana and I glanced at each other.

This was the second death in this house within twenty-four hours. Doctor Fulton's passing so soon after Mrs. Robinson's was too coincidental. I didn't believe this was just another natural death.

"Everyone out!" shouted the pastor, shooing everyone out the door. "Out, out!"

I frowned at the man. Why was he sending everyone scurrying off? Now was the time to check for evidence and ask some serious questions.

But Caril and Charles were already out the door, and Nancy had grabbed Jim's arm and was pulling him toward the entrance.

Barry didn't need to be told twice. He turned around so hurriedly, he sent his chair crashing to the floor. He stumbled out, pushing the others rudely out of the way.

"Pastor Graham," I called above the din. "What are you doing?"

He turned to me and glared.

Tetyana, Katy, and I had gathered around Doctor Fulton. I felt obligated to protect this man, or protect his dead body, and it seemed like my friends felt the same way.

"What are you lot hanging around here for?" snapped the pastor. "Leave! Now."

"What are you planning on doing, Pastor Graham?" I asked. "We need to make sure we preserve the evidence."

"Evidence?"

He took a step back, startled, and shot a perturbed look at the dead doctor.

Did he really think the doctor just had a heart attack?

"Poor Fulton," said a small voice next to me.

Lisa was still in her chair, staring at the doctor, her face contorted into a mixture of pity and sadness.

"Poor, poor man," she said. She looked up at me. "He was a good doctor, you know?"

"Lisa, go to your room," said the pastor, sounding like a schoolteacher scolding their pupil. "We'll take care of this."

Lisa didn't answer. She didn't even budge, like she was glued to her chair.

I turned away from her and back to the pastor. It was time to ask some tough questions.

"Mrs. Robinson died only a few hours ago. The doctor said she'd been in excellent health and her death was a surprise to him."

He stared at me.

"This morning Doctor Fulton said he was going to ask for an autopsy on her," I said. "And tonight, he dies. A second sudden and unexpected death so soon."

The pastor's eyes grew wider.

"Where are you going with this?" he stammered.

"You're a smart man, Pastor Graham. You have probably come to the same conclusions we have."

"I don't know what you're talking about."

Why is he so defensive?

"Why did you ask everyone to leave the room?" asked Tetyana. "What do you plan to do with Doctor Fulton's body?"

The pastor turned to her in surprise.

"Why? Because, this is a terrible thing. Death can be so difficult," he spluttered. "We can't have everyone freak out. We need to—"

"What we need to do right now," said Tetyana, cutting him off, her voice calm but firm, "is to contact the authorities."

"The authorities? Why in heaven's sake?"

"And this room needs to be secured."

"What are you going on about?"

"Pastor Graham," I said, "I'm sure the police will have many questions."

"The police?" He gave me a wild look. "This is preposterous."

A rustle by the doorway caught my eye. I thought I glimpsed a shadow lurking near the entrance.

Is that Nancy? Caril? Or Charles?

I couldn't say, but I was sure someone was out there, listening in.

"What we're saying, Pastor, is we can't rule murder out."

"You can't be serious. This is blasphemy. How can you even fathom such madness!"

He glared at us, his face turning purple.

"The only people who'd think of such an incredibly ludicrous story would be meddlesome, busybody strangers."

He spat that last word out.

A high-pitched cry startled me.

It was Lisa.

I'd forgotten she was still here.

She threw her napkin on the table and stood up shakily. She careened for a second, and Katy leaned across to steady her.

Pushing her away, and letting out another strange, animal-like cry, Lisa ran out of the room, as if she couldn't take this anymore.

"Who are you to talk to our pastor like that?"

I looked up.

It was Jim, hovering near the entrance. I was right. I had seen a shadow near the threshold. I guessed he'd escorted Nancy to their room and returned.

His friendly demeanor had vanished. His eyes flashed in anger.

"Why are you trying to upset everybody?"

"I'm sorry, Jim, that wasn't my intention—"

"Mrs. Robinson and Doctor Fulton were friends. They were family," he said, glaring at us. "Who are you to come here and tell us what to do?"

The pastor jumped in.

"I suggest you all leave this room right now. If the bridge was in working condition, I'd ask you to leave this house. We don't need strangers here accusing us of such heinous things."

"But Madame Bouchard wrote a—" Katy started.

I laid a hand on her arm to stop her.

This was not the time to tell them about the codicil. That conversation was best had with lawyers in the room. Maybe even the police. Otherwise, I was sure we'd see more violence in this house.

It was time to regroup.

There was not much we could do here. Without an easy connection to the outside world, we couldn't even warn the authorities.

"We're leaving," I said, glaring back at the two angry men.

I walked toward the door, gesturing to my friends to follow me.

Chapter Forty

We stumbled out in a daze.

"I don't like leaving them with Doctor Fulton," whispered Katy as we walked away from the dining room.

"We could have stayed and fought," I said, "but I'd rather keep things discreet for now."

"Discreet?" she whispered back hoarsely. "The doctor just died. And you both have guns, for goodness's sake. Why didn't you use them?"

"It's a last resort, Katy," said Tetyana. "Our lives weren't in danger."

"Who knows how long we'll be stuck in this house with these people," I said. "We need to be smart now, not rash. That'll just make the killer clam up or become even more dangerous."

"This way," said Tetyana, signaling to us. "It's a good time to search the kitchen for those letters."

We took the main stairway from the second floor back to the kitchen.

"Was it poison, do you think?" asked Katy as we climbed down.

"He wasn't shot or stabbed," said Tetyana grimly. "Whoever did this was very careful."

"I didn't see him eat or drink anything we didn't," I said, "makes me wonder if someone gave him something earlier."

"In the kitchen maybe?" said Katy. "Nancy served him that beer he was nursing all afternoon."

"Let's go find his glass and the beer bottle," I said. "We can put them away till the authorities come."

"But why would anyone want to kill Doctor Fulton?" asked Katy.

"He knew something," I said, "he knew how or why Mrs. Robinson died."

Tetyana made a "quiet down" motion with her hands.

"Someone's inside," she whispered.

We stared at the main door to the kitchen. It was ajar and we could hear the tap running. Tetyana opened the door and stepped inside.

I'd expected to have the kitchen to ourselves, but Nancy was there, cleaning up.

She looked up when we trooped in.

"You doing okay?" I said, walking toward the counter.

"No," she said, her voice harsher than usual.

Her hands were a blur as she put the dishes away. It was like she hoped all this activity would help her forget what had just happened.

"Need any help?" I tried again, as I reached for another dishcloth.

"Leave that be," she said, not looking up. "I'll take care of this."

"Nancy," I said, putting my hands on the counter. "Can we talk?"

She didn't answer.

"Don't you think it's strange that Doctor Fulton died so suddenly like that?"

She looked up only for a second. Her eyes flashed, just like Jim's had only moments ago. When she spoke, her voice was so venomous I took a few steps back.

"I heard you talking to the pastor. You people come here and accuse us of all sorts of things. Who do you think you are?"

I stayed my ground.

"I'm not sure Mrs. Robinson mentioned this to you, but she invited us over."

"You're lying!"

Katy came up. "Nancy, how can you not find it strange that Mrs. Robinson and the doctor passed away so close together like this?"

Nancy slammed a dish on the counter.

"Maybe it was something he ate," she said. "Indigestion gone bad. He's an old man. Maybe he was allergic to something and didn't tell me."

Her voice was low, like she was talking to herself, trying to convince herself rather than us. She looked up, that nasty scowl back on her face.

"What's it to you people, anyway? You're not family."

"You aren't either," said Katy.

It was like Katy had slapped her.

Nancy took a step back, her face red in fury.

"Get out!" she screeched, pointing at the door. "Get out of my kitchen!"

＊——◆——＊

"What a mess," said Tetyana, shaking her head.

We were huddled upstairs in our bedroom, trying to think of our next steps.

We didn't have many options.

With the bridge down, our car was stranded on the grounds. The only way out of this house was through the woods along a trail that led to the old riverbed. From there, we'd have to find a way back to town in the dead of the night. A risky journey, if our guess had been correct.

Who knew where that riverbed led to?

Besides, none of us were ready to leave.

Tetyana kept reminding us that this house, these grounds, this entire estate may now belong to us, or technically, my company, the Red Heeled Rebels Group.

As far as I was concerned, we couldn't abandon this house without having made good on our promise to the woman who had called me for help.

"Mrs. Robinson wanted us to find the letter writer," I said. "That person could be, in all probability, the killer. For her sake, we've got to find out what's going on."

Tetyana nodded.

"I bet you this entire inheritance those two were murdered in cold blood by someone who sat around the table tonight."

"But how?" said Katy. She was sitting cross-legged on the floor, leaning against the bed, absentmindedly playing with the Care Bear on her lap. "I know we think it's some sort of poison, but they both looked like heart attacks to me."

"Nancy may be right," said Tetyana, leaning against the wall and crossing her arms. "The doctor could have ingested something in his food or drink. They'd have had to be real careful to make sure he was the only person who'd eat it or drink it."

"But we prepared the food," I said, "we used the same dishes to plate the food for everyone. Unless…" I paused to think. "Unless someone added it *after* we served him."

"The pastor poured the wine," said Tetyana, "and he was the most adamant for everyone to leave at the end."

"I am sure he used the same bottle for all of us," I said, trying to remember.

"Don't forget Caril and Charles," said Katy. "They set the table before anyone came to the room. They could have put something transparent into his glass or plate and no one noticed."

"Cyanide or something similar would have done the trick," said Tetyana, nodding.

"He'd have tasted or smelled cyanide, wouldn't he?" I asked.

"Maybe that cut on his nose temporarily damaged some nerves," said Tetyana and let out a loud sigh. "These are all suppositions. What we need is hard evidence."

"Wait," I said, realizing something. "Lisa was sitting at the table when I ran up with the veggie platter. She was in her seat all by herself before anyone else. She didn't move when Charles set her place. She didn't even acknowledge him."

"That woman gives me weird vibes," said Katy.

"Nancy asked her if she was hungry, but she didn't answer," I said, recalling the conversation, "she just sat there."

"Strange," said Tetyana.

A shudder went through me as I remembered the cold and clammy feel of her skin.

"There's something badly wrong with her," I said.

"Mentally or physically?" said Katy.

"Maybe both." I paused as the book sitting on the bed caught my eye. "I can't help but feel that diary holds all the clues. Mrs. Robinson wanted us to find that book."

"A murderer's clue?" said Katy, picking up the diary. "From a nine-year-old girl's drawings?"

Pastor Graham's nasty tirade in the dining room flashed to mind. Yes, we were strangers here, but it wasn't strangers they needed to be afraid of. It was much easier to be killed by your own family.

Much easier.

I knew this from my own past.

Chapter Forty-one

"But what about Mrs. Robinson?" said Katy. "How did she die?"

"Those letters," I replied, "carried the actual threat. I'm sure of it."

"How?"

"Remember, the white powder I saw on the letter she showed us? Mrs. Robinson thought it was baby powder or something. But the originals could have carried a poisonous substance which she inhaled and made her sick."

Tetyana nodded.

"She said she hadn't been feeling well for the past four weeks. That's exactly when she started getting the letters."

"But who'd want to kill her?" asked Katy.

"That ball was rolled before we got here," said Tetyana. "Someone had a grudge against her, wanted revenge, or planned to silence her, so they sent those letters to kill her over time and minimize suspicion."

"Then Doctor Fulton figured out Mrs. Robinson didn't die of a heart attack," I said. "So the killer got rid of him too."

"How do you know he knew?" asked Katy.

"I talked to him this morning. He was cagey, confused, and sounded like he didn't want to even contemplate whatever it was he'd found. But he finally said he would ask for an autopsy to confirm how she died."

I paused.

"I don't want to sound paranoid, but I thought I heard someone behind us when we were talking. I didn't see anyone, but the killer could have been there."

"That sealed the doctor's fate," said Katy glumly.

"Remember, the doctor didn't want to be left alone all day?" I said. "Maybe he was scared the killer knew and would go after him."

Katy raised her eyebrows. "Which they did."

I felt that all too familiar sinking feeling in my stomach. If the killer had heard me talk to the doctor, that meant I could be their next target.

Tetyana straightened up and gave me a concerned look as if she read my mind. She reached into her holster and pulled out her side arm.

"You have your piece on you?" she asked.

I patted my vest and felt the comfort of the pistol snug in my pocket.

"Good," she said. "Keep it close and don't hesitate to use it."

I nodded.

"It's time to do some sleuthing—" she started, but a single knock on the door stopped her.

We froze in place, staring at our door.

I looked at my phone. It was almost midnight. What was someone doing in the corridor at this time of night?

Tetyana put her finger to her lips and stepped toward the entrance. She put an ear on the door to listen. I tiptoed over and took position behind her, my weapon in my hand, ready for anything.

It was strange the person only knocked once.

Were they waiting behind that door?

Giving me a quick nod, Tetyana turned the lock and flung the door open in one swift move. She vaulted out, gun aimed forward, crying, "Freeze!"

I jumped after her, but the corridor was empty.

We scanned both sides, but either the door-knocker had run away or was hiding in the shadows.

Katy stumbled out of the room and peeked out.

"Who is it?" she whispered.

Tetyana turned to us.

"Someone's stalking us. Let's go find out who is playing these games."

"Right now?" said Katy, appearing unsure if she wanted a midnight expedition.

Tetyana nodded firmly.

"You two go down to the west wing and check for anyone roaming around. I'll go check the stairwell. I have a feeling they went toward it. Easiest place to hide and fastest place to get away."

"Be careful," said Katy.

"Don't shoot unless absolutely necessary," warned Tetyana. "If you see anything strange, shout."

"Will do," I said.

"Let's go, Katy," I said, turning around and heading toward the main section of the house. "Watch my back."

Sticking to the shadows, Katy and I tiptoed along the hallway, checking each room, one by one.

I had suspected Mrs. Robinson had given us the sole furnished room on this wing, and I was right. All the other doors on our wing opened to vacant, empty spaces.

Katy and I slipped through the corridor without seeing or hearing a soul. Other than the sound of the wind whipping around the cupolas on the roof, it was eerily quiet.

It was also dark, the only illumination coming from a bank of vintage spotlights affixed to the ceiling.

I turned back and scanned the corridor behind us. Tetyana was nowhere to be seen. She'd already searched the corridor and was probably climbing down the back stairway. I hoped she was okay.

Katy and I approached the west wing and glanced around cautiously.

The main stairway of the house was built like a Cinderella staircase that swirled all the way down to the first floor. The stains and scratches on the pine told us this staircase needed a good wax and polish, but it would have been beautiful in its time.

"Nobody's around," whispered Katy as we walked up to the top step and surveyed the landing.

We stood near the banister, straining to hear sounds of anyone walking or talking, but the house had fallen silent.

"This way," I said, walking toward the west wing on the third floor.

"What are you doing?" whispered Katy, pulling on my vest.

"Let's see who's in their rooms."

When the pastor shouted for everyone to vacate the dining room, Barry, Caril, and Charles had scooted out, followed by Lisa, later on. Nancy had probably finished her duties and also returned to her room like the others and shut herself in.

The two people I wasn't sure about were the pastor and Jim.

I couldn't but help feel like those two shared a secret. They were constantly defending each other, glancing at each other before speaking, like they had a secret code. The way Jim deferred to the pastor was a bit too much to be natural.

Katy and I tiptoed through the west wing, looking for signs of life.

"They renovated this part," whispered Katy, as we stepped over the new carpet. "It's much nicer here."

"Guess someone finally decided this needed an upgrade."

I had no idea who stayed in which rooms, but there were four rooms on this wing. All four had light coming from under the door.

They were still awake.

"What do we do?" said Katy. "Knock?" She made a face that clearly said she'd prefer we didn't.

I shook my head.

"Let's check the second floor. Maybe the pastor and Jim are still there."

With a sigh of relief, Katy turned around and stepped ahead of me.

"This place gives me the creeps."

"Me too," I said as I followed her back toward the main staircase.

"Who do you think knocked and ran?" said Katy. "And why? It's a kid's game."

It was getting more and more difficult to know what everyone's intentions were. That nagging feeling came back to me. Everyone was putting on a show here. Either for each other or for us. I wished I knew more.

"Maybe someone wanted to alert—"

I stopped as soon as I saw it.

"Hey!" I called out. "Stop!"

But it was too late.

Katy lurched over the trip wire and stumbled headfirst down the stairs.

<h1 style="text-align:center">Chapter Forty-two</h1>

"**K**aty!"

I leaped over the wire and dashed down, taking three steps at a time.

A low moan came from below.

My heart jumped to my throat as I saw the body lying on the second-floor landing. I bounded down the stairs and reached for Katy's shoulder, my heart thumping like mad.

"Oh, my goodness. Katy, are you okay?"

She groaned.

"What... happened?"

Her voice was feeble but audible.

I kneeled beside her and put my gun on the floor.

Katy was twisted into an awkward position and was gripping onto her right leg, like it hurt badly.

I clutched her shoulder and gave a short prayer to whoever had been watching over her.

Thank you. She's alive.

"You tripped over a wire. It was on the first step. I didn't see it in the dark."

Another groan.

"You okay, hun?"

"My ankle...."

I looked over her, gently feeling her limbs.

"No broken bones?"

"Nope."

"Blood?"

"Don't think so..."

I sighed with relief.

A twisted ankle was better than a broken neck.

Katy turned around, positioning herself to sit up.

"Don't move," I said.

Ignoring my advice, Katy sat up slowly and leaned against me for balance. I reached around her shoulders and gave her a tight squeeze.

"I'm so sorry."

"Not your fault."

I tried to collect my thoughts.

Who did this?

And why?

I would never forgive myself if anything happened to Katy or Tetyana.

When I'd packed my bags for this trip, I'd thought this case would be a breeze. A fast way to earn our charity money. It would be a simple question of figuring out the spiteful family member who wrote those nasty letters, I'd innocently thought.

But this had turned into a double-murder investigation, and it was us who were being targeted now.

"I didn't expect them to come after us," I said. "Maybe I did intellectually, but I wasn't prepared for it."

Katy pulled her foot to the side, grimacing in pain. "Should have seen that stupid wire."

"No one would have seen it in the dark," I said. "Whoever it was, did a good job."

"Good thing I caught the railing, or I'd have gone tumbling all the way down."

I looked up and scanned the third-floor landing.

My stomach fell as I saw a shadow cross the corridor upstairs. I grabbed my gun and spun around.

"Stop right there!" I yelled.

When the figure bent down to peer at us, the corridor light fell on her face.

"Tetyana?"

She didn't answer.

"Watch the wire!" I called out.

But she'd already spotted it. She was kneeling down to examine it. Then, pulling out an army knife from her vest, she reached over and snapped it in two.

While Katy and I watched, she climbed down slowly, feeling her way, searching for more booby traps.

"You okay?" she said, when she got to the second-floor landing.

"They didn't kill me," Katy replied with a wonky smile. "Whoever tried that will be mighty disappointed."

"A twisted ankle, but it could have been worse," I said, looking at Tetyana. "Much worse."

She nodded, a grave look on her face.

"Didn't see who it was?"

"The floor was deserted." I glanced up at the third floor. "Where is everyone? Katy falls down the stairs, I run down shouting, and nobody comes out to check?"

"I heard you yell," said Tetyana. "Heard you from near our bedroom."

"Maybe everyone's scared to death now," said Katy, trying a feeble smile. With a painful moan, she tried to stand up, holding on to my shoulder.

With help from Tetyana and me, she made it to her feet, leaning against us.

"You need to lie down, my girl," I said.

"What you need is ice," said Tetyana.

"Can you take me to our room?" asked Katy. "Sitting in a quiet spot for a little while would help."

Supporting her on both sides, Tetyana and I took her up to the third floor and back into our room.

We moved slowly, using Tetyana's torchlight to check for any more wires. I was beginning to feel like there were death traps everywhere in this house.

Once Katy was tucked in bed with the Care Bear, I turned to Tetyana.

"There's ice in the freezer downstairs," I said. "I'll go get some."

"Wait," she said. "I'm coming with you. Not a good idea to roam around the house alone right now."

I turned to Katy.

"You're going to be fine?"

"Don't worry about me," she said, but I could see the pain in her eyes.

"We'll lock the door behind us," said Tetyana. "It will be just for two minutes, okay?"

She gave a feeble nod.

Poor Katy. She didn't have a choice.

After closing and bolting the windows in the room, Tetyana and I exited. We locked our door and walked toward the back stairway, stopping every few seconds to check for traps that might have been laid for us.

Someone in this house meant business.

Dirty, ugly, deadly business.

"Do you think that wire was meant for us?" I asked.

"Definitely," said Tetyana, as she scanned the stairwell. "I found a wire trap on the top of these stairs too."

"Are you kidding me?"

"Saw it just in time and cut it in two. Whoever knocked on our door wanted us out and walking around." She shook her head and gave me a stern look. "I'm no longer playing the polite guest."

"I agree," I said. "This just leveled the game up."

Once we got to the kitchen, Tetyana switched the light on and we glanced around us.

Thankfully Nancy had left the room after a cursory tidy up. There was still a pile of dirty dishes in the sink and dirty glasses on the counter.

But now it was hard to say which glass belonged to whom. I reached over to the wine goblets, trying to recall which ones had been Doctor Fulton's, but realized any one of them could be laced with poison.

I walked over to the freezer, opened the door and fished out the ice tray. While I twisted the tray to pop out the cubes, Tetyana waited by the window, intermittently scanning the entrances.

"Done," I said, picking up the two ice packs I'd made using plastic bags. "Let's go—"

That was when the kitchen lights turned off.

"Hey!" I said, twirling around. "What's going on?"

"Shh…," said Tetyana from near the window.

I stared at her silhouette, waiting for my eyes to adjust to the sudden darkness. She was standing next to the window, peering out.

"What are you looking at?" I whispered.

"Just like last night," she replied.

I flattened myself against the wall and inched toward her.

"Someone's walking across the grounds toward the barn," she said in a low voice. "They're not looking this way, but I can't say they didn't notice the kitchen light."

I felt the hair on the back of my neck stand up.

I tiptoed closer and peered out.

She was right.

It was the same image we saw the night before from our room upstairs. A lone male was walking toward the barn. A sliver of yellow light fell on the ground when he opened the barn door.

"It's a man, that's for sure," I said, "is it Jim? The Pastor? Barry?"

"Walking too straight to be Barry," said Tetyana, "he stayed the course. Didn't even look back."

Within seconds, he slipped in and closed the door.

"Look, there's someone else," said Tetyana.

We watched as a second person walked over to the barn, opened the door and stepped inside.

Just like the night before, the lights inside the barn switched off, and the grounds plunged into darkness.

Chapter Forty-three

"I bet you that second man was Pastor Graham," whispered Tetyana.

"What's he doing there at this crazy hour?" I whispered back. "And who's he with?"

We stayed still, watching the barn for any more signs of life, but things had gone silent. A winter owl swooped by the window, swishing through the air, startling us. But other than the bird, things had quietened on the grounds again.

The ice packets in my hand were sticking to my skin now, and Katy was still waiting for us upstairs in a locked room.

"We need to go," I said. "Katy's still in pain."

"Roger that," said Tetyana, stepping away from the window. "Then, we're going to find out what's going on in that darn barn tonight."

We climbed up the stairwell, walked through the corridor and got back into our room. The trip took longer than usual as we stopped every few feet to make sure someone hadn't followed us down and was lying in wait to ambush us.

"Do you think this barn has anything to do with the murders?" asked Katy when we told her what we'd seen.

She still looked in pain, but she was at least comfortably snuggled against the pillows with ice on her ankle.

"To tell the truth, I don't know what to think right now," I said.

So many strings had unraveled in the short time we'd been in this house. Things had happened so fast, I wasn't sure if these strings even belonged to the same piece of cloth.

I sat at the edge of the bed.

"Here's what we know so far," I said, trying to sort it out in my head. "Two people have died within hours of each other, and they both happened under mysterious circumstances."

Katy and Tetyana nodded.

"There's a weird dynamic here. The owners act like they're children. They don't seem to have much agency and may even be mentally and physically unwell. Meanwhile, the pastor who has no ownership of the house, acts like he's the master of this place."

"And everyone in this house seems to have secrets they're not ready to tell," said Katy. "That included Mrs. Robinson and Doctor Fulton."

"Not to speak of losing Internet and phone connections just as Mrs. Robinson died," said Tetyana, "and the sudden arrival of the *Natural Born Killers* doppelgangers."

"Don't forget the argument we saw in the woods," said Katy. "That could have something to do with what's going on here too."

"As if that's not enough," I said, "we have the codicil from Madame Bouchard saying we inherit this estate."

Tetyana nodded.

"Then, someone tries to either hurt or murder one of us with a tripwire."

I sat back and massaged my temple.

"Too many questions and not one answer."

I looked up at my friends.

"Don't you find it strange no one came out of their rooms to check when Nancy yelled last night? Then tonight, they must have heard Katy stumble down the stairs. So, either they're hiding in their rooms, too afraid to come out or...."

"They planned it," said Katy, sitting up quickly and wincing as her ankle moved.

"What do you mean?"

"They're in this together. They *all* wanted to get rid of Mrs. Robinson for some reason. They did it successfully, but then we showed up. Remember how the pastor wasn't too keen to call the official emergency line but sent Jim to get Doctor Fulton? The doctor came, saw something suspicious, and now he's dead." She paused. "We're next."

We stared at each other, mulling over this possibility.

"A scary thought," I said. "If they find out about the codicil, they'll definitely want to eliminate us."

Katy patted her pocket. "I have it right here. Nobody has seen it except for us."

Tetyana had been shuffling her feet for a while now like this talk was driving her up the wall.

"Our next step is to check the barn," she said. "We'll either learn something or eliminate someone as a potential killer." She turned to me. "You coming?"

I put a hand on Katy's shoulder.

"You going to be okay, hun?"

Katy nodded and gave a rueful smile.

"I want to come with you, but I guess I'll hang out here." She turned toward the bookshelf and scanned the shelves. "Can you pass me the girl's diary, please? There might be more clues inside."

Tetyana walked over and picked up the book and handed it to her.

"Be careful, you two," said Katy, as she took it.

"We're both armed and trained," said Tetyana to her. "I don't want you worrying about us."

Katy nodded.

I placed her mobile phone on the bedside table. "Monitor it, in case the network comes on again."

"Thanks," said Katy, taking the phone and tucking it under her pillow.

Tetyana walked over to the windows to check the locks.

"Don't open the door if anyone knocks, okay?"

"Won't even get out of bed," replied Katy, making a face. "Promise."

"Don't leave the room even if they pretend to be us or say we need help."

"Aye, aye, Captain."

After saying goodbye to Katy, Tetyana and I slipped out, bolting the door behind us and taking the key with us.

I felt bad locking our friend up like this, but it was for her own safety. My only consolation was Katy's fighting Irish blood.

Anyone who put her in the corner found out swiftly not to mess with a redheaded woman like her.

Chapter Forty-four

T etyana and I walked toward the stairwell at the back.

We were getting to know this route well now, but we moved deliberately, checking the floor, the walls, the light fixtures, and even the ceiling.

There was no one in the kitchen when we got down there. We slipped out of the side door and walked toward the barn, keeping to the shadows. We had no idea if anyone was watching the grounds from their bedroom window.

The barn was dark. We circled the structure, trying the windows and doors. Everything was fastened tight, and it seemed like no one was inside.

"You think they left?" I whispered to Tetyana.

She shook her head, frowning.

"Someone or some people are still inside."

"How do you know?"

"Gut feel."

The barn was on slightly elevated grounds, which backed on to the woodlands. We positioned ourselves behind the pile of lumber beside it, as it kept us hidden, and also gave a good vantage point to the house and the driveway.

We squatted on a log and kept watch, waiting, wondering what would happen next.

"This might be a long wait," I whispered as I tried to get settled on the uncomfortable tree trunk, its sharp bark pricking my thighs.

"We can barge in now and make them talk," said Tetyana, holding up her Glock. "What happened to Katy gives us just cause."

"That's our last resort," I said in warning.

We sat still for about half an hour, though it felt like an eternity. My imagination ran wild, wondering what was going on inside the barn.

Were they having a party in there? Or was this where a cult held their rituals and seances? Maybe a ritualistic killing?

That last thought sent a shudder through me.

The night air was cooling. Staying motionless with our backs to the woods wasn't the most pleasant way to spend the night. I wiggled my toes and warmed my hands by blowing warm air into them. It took effort to keep my teeth from chattering.

Tetyana, on the other hand, was sitting on the log as calm as a yogi at a meditation retreat. Her eyes were focused on the manor, but I knew all her senses were on full alert.

I wondered why she was so adamant about us inheriting the house. It was unusual for her. Tetyana wasn't the materialistic type.

I nudged her. She turned, a questioning look on her face.

"Why is it so important to you that we get the house?"

She stared at me for a while, then looked down at the ground.

"I've lost everything in life. My brother, my mother, my village, my country." She paused and looked up at the sky as if she was seeing her dead family members up there. Somewhere.

"You have us," I whispered. "We'll always be here for you. We're family now."

"I know that." She gave me a playful nudge with her elbow, but I saw her other hand go up to her face and wipe her eyes. I'd only seen her cry once, and that had been the first time she'd told us about her violent past.

"I've dedicated my entire life so other kids wouldn't end up like we did," she said.

Stolen. Beaten. Tortured. Trafficked. I wouldn't wish our past on anyone, not even my worst enemy.

"We fought back and got out," said Tetyana. "We were the lucky ones."

"We turned out all right, didn't we?" I said. "Sure, we cope in our own ways, but we keep ourselves busy and stay sane."

That much was true.

Luc was obsessed with his cakes, David with his Krav Maga training, Peace with his high-powered job, Katy with her daughter, Chanda with running the orphanages, Win with her computers, Tetyana with her guns and me with my baking business.

David called it post-traumatic growth.

I gave Tetyana a nudge back.

"A bunch of weirdos, but we're normal, if you ask me," I said.

"Normal?" said Tetyana, shaking her head. "What's normal, anyway?"

"But what does this house have to do with us?"

She sighed.

"This is going to sound merciless, but I hate to see rich, entitled, privileged folk not appreciate what they have. I don't know what these people have gone through, but they live in a safe country with opportunities we could only dream about. I'd have killed to grow up here. But they've all ended up bitter, drunk, and so ungrateful."

It was a brutal thing to say, but I couldn't disagree with her.

"Imagine how many stolen children there are in America?" she said, suddenly getting animated. "We can renovate this place, get some help to run it, hire teachers and nurses, and give those kids a better life. They'll have all this space to run free and learn to be kids again."

She looked at the house, a dark monolithic shadow on the grounds now. "It's such a waste," she said, shaking her head. "Such a bloody waste."

"You're still angry, aren't you?" I said, putting a hand on her arm.

"Guess I am," said Tetyana, looking away. "Maybe I haven't gotten over it all."

I sat back to think. I didn't think any of us had.

We let our obsessions keep our minds occupied, away from our dark memories, but nothing could erase our pasts. They'd always be with us whether we liked them or not. Without them, we wouldn't be where we were today, anyway.

My mind wandered to the inhabitants of Cedar Cottage. We didn't know anyone's history in this house. I couldn't help but think their secrets were deep, perhaps even darker than ours. I just wished I knew what they were.

What we needed was to find a way to have them open up to us, one by one.

Tetyana and I sat quietly after that. It was like we'd said everything we had wanted to say.

After another hour, and another painful prick of the tree bark on my thigh, I stirred, desperately wanting to get up and stretch my limbs. I was wondering if walking in a small circle behind the logs to let the blood flow again would be a bad idea, when I spotted the flicker of light in the woods.

I turned to Tetyana.

She nodded.

"Someone's in the cabin again," she whispered.

"What are all these people doing outside at this time of night?"

"The question is," said Tetyana, "is it someone from the house, or is it someone we haven't met yet."

A chill went through me.

How many more strangers are hiding in the shadows of this estate?

I was just about to suggest that we walk over to check the cabin when the barn door creaked open.

Tetyana and I whipped around and peeked out from behind the lumber stack.

The barn door had opened halfway.

There was no party going on inside, or a seance, or a killing ritual. It was just one lone man. He turned around, wished someone goodnight in a quiet voice, and walked out. We watched him navigate his way through the darkness.

This was a man familiar with the grounds.

"Graham," whispered Tetyana when he was partway up the driveway.

Yes, it was him all right. I'd recognize his figure now. He had the confident walk of a man who knew his position in this house.

Pastor Graham strode back to the manor, heading toward the side door. He didn't look back or even appear concerned if he was being seen out and about like this.

The house was dark and silent, except for the faint light from our bedroom window. Katy was in bed, still reading, I supposed.

The pastor walked up to the side door, opened it, and disappeared inside.

Like the last time, no lights went on inside the house. It was like he was feeling his way to his room in the dark.

"There's one more person inside the barn," I whispered.

Tetyana nodded.

"We could wait for them to come out, which could be tomorrow morning, or we can go in and ask them what they're doing here."

We slipped out from our hiding spot and walked to the barn.

Tetyana brought her gun out of the holster and pointed it at the door.

"Put that away," I whispered, turning to my friend, "we're not going in guns blazing."

She gave me a surprised look. "They could be armed."

"I doubt it," I said. "Besides, we can't threaten them. We need them to open up to us and talk."

She didn't change her posture.

"You forget there's a serial murderer running around here," she said, gritting her teeth. She motioned me toward the door.

"You knock. I'm standing right here and won't hesitate to blow their heads off if they make the wrong move."

With a sigh, I turned around and rapped on the door, knowing whoever came out was bound to see her standing behind me, her sidearm aimed at their face.

But there was no sound from inside the barn.

I knocked again, louder this time.

A noise came, like someone was scraping back a chair. Then, footsteps near the door.

I stepped back.

The barn door flew open, and a surprised face popped out.

Chapter Forty-five

"Jim?"

He stood at the doorway with no shirt on, his hair tussled, like he'd just woken up.

"What in goodness's sake are you doing here?" I asked.

He rubbed his eyes. "What's going on?"

"That's what we'd like to find out," growled Tetyana from behind me.

Jim stepped back in alarm as he spotted her and jerked his hands up. He stared, open-mouthed, at the end of the gun barrel pointing at him.

He was fully awake now.

"May we come in?" said Tetyana, stepping around me and walking inside, making Jim stumble backward.

I caught a movement near my feet. It was the feral cat slinking in between my legs and disappearing into the barn.

I closed the door behind me and turned on the switch next to the door. The barn flooded with light, making us all blink.

"Stand still," commanded Tetyana.

Jim stood rigidly in place while she patted him down.

He shot me a frightened look over her shoulder.

"Who are you people?" he said. "What do you want with us?"

"Turn," instructed Tetyana.

I felt bad for Jim. He seemed like a good man, despite those glassy eyes and those funny feelings I got about him playing a role. There must be a reasonable explanation for him being here in the barn at this time of the night.

"Clear," said Tetyana.

Jim turned back to us, his arms still in the air, eyes wide as saucers.

"Anyone else in here with you?" asked Tetyana.

"N... no... no."

"You can put your hands down," I said, softening my voice.

Though I was playing good cop, I was on guard. We still didn't know how Jim would react to our questions.

I glanced around inside the structure. So, this was the mysterious place Pastor Graham didn't want us to enter. At first glance, it looked normal enough.

What was he hiding?

Near the entrance was a large sofa bed, which had been pulled out. That was probably where Jim had been sleeping when we knocked.

To the right was an open warehouse area which held yardwork tools, snow removal equipment, various plumbing apparatus, and other bits and ends you'd find in any work shed.

Next to the yard equipment was a workbench with four chairs scattered around it. On the bench was a pile of nails and half-cut wood planks. It seemed like sawdust covered almost everything here, even, I suspected, the sofa bed.

To my immediate right was a small office den with a desk and a stiff-backed plastic chair.

I stepped up to the den and peeked in. On the desk was an ancient beige computer and an ink-jet printer-copier that had seen better days.

"Did you see this?" I said to Tetyana.

She poked her head in for a second and we exchanged a quick glance. This could be where Mrs. Robinson copied her poison pen letters for us.

I turned to scan the rest of the building. To my left was a long white corridor from where the distinct smell of horses came. A breathy snort told me they were nearby.

"How many horses do you have in here?" I asked.

"Er," Jim stammered, his eyes flitting from Tetyana's pistol to me. "T... t... two for now."

I walked over.

There was a row of six stalls on either side. I strolled toward the animals, my eyes sweeping the surroundings.

All the stalls were empty except the last two.

The animals were wide awake and stared at me when I got to the end of the corridor. They were two adults, one dark brown mare and one black stallion. They seemed as surprised to see me as I was to see them.

With their shiny coats and those large horsey eyes with long lashes, they could melt any heart.

"Beautiful," I said, reaching over to the mare. She inclined her head and sniffed my hand, blowing warm air all over me. I wished I'd brought an apple for her.

"Looks like someone grooms them."

Jim mumbled something incoherent from behind me, then cleared his throat.

"Barry helps a lot," he said, "always here making sure they're okay."

"Barry?" I said, turning to him in surprise.

"He'd do anything for the animals."

He pointed at something in the corner of an empty stall.

"Took that ugly thing in even with its fur all falling out. Found it half dead in a ditch. Lisa wouldn't allow it in the house so it sleeps in here. Barry couldn't bear to see it suffer."

I peered into the corner Jim was pointing at to see a small ball of mangy fur. It was the feral cat, staring at me, suspicion in its eyes. As soon as I took a step forward, it let out a hiss and slunk farther back into the shadows.

"Barry?" I said again.

It was hard to believe that man had any good streak in him. People surprised you in the most unexpected of ways sometimes. Tetyana shrugged as if to agree. Jim merely sulked in his corner, unhappy.

I turned back to the horses.

They already had their winter fur. They shouldn't be cooped up in these tiny stalls all day and night, I thought, suppressing an urge to pull open the stall doors and let them go free outside.

I faced Jim.

"How come we didn't see them out in the paddock today?"

His eyes flickered nervously. "They, er, hate going out in the winter... too cold... so we, er, keep them in."

"Who do they belong to?"

"Lisa."

Something in his voice made me stop.

"Really?"

He looked away.

Why would he lie about the horses? These were the most innocuous questions we would be asking him that night. We hadn't even got to who murdered Mrs. Robinson and Doctor Fulton, and why, yet.

Jim turned and looked at Tetyana, then back at me.

"What do you want from me?"

"Information," I said.

Jim stared for a second. Then, like he had a sudden boost of gumption, he straightened up and glared at us.

"You were stranded. We gave you a place to stay and food to eat. And this is how you treat us? With that thing in my face?"

Tetyana took a step toward him.

"Someone put a tripwire on the stairs tonight. Katy fell over it and almost broke her neck. So yes, I'm justified in coming here to ask a few questions with a gun in my hand."

Jim stared at her, bewildered.

"A tripwire?" he said. "Are you joking?"

I examined his face. He wasn't acting.

"There have been two sudden deaths in this house, one after the other," I said. "Doesn't that unsettle you?"

Jim opened his mouth and closed it, as if unsure what to say.

"They were both older, and I thought... heart attacks... you know, like the pastor said...." He frowned, turned to Tetyana, then back at me. "Why? What are you saying?"

"What I want to know is where you were when Katy stumbled down the stairs about an hour ago," snapped Tetyana.

Jim gave her a terrified look.

Chapter Forty-six

"I was here," he said, gesturing wildly. "Came here right after dinner. But I'd never do anything like that. I mean, anyone could have... oh no, Nancy. Is she all right?"

"She's in her room as far as we know," I replied.

"This is crazy—"

"Jim," said Tetyana, "what do you do here at night?"

He turned away and let out a heavy sigh. His shoulders drooped and his face turned a slight pink. "I... I have a hard time sleeping in the house, so I come down here."

Right.

I knew there was more to the story than that. Jim and Nancy had a fight, and she'd sent him to the doghouse, but he was too embarrassed to admit it to us.

"Jim," I said, beginning to think he wasn't the killer. "Can you tell us what's going on in this house?"

"Nothing," he said, his voice higher pitched than before. "I don't know. I mean, nothing's going on."

Though Jim may not be killer material, he wasn't telling us everything.

One of the horses grunted.

"Let's go find a place to sit and talk," I said, "and let the animals sleep."

After a moment's hesitation, Jim turned around and retraced his steps toward the front entrance. We followed him, our eyes and ears peeled for any suspicious sights or sounds.

Jim walked over to the workbench, scraped back a chair and gave a befuddled look at Tetyana, who was still pointing her sidearm at him.

"Sit," commanded Tetyana, as she took a chair across from him.

Jim sat down.

"Place your hands on the table where I can see them."

Jim did as he was told.

I took a chair next to Tetyana and waited.

Jim gave us a baffled look.

Silence can be a powerful weapon. When used strategically, people spilled their guts.

"What do you want with me?" he blurted after a few moments of quiet. "I've done nothing wrong. I'm just a worker here. I do what they tell me."

I do what they tell me?

"How long have you been staying in this house?" I asked.

"I don't know, five months. Maybe six."

"How did you find a job all the way here? Who told you about this place?"

Jim looked down.

We'd touched on something, something he didn't want to reveal.

He sighed. "It was Graham, I mean Pastor Graham, who told us about an opening here."

"Were you with Nancy, then?" I asked.

Jim looked away again, the pink flush coming over his neck and face, this time.

"I've been with her for three years."

"So you and Nancy came all the way from Iowa?"

"Iowa?" he said in surprise.

"That's where Nancy said you're from."

He shook his head. "Maybe... maybe she didn't want to.... Maybe you didn't hear it right. We're from Falcon Hills."

"Why would she lie?"

Jim let out a despondent sigh and looked down.

"Nancy's father is in prison for drinking and driving. Killed two kids from our school a while back. He used to be a schoolteacher so everyone knew him and she got bullied badly for it. She thinks the whole world's out to get her, so she doesn't like people prying, you know?"

Nancy's antagonistic attitude made more sense now.

"Did you both get along with Mrs. Robinson?"

Jim looked up in surprise.

"Of course. I liked her. We all liked her. She was a really nice lady. She made us feel like we weren't alone here and she never treated us bad. It was what Nancy needed."

He was finally telling the truth.

"Do you know if anyone had a disagreement with her?"

Jim gave me a blank look.

I tried again. "Did anyone in this house not like her?"

He shook his head, a dazed expression on his face. "I can't imagine it. She did so much for us...."

His face scrunched up, like he was about to cry. He put his head in his hands and stayed in that position for an entire minute.

When he looked up, his eyes were red.

I softened my voice. "Were you close to her?"

"Yes… I mean… we were all living in the house so, we were as close as we could get." He paused and wiped his face. "I miss her. She kept everyone together. When Barry got crazy and went on his rages, she calmed him down. She'd talk to Lisa when she got in one of her moods, and she was always watching over Nancy. I don't know how we're going to cope without her."

"What about Pastor Graham?" I asked. "Did he get along with her too?"

Jim flinched at the mention of the pastor. That's strange, I thought.

"Yes," he said, collecting himself. "She used to make his favorite blueberry pie, and he'd bring her flowers from the market as a thank you for letting him stay over on weekends."

"Why did Pastor Graham stay over every weekend?" asked Tetyana.

Jim looked down and swallowed hard, his Adam's apple moving up and down. He stared at his hands. I wondered why he was having such a hard time answering a simple question.

"He… he wanted to get away from town. He called this place his retreat…"

"Every weekend?" I said. "That's a bit unusual, isn't it? Doesn't he have an office and home in town?"

Jim sat clasping and unclasping his hands in front of him, pointedly avoiding eye contact. The man was nervous.

I tried again. "What was the pastor doing in the barn right now, Jim?"

He didn't reply.

"Answer the question," snarled Tetyana, the light from the naked bulb above us glinting off her gun.

Jim went silent for a few seconds before he spoke. When he did speak, his voice cracked, and he didn't look up.

"He was here because he's my lover."

Chapter Forty-seven

Tetyana and I leaned back in our chairs in shock.

This was unexpected.

Now that Jim had confessed to his worst sin, he was ready to talk. I didn't even have to probe.

"I knew him from way back. He used to teach in my elementary school," said Jim. His eyes were glassy and his tone was deadpan, like all the emotion had been drained from him.

"He liked to make friends with the choirboys in school. Boyfriends, I mean. I used to sing in the choir. I didn't know it then. I was just a kid. Anyway, that's where I met him."

He took a deep breath in.

Tetyana and I listened silently.

"When Pastor Graham asked you to do something, you just did it. Everyone told you that was the way it was. No one said no to him."

Jim stopped and fiddled with an errant nail on the table, his eyes down, his face pale.

"He never left you alone either. It didn't matter how old you were or where you lived. He found you. And when he found you, you just did what he asked again…" He trailed off. "Otherwise, he'd tell…"

My head baker and dear friend Luc's face flashed into mind as Jim told his story. I knew all too well about older men preying on young boys in choirs and orphanages. The word *boyfriend* was an ugly misnomer. This was child abuse in the most awful way possible.

I bent down, settling my arms on my thighs, and lowered my voice.

"How old were you when it started?"

"Ten."

The three of us sat without speaking for a minute. It was hard to respond to that. I wondered if he'd ever shared this story with anyone before. After all, he'd confessed to us at gunpoint.

Jim's face was taut and his shoulders were stooped, like he'd been defeated.

If Tetyana was right, and Jim took drugs, it now all made sense. Most people got addicted to alcohol or drugs to stave off emotional or physical pain. In his case, it was probably both. I wondered where he kept his stash and if Nancy knew.

Jim looked up, a distressed expression on his face.

"Please," he whispered, "please, promise me you won't tell Nancy."

I leaned across the table. What I really wanted to do was reach over and touch his arm, to reassure him, but something stopped me.

I still didn't know what had happened to Mrs. Robinson and Doctor Fulton. I still had to identify the insidious letter writer. While Jim looked vulnerable and frightened, I had no idea what his role was in all this. Pastor Graham could have put him up to the murders, for all I knew.

"Absolutely," I replied. "You have our word. We didn't come here to dig any of that up. I'm so sorry about what happened to you."

He turned back to his nail, impulsively tapping it on the bench, his mind elsewhere.

I noticed Tetyana had holstered her weapon now. We sat around the table for a long time, not speaking, listening to that melancholy tick-tick sound of the nail against the wood.

Now that Jim had devolved his darkest secret to complete strangers, I could only imagine what was burning through his mind.

Part of me wanted to let him be, let him go away and deal with his personal demons, but I also had a mission to accomplish.

"Jim," I said, "would you mind if we ask you a few questions about this family?"

He shrugged.

"Fire away," he said in a tired voice, not looking up. "Not like I have a choice, do I?"

"You do," I said, "we're not the police. But I think you need to know why we're here."

He looked up, a curious expression in his eyes.

"What do you mean?"

"Did you know Mrs. Robinson had been getting death threats?"

His eyes widened.

"Death threats?"

"She showed one to us. We have copies of all of them and they're pretty nasty."

"Who'd do something like that? To Mrs. Robinson, of all people?"

"That's what we were wondering," I said. "She called us down here to help her find the person who was doing it."

He stared at me for a moment.

"So, you weren't really lost then?"

I shook my head.

"You aren't the FBI or anything?"

I shook my head again.

"You... you're like private investigators or something?"

"Or something," said Tetyana before I could answer, shooting a warning look my way.

We might just be the new owners too.

I bit my lip and continued.

"Do you think Pastor Graham would do something like this? Do you recall seeing anything that might lead you to believe he wrote those letters?"

Jim shook his head, but that was more a gesture of confusion than an outright no.

"He liked Mrs. Robinson. Used to say she was the best thing that happened to this house. He's respected in town and here. I can't imagine him doing anything like that."

Tetyana glared at him.

"There's no reason to defend that pedophile," she said, spitting that last word out as if she'd bitten into something bitter.

I was sure if Pastor Graham had walked into the barn just now, she'd have pulled him into a corner and walloped his head with her gun.

"He hurt you when you were a child, Jim," said Tetyana. "He's blackmailing you now. He's not your lover. He's a sadistic ass clown who needs his head whacked in."

Jim rubbed his face. If ever a man looked miserable, it had to be him right now.

"I'm not defending anyone," he said in a cracked voice. "I'm not lying. I've told you things I've never even told my wife...."

I leaned across the table.

"If anyone found out about the pastor and you, would he try to silence them?"

Jim sat quietly, his eyes darting back and forth, like he was thinking this through.

We waited.

He shook his head. "I don't think he's a murderer. I can't see him sending nasty letters to Mrs. Robinson."

I gritted my teeth. Why was he so adamant to protect the man who robbed him of his childhood? Maybe it was Stockholm syndrome. Maybe it was blackmail. My gut said he was telling the truth, but he was clearly under the pastor's influence.

"The only person I can imagine getting poison letters is Barry," said Jim.

"Why?" I asked, though I had a pretty good inkling.

"He can get real nasty when he's had too much, which is pretty much every day. He's got a mean streak. Secretly, I think everyone wishes he'd just drop dead and save us all this misery." He paused. "But I can't imagine anyone trying to hurt the doctor or Mrs. Robinson."

"No one?" I asked with a sigh. "You know, Jim, ever since I got here, I felt like this house holds too many secrets."

Jim looked away, that evasiveness coming over him again.

"Anything else you'd like to share?" said Tetyana in an impatient voice.

Jim looked up. "You're not cops?"

We shook our heads.

He let out a sigh.

"Look, I don't know anything about these letters. I know nothing about that wire on the steps. And I have no idea what happened to Doctor Fulton and Mrs. Robinson. I just keep my head down and do my job, okay?"

Tetyana and I nodded.

"You saw those horses?" he said.

"What about them?" I said.

"They're not Lisa's. She's allergic to animals, so she never comes here."

"Do the owners rent your stables?"

Jim shook his head.

"They're not ours. We don't let them out because… because they've been kidnapped."

Tetyana let out a low whistle.

"Kidnapped?" I raised an eyebrow. This was a night full of surprises.

"These aren't just any horses, you know," continued Jim, fidgeting in his seat. "They're thoroughbred racehorses."

"How much are they worth?" asked Tetyana.

"I dunno. One day I heard Lisa say they had a buyer in Dubai or someplace like that. I heard something like a half a million dollars for four."

"Lisa has a horse-napping racket going on?" I said. *"Lisa?"*

"It wasn't her who came up with the idea," Jim replied, his shoulders stooping again. "It was Pastor Graham who made her do it. He brought them over one day in a big trailer and asked us to hide them. No one questions him. I constructed the stable extension to the barn this summer, like he told me to."

"Haven't the owners contacted the police? Aren't they searching for them?"

"They won't."

"Why not?"

"Because they don't want the horses to get hurt, and because…"

He fell silent again.

We waited.

His face flushed when he spoke again.

"Because he's blackmailing us. All of us!"

Suddenly it dawned on me.

"The owners of these horses were your classmates, weren't they?" I asked. "Graham's victims from the past?"

Jim nodded.

"He threatened them, like he's doing to me. That's why they'll never tell the police."

"Did this pastor fellow abuse Lisa and Barry when they were kids, too?" asked Tetyana.

Jim shrugged and swallowed a sob.

"Maybe Barry. Maybe that's why he drinks so much. I dunno."

I remembered how the pastor had groped Katy at dinner our first night here. Maybe, I thought, he abused both little boys and little girls.

Mrs. Robinson had been correct. This house held many mysteries, mysteries I wasn't sure I could stomach any more. But I had a job to do. I pressed on.

"Mrs. Robinson said they never went to school. Where did young Barry and Lisa meet the pastor?"

"He came every weekend to give them lessons when they were kids. He was just a teenager back then. Their parents arranged for tutors because they were never around. Anyway, that's what Lisa said once."

Even at a young age, Pastor Graham had found the perfect career that would give him access to young victims. *What a sick creep.*

Tears rolled down Jim's eyes, falling on the sawdust on the table.

"We were just kids," said Jim, his hands curling into fists and his face red in embarrassment or anger. "When we grew older and left school, he followed us. He found us and told us he'd share our secret if we didn't listen to him. He took pictures every time. We have no choice—"

He stopped abruptly and put his head on the table.

Tetyana and I stared at this grown man who was now crying like a child.

Perhaps for the first time in his life, he was releasing all the trauma from his horrific childhood.

Chapter Forty-eight

"What the hell is going on over there?" said Tetyana.

We had just stepped outside the barn. Jim was shutting the door behind him when Tetyana and I noticed the house.

All three floors were lit up.

I checked my watch. It was two in the morning.

Is the entire household up?

Only an hour ago, the manor had been plunged into darkness. I was sure everybody had trudged up to their rooms after the pastor had shooed them out of the dining room.

"Stay behind me," instructed Tetyana as she pulled out her weapon and slid into the shadows.

I turned to Jim.

"Any idea what's going on?"

He shrugged, looking as perplexed as we were. And scared.

I pulled out my gun and gestured to Jim to follow me.

Tetyana was already halfway down the driveway. I could see her silhouette slinking along the side of the house, moving toward the side door.

My mind flashed to Katy.

Our bedroom light was on, but I knew she had planned to stay up reading the diary. I felt the bedroom key in my pocket with relief. She was safe in there.

I could hear Jim's laborious breathing behind me. "Hurry!" I said, as I ran to catch up with Tetyana.

Tetyana kicked the side door open, and I jumped in behind her.

We spun around, guns aimed forward. But the kitchen was empty, though the lights had all been turned on.

The row of dirty wine glasses had fallen to the floor from the counter and smashed into pieces. I moved away from the shards and pointed the mess out to Jim, so he wouldn't step on it.

Someone, I was sure, had been in such a hurry they'd knocked over the glasses.

But something else was amiss.

The knife block, the one with Mrs. Robinson's red-handled designer kitchen knives, had been turned on its side. Two knives were missing.

A muffled sound came from somewhere upstairs.

"Katy?" I shouted out, my heart leaping to my mouth.

The sound came again, like a soft thud against a wall.

I didn't wait another second. I whirled around and ran up the back stairwell, with Tetyana and Jim at my heels.

"Katy?" I hollered as I ran up.

"Watch for traps!" yelled Tetyana after me, but I barely heard her.

As soon as we got to the top floor, my stomach turned queasy. Something was wrong. Very wrong.

We quickened our pace.

With every step closer to our room, my throat felt drier and my stomach more nauseous.

"Frigging hell!" shouted Tetyana, breaking into a run.

Our bedroom door had been flung open.

I dashed after her.

But Katy was no longer inside.

"Katy!"

"She struggled," said Tetyana, surveying the room.

Someone took her.

The bedside lamp was lying on its side, and the plush toys had been scattered across the room. The comforter and bedsheet had been ripped away from the bed, like Katy had either flung them off to jump out, or someone else had done it before snatching her.

I wanted to cry out, but my mouth seemed to have been clamped down. All I could hear was my heart pounding in my chest.

Katy. What happened? Where are you?

I whirled around in one spot, hoping to see her. I knew how ridiculous it would be to think she was still in this compact room with no space to maneuver, let alone hide. But I kept looking.

Tetyana was checking the windows. She rattled the latches to confirm they had remained locked. Katy couldn't have disappeared through the window, I thought. They took her out the door.

Who unlocked the door? And how?

"Either someone had an extra key and got in," said Tetyana, reading my mind, "or she opened the door and let someone in."

"She'd never let anyone in," I said. "She's smarter than that."

"Maybe someone pretended to be one of us."

"Impossible. Remember? She could barely walk."

As we were talking, Jim stepped up to the bedside table and straightened up the lamp. Then, he bent down and picked up a small object from under the bed.

"Hey," he said, waving it at us.

"Katy's phone!" I said, swiping it from him. It was locked, but finding it here confirmed she hadn't left willingly. She'd never drop it and run out like that.

Tetyana was examining the carpet near the bed, and for a moment, I wondered if she was looking for bloodstains.

I tried in vain to not let wild thoughts of Katy being shot, stabbed, or worse, enter my head. I didn't know what I'd do if she'd been hurt. But I needed a cool head to find her.

I turned back to the bed.

Something else was missing in this room. I scanned the space, racking my brain. Something bothered me, but I couldn't put a finger to it.

What is it?

Think, woman, think.

I stepped up to the bed and stripped the comforter and bedsheets. Then, I pulled away the fitted sheet on the mattress.

"What are you looking for?" I heard Jim say behind me. Without answering him, I picked up a pillow, ripped off its cover and looked inside.

Nothing.

I threw the pillowcases on the naked mattress and turned around to see Jim and Tetyana staring at me.

"The book," I said to Tetyana. "It's gone."

"What book?" asked Jim.

The photocopied letters had disappeared too, together with the girl's diary, but I wasn't about to divulge any more information in front of him.

As I surveyed the room, my fighting spirit grew stronger inside of me.

My eyes narrowed, and I gritted my teeth. I raised my arm and aimed my weapon at Jim.

He stared at me with a stunned expression on his face.

"Do you know who took her? Do you?"

He stepped back, shaking his head, arms raised in the air.

"No, I never even knew she was gone... I have no idea... Please don't...."

"Asha," I heard Tetyana say, but my eyes were on Jim.

"I swear if you had anything to do with Katy's disappearance, I won't hesitate to put a bullet through your head."

Chapter Forty-nine

"Asha!"

I turned around to see Tetyana leaning toward the entrance, her face taut, her ears and eyes on alert.

"Second floor. Something is going on. Maybe Katy's down there."

That was when I heard the low hum of people talking. I could feel the urgency in their voices.

One voice got louder. It was Nancy. She was objecting to something, but it was hard to make out the words. Then Barry let out a deafening yell.

Jim didn't hesitate.

Pushing me aside, he darted out the door.

With a curse, I scooted after him, Tetyana right behind me. Jim scrambled down the stairs, calling Nancy's name, panic tinged in his voice.

Within seconds, Tetyana and I burst into the second-floor dining room after Jim.

It seemed like everyone, except for Katy, was inside the dining room.

They all turned and stared.

We stared back.

Jim ran up to his wife. She'd been standing by the table, looking like she was having a panic attack. She fell into Jim's arms with a cry.

That was when I saw it.

In the same chair where Doctor Fulton had sat just a few hours ago, was Pastor Graham. His head was slumped over. Protruding from his back was a butcher's knife. It was the same red-handled knife I'd seen Nancy use in the kitchen to slice her meat.

I stared at his body in shock.

Even from where I was standing, I could see the deathly yellow pallor that had come over him.

For the past hour, as Jim had shared his story with us, I'd been building a case against this despicable man. I'd been relishing the thought of outing a blackmailing pedophile who'd been terrorizing so many innocents.

While I had no proof he was behind Mrs. Robinson's or Doctor Fulton's deaths, I was sure I'd find one. Plus, I had zero sympathy for this man who'd groped Katy at the dinner table.

Pastor Graham had been my prime suspect.

But now he was dead.

This meant there was another killer in the house.

I glanced around the room, my heart racing.

It was like we'd walked into a room under a spell. Everyone was standing frozen in place, completely mute, shocked expressions on their faces.

What's going on in this mad, mad house?

Tetyana marched up to the table. She reached over to the pastor's wrist to feel his pulse, then holstered her weapon and bent down to scrutinize the knife wound in his back.

She straightened up and didn't say anything.

She didn't need to.

I slipped my gun into my vest pocket, feeling numb. This made three deaths in twenty-four hours.

No one said a word.

They were all staring at the pastor's body, as if they couldn't believe what they were seeing.

And now Katy's missing. Where is she? Who took her? What happened?

My mind whirled, and my stomach churned.

Did Katy have something to do with this? Did the pastor try to attack her, and she fought back? But she'd never stab a man in the back.

I looked around the room.

Barry was in striped blue pajamas, his hair standing straight up as usual, his bloodshot eyes looking like he hadn't slept in days and his bushy eyebrows making him appear more menacing than ever.

There was a bruise on his left eye and a scarlet mark on his face. I wondered if he'd fallen down and scraped himself in a drunken stupor and we hadn't even noticed.

I had expected him to be frothing with fury, but the man standing by the liquor cabinet was a frightened one. The third death had finally subdued him.

Lisa was by her chair, looking down at her hands. Her hair was standing in clumps, like she'd forgotten to smoothen it down when she got out of bed. I noticed she kept her face down, staring at the table, like she couldn't bear to see the dead man.

Charles, one half of our hiking couple, was standing by the door, clutching the wall for support, still in his jeans and T-shirt, as if he'd never gone to bed. He looked pale, like the blood had drained from his face.

Where's Caril?

I looked from one person to the next.

"Anyone know how this happened?" I asked, hearing the strain in my own voice.

Silence.

"Who found Pastor Graham?" I asked again.

"I didn't see a thing," said Charles finally.

I turned to Barry.

"Me too," he replied in a flustered voice. "Never seen nothing..."

How fast a coward falls.

I turned to Lisa, but she wasn't looking up.

"What about you?" I said.

She shook her head and looked down, her lips pursed. I doubted I was going to make her talk right now.

I turned around, looking everyone in the eye.

"Katy fell and twisted her ankle on the stairs and couldn't walk, but now she's disappeared."

They stared back at me, blank expressions on their faces.

I raised my voice. "Did anyone see her?"

No one replied.

I pulled my gun out.

"Answer me!"

Charles and Nancy recoiled at the sight of my weapon. Lisa shook her head while Barry turned a bewildered face to me.

"You mean the redhead?" he said.

"Yes, the redhead," I said through gritted teeth. *The one you tried to slap around this morning.*

"Never seen the wench."

I wanted to pistol whip the man, but I knew that would only make things worse. Besides, we needed him to talk.

I took a deep breath in to rein in the anger threatening to explode from me. I turned to the room.

"If any of you have harmed even a hair on Katy, I swear—"

"It was her!"

I whirled around. Barry was pointing an accusing finger at Nancy.

Nancy raised her face from Jim's chest, wiped her eyes and gave him a scared look.

"Didn't hear no one stumbling down the stairs," said Barry, "but I heard her. She's the one who banged on my door."

"She banged on my door too," said Charles.

Lisa nodded, still keeping her face down. "Mine too," she said in a quiet voice.

All eyes turned to Nancy.

"She did him in!" screeched Barry. "She's the one!"

Chapter Fifty

"I didn't kill him!" shrieked Nancy.

Jim pulled her in closer.

"You have the wrong person," he said, his face turning a tinge of purple. "Stop picking on her."

"It was her, I tell you!" bellowed Barry.

"You're lying!" yelled Jim.

I turned to Nancy, who was shaking in his arms.

"How about you tell us how you found him?" I asked.

She looked up, her eyes red.

"I know nothing about Katy falling down the stairs, but I heard loud noises downstairs just a few minutes ago and came out to see what it was."

"Noises?" I said. "Like what?"

"Like people having a bad fight. It was so bad it made the hair on my arms stand up."

"Was it Pastor Graham's voice?"

"I thought I heard a woman, but maybe it was him...." She gave a petrified side glance at the dead body at the table.

"A woman? Was it Katy?"

Nancy shook her head.

"I don't think so...."

"When did this happen?"

"I dunno."

"Try."

"Guess it was a good ten or fifteen minutes ago," Nancy replied, sniffing. "I couldn't find Jim, so I came down to see what was going on, and I saw this... he... it was horrid!"

"Did you see anyone else on the landing or the corridor?" I asked.

She shook her head.

"Nancy, I need you to be absolutely frank with us," I said. "Can you tell us what you were doing at Mrs. Robinson's room when she died?"

She shot me a terrified look.

"I, er..."

I waited.

Nancy moved away from Jim and leaned against the wall.

"It was about Jim," she mumbled.

Jim gave her a horrified look.

"Me?"

Nancy turned to the room, her eyes filled with tears. "Look, you all know we're having trouble. It's not a secret. I went to Mrs. Robinson for advice. Whenever I couldn't sleep, I went down to talk to her, and she made me tea. She helped me."

"But... but, I...." Jim tried to speak, but was faltering.

"Thank you, Nancy," I said quietly.

I glanced around the room. There were two people missing from here: Katy and Caril. I was about to ask Charles where his partner was, when Tetyana, who'd been circling the pastor's body, looked up with a deep frown on her face.

"What happened to Doctor Fulton?" she asked.

Jim cleared his throat and opened his mouth, but nothing came out.

"What is it, Jim?" she asked.

"It was me and Pastor Graham," replied Jim, giving a furtive glance at the body of the man who'd terrorized him for so long. "He told me to help him take the doctor downstairs."

"Downstairs? Where?"

"To the..." He swallowed. "To the wine room."

Tetyana glared at him.

"Why in hell would you move a dead body?"

"Because he said so," said Jim, his voice rising defensively. "It's too warm up here. We had to keep him cool, like with Mrs. Robinson. He said if he stays here, who knows what will happen. So I helped him move the doctor."

"Nancy, did you touch or move the pastor's body too?" asked Tetyana.

Nancy flinched, as if she was repulsed by the very thought.

"Is this how you found him?" Tetyana asked again.

"I didn't even come into the room. Spotted him from the doorway. So, I ran up and banged on everyone's door...." She choked back a sob. "I didn't do it. I swear to you. It wasn't me!"

She burst into tears.

I looked over at Charles, clutching at the doorway, like he wished he could run away but knew he shouldn't.

I spun around, glowering at the room.

"Someone put a tripwire across the top step in the main staircase and the back stairwell. They meant for one of us to fall over and break a neck. That's what Katy tripped over."

I whirled around to make sure I looked everyone in the eye. "Who did it? Who put that death trap in place?"

They looked at me with shocked expressions on their faces, but no one spoke.

"Where were you all in the past hour?"

"Sleeping," said Charles, answering swiftly. Too swiftly. "In my room."

"Me too," said Nancy through her tears.

Lisa nodded.

"I was with you," said Jim to me in a small voice.

"I was in my damn room," shouted Barry. "What's with all these questions?"

"We've had three murders in the past twenty-four hours and our friend Katy has vanished, and you're not even remotely concerned—"

"Shut up!"

Barry stomped toward me, his tumbler raised in his hands.

"You!" he thundered, swaying like a zombie. "Throwing your weight around, pulling out guns and asking questions like you're the damned FBI!"

I stepped back. Even from halfway across the room, I could smell his whiskey-fumed dank breath. I had no intention of being on his warpath again.

"Who do you think you are?" he hollered. "Showing up like the witches of Macbeth and all hell breaks loose. You have a lot of explaining to do. How do we know it wasn't that redheaded pal of yours who killed Pastor Graham?"

He stopped and swayed in place, his face red with fury.

"This is your damn fault," he said in a slurred voice. "You come in here sticking your noses into things you shouldn't."

He took another swig of his drink and glared at me. "I don't know what you people are up to, but I tell you, you have cursed this place!"

I racked my brain, trying to think of how to best subdue this man. He was twice my size, but he wasn't in control of his physical capacities right now.

"Barry," I said, mustering my calmest voice. "This has been a shocking day for all of us. I'm as horrified as you are—"

"Don't talk to me like I'm a stupid child!" yelled Barry, spitting his alcohol -fumed drool all over himself.

"It was Mrs. Robinson who invited them here."

All eyes turned to Jim, even Barry's.

"She was getting death threat letters," continued Jim in a quiet voice. "She hired them to help her find who it was. They're private investigators or something."

Silence.

Everyone stared at Tetyana and me.

For the first time, Lisa raised her head and brushed her hair back.

"Mrs. Robinson asked you to come?" she whispered.

I nodded.

"Lies, damn lies!" shouted Barry.

"She showed us her letters," I said, ignoring Barry. "All she wanted was to make them stop. We didn't realize this was going to turn into a triple murder investigation."

Lisa flinched again, like I'd hit her.

"They're lying," shouted Barry. "It's them who did this. They came here and killed everyone!"

Before I could react, he threw the whiskey-filled tumbler at me. I ducked, but I was a split second late. The tumbler smashed against my head, making me reel back.

With another roar, Barry came at me like an angry bull, his fist raised high.

I stepped aside, ignoring the searing pain spreading across my temple, and braced myself.

Barry got to only two feet from me when he crumpled on the ground with a surprised bellow, bringing me crashing down with him.

It was Tetyana.

She'd pistol whipped Barry on the head.

"Get off her, you frigging dufus," I heard her growl as she forced him to his feet.

I pulled my feet from under his bulky body and stood up. Barry got up shakily, groaning.

I stepped back while Tetyana pushed Barry toward a chair and shoved him into it. He plopped down, protesting noisily. She placed her hands on his shoulders and pinned him down.

The left side of my face was wet, and my head was throbbing. I wiped the whiskey from my hair, feeling nauseous at the sickly smell.

"You all right?" said Jim.

I nodded, trying not to think of the migraine threatening to break out any moment.

"Anyone else try funny games like that," said Tetyana, "and you'll feel the butt of my gun."

"There's a killer roaming around this house," I said. "Figuring out who they are should be our priority."

Nancy turned a panic-stricken face at me.

"Are we all a target now? Who's going to die next?"

Chapter Fifty-one

I looked around the room, gauging everyone.

On the surface, it seemed absurd to think Barry the drunkard could kill three people in a row in cold blood and get away with kidnapping Katy. He was too loud, too brash, and too clumsy, with the manners of a bull moose in heat.

Then there was Lisa.

She was standoffish and distant, but if I'd have to bet on it, I'd say she wouldn't be able to find her way out of a paper bag even with directions. She had a peculiar personality, but I wondered if she had the wherewithal to pull my friend off her bed and take her somewhere. Katy would have fought back like a mad cat.

Nancy and Jim looked genuinely distraught. *Did Nancy have something to do with Katy's disappearance?* Though Jim had opened up to us in the barn, and had us for an alibi, I wasn't about to trust him yet.

They could all be the best actors in town for all we knew.

It was Charles who concerned me the most. He was a stranger, or so he had told us, but I had a funny feeling he knew this house.

I suddenly realized what had bothered me earlier.

I remembered how he and Caril had walked directly toward the staff entrance when Nancy had asked them to wash up. The kitchen had two doors that lead to the rest of the house. Any normal guest to this house for the first time would have asked where the washrooms were.

I was about to ask Charles about Caril, when Barry yelled.

"What do you want to do now?" he shouted. "You talk like you know everything. Hang everyone we suspect? I vote we hang you!"

I was glad Tetyana was holding him down. There was nothing more I wanted to do than to punch him in the face and tell him to shut up. Katy was missing, and he was playing childish games.

"What we're going to do now," I said, "is to contact the authorities and let them do their job."

No one spoke.

"Tetyana and I will search this house and the grounds from top to bottom for Katy tonight."

"Like hell you will," grumbled Barry.

"We're going to lock the dining room as it is, so we don't interfere with the evidence," I continued, ignoring Barry's glares. "Then, we'll ask you all to go to your rooms and stay there until we get the police here."

"That might take days," said Nancy, a horrified expression on her face. "You can't lock us up like that. Besides, we can't leave Pastor Graham... sitting here till then."

"Officer Jensen said he'll come tomorrow morning to check on us," I said, "he's our best hope right now. We can set up a footbridge so they can—"

"You're a fool to trust that incompetent piece of a man who calls himself an officer," Barry exploded. "It'll take him weeks to find reinforcement."

"He'll come," I said, not feeling confident in my own sentiments, but I wasn't going to show it to them.

I turned to Charles.

"Where's Caril?"

He shrugged. "In bed, sleeping, I suppose."

"Was she sleeping when you came down?"

"I... I...," he spluttered. "She said she was thirsty and went downstairs to get a glass of water. So, when Nancy banged on my door, I didn't look. She might have come back. I don't know."

"Wouldn't you have noticed if Caril wasn't sleeping next to you?"

"I... just ran out. There was all this noise outside and everyone was shouting about the dead pastor. I didn't have time to think."

Charles was scrambling all over the place. He was a liar and a bad one at that.

We had to locate Caril. I was sure she had a connection to this house. The way she behaved was too unusual, not like a lost hiker with a twisted ankle.

It was also strange the only two people missing were Caril and Katy. Something told me finding Caril would lead us to Katy.

My mind whirred. If someone took Katy, where would they take her? The barn? The cabin? The woods? I felt heart palpitations thinking of all the dangerous places she could be.

I turned to the room.

"We saw tire marks on the old riverbed just outside the tree line. Does anyone know where that leads?"

No one answered.

"It's not that far from the cabin. If you follow the trail to the end, you'll see it."

I watched Jim, Nancy, and Charles closely, and hoped Tetyana was focusing on Barry and Lisa.

Nancy shrugged.

Jim shook his head.

Charles didn't even look up.

He knew something, but he wasn't talking.

"You people are mad," muttered Barry. "That goes nowhere."

I turned to him.

"Do you know that road?"

"Bosh. It's not a road. Not even a trail. Why don't you listen when I tell you?"

"We're listening, Barry."

"That riverbed stops halfway to town. It was closed down years ago."

"Sounds like you know it well."

"They built a dam twenty years ago and there's no way to cut across that, unless you're planning to die drowning."

He looked down, shaking his head, all of a sudden melancholy.

"I used to run around over there when I was a little boy," he said, his tone softer. "Some weekends, I went to town all by myself, bought candies and walked back. Took me all day, but I loved it. Then those bastards came and built that dam. It's a dead end. Those good for nothing..."

Tetyana and I locked eyes.

It was time to stop talking and start moving.

Tetyana let go of Barry and stepped away.

"Jim, you're with us," she said. "We'll need some extra muscle power for the bridge. Everyone else, go to your rooms until we give the all-clear."

We were risking it by bringing Jim with us. He had been willing to take instructions so far, but I couldn't let my guard down. For all I know, he was the killer among the group.

But Jim also knew the area, the town, the people, and he knew where to find the equipment for repairing the bridge. If it came to it, Tetyana and I could tackle him.

No one moved.

Tetyana raised her voice. "Anyone here looking forward to being the fourth body or discovering it?"

No one even twitched a muscle.

Tetyana screwed her eyes tight. "Are you all going to go up on your own volition or are you going to make me force you?"

Nancy shot her a frightened look. "You're not the police."

"We're trying to stop a fourth killing here," I said.

"You're not seriously going to jail us in our rooms, are you?" said Charles.

"It's for your own safety," I said.

Barry thumped an angry fist on the table, making us all jump. "Madness. I tell you, you're all mad!"

"We don't have all night." Tetyana waved her gun, her voice tinged with impatience. "Since you all seem so reluctant to follow instructions, I'm locking you in."

"Who the hell are you to push me around in my home?" hollered Barry. "You rat-faced whores. You will regret this!"

It took five seconds of strategic prodding with Tetyana's handgun to escort a raging Barry up to his room. After that, Lisa and Nancy went to their rooms without a fuss.

Before locking them in, Tetyana and I checked each room, looking under the beds, inside the closets, behind the curtains, in the showers and bathtubs just to make sure Katy hadn't been shoved in there.

My friend was nowhere to be found, but we made other discoveries.

On a table next to the sink in Lisa's bathroom was a jumble of bottles, jars and even a mortar and pestle. Small clay pots of garden-variety herbs lined her windowsill. *An herbalist?*

I picked up a small brown bottle whose label had an X on it. I popped the cork and sniffed the contents. Almonds. I put the bottle down, puzzled why she would have baking ingredients in her room.

I found a small packet of white powder in the bathroom cabinet of Nancy and Jim's room. Was this why she shouted in anger the night before? Because she found this packet here?

Both Lisa and Nancy glared at me as I took the key from the other side and closed their doors. I felt bad for locking them in, but they each had a comfortable bed and their own things.

Then we took Charles to his bedroom.

His room was empty. Something told me he had been humoring us all along. He'd known his partner wasn't here.

We stepped inside and checked the usual places.

"Where's Caril?" I asked.

"I told you I don't know."

I stared at him. Katy was missing, and I was freaking out. In contrast, he seemed to take his partner's disappearance in stride.

"Your girlfriend's vanished in a house where three people have suddenly died, and you're not troubled?"

He looked me in the eye. I thought I caught a glint of amusement. "Like I said, she probably went to get a glass of water from the kitchen."

"We didn't see her when we came in."

He shrugged. "Maybe she's in the downstairs bathroom."

I squinted at him.

"What are you and Caril doing in this house?"

"I already told you. We got lost."

"I don't believe you."

He gave Tetyana and me a sick smile.

"Look, I know you're trying to find a killer, but it ain't me. It ain't Caril either. You people are barking up the wrong tree."

"Do you know who it is?" I asked.

He shot me an impatient look.

"I don't have to answer any of your questions. I'd be happy to talk to the police, but right now," he gave me a steely look, "damned if you think you're going to lock me up in this airless room."

Before I could react, he pushed me roughly aside and made for the door, but Tetyana grabbed him by the collar.

"Where do you think you're off to?"

"Off to find Caril," he snarled, struggling to push her hand away. "Let go of me. You don't know who I am."

Tetyana shoved him on the bed, making him fall on his back.

"I don't care if you're the Prince of Wales, bud. You stay exactly where I tell you to stay."

Chapter Fifty-two

"We're going to go room by room," said Tetyana. "We'll start on the third floor."

I pulled Mrs. Robinson's master key ring from my pocket. "Here."

She plucked them from my hands.

"Good. I don't have to smash the doors down now."

Jim gave her a fearful look.

"Stay in my line of sight and no funny moves, got it?" I said to him.

He nodded.

For the next fifteen minutes we followed the same drill.

I kept a sharp eye out, my gun at the ready, while Tetyana opened each door. All the while, Jim stood quietly, not more than three feet from me, staring at his shoes, looking like the world had ended for him.

It took Tetyana minutes to search each room. Since they had been built and decorated similarly and some were only sparsely furnished, her job was faster than I expected. Our only delay was in trying to figure out which key fit which lock.

From the third floor, we walked down to the second landing, watching out for booby traps along the way. Other than the dining room, there was just one room on the east wing of the second floor. It was the immense living area connected to the dining room.

We walked in cautiously.

It was bizarre to see the pastor's lifeless body at the table with that knife sticking out of him. For one brief moment, I felt bad for barging in, like we were intruding on the dead.

I tried to not look that way while Tetyana searched all the alcoves and nooks where a human being could be hidden.

We were just about to depart through the living room entrance, when Jim turned to Tetyana.

"You missed something," he said.

"Oh, yeah?"

"There's a secret closet in here."

Tetyana merely raised an eyebrow.

I scanned the room. "Where?"

"Behind the liquor cabinet."

Tetyana gave him a look over, as if she was trying to decide whether to trust him.

"All right then," she said, "why don't you show us?"

Jim walked over to the liquor cabinet while I aimed my gun at his back. I didn't know if he was playing a game, but if he was, I was going to have control over the situation.

But Jim seemed focused on his task. He opened the wooden doors, shoved his hand inside and moved it around as if he was rummaging for something.

"You'd better not be looking for a weapon," growled Tetyana.

Jim didn't look up.

"There's a latch in here," I heard him mumble. He was feeling the back of the cabinet now. "I saw Barry open it once."

After a minute of searching, Jim pulled his hand out with an exasperated sigh. One by one, he took out Barry's whiskey decanters and tumblers. After placing them all on the dining table, he reached in to feel the back panel again.

A hollow click came from somewhere. I felt goose bumps rising at the sound.

"Found it?" said Tetyana, getting closer to look.

A second click came as Jim fiddled with a mysterious latch inside the cabinet. Then, to my surprise, he stepped back and pulled the cabinet away from the wall.

The entire liquor cabinet acted like a door, an entrance to a concealed secret room.

I stepped up to see.

It was an open space built into the wall, about five feet wide and five feet deep, the size of a small closet you'd find in a decent city apartment.

I peered inside.

"It's tiny," I said.

It was also empty.

"What did Barry keep in here?" asked Tetyana, stepping inside to examine it closer.

Jim shrugged.

"No idea. When I saw him open it the other day, I was sure this was where he hid his whiskey stash. Lisa doesn't like him drinking much, and Mrs. Robinson and Doctor Fulton were always trying to get him weaned off the stuff."

Tetyana bent over and reached for something on the floor. She turned and held out a lone bottle of whiskey in her hand.

"Just one left," she said. She turned the bottle in her hand and held it up to the light to examine it.

"Nothing special about it. A ten-year-old bottle of scotch. Probably worth twenty-five dollars at most."

She looked at Jim.

"Did he take out anything the last time?"

He shook his head.

"I thought he put something inside, but I didn't see what it was. He walked in and after a few minutes came back out and closed it up."

"He didn't spot you watching?"

Jim gestured at the large windows behind the sofas. "I was cleaning them from the outside, on a ladder. He was too busy or too drunk to notice me. But I definitely saw him."

Tetyana walked back into the space and placed the bottle exactly where she'd found it. Then she began to feel the walls inside.

I realized that while the decor was from the sixties and seventies, the house had been built much earlier, possibly a hundred or more years ago. This hidden closet could be the entrance to a secret passageway. There could also be more secret rooms on other floors.

Anything was possible in an old manor like this.

For the love of all things, I hoped Katy wasn't stuck somewhere we wouldn't be able to find her. I leaned against a chair, feeling nauseous at the thought her alone and scared in a deep dark place inside the bowels of this house.

Please let Katy be okay, I said to myself for the hundredth time that evening.

Tetyana came out, looking disappointed. "Nothing. No secret doorways in here." She turned to Jim. "Close it up."

Jim pushed the liquor cabinet back against the wall and placed Barry's treasure trove back on the shelves where they belonged.

"What's on the west wing of this floor?" I asked Jim.

"Used to be smoking and reading rooms and such. There's a small library, but no one goes there."

"We're going to change that," said Tetyana, ushering us out and into the main corridor again.

As we scoured each room, Tetyana and Jim searched for more secret hideouts, but they found nothing. Heavy drapes covered most of the furniture and the dust settled on them told us it had been years, maybe even decades, since anyone had walked into this wing.

From the second floor, we trooped down to the first floor where the kitchen and staff quarters were. Other than the broken glass lying on the ceramic tiles of the kitchen and the missing knives, nothing else seemed out of the ordinary.

We walked into the staff quarters, with Tetyana leading the way.

Except for Mrs. Robinson's room, the staff rooms were mostly unfurnished. Other than a bedframe, a lone chair, and a frayed rug or two, there wasn't much to see, which made our search go quickly.

"Why did Mrs. Robinson sleep on this floor when everyone else slept upstairs?" I asked Jim, as he tapped on the walls, searching for potential hidden entrances.

"She used to sleep upstairs at one point," he said. "Way before we came here."

"Any idea why she moved down?"

He shook his head.

"Never told us, except this was her room when she was a girl. If you ask me, she was tiring of Barry's rumblings in the middle of the night."

I raised an eyebrow.

"A sleepwalker?"

"He's always awake and knows exactly what he's doing. Whenever he gets thirsty in the dead of the night, which happens often, he stumbles to the dining room to his whiskey cabinet. He never does it quietly."

I thought of Katy stumbling down the stairs and wondered if that was why no one had come out to check. Did everyone think it had been Barry careening around on his way to a midnight drink?

"Next stop," said Tetyana when all the bedrooms were done, "is the wine room."

Jim gave a shiver. "Do we have to?"

Without answering him, Tetyana and I moved toward the small steel door next to Mrs. Robinson's. It was the only room we hadn't checked yet.

"Ready?" said Tetyana, as she turned the key and pulled open the door.

We stared.

"Oh, man," said Jim from behind me. "Oh, man."

The wine room was a simple musty closet with stainless steel shelves lining its back wall. A dozen dusty bottles of wine lay on their sides on a middle shelf. It didn't look like a place that was used often.

Except for the floor.

On the ground, next to each other in that small space, lay Mrs. Robinson and Doctor Fulton. Their skin was a deathly gray-blue hue. Their eyes were closed like they were sleeping, but their bodies were rigid. Molted discolored spots had started to appear on Mrs. Robinson's face and neck. Her body was already disintegrating.

With a shudder, I looked away.

Tetyana closed the door and locked it. We stood by the room without speaking for a minute, like we were compelled to show deference to the dead we just saw.

"All right, folks," said Tetyana in a quiet voice, after a moment. "Let's resume the search."

Jim and I followed her out, and walked toward the kitchen without speaking.

Seeing the dead bodies had rattled all of us. It made me realize what we were up against. Someone had gone to great lengths to take the lives of three people.

I felt a cold sweat break out.

Where's Katy?

"There are flashlights in the utility cabinet," said Jim, walking up to what looked like a small pantry in the kitchen. "They'll help when we search the grounds."

A jumble of black wires fell out as he opened the pantry door. He picked up the tangle of wires and shoved them back inside.

"Someone's been stuffing all this crap in here," he said.

I peered inside.

Stashed inside were small home electronics, wires, batteries, a toolbox, and a pile of plastic Tupperware containers.

"Who put this in here?" said Jim, pulling out a small canister of beans. He put it on the counter and turned back to the closet.

I peered at the transparent jar filled with dark brown beans. Tetyana was also staring at the jar.

"These aren't kidney beans, are they?" I said, turning it around.

"They look familiar," she said with a frown. "I wouldn't touch those, if I were you."

Jim pulled out three flashlights from the cabinet and handed one to Tetyana, the second to me and kept the third for himself.

The door caught on something as he tried to close it. He bent down to see what it was when the tangle of wires he'd shoved in earlier fell on his head.

With an exasperated sigh, he scooped them back up, but stopped in mid-motion.

"Jeepers."

"What is it?" I said, bending down to look.

He turned to us, his face pale.

"A bomb."

Chapter Fifty-three

Tetyana pushed him aside and looked in.

She reached in and pulled out a black electronic device with a row of short antennas.

Jim turned to her, his face completely white.

"What if it goes off?" he whispered hoarsely.

She shook her head.

"Relax, it's not a bomb. But we now know why our phones stopped working."

She turned the device around in her hands.

"A cellular phone jammer. It's illegal to operate one but not to buy one."

I stared at the metallic device.

"This has a good range," said Tetyana. "Whoever got this knew what they were doing."

"How can you buy one but not operate it?" asked Jim, puzzled.

"You just don't turn it on," replied Tetyana.

"Can you get one online?" I asked.

"Probably where they got it from," said Tetyana, examining the back of the device. "Now who would that be?"

"I swear it isn't mine," said Jim. "Never seen one before in my life. Someone put it in here."

"Who has access to this cabinet?" I asked.

"Everybody. Anyone who comes to the kitchen could have shoved that thing inside. Normally, I'm the only one who uses it. It's where I put extra stuff I don't use often."

Tetyana switched a knob on the device and turned to me.

"Want to try your cell, Asha?"

I reached into my vest and pulled out my mobile.

The signal bars were all green, but I knew I couldn't rely on that. I auto dialed Katy's phone, which I held in my other hand.

It rang instantly.

"My goodness," I said, in relief, "you're right."

Jim pulled his phone out to check too.

"All good and in working order now," said Tetyana, pushing another button on the device. "Wi-Fi's back on again too."

"Time to call the cops," I said, punching in nine-one-one.

"Nine-one-one. For what city or town please?"

A flush of relief went through me to hear the dispatcher's voice.

"I'm calling from Cedar Cottage in Falcon Hills."

"Do you require police, fire, or an ambulance?"

"Police, please."

"What's the nature of your emergency?"

I was about to say *triple murder homicide* when I stopped myself. The pastor had definitely been killed, but the other two? Did I want to go on record saying I knew what had happened to them?

I wasn't sure if the dispatcher would consider this a prank. To even think of saying those words seemed unimaginable, and I'd seen the three dead bodies.

"A missing person," I said, crossing my fingers. "I'd like to speak with Officer Jensen from Falcon Hills."

She put me through.

I turned the speakerphone on so Tetyana could also hear the conversation. I knew I was risking Jim listening in as well, but I had no choice.

"Officer Jensen."

"We met on the dirt road to Cedar Cottage on Friday afternoon. The three women with the flat tire? We spoke to you across the broken bridge yesterday."

"Yes, I remember. What seems to be the problem?"

"There's been a murder at Cedar Cottage."

"Mrs. Robinson?"

He didn't sound surprised, but then again, he'd heard of her death. Still, it was a strange way to respond. I filed it in the back of my memory banks.

"Two more people died since Mrs. Robinson. Pastor Graham and Doctor Fulton."

The line went silent.

I thought I heard a thud, like he'd jumped out of bed. Then a rustle, like he was struggling to put clothes on while holding the phone.

"*Who?* Who died again?"

"Doctor Fulton and Pastor Graham. Doctor Fulton died during dinner in front of everyone. We thought he was choking on something, but it could be more than that."

"And the pastor?"

"We found him a half an hour ago, sitting at the dinner table. He had a kitchen knife in his back."

Again silence.

The man was a rookie. I could just see his brain whirling, trying to remember what he'd learned at the police academy.

"Officer, I think you'll need to come down and bring the sheriff too."

"I am the sheriff," he said, his breath coming fast and shallow. "Why did it take you half an hour to call me?" he demanded.

"Our phones and the Internet were down, remember? We just found a phone jammer in the kitchen."

"*A what?*"

"A phone jammer."

Silence.

"Could you get reinforcement quickly?" I asked. "Perhaps ask a neighboring county department for help? We have three dead bodies in the house, two in the wine room and one in the dining room. We didn't want to disturb the scene. You'll need forensics here," I said, feeling vaguely silly to be telling him how to do his job.

He didn't protest. I heard a snapping sound like he was putting on his utility belt.

"Everyone else okay?" he asked, his breath loud and fast over the phone. I heard footsteps, like he was stomping around, looking for his shoes.

"No, I'm afraid not. Our friend, Katy, has gone missing. About an hour ago. She was in her room with a twisted ankle, but it seems like someone took her."

"*Took her?*"

"We searched the house, but we didn't find her. We're going to check the grounds next."

"You all stay put right where you are," he said, confidence returning to his voice. "Don't you move. Lock yourself up in your rooms, and just wait till we get there."

"How soon can you get down here?"

"I'm calling the local counties as soon as I hang up." His voice was rushing now. I heard a door bang shut. "And don't touch anything!"

"Just so you know, the bridge is still down."

I heard a loud groan. "Damn. Damn. Damn."

Tetyana gestured to me.

"Wait, my friend wants to talk to you," I said, and thrust the phone near her mouth.

"Officer, I'm going to see if I can put some lumber across the narrowest part of the gully," said Tetyana. "That way, you can at least walk over."

Silence.

"Roger that," he said finally. "Thanks. We'll figure it out. Could take me an hour to rustle everyone up. Important thing is for everyone to stay safe, you hear me?"

A car door slammed, and an engine started.

"Loud and clear," I said, giving Tetyana a look. I wasn't about to stop searching for Katy now. "Thank you, Officer."

I heard him swear as I hung up.

Tetyana walked over to the stove with the phone jammer in her hand. She opened the oven door.

"Are you planning to burn it?" asked Jim.

Without replying, she threw the device on the bottom shelf.

"I'd normally leave it for the police, but don't want anyone using it soon."

She turned the grill on at high. The oven started a slow hum, signaling it was warming up.

Gesturing us to follow her, Tetyana opened the side door, and we spilled out.

Our first stop was the parked vehicles. While I kept watch of the surroundings and Jim shone the flashlights for her, Tetyana methodically checked the inside of each car.

My heart jumped to my mouth when she opened the boot of our rental. Wild images of Katy trussed up in the back flashed to my mind. I shook my head to clear it. I always came up with the worst-case scenarios at the worst possible times.

Katy, where are you?

Tetyana slammed the boot shut, shaking her head.

"Nothing here."

I glanced around the grounds. She could be anywhere. Whoever had taken her could have tied her up and pushed her under a hedge.

But why would anyone take her?

Katy had no connection to this family. This was the first time she'd even come to this state.

If this had anything to do with the codicil, it hadn't referred to any of our names, only that of my company. I was sure none of us had mentioned my bakery name to anyone in this family.

A chill went through me as I remembered that piece of paper was in Katy's pocket. If whoever took her searched her, they'd find it easily.

"We need to hurry!" I said, turning to Tetyana.

It took us minutes to get into the barn. As I kept vigil near the main door, Tetyana and Jim searched the place together.

I'd thought the barn would be easy and fast, but I'd forgotten all the hiding spots in this place, including the empty stalls, and the cupboards that held the mulch and manure bags.

Jim moved the horses out of their stalls so Tetyana could search their space as well. The horses didn't seem too upset by our intrusion. I wondered if they welcomed this attention, after being cooped in for so long.

"Nothing," said Tetyana, after a thorough search.

"Next stop, the cabin," I said, urgently reaching for the door.

An alarmed expression came over Jim's face.

"But there's nothing there," he said.

Tetyana turned to him. "Something in there you don't want us to see?"

"They probably took her to the woods," he mumbled, blinking, as if he was trying to come up with a fast answer. "They could have taken her up the mountains."

"I don't think so," said Tetyana. "It's cold, dark, and slippery out there. Unless the person who took her was a lunatic, no one would risk their own lives like that."

"Jim," I said. "What are you hiding?"

"Nothing," he said, looking away. "We'll be wasting our time, that's all. I tell you there's nothing there. Besides, it's locked—"

Tetyana turned the gun on him.

"Move," she said. "Now."

Chapter Fifty-four

"Someone's inside," I whispered.

The eerie yellow light flickered in between the trees, disappearing one moment and appearing again, as the cold wind rustled the leaves.

Someone had lit the candles inside the cabin. But as we marched through the trail with Jim trudging reluctantly between us, it felt like a menacing signal, like a spotlight from a lighthouse, warning us to stay away.

My mind was buzzing nonstop. All I could think of was Katy.

We'd watched each other's backs since high school. We'd been there for each other, through the most unimaginable horrors of our lives.

Katy was the most trusting and kindest one of us too. She'd got into trouble before by being at the wrong place at the wrong time with the wrong people. I wondered who had tricked her into opening the door.

And why?

I gritted my teeth as I felt a red-hot flash of anger unfurl inside of me. If anyone had touched a hair on Katy's head, I'd make them pay so badly, they'd wish they were never born.

When we reached the cabin, Tetyana instructed Jim to walk up to the front door until she gave the signal.

I waited at the bottom of the steps, my gun trained on the door while Tetyana slunk around the cabin to look through the window.

The woods were quiet.

I remembered the haunting sound of a night owl hooting among the pine trees the night before. But now, it seemed even the bird knew something was up. I imagined the trees surrounding the cabin holding their breaths, as they waited, like us, to see what would happen next.

Other than the flickering light from the cabin windows, there weren't any other signs of life. But someone was inside the shack.

Why wasn't Katy making any noise? Wouldn't she have fought back and screamed by now?

I shuffled my feet impatiently as I waited for Tetyana to return from her reconnaissance.

"Caril," she whispered as she came around the corner.

"Katy?" I asked.

She shook her head.

She leaped up the steps, pushed Jim aside and rapped on the door sharply.

I could imagine Caril staring at the door, wondering who it was coming at this time of night. After what felt like ages, I heard footsteps near the entrance.

The door flung open.

"Oh!"

Caril stared at Tetyana, who was standing at the threshold with her gun pointed at her head.

For the first time since we'd met her, Caril wasn't wearing her shades. The only illumination inside the cabin came from two candles on the table. Outside, among the trees, it was dark and hard to see.

But Caril's eyes swept down toward me, then back up at Tetyana. Her eyes widened as she spotted Jim standing quietly in the shadows of the porch.

So she can see without those glasses.

"What are you all doing here?" she asked in a trembling voice.

"May we come in?" said Tetyana. It wasn't a question.

Without waiting for a reply, she walked inside, forcing Caril to the back of the cabin.

I jumped up the steps toward the entrance. I pulled Jim inside, closed the door, and positioned myself where I could see everything.

Caril stepped backward and toward the kitchen sink until she hit the counter. She gripped the edge of the counter, her face white.

"How... how did you know I was here?" she asked.

"The question is, what are you doing here?" I said. "And where's Katy?"

Caril scrunched her forehead. She looked from me to Tetyana to Jim.

"What do you mean?"

"Our friend. She's missing. Where is she?"

"I've no idea what you're talking about."

"She fell down the stairs and twisted her ankle." My eyes fell on Caril's feet. "A real ankle twist, unlike yours," I said with a snarl. "So she couldn't have walked out. That means, someone carried her out or forced her to walk out."

Caril opened and closed her mouth like a fish out of water. It seemed like she'd lost her voice. She shook her head mutely.

Tetyana turned to Jim and motioned him toward the bed.

"Sit where we can keep an eye on you."

Jim didn't wait to be told again. With a scared glance at her, he moved toward the bed and perched on the edge.

Tetyana turned to Caril.

"Anyone else in here?"

Caril's eyes widened.

"I asked a question."

"No," said Caril, shaking now. "No. 'Course not. Just me..." she stammered. "Who are you people?"

Without answering her, Tetyana started working her way from the entrance. She checked the small closet, all the kitchen cabinets, under the bed and even the stove.

Jim sat at the edge of the bed, his head in his hands, as if he couldn't take it anymore. That was when I saw the small square object near his feet, half hidden under the bed.

I didn't need to see it up close to realize this was the girl's diary Katy had been reading up in our room.

That was when I realized who the woman was. There was only one answer to her strange behavior, and now I knew.

Once Tetyana was done inside the main cabin, she moved into the bathroom. My heart dropped to hear her rip open the shower curtain. I half wondered if Katy was tied up and trussed in the shower.

"All clear," said Tetyana, coming out of the bathroom with something in her hand. "No weapons. No ammunition. No bodies."

She held a plastic package up and turned to Jim.

"Except for this."

I peered at the small white packet in her hand. I noticed Jim's face had gone pale.

"There's a stash of these in the bathroom cabinet," said Tetyana. "Jim, you want to tell us what this is, or should I?"

His shoulders dropped. He looked down at his feet and let out a defeated sigh.

"What is it?" I asked.

"Cocaine," said Tetyana.

Caril gasped. "I thought it was bath salts."

"Gift from the pastor?" said Tetyana to Jim.

He let out another desperate sigh. His eyes were red, lined with stress. He's about to cry, I thought.

"He got me hooked on it early."

"Pastor Graham?" said Caril in shock.

No one answered her. This was not my or Tetyana's story to tell. Jim gave Tetyana a pleading look.

"If Nancy ever found out, she'd leave me. She doesn't know about my... other side...." He paused and swallowed hard.

"She already suspects something. She found a small packet in my trouser pocket yesterday. I told her I was hiding it for the pastor, but she didn't believe me. She's spitting mad at me right now. I just can't tell her about the pastor too. It'll kill her to know...."

"What's all this about the pastor?" said Caril, straightening up. "What are you all talking about?"

"It's fine, Jim," said Tetyana, ignoring Caril, her voice uncharacteristically soft. "We're not here to judge you. All we want you to do is tell the truth. Thank you."

Tetyana looked at me.

"Now we know why Nancy screeched in the middle of the night. It was no nightmare."

Jim put his head in his hands again. His shoulders shook, like he was crying silently.

My mind whirred. Jim had a good reason to get rid of the pastor, but he'd been with us that hour, so he couldn't have done it. This still didn't exonerate him from Mrs. Robinson and Doctor Fulton's murders, if they were truly murders.

I turned to Caril.

"All right," I said. "Your turn. Start talking."

She gave me a scared look.

"What do you want me to say?"

"Let's start with your real name."

Caril's jaw dropped. She stared at me in shock.

I tried again.

"Caril's not your name, is it?"

She looked away.

"Charles said he'd never been to this house before," I said. "But you have. In fact, you were born here. Am I correct?"

Chapter Fifty-five

S he blinked rapidly.

"Jim," I said, pointing at the floor near his feet. "The book, next to you."

He reached down and pulled the book out from underneath the bed. I leaned over and plucked the diary from his hands.

"This diary," I said, turning to the woman. "It's yours, isn't it?"

I squinted at the woman standing in front of us. She stared at me like an animal caught in the headlights of a car.

"Your real name's Victoria."

Even in the dim candlelight, I could see her neck flush deep red. Her hands were gripping the counter so tightly, her fingers had turned white.

"Why did you choose the names Caril and Charles to introduce yourself to this household?"

She flinched like my words had been daggers.

"The *Natural Born Killers*," I continued. "You thought you were being smart, weren't you? Or did you think it would be funny?"

Jim turned a startled face toward me.

"Natural Born Killers?"

I didn't answer. Neither did Victoria.

She stood scrunched up in the corner, withering like a leaf on fire.

"I think you wanted to scare someone in this house," I asked, "that way, they'd know you weren't returning home for just a tea party. You meant business."

Victoria had her head down now. Her chest was heaving, and I saw a tear fall to the ground.

"Who did you want to scare?" I said. "Your mother, Lisa? Your uncle, Barry? Or was it Mrs. Robinson who took care of you as a child?"

With a shriek, Victoria brought her hands to her face. Then she burst into tears.

I waited for her to let it all out. We listened quietly to her gut-wrenching sobs, watching the tears roll down her cheeks, her face partially hidden behind her trembling hands.

I looked over at Tetyana, who was standing on guard near the door.

"Katy," she mouthed.

I nodded. Katy was our priority.

I took a step closer to the woman.

"Victoria, our friend is missing and may be in danger. We need to know where she is and why anyone would take her."

She didn't answer.

I tried again.

"We think all these events are connected, and I think you can help us figure it out."

"I'm scared," she stammered in between her sobs, "I don't know why everyone's dying like flies. I'm so scared."

"Victoria, I need you to pay attention," I said, my voice firm. "Can you do that?"

What I really wanted to do was to walk up to her and shake the answers out of her.

Jim picked up a towel that had been lying on the bed and handed it to her. She took it from him and wiped her face clumsily.

"Can you tell us the truth?" I asked.

She gave a small nod.

I felt sorry for her. She was a broken woman. Victoria had a role to play in the events, but I was sure she wasn't the killer now.

"Why did you come back home?" I said, keeping my voice as gentle as I could.

"Mrs. Robinson," she whispered, wringing the towel in her hands. "She told me it was time."

"Time for what?"

She took a deep breath and swallowed. Jim stood up, walked over to the sink and poured her a glass of water. We waited for her to drink.

"She said my grandmother died," she said, putting the glass down with a shaky hand. "I never really knew her, but Mrs. Robinson said she most probably left the estate to me."

I raised my eyebrows. I wanted badly to look at Tetyana, but I kept my focus on the woman in front of me.

Victoria swallowed a sob and took another breath in.

"She knew Grandmother hated my mom and uncle. She called them devil's children. So, Mrs. Robinson told me to come and claim what I own."

I felt my stomach sink. If that codicil was legal, we'd be stealing the childhood home from this woman who'd spent most of her life in an asylum.

"It was you who we saw in the woods two days ago, wasn't it?" I said.

Victoria turned to me and blinked.

"You were arguing with a man in the clearing out there near the river. Who was it? The pastor?"

She shook her head. "Doctor Fulton," she whispered.

"We saw you take a knife out and stab his face."

A surprised gasp came from Jim.

"Why did you do that?" I asked.

"He wanted me to go away. He wanted me to leave this place."

"Why?"

She looked up.

"Because he didn't want me to get hurt. He said I wasn't safe here."

"And you stabbed him?" said Tetyana, frowning.

Victoria buried her head in her hands. "I didn't want to hear it. I was angry. I thought he was pushing me away from what was rightly mine."

"Do you know who killed Mrs. Robinson?" I asked.

She stared at the floor for a while.

"No." She shook her head. "I only came back because... I wanted my childhood back."

"Why take on serial killer names then?" I asked. "And why come in the middle of the night, wearing shades, telling a dubious tale of getting lost on a hike in the mountains during off season?"

"I don't know. I didn't mean to...," said Victoria, her hands gripping the counter again, as if that was the only thing keeping her up. "It was Charles' idea."

"Who's Charles?" I asked. "A friend? Family?"

"Boyfriend." She paused and shrugged. "Kind of, I guess."

"Where did you two meet?"

Victoria looked down and shuffled her feet.

"He worked at the hospital."

"What did he do there?"

"A cleaner. Custodian. He also did magic tricks for the kids to make extra money. They didn't treat me very nice there. He helped me a few times. Then he, er...." She stopped and buried her face in the towel again.

"What did he do?" I asked.

"He asked me to do him favors."

Tetyana grimaced. I could only guess what favors they would be.

"You never reported him to the doctors or the nurses?"

"He said everyone was against me so, I never..." She looked down, a despondent expression on her face. "He was the only friend I had."

Victoria had turned silent again.

"Then one day," I said, trying to put together the pieces of the puzzle myself, "Mrs. Robinson called you or wrote to you to give you news of your grandmother's death?"

She nodded.

"How did you get out of the hospital?"

"I asked Charles to help me. He said no at first, but when I told him I was going to inherit tons of money, he said he'd help, but he made me promise to give him half the money and half the house."

"Some boyfriend," muttered Tetyana from behind me.

"And you said yes?" I asked.

"He helped me." Her voice rose in pitch.

"How?"

"He wrote a letter, pretending to be my doctor."

"He forged a discharge letter?"

She nodded.

"He said they'll never find out. And if they did, we'd be long gone, anyway."

"Then you both came here?"

"Not right away." Her eyes were studiously scrutinizing the floor, like she was too ashamed to tell the story.

"He took me to a bar, and we got drunk. *I* got drunk. I'd never had anything stronger than cough syrup before. Anyway, I don't remember much, but he wanted me to do all these things."

"Like what?" I asked gently.

"He came up with this crazy idea of Caril and Charles, and said we'd come up here and surprise everyone, you know?"

I nodded.

"He told me that's the way to make an entrance."

She looked up at me.

"That way they'd know I'm not a scared little girl anymore. They can't get rid of me again."

Chapter Fifty-six

"How did you two hike through the mountains in the middle of a storm?" I asked.

Victoria shook her head.

"We didn't. We came through the back road. It's an old road I used to play on when I was little."

"The one along the dried riverbed?" asked Tetyana.

Victoria wiped her eyes and nodded.

"I thought if we pretended to be lost hikers, they'd let us in and we'd have time to figure something out once we were inside."

"Barry said that back road was barricaded," I said.

"The dam went up the year I left. I used to play around that place. Uncle Barry got so mad at the city about the construction, he threatened to blow everything up. So the city said if he ever came near the dam, they were going to arrest him and put him in jail."

She took a deep breath.

"But I hung around and saw them make the temporary road to bring the heavy equipment. That goes down to the valley below and to town."

"You were the only one who knew about it?"

"I think so. The construction company never needed to use it again. It's overgrown now and you need a good truck to come up it."

"Where's the truck you came in?"

"I asked Doctor Fulton to bring us here in his SUV. He didn't want to, but I begged and pleaded and cried. I told him I wanted to reunite with my family. But he came back a day later to tell me to leave. He said I was playing a dangerous game. That's why you saw us arguing in the clearing."

"Did you stay in the cabin for the first few nights?" asked Tetyana.

Victoria nodded. "Mrs. Robinson knew I'd come. She even brought us food."

"How did you know about this place?"

"I used to come here when things got really bad at home," she said, looking down at the floor. "Uncle Barry made this cabin for me. He told everyone it was for lost hikers, but he told me it was my sanctuary."

"Didn't you worry someone would see the light and ask questions?" I asked.

Victoria shrugged.

"We had to take a chance. We only lit the candles for a short time at night."

I took a deep breath in to clear my head.

"So, who sent Mrs. Robinson those death threats? It wasn't you, I gather?"

"She was my friend!" Victoria wailed. "She was there for me from the beginning. If it hadn't been for her, I'd have killed myself. I wouldn't have survived this house."

She looked at me through her tears.

"Someone wanted to get rid of her. She knew everyone's secrets. She knew who...."

She glanced at her diary lying open on the bed. Jim had taken it from me and had flipped through it. It now lay on the comforter, opened to the middle page with the macabre childish drawings. My eyes fell on the image of the bleeding knife over the stick girl's or woman's body.

"Victoria?" I asked softly. "Who hurt you in this house?"

In response, she burst into tears again.

I turned to Tetyana, who was looking impatient by the door.

"Katy?" she said. "She could be anywhere, maybe even in the woods."

"Could have been any of them," I said, "Charles, Barry, Lisa, Nancy—"

Jim turned to me in shock.

"Nancy wouldn't hurt a fly. She's moody, but she's harmed nobody in her life. Please believe me. I'd take a bullet for her. She's the only sane person I've had in my life. She'd never do anything like this."

I said nothing.

Though Nancy was an emotional basket case, I was also beginning to think she was incapable of carrying out a kidnapping or murder.

"It couldn't have been Graham," I said. "He was dead."

Victoria looked up in shock.

"The pastor's dead?"

I turned to her.

"Where were you an hour ago? You weren't in your room, were you?"

"I went down to Mrs. Robinson's room."

"What for?"

"I was sure someone killed her, so I went to check and see if I could find anything." She choked back a sob. "When I came down the stairs, I heard strange noises in the kitchen. I sneaked in to see what was going on but the kitchen was empty."

I pointed at her book on the bed.

"Where did you find the diary? Katy had it with her in our bedroom."

"It was on the floor in the kitchen. Next to the counter."

"Was it you who knocked the glasses over?"

"I might have. I heard a crash, but all I saw was my secret book and I ran to pick it up."

"Where did you go from there?" asked Tetyana.

"I couldn't stay in the house any longer. It was suffocating me, so I ran out. I ran and ran through the woods till I came here."

I shot her a frustrated look. We were learning a lot more about this strange family, but none of this was helping us locate Katy.

I looked at Victoria and Jim. They both looked beaten up, crushed.

"Do either of you have any idea where Katy is?" I asked.

Victoria stared at me for a moment, then her face cleared.

"I think your friend is still in the house."

"Oh, really?" I said, straightening up.

"I think I know where she is."

Chapter Fifty-seven

"We searched everywhere," I said, "all the rooms on all floors. We even found the hidden closet in the dining room."

Victoria looked up with a gasp.

"You found the secret room?"

"What do you know about it?" asked Tetyana.

"It goes down to the basement."

"What basement?" said Jim. "There's no basement in this house. Even the wine cellar is on the first floor."

"It's under the staff quarters. That's where…" Victoria looked away, a mixture of fear and shame on her face.

Tetyana's face turned dark.

"I checked that hidden closet. I couldn't find a darn thing. No secret handles or knobs or latches. Are you telling me I missed it?"

"Barry boarded it up," said Victoria. "After—"

"Are you sure you're remembering things right?" asked Jim. "I'd know if there's a basement in this house."

"It's an empty room. An underground cellar with stone walls and a cold stone floor." Victoria shivered and hugged herself.

"Maybe no one remembers it anymore, so no one told you about it."

I heard the cabin door open. Tetyana was already on her way out.

"Coming?" she called out.

"Do you know how to get to this basement?" I asked Victoria. She stared at me.

"Please, help us. Maybe that's where Katy is."

With a start, she stepped away from the counter, a strange look on her face. Without saying a word, she rushed out the door, past Tetyana.

Tetyana and I leaped down the steps to follow her. From behind me, I vaguely heard Jim shut the cabin door.

Victoria was already on the trail, power walking ahead of us, as if in a trance. Something was pulling her back to the house.

I was about to run and catch up to her when I saw Tetyana grab Jim by the elbow.

"Wait," she said to him.

I stopped in my tracks.

What's going on now?

"Get your truck," she said to him. "We need more lumber from the barn. Haul some to the end of the driveway for the footbridge."

"The footbridge?"

"I set up a skeleton frame this afternoon. You just need to reinforce it. You'll need a few strong spotlights and a pulley. The oak tree next to the bridge is strong enough to handle the weight. When Officer Jensen comes, ask him to help you from the other side." She paused. "Try not to fall into the river, will you?"

Jim stared at her.

"Just do as I say," said Tetyana.

"And... and you?" he said, finding his voice.

"I'll join you soon," said Tetyana. "Go! Now!"

He turned and fled down the path, taking a sharp right in the direction of the barn.

"Do you trust him?" I asked.

Tetyana shrugged. "We'll have to risk it."

Victoria was almost at the end of the trail now.

We raced to catch up with her.

From there, it took us five minutes to get to the house. When we reached the side door, Tetyana yanked it open, and the three of us stumbled into the kitchen.

The last person I had expected to find inside was Barry.

He was sitting on the counter, hugging a decanter of whiskey with one hand and holding a tumbler with the other. His bruised eye was now swollen and turning a purple hue.

He looked up and peered at us as we walked in.

"What in tarnation are you people doing here?" he asked in a slurry voice.

"How the heck did you get out?" asked Tetyana, walking up to the counter.

"You think you can hold me a prisoner in my house!" he roared.

With no warning, he picked up the jar of beans on the counter and hurled it at Tetyana. She ducked just in time. It crashed against the wall, breaking into pieces and spilling the beans all over the kitchen floor.

"Hey!" yelled Tetyana angrily. "What the hell are you playing at?"

But Barry was just starting.

He picked up an empty tumbler and threw it at Victoria, who had been staring at him from the doorway. Then he lobbed another my way. I stepped aside just as it crashed against the window.

"Stop this right now!" shouted Tetyana.

But Barry seemed to have remarkable stamina despite his drunken state. He grabbed an armful of wine goblets and pelted them her way like they were hand grenades.

Ducking this way and that, Tetyana advanced on him, her face contorted in fury.

I grabbed Victoria's arm, but she struggled and pushed me away.

"Uncle Barry!" she screamed. "It's me!"

Barry had just raised his hand to throw another glass at Tetyana when he stopped and turned toward her.

"Don't you remember me?" asked Victoria.

Barry snorted.

"Why am I supposed to remember any of you tramping, intruding, backwater miscreants!"

His niece stepped closer to the counter.

"Uncle Barry, it's me, Victoria. Remember? You taught me to ride my pink bike. You taught me to rescue baby birds. It's me. I'm back."

I didn't know what I'd expected to happen, but it wasn't this.

With an ugly yell, Barry picked up the nearest stool and threw it at Victoria.

I pulled her down, but not before it grazed her shoulder. She fell to the floor with a thud.

"You're not her!" he bellowed. "They told me she's dead!"

"I'm not dead, Uncle Barry!" screeched Victoria, struggling to get away from me. "It's really me!"

I held on to her with a firm hand and hissed at her. "You'll get yourself killed."

"Let me go!" she said, slapping my hand away and getting up.

That was when I saw Barry pull out a kitchen knife from the counter block.

"Get down!" yelled Tetyana as she slammed on the floor behind the counter.

I dove to the floor, bringing Victoria crashing down with me. The knife hit the wall, two inches from her head.

"Get out now!" I heard Tetyana holler. "I'll handle him! Get out of the kitchen!"

"This way," I said, army crawling toward our nearest exit, pulling a shocked Victoria by the arm. "Come!"

A crash came from behind us, followed by an angry roar.

"Frigging hell!" I heard Tetyana yell behind me.

A quick glance back told me she finally had Barry in a handcuff hold and was struggling to control him.

"Let's go!" I shouted, as I kicked the door and rolled into the corridor that led to the staff quarters.

I jumped up to my feet and pulled Victoria up.

"We need to get to that closet now."

She gave me a wild look.

I pulled her in by the shoulders and shook her.

"Katy's probably in this dungeon right now. Was it Barry who took her down? I swear if he did anything—"

Wordlessly, Victoria pulled away from me and dashed down the corridor.

"Wait!" I shouted, running after her. "Get back here!"

But she was running straight toward Mrs. Robinson's room.

"The other way!" I shouted. "We need to go up to the dining room!"

She slammed open Mrs. Robinson's door and vanished inside. I rushed in after her, to see her pulling the frayed bedside rug off the floor.

"What are you doing?"

"This," she said, pointing at the opening she'd just uncovered.

I stared at the gaping hole in the floor.

Chapter Fifty-eight

Victoria and I stood shoulder to shoulder, staring at the hole.

"Mrs. Robinson came to rescue me, one day," she said, "that's how I found out there was another way down."

"Is this why she took this room? To watch over the entrance?"

She nodded.

Next to the bed was a round steel slab with a handle on top. That had probably covered the hole. Barry must have removed it when he took Katy down.

I peered inside. A narrow concrete stairwell wound down into a dark subterranean part of this house.

Back in the kitchen, it sounded like Tetyana was wrestling a herd of bison. Part of me wanted to run back and back her up, but if she could fight the Russian militia, she could surely subdue a raging Barry. I'd only be in the way.

I pulled my Glock out of my vest and turned to Victoria.

"Follow me," I said.

I turned around and stepped into the hole.

It was dark in the underground stairwell.

I felt my way down a few steps before remembering the flashlight Jim had given me in the kitchen. I had stashed it in my back pocket.

I pulled it out and turned it on. From behind me, I heard a sigh of relief from Victoria.

Shining my torch in front with one hand and training my Glock forward with the other, I climbed down, one step at a time.

The stairwell seemed to go on forever, constricting as it wound its way down. I imagined the walls closing in and forced myself to keep breathing.

I suppressed the urge to run down, but the stairway was slippery, which meant water was leaking in from somewhere. The last thing I needed now was to fall and sprain an ankle.

This wasn't a basement we were climbing down to. It felt like we were descending into hell.

If I hadn't suspected Katy was alone somewhere down there, I'd have felt sick to my stomach. But I didn't have time to think of anything but her.

"How far does it go?" I asked, cringing as the echo boomeranged back. I hadn't expected an enclosed space like this to have an echo, but that partly answered my question. It was a long way down.

"I don't remember," whispered Victoria from behind me. I could hear the subdued panic in her voice.

I didn't know what had happened to her down in the basement. I could only imagine that experience had haunted her so much, it had compelled her to draw those disturbing images in her diary.

But this was not the time to ask. I had no idea how she'd react to me digging up more about her past, and right now, I needed to find my friend.

Please be okay, I prayed as I climbed down, gritting my teeth as I thought of all the ways I would make Barry pay.

That man is mad. Completely and utterly mad.

I thought of poor Katy being dragged down here with her foot injury and swore. I was going to throttle Barry when we got back up. I was going to have that man's alcohol-soaked head on a platter.

I kept pushing onward.

"We're almost there," said Victoria from behind me.

I slowed down and shone my flashlight around. The torch light fell on a small steel door at the bottom of the stairwell, about fifteen steps down.

With my heart in my mouth, I climbed down and yanked the door open.

Katy was sitting in a small wooden chair in the far corner of the room.

Her hands were tied behind her and her legs were bound to the feet of the chair. Around her mouth was a gag made of a yellowed cloth.

"Katy!" I shouted as I ran up to her, my heart pounding.

Tears were rolling down her cheeks. She looked relieved to see me, but I could see the desperation in her eyes.

That was when I noticed her hair.

Someone had taken shears to it. It was now sticking out haphazardly in rough, pointy ends. Scattered around her feet were her gorgeous red curls.

Barry slashed her beautiful hair. That sick, sick man.

Next I saw the deep cut on her forearm. It was a knife wound.

"Oh no! What did that sick man do to you?" I said in shock.

Katy struggled in her chair.

"Hmmm..."

I fell to the floor, placed my gun down and started to untie the rope to her left foot.

"You're going to be okay," I said, as my shaking fingers fumbled to untie the knots. "I'm going to get you out of here. If he has hurt you, Katy, I swear, I'm going to cut his head off myself."

"Hmmm..."

"That's one leg free," I said, pulling the rope away.

Katy nudged me hard with her freed foot.

I looked up in surprise.

She kicked me again.

I suddenly realized she was trying to signal something.

"What is it, Katy?"

In my panicked state, I'd forgotten to take off her gag first. Cursing myself, I leaned over to remove it. That was when I noticed she wasn't looking at me.

I sprang up.

She was staring at something behind me, her eyes filled with terror.

I spun around.

Chapter Fifty-nine

It was Lisa.

She was standing near the door to the basement with one arm around Victoria's shoulder.

In her right hand was a bloodied kitchen knife, which she was holding to her daughter's throat.

Lisa cackled when she saw me look.

How did I not hear her come in?

Lisa's grip was so strong, Victoria's bare arm had turned white where her mother was digging her fingers into her skin.

Victoria had turned a ghostly white, and she wasn't even trying to fight back. It was like she'd become a scared little nine-year-old girl again.

Now that I was seeing Lisa fully, I noticed she looked like she'd been in a fight. There were scratch marks on her face and her forehead. I'd thought her hair standing in clumps was from her jumping out of bed half-asleep. But now, it looked like someone had pulled at it.

Good. Katy had put up a fight.

I felt a chill as I remembered the fresh bruises on Barry.

I stared at the bloodied knife.

Whose blood is it? Katy's?

Did they both drag Katy down here? We left her all alone, handicapped by a sprained ankle, while these two crazies snatched her.

That was when I noticed the thin red line on Victoria's neck. Lisa was cutting into her.

Suddenly everything clicked into place.

How could I have been so stupid?

"It was you!" I said. "You're the one who killed Mrs. Robinson. You're the letter writer."

"Clever girl," said Lisa.

Her voice was timid and soft, just like it had been when she spoke to me in the dining room upstairs. But there was an ugly glint in her eyes, one I could see even through the dim light from the lone naked bulb above us.

How did she get out of her room?

I was the one who'd locked Lisa's door. I still had her room key in my pocket. I wondered if this entire family had Houdini skills I hadn't known about.

I stepped in front of Katy to shield her, a sinking feeling in my stomach. I kicked myself for not checking the basement before running in.

That was when I realized my second dumb mistake.

My gun was lying on the floor next to Katy's chair.

I would have to move at lightning speed to pick it up, but that could endanger Victoria's life.

I felt my entire body shake. I wanted to shout at Lisa, but my throat had gone dry. I swallowed hard. I cursed myself.

Lisa smiled a satisfied smile, like she knew my dilemma.

I had to think fast.

"How did you get out of your room?" I asked, keeping my voice steady.

Lisa smiled again, that sickly smile.

"Don't you think I have a master key set in my room? This is my house after all."

I grimaced. I'd slipped badly.

Another chill went through me as I realized what Katy had on her.

Where's the codicil? Is it still on her? Does Lisa know about it?

My eyes swept the room, but there was no letter or paper anywhere to be seen.

"I knew you girls were hatching something," said Lisa, seemingly amused at my expression. "I waited for you and that tall one to leave your room." Lisa gave a look behind me at Katy. "Found that spitting cat all by herself, but when she put up a fight, I had to get Barry to help. A few smacks to the head and she stumbled out of bed dragging that ankle. Didn't you now?"

I felt angry goose bumps on my arms.

Oh, my goodness. What did I get you into, Katy? I'm so sorry.

Behind me, Katy remained silent.

"You let Barry out too?" I asked, keeping my eyes on Lisa.

I wasn't sure what her next move would be, and I wanted to be prepared.

"Poor man," she said, "he was going mad locked up in his room like that. I had to let him out." She gave another glance behind me. "Plus, I needed help to bring that caterwauling thing down here."

I narrowed my eyes.

"Why did you take Katy? She has done nothing to you."

"She was in the way. You all were. You didn't listen to me the first time I told you to leave, so I had to send you a stronger message."

"So it was you who vandalized our car?"

"You mean, that message I left for you?"

I nodded.

"Why didn't you listen to me?"

I looked away, trying to collect my thoughts.

I wondered how Tetyana was faring with Barry upstairs. I wondered if Officer Jensen had come, with or without reinforcement. And I wondered if Jim had made good on his promise and not turned on us for whatever reason.

That was when it dawned on me.

No one knew we were down here. No one knew of this secret entrance. Victoria had said they boarded the hidden entrance on the second floor a long time ago.

Barry knew of it, but he'd never betray his own sister. They were in this together. She was the mastermind, I was sure now. He was just her flunkey.

My only hope was they would start checking the servants' quarters first and discover the gaping hole in the floor of Mrs. Robinson's room. Either way, our rescue was going to take a while.

I turned to Lisa.

"Do you know who this is?" I said, keeping my voice steady, despite my heart hammering inside of me. "This is Victoria, your daughter."

Lisa laughed.

"Do you think I'm that stupid? I knew it was her the moment I set my eyes on her, even with those ugly dark glasses. A mother always knows her children."

So she knew?

Victoria's face was so white now, I worried she might faint.

"I used to love her at one time," said Lisa softly.

Half my brain was furiously thinking of how to keep her occupied till the others found us, while the other half was racing, trying to figure out how to pick up my Glock.

Lisa brushed the knife against her daughter's neck like she had a feather in her hand, not a deadly weapon that could easily decapitate her own child.

Victoria's chest heaved up and down, and tears streamed down her face.

It's not Barry who's mad. Lisa's the one who's completely gone in the head.

"I loved her so much when she was a wee little one," cooed Lisa, making me want to vomit.

A little color came to Victoria's face at those words. It was like her fear was slowly being churned into anger. I watched her closely. Maybe, just maybe Victoria had a fighting spirit inside of her.

Good, I thought in relief. *Summon your inner warrior, Victoria. Now is the time. Don't succumb to this madwoman.*

"You never loved me!" shouted Victoria, startling me. "You bitch!"

Lisa drew back as if in shock. "How dare you!" she screeched.

Then, to my horror, she brandished the knife in the air.

"No!" I yelled. "Stop! Put that down!"

"I loved you once," said Lisa to Victoria, ignoring me. But her arm raised high with that knife didn't lower. "But then, you became the daughter I never wanted. Everyone doted on you. Even my own mother. She hated me. So why should I love you?"

I was just about to drop and pick up my weapon when Lisa turned to me, her hand still in the air.

I stopped breathing.

One swift swipe and Victoria's life would be over.

"I hated that woman," said Lisa, an ugly fire flashing in her eyes. "She didn't like how my father and Barry paid attention to me. My father treated me like a princess. So, she goes and abandons me. What a righteous, nasty witch!"

I waited for her to stop hyperventilating and lowered my voice.

"Lisa, your mother is dead. Is all this worth it now? Why don't you let Victoria go? We can go upstairs and have a chat over a cup of tea. You can tell me all about your mother and your childhood."

My eyes went to Victoria. I wondered how I could signal to her to keep her mother occupied while I reached for my gun.

"I know exactly how you feel," I said. "I knew your mother well. She had a dark side to her. Everybody feared her and what she could do if you crossed her. I feel bad for you, to have a mother like that."

Lisa smiled.

"You understand me better than my own family."

Despite her soft voice, I knew this woman had sharp claws. Her nerves were wound so tightly, she could spring out and cut us to pieces at any moment.

Victoria's face was slowly turning purple now and I could see her hands clench and unclench, like she was gearing up to fight. But she was weaponless and vulnerable, while Lisa wouldn't hesitate to slash her in an instant.

"I hate you!" yelled Victoria.

Lisa turned to her daughter.

"How can you speak to me like that?" she said. "After all I did for you?"

"For all you did to me?" shouted Victoria, her voice echoing across the empty chamber. "I was just a little girl. What did I do to deserve that?"

Lisa turned to me.

"What an ungrateful child, isn't she?"

"You tied me to that chair and beat me every Sunday!" cried Victoria. "You left me here for days without food, alone. You said you hated me! You punished me because Grandmother and Uncle Barry loved me. He tried to protect me from you. You call yourself a mother? How dare you?"

I wondered how long Victoria had waited for this confrontation with Lisa. She was frothing at the mouth and struggling, but Lisa's grip was strong.

"Uncle Barry tried to stop you, but—"

"That man isn't your uncle."

Victoria stopped moving. She turned to Lisa, stunned.

"What do you mean?"

"He is your father, my child."

Chapter Sixty

I took a startled step back.

"What are you saying?" stammered Victoria.

Her voice was hollow, and her face was crumpled. She'd gone limp in her mother's clutches, like her spirit had vanished from her.

"You told me my father was from town—"

Lisa let out another cackle.

"You know so little."

"Tell me!" screeched Victoria. "How is Uncle Barry my father?" Her high-pitched voice echoed across the room and up the stairwell.

Good. I crossed my fingers behind my back. Hopefully, someone heard that.

Shout some more, Victoria. Louder.

"Do you really want to know?" said Lisa.

"Yes!" cried Victoria.

"Pastor Graham liked to play with us when we were little. He was no pastor then, just a little boy who... let's just say he was very friendly."

I felt a nudge on my leg. Was it Katy? But the story unraveling in front of me was so morbidly fascinating, I didn't turn back.

Lisa smirked. "He made Barry and me play together whenever he came over."

Play?

I braced myself for the sick story she was about to divulge.

Victoria's brow knotted. "What do you mean?"

"You don't need the details, honey. Let's just say, we didn't know any better. What Graham told us to do, we did. He loved to take pictures with his old-fashioned camera."

My stomach turned.

"No!" asked Victoria, her face a picture of confusion and distress. "That's not true. Don't tell me!"

"One day," continued Lisa, impervious to her daughter's agony, "Barry and I were pretend-playing in my bedroom, your old room, and your grandmother caught us in the act."

I looked at her in shock.

"I was only eleven and Barry was nine, but your grandmother ran screaming and never talked to us after that again."

So, that's why Madame Bouchard had abandoned them and eventually disinherited them. That's what she meant in the codicil, when she'd said *Only God can help them for the sins they have committed.*

"But I was a better mother to you than my mother ever was," said Lisa, a sad look in her eyes. "She dumped me. So ashamed of me, she was. Pretended I didn't exist. And I was just a little girl. Compared to her, I treated you like a princess."

"You're sick!" said Victoria, almost choking on her anger.

Lisa drew back like Victoria had stung her.

Victoria was shouting through her tears now. "You beat me every week. You tortured me and you sent me away because you hated me. You killed Mrs. Robinson because she knew what you did to me. Maybe she knew about you and Barry too.

"Did she? Did she?" screeched Victoria.

"She was a busybody, that nosy old woman," said Lisa, her soft voice laced with venom. "It was time for her to go."

"You killed Doctor Fulton too, didn't you?" cried Victoria. "He found out what you did to Mrs. Robinson, and he was going to tell everyone. That was your work, wasn't it?"

Lisa didn't answer. But her murderously calm face told me everything.

Victoria had hit all the right notes, one after the other. But she was playing a dangerous game. I had been wrong. Lisa wasn't insane. She had all her faculties about her.

She knew exactly what she had done. And what she was about to do.

"What about Pastor Graham?" I said, speaking fast, hoping to deflect Lisa away from Victoria. "Do you know what happened to him?"

Lisa didn't even look at me.

"That was Barry," she said with a smug smile, her eyes still on her daughter. "It was your father who did that."

I felt another nudge on my leg and noticed a movement on the floor. I looked down.

With her free foot, Katy had kicked my gun closer to me. All I had to do was bend down and pick it up.

Thank you, Katy.

This was my chance. I had one split second.

I bent down and yanked the weapon from the floor.

Chapter Sixty-one

I gripped my gun behind my back.

My heart was hammering so loudly, I was sure the entire world could hear it. If Lisa had noticed my sudden movement, she didn't show it.

I knew what I had to do, but it seemed like something stronger than me was restraining my hand.

I'd killed enough men before I hit twenty. I knew what it was like to watch the ugly, contorted face of a dying man as he took his last breath. However evil that man had been, those images haunted me at night.

Now, faced with another death on my conscience, my hands felt like lead.

My heart was racing a thousand miles a minute. My hands were shaking and my palms were sweating.

Lisa doesn't deserve to live. She doesn't. She doesn't.

"Why did Barry kill Pastor Graham?" I asked, my heart pounding.

"Because I told him to," said Lisa with another laugh. "He always listens to me. Ever since we were little." She paused. "Besides, it was time for that old man to go too. He was always pulling on our strings and I was getting tired of it."

"You're mad," said Victoria.

She looked like she didn't care what her mother said anymore. I'd probably feel that way too, if my estranged mother was holding me at knifepoint, sharing such vile secrets.

A faint thumping sound came from somewhere. I wasn't sure if it was my imagination, but it sounded like footsteps running above us.

Is that the police? Is it Tetyana? Jim? Did they find us?

But Lisa didn't seem to notice, engrossed in a mad conversation with her daughter.

Tears rolled down Victoria's dejected face.

"Uncle Barry drank to forget what happened to him," she said.

"Don't be silly, child. Barry needed little encouragement. He did the drinking all on his own. He's a bit thick in the head."

I gripped my gun tighter. I couldn't have it slip and fall on the floor now.

All I had to do was make sure Victoria wasn't in the line of fire.

You can do this. So what if Lisa dies? The world doesn't deserve her kind. Take the shot. End her now.

There was a rustle near the door. I thought I saw a shadow fall across the threshold.

Tetyana?

"Lisa," I said, "please put that knife down. Mrs. Robinson and Doctor Fulton are both gone. Pastor Graham is also gone. What else do you want? What do you hope to get from hurting Victoria?"

"She wants attention," cried Victoria, "that's what she always wanted!"

"Really, child. You hardly know me."

"I'm not a child anymore!"

"You got your stubborn streak from your father's side, didn't you?" said Lisa, smiling at her own sick joke. "Should have locked him up at the hospital, like I did you, a long time ago. I'll cut his throat after yours. You're both useless to me now."

"Lisa, please—" I said, stepping forward.

"You narcissistic bitch!" screeched Victoria. "I hate you!"

Lisa leaned away, like the words were physical blows. With a bloodcurdling scream, she raised her knife in the air.

I whipped out my gun and fired.

The sound of my weapon echoed across the chamber, deafening my ears.

Lisa crumpled to the ground, her knife falling with a clatter to the cold stone floor.

I hit her!

That was when all hell broke loose.

Suddenly Tetyana, Jim, and Officer Jensen were all inside the basement.

Tetyana ran up to us.

"Katy!" she shouted. "You okay?"

I turned around to untie Katy's gag while Tetyana worked on the knots on her hands. I pulled the gag off, bent down and threw my arms around Katy's shoulders.

"Katy," I said, as I held my friend tightly. "Are you okay?"

I don't know how long we were in that awkward position, when I felt Tetyana's hands on my shoulder. She pulled Katy to her feet and looked her over with a critical eye.

"No bones broken?"

"I'm good. I'm fine," babbled Katy, wincing as Tetyana bent down to examine the cut on her arm.

I turned around to see what was happening with Lisa.

Officer Jensen and Jim were on the floor next to her. Jim had pulled his T-shirt off and was ripping it into strips to bandage her leg, while the officer was putting pressure on her wound to stop the bleeding.

She was still alive.

Jim took over Lisa, and Jensen stepped back. He pulled out a pair of rubber gloves from his pocket and once gloved, bent down to pick up the bloodied knife and slip it into a plastic bag.

"Officer Jensen," I called out, "check her pockets."

He gave me a questioning look.

"I think there's something in there you'd want to see."

Without interfering with Jim's work, Jensen reached into Lisa's dress pockets. There was nothing on the left pocket but he found something on the right.

He pulled out a crumpled beige envelope and held it to the light.

"There are at least four more of those," I said.

Jensen nodded and put it into another plastic bag. He didn't look surprised at his discovery. Something told me he already knew what that envelope contained.

A whimper in the corner made me turn. It was Victoria, slouched against the wall, hugging herself, staring at her mother in shock.

I walked over to her.

"Hey, Victoria?" I said. "You'll be okay. She can't hurt you anymore."

She gave me a hazy look, like she had hardly registered what I had said. I pulled her away from the wall.

"Come. Let's get out of this place. We need to have someone look at the cut on your neck."

Like a zombie, she followed me to the door where Tetyana and Katy were waiting.

"Ready?" Tetyana said, taking Katy by the arm.

I put my arm around Katy's shoulder and gestured to Victoria to follow us.

Leaving the men behind with Lisa, we stumbled out of the dank basement and back up the stairwell.

It was a relief to leave behind this torture chamber that had haunted a little girl so many years ago.

Chapter Sixty-two

"Ricin?" I said.

"That's what the lab said," said Officer Jensen, flipping through his notepad. "I have the preliminary report back at the office. We found fingerprints on one letter. Lisa wasn't as careful as I thought."

It had been a hunch, but we now had confirmation of how Mrs. Robinson had died.

This also confirmed Mrs. Robinson had shared the original letters with Jensen before we came over, albeit reluctantly, I supposed. No wonder he had wanted to stop us from coming to this house.

"So, it's these beans?" said Nancy, pointing to the broken jar lying on its side next to the window where Barry had smashed it only a few hours ago. "They look pretty. Harmless."

The officer reached over and picked one up.

"Castor beans," he said, rolling it on his palm. "If I had to guess, Lisa made the ricin powder in her room and stuck it in her letters. No one knew what she was doing."

"They'll find a mini lab with a stash of medicine bottles when they search her room," I said. "She even has a mortar and pestle to smash those beans to powder."

"Killer beans," said Tetyana. "Sure you want to touch those?"

Jensen promptly flicked the bean away.

Next to me, Victoria shuddered and pulled her blanket around her closer.

We had all gathered around the fireplace in the kitchen.

Around us and above us, we could hear heavy feet stomping all over the place. A team of detectives and officers were swarming the house, taking photos and processing the three dead bodies.

Jensen had brought us to the kitchen to take our statements and keep us out of their way.

Katy was sitting in the rocking chair near the fireplace, her leg elevated on a cushion, nursing a hot cup of chamomile tea. It was going to take time for her to recover from her ordeal, longer than it would take for her beautiful hair to grow back again.

The first responders had cleaned and bandaged her arm, and had administered painkillers, but she was still hurting. I was thankful the knife wound and her sprained ankle had been the worst of her injuries.

Victoria had escaped with a cut to her neck where Lisa had pushed the knife in. The red mark looked nasty, but I could see she was having a harder time coming to terms with the shocking secrets she'd learned in the basement than any physical wound she'd have incurred during that final melee.

I wasn't sure if anyone could fully recover from that kind of past.

"I never expected Lisa to be so..." Katy stopped to search for the right word. "So innovative."

"Bah," said Jensen. "She could have easily got the ricin recipe off the Internet and convinced the pastor to get her the ingredients. Nothing enterprising in this."

"She's seriously deranged to slash your hair like that," said Nancy to Katy. "I knew she was a little off, but this is crazy stuff, like that horrible hand-chopping woman from *Misery*."

I shuddered to think how much worse it could have been.

"She said it was to punish me," said Katy, sadly pulling at the ends of what was left of her hair. "She said I needed to learn a lesson because I fought back when she came to get me."

Victoria shook her head.

"She used to take a scissor to my hair too, when I was a kid. She knew I liked to have my hair long. It was her way of punishing me."

"Oh, my gosh," said Nancy. "That's sickening."

"That woman knew exactly what she was doing," said Tetyana. "I'd say all her moves are calculated for effect." She turned to Jensen. "You'll have your hands full with her in your jails."

Jensen sighed. "My first arrest, to tell you the truth. Good thing I only have drunk tanks, so she's going to a bigger free hotel, courtesy of the next county. I'll owe them one."

"What about Doctor Fulton?" I asked. "How did she kill him?"

"Detective Peters says they suspect cyanide in his water glass. She probably put it in when you weren't looking. They'll be checking the glasses at the lab. Or whatever is left of them."

"Cyanide?" I said, sitting up. "I smelled one of Lisa's bottles in her room and I was sure it had a faint hint of almond."

"Are you saying we'll find your fingerprints on that bottle?" said Jensen, his eyes narrowed.

I nodded, sheepishly. "I didn't know. I thought it was baking extract."

"*Baking* extract?" said Jensen, blowing a raspberry. "Good thing for you Lisa's talking."

I was glad too.

The past few hours had been a whirlwind.

Tetyana had subdued Barry and locked him up in his room, and Jim had kept true to his promise and had strengthened the footbridge for the first responders to walk across. When they finally came through, they'd arrested Lisa alive, with a bullet lodged in her thigh.

Falcon Hill's fire truck, ambulance, and the local sheriff's vehicle were parked on the other side of the gully. Behind them were a half a dozen squad cars from the neighboring counties that had come to aid Jensen.

An emergency crew was constructing a larger makeshift bridge so the responders could carry a stretcher with Lisa to the other side and into the ambulance.

I didn't care if she came out of her surgery dead or alive. All I cared about was she had confessed. It had taken little for Barry to spill the beans after that. And now, a judge and jury would decide their fate.

Whatever happened, the house already felt lighter with those two out of it.

"This place will be swarming with investigators for the next few days," said Jensen. "You all will have to find another place to stay. There's a motel in town with empty rooms if you need."

"You tried to discourage us from coming here on the first day, didn't you?" I said, looking the officer in the eye. "It was you who slashed our tire, wasn't it?"

Jensen sat up and slapped his notebook shut.

"No, ma'am. That would be illegal."

"It was you," I said. "You just can't admit it."

"You got cold feet," said Tetyana, giving him a wink. "You jammed the spike belt as soon as it went out, so it only cut into our back tire. Couldn't follow through, could you? You knew what you were doing was wrong."

Officer Jensen glared at us, but I could see a hint of guilt in his eyes. He'd been acting out of desperation, I gathered.

"When Mrs. Robinson showed me the letters," he replied in a sober voice, "she said it wasn't a big deal. She was embarrassed. But I knew it was a serious affair. I knew this wasn't going to come to a good end."

He paused and shook his head.

"She told me she didn't want to bother the police, and she was going to get outside help. Said she had this secret number to call for help. I tried my best to stop her. Told her what she needed was proper police help, not some..."

He stopped and glowered my way.

"Private investigators who saved Victoria's life and got Lisa to confess?" piped up Katy.

"We're talking triple homicides here, folks," said Jensen, his shoulders stooping. "This was a dangerous game. Besides, you didn't stop it all from happening, did you?"

"Neither did you," pointed out Tetyana.

Jensen shrugged.

"The point is, you need to leave these things to the professionals. Going around pretending to be Sherlock. Touching things you shouldn't have. Should have called me as soon as you saw Mrs. Robinson was sick."

"We didn't know what was going on then, and when we did, the phones were jammed," I said. "Anyway, if it wasn't for us, who knows what else could have happened here?"

Jim, who'd been listening in quietly, let out a sigh.

"Probably Nancy and me dead and gone too. I, for one, am happy you came. You saved our lives."

"More tea?" said Nancy, walking over with a teapot.

"Yes, please," said Jim, reaching out with his mug and giving his wife a sheepish look.

He had a lot of explaining to do and, thankfully, Nancy was still on talking terms with him. I wondered if he would ever tell her his full story, or if he'd keep it a secret for the rest of his life. At least the man who'd terrorized him was now gone for good.

"I sort of feel bad for them," said Nancy, pulling a chair next to her husband and sitting down. "They had rough childhoods. Their parents abandoned them. They were left to fend for themselves in this big house in the middle of—"

"Poor little rich kids," said Tetyana with a snort.

"Not an excuse for murder," said Jensen. "I know folks who grew up in worse conditions. They didn't grow up to become serial killers."

"What about the horses?" I said, turning to Jim. "What's going to happen to them?"

"We'll send them to their owners. I'll take care of them till then."

"Do you know who they belong to?"

"Phillip Tanner. He used to be a tenor in my choir. Was a talented singer too. Then he hit eleven and stopped coming to rehearsals. He was changed...."

He stirred as if to shake old cobwebs off. He cleared his throat and turned to the police officer.

"I have his address. He used to race the horses at Belmont Park every year. I guess they're still good for a few more races. I've done my best to take care of them while they were here."

Jensen scribbled a note on his notepad and rubbed his eyes.

"I'll be doing paperwork on this case for weeks."

"Speaking of paperwork," I said, looking at my friends.

Katy nodded. Tetyana looked away. She'd finally agreed to my proposal, but I knew she felt there were better ways to help.

I turned to Victoria.

"This house is yours now."

She looked at me in surprise. Katy pulled out the codicil from her pocket and handed it to her.

"What's this?" asked Victoria.

"Your grandmother was an eccentric woman," I said. "This codicil means this house now belongs to my company. Our attorney in New York just confirmed its legitimacy."

Victoria's face fell.

"But we've decided there's no one better suited to inherit this home than you," I continued. "As soon as we get things sorted out with the lawyers, this title will be reverted to you."

Victoria looked at me in shock. Then, a small smile broke out on her face.

"You're not joking, are you?"

"We don't joke," said Tetyana in a firm voice.

I sighed in relief. She'd argued and pushed back. If we took ownership, she'd said, more children in need would get a place to sleep. She was right. But that was a decision for Victoria to make when she was ready. Not us.

I was glad Tetyana was coming around. I knew she would.

"Is this for real?" squealed Victoria, unfolding the codicil.

"It's your childhood home," I said.

Katy reached over and squeezed her arm.

"Better believe it, hun."

"Hey, Victoria," I said. "My only suggestion is to keep Jim and Nancy on here to help you." I turned to the couple. "That is, if you want to stay."

Jim opened his mouth and shut it, and turned to Nancy.

We all waited.

After a long pause, Nancy nodded. "That would be good. I don't want to go back to town."

Victoria put her palms together. She looked like she wanted to jump up and embrace Nancy but was restraining herself. "I'd really like that. Thank you, Nancy and Jim. This can be your home too."

Jim scanned the kitchen and turned to Victoria. "This place needs a lot of work. I can spruce it up for you, if you'd like."

"I'd love that!"

"I'll clean up the cabin too," said Jim. I noticed his eyes turn down, as if he was searching for something at his feet. "I'll get rid of the old bath salts in the washroom. Flush it down the toilet."

I jerked back in surprise to hear that. Everyone gave him a confused look but Tetyana's face remained stoic.

I gave a discreet glance at Nancy and saw her shoulders relax. A flicker of relief crossed her face. So, she had known about his drug abuse all along.

I turned to Jim who was now watching his wife, a sad look on his face, as if he was remorseful for the hurt he'd put on her. Jim would need time to adjust and those two would have some work to do, but at least they were heading in the right direction.

"Excuse me, Sheriff?"

We turned around.

It was one of the junior officers who'd come with the investigation team.

"Someone's locked up in a third-floor bedroom upstairs. Can't find the key. Man's been banging about for a while now."

"Oh!" I said, pulling out the room key from my pocket. "I totally forgot about Charles. I'm so sorry—"

Before I could finish, Victoria swiped the key from my hand and hurled it into the fire.

"Whoa!" said the constable, scrambling after it.

"What did you do that for?" asked Jensen, turning angrily to Victoria.

"Won't hurt him to stay in there for a little while longer," she said. "When you do get him out, would you escort him off my premises, please?"

My premises.

I smiled at those words. *Good for you, Victoria.* If anyone deserved a life of freedom and peace, it had to be her.

Victoria got up from her chair and plucked out the diary she'd been keeping hidden under her blanket. Without any warning, she stepped up to the fireplace and chucked the book in too.

Jensen swore. "For crying out loud, that could be evidence."

Victoria shrugged. "I think you have enough to make a case against Lisa."

Shaking his head, Jensen got up to help the constable open Charles' bedroom door, leaving us alone in the kitchen.

We huddled close together, watching the fire flicker and grow, eating the pages of Victoria's old diary.

A ping from my phone made me look down at my lap. I picked up my mobile to read a text from Peace.

"Madame Bouchard's lawyer confirmed the case is now closed. Check the orphanage account for a generous donation transfer on Monday."

Madame Bouchard had been serious after all.

I couldn't wait to share the news with my friends, but now was not the time.

I leaned back in my chair, feeling like I had gone full circle.

When I had met Madame Bouchard decades ago, I'd been a scared, orphaned girl, desperate for help, pleading for her to give me a break. And now, I'd paid it forward by sticking to my promise to help sort out her own family affairs.

Knowing her, I was certain she'd approve of my methods, as unconventional as they might be. I knew she'd be happy her granddaughter was a free woman now and would take on the ownership of her childhood home.

Justice had been restored. That was all that mattered.

I leaned forward to warm my hands over the fire, wondering where in the world Madame Bouchard was going to send us next.

The pages in Victoria's diary were shriveling up one by one, disintegrating into hot cinders. It was cathartic to watch the fire devour the past.

Through the crackling of the fire logs, I could hear another message.

Our job here was done.

It was time for us to head home and rejoin our own families.

Back in New York

Chapter Sixty-three

Katy's phone rang, silencing Tetyana and me in mid-argument about which ramp to get off the highway.

In the backseat, behind us, Katy fumbled to turn her phone on.

"Hey, sweetie," came her voice, guarded, but with a tinge of hope.

Tetyana and I exchanged a quick glance.

That had to be Peace.

"No, I'm okay, everything's fine," said Katy, her mouth turned to the phone. "How's Chantelle doing today?"

I tried not to listen in, but I couldn't help it.

Katy and Peace weren't just my close friends, but, like Tetyana, Luc, Win, and everyone else who had joined our missions over the years, they were my family. When they hurt, I hurt too.

"Yeah, I know," said Katy, her voice low. From the rearview mirror, I could see she was trying to hold her tears back. "No, it's just my hair. I look very different now. It'll grow back, I guess, but I look awful."

There was a long pause as Peace talked at the other end.

"I know, sweetie," said Katy, finally, her voice breaking up. "I love you too."

I glanced at the rearview mirror to see tears roll down her cheeks.

Something caught in my throat. Next to me, I heard an audible sigh of relief from Tetyana. I felt my shoulders relax as I turned my attention back to the road.

After talking with Chantelle for another ten minutes and telling her and Peace she was coming home, Katy hung up.

Silence echoed in the car.

No one spoke for the next little while.

In the back, Katy was wiping her eyes, and trying not to sniffle too loudly. I wanted so badly to turn around and give her a big hug, but I knew she liked her privacy and would tell us everything at the right time.

"So," I said after a few minutes. "Do I drop you off at home, Katy?"

From the rearview mirror, I saw her nod.

"Yeah." She was trying hard to sound nonchalant when I could hear the strong emotions bubbling inside of her. "I miss them so much," she said, her voice trembling. "I feel so bad for leaving them."

"Oh, honey," I said. "Don't be so hard on yourself. Besides, you needed some time away, and it was important to let Peace know how you felt, right?"

"Long-term relationships aren't easy," said Katy, blowing her nose in a tissue. It seemed like she was talking to herself more than us. "It takes so much work some days, you know?"

Tetyana and I nodded.

"He said he's not going to bring work home anymore. And we're going to get back to our Friday date nights. We stopped last year. I don't think that helped. I really missed them."

"That's wonderful news," I said. "See? It turned out all right."

"I hate fighting, though," sniffed Katy.

"David and I get into scraps too," I said. "Once I was so mad at him I told him to get his own apartment, but we talked and made up before we went to bed. Relationships aren't easy."

"I guess the trick is to listen," Katy said as she wiped her nose. "I suck at listening. I don't let him get a word in when I'm mad."

"That's what I like about you," said Tetyana, turning around with a grin. "You can be a firecracker when you get pissed off."

"Nothing wrong with getting mad when you feel like someone wronged you," I said. I smiled at my friend through the rearview mirror. "I think you did the right thing. You have to say what you feel or you'll end up miserable. You guys will work through this. I know you will."

Katy smiled back.

"This is why I never put up with long-term relationships," said Tetyana, shaking her head. "Married life is not for me. All this communication stuff and working things out before going to bed is fine, but I don't have that kind of patience."

"As long as you're happy," I said, "that's what matters." I paused, wondering if this was a good time to ask the question we were all dying to have answered. "Hey, so who are you seeing these days?"

Tetyana turned to me, a stern expression on her face. "If I tell you, I'd have to kill you."

"Don't tell me you're dating a spy again," said Katy.

"I never said that."

"Sometimes I feel like you treat dating like you're fighting a war."

"Different strokes," said Tetyana with a shrug.

"Come on," I said. "Stop stalling. Who are you dating?"

"Look, I don't want to have to bring them over for dinner, make small talk, and pretend to be lovey-dovey. That's not me."

"Can you at least tell us his name?" asked Katy.

"Or her's, if it's a her," I said. "We love you either way, you know that, don't you?"

"What about you?" said Tetyana, poking me on the shoulder. "When are you and David going to have your wedding?"

"Wedding?" I gulped.

Why did she have to bring this up now?

"Yeah," said Katy, poking her face in between the seats and turning to me. "When is the big date?"

"I er... guys, I'm driving. Stop distracting me."

"What a lame-ass excuse," said Tetyana, shaking her head.

"You, my girlfriend, have serious commitment issues," said Katy. "Either that or it's David."

"Who said we can't commit? We've been engaged for..." I stopped as the GPS monitor on my dashboard pinged loudly.

"Would you two stop picking on me?" I said, signaling and moving over to the right lane. "I missed our exit."

"You're changing the topic," said Tetyana.

"Am not," I said.

"Are too," said Katy. "Like Tetyana did just now."

"Did not!" said Tetyana, turning around and punching Katy playfully on her knee.

I listened to the banter between my friends, one eye on my GPS, glad we were finally heading home.

❖——❖

The first thing we did when we returned to our neighborhood was to drop Katy off at her house.

Tetyana and I waited in the car and watched Peace fling open the door and embrace Katy.

Archie, their three-year-old golden retriever, dashed out the door, almost knocking them over. He whirled in excitement around the front yard, barking indiscriminately at an imaginary squirrel or the other. Chantelle shot out soon after and skipped around her parents' legs, laughing and giggling to herself.

"I'm so glad they're together again," I said, a sense of immense relief wash over me. I felt my eyes well up.

"They were never going to break up for good," said Tetyana. "You worry too much, Asha."

I watched Katy and Peace silently, thinking there was truth to that old saying. Sometimes, a bit of distance can make the heart grow fonder.

"They'll be fine," said Tetyana, putting a hand on my shoulder. "Let's leave them be."

I rolled down the window and waved.

"See you all tomorrow!" I hollered and blew them a kiss. "Love you!"

Chantelle let out an excited shriek and waved madly. She made a move to run toward the car, but Katy held her back, smiling. With a happy sigh, I rolled back on the road and Tetyana and I waved out the window till we turned the corner.

I was going to miss my friend.

For almost two weeks, Katy had been staying at my home, in our guest bedroom. I hadn't wanted to interfere, but I'd fervently hoped Peace and her would make up and rediscover the love they'd found so long ago in the middle of one of our crazy missions, traveling across East Africa.

"It feels like forever, doesn't it?" I said, turning to Tetyana. "Since we were running around in Peace's open Jeep across the savannas?"

She leaned back in her seat. "Those were the days," she said. "We were brash, foolish, and young."

I jabbed her with my elbow.

"We're still young," I said, giving her a side glance. "Young enough to hook up with hot guys every week."

"Hot? Who said hot?"

"I know you. You'd never go out with anyone who's not ripped, toned, and looks like a cover model for a muscle and fitness magazine. Am I right or am I right?"

Tetyana smiled, but didn't say anything.

I dropped her off at her apartment and turned around to head back to my own house, only a few blocks away.

I parked the car and walked up the steps to my small brownstone home. The door banged open before I could get to the top of the stairs. David jumped out and picked me up, without even saying hello, and twirled me around.

"David," I said, laughing. "Put me down."

Instead of answering me, he pulled me in for a kiss. I don't know how long we stood at our doorway kissing, but I pulled back realizing we were in full view of all our neighbors.

"This is very nice, but my suitcase is still in the car," I said, snuggling up to his chest.

"I'll get it for you later," he said. "But right now, I made dinner for us. I've been cooking all day."

I cocked an eyebrow. I was the officially trained chef in the family. David usually stuck to making sandwiches, soup, and coffee.

"You? You were cooking all day?"

"Better believe it. I tried something from one of your Chef Pierre recipe books."

"Chef Pierre? Honey, are you feeling all right?"

"Yeah, why?" said David, looking slightly offended. "Don't you think I can do it?"

"No... it's just that... that's serious gourmet cuisine."

"Give me a chance, will you?"

I sniffed the air. "Whatever you did does smell good."

With a grin, he pulled me inside and closed the door behind us.

My jaw dropped as I saw the dining table in the corner of our open living room.

He'd set it with our finest cutlery and dishes and my best blue table cloth. A champagne bottle sat patiently in a silver bucket filled with ice, next to a vase filled with baby white roses. Set around the room, on the coffee table, dining table, and window sill, were small glass candle holders with lit candles.

"Sweetie, this is beautiful," I said, taking it all in.

Suddenly, a jolt of worry went through me. I pulled out my phone.

"What's the date today? It's not our anniversary, is it?" I said, feeling my stomach sink. "It's not my birthday, and it's not yours either...."

David pulled out a chair and grinned. "It's a new day I made up."

"Oh, really?" I said, cautiously.

"It's our I-wish-you-didn't-go-on-dangerous-missions-but-I'm-glad-you're-home-in-one-piece-and-now-we're-gonna-have-an-awesome-evening day."

I laughed, more in relief than anything, and took my seat.

"That's a mouthful," I said, turning around to kiss him. "I'll take it though. Should I have brought a bottle of wine or something for the celebration?"

"You just sit right there," said David, turning around and walking into the open kitchen. "I've got everything."

My phone buzzed.

My eyes widened as I read the text message that had just come in.

"You are invited for a weekend at the exclusive resort on Coffin Island. I look forward to meeting you shortly."

The signature line at the bottom simply said, *A friend of Madame B.*

I looked up. David was busy at the stove, whistling to himself.

"Hey, David?"

"Yup?" he replied, not looking up.

"Did the bakery get any more prank calls while we were away?"

"Nope," he replied, shaking his head, peeking through the oven's glass door. "Probably some bored kid. Wouldn't worry about it."

I turned back to my phone.

That prank call had annoyed me at first. Then it had unsettled me. I was suspicious of everything, even this text I'd just got.

But maybe I was over-thinking things as usual. Maybe this was just spam. Nefarious Internet marketers were always pretending to gift you things while they were really setting the stage to harass you for money later on.

My finger hovered over the delete button.

Something made me stop. I reread the note.

Madame B.

I scrunched my forehead. This had to be a call for help from a friend or colleague of Madame Bouchard. *Who else would it be? Should I respond?*

Without deleting it, I closed the app and slipped the phone in my pocket.

Those were questions for another day. Right now, I had more important things to attend to.

I sat back in my seat. The smell of something delicious wafted from the oven. Nothing was burning. Maybe David had a special talent for cooking, after all.

The candles on the table winked at me.

For one blissful moment, I forgot about my worries and constant speculations about where Madame Bouchard was going to drag me next. I took a deep breath in, thinking what a lucky woman I was to have David to come home to.

❖———❖

Continue the adventure!

Read the next Merciless Murder Mystery Thriller and find out what Asha and Katy confront next on an isolated resort island off the wild coast of Oregon.

Lock your door. A killer is on the prowl. He's taking each guest, one by one...

Flip the page to read the first chapter.

Or, get Merciless Games right now, here:
www.tikiriherath.com/mysteries

Merciless Games - Chapter One

The Photo

It was an image of a bloated, dead body. He lay naked, sprawled over a cluster of rocks on a deserted and remote beach. The gruesome blood splatters on his back said he'd been shot multiple times. Whoever killed him had been vicious. Boiling with the desire for revenge.

They'd made sure he was dead.

✦━◆━✦

"It's spooky here," said Katy. "I don't like this."

"It's just a short trip," I said.

"Famous last words," she said, making a face.

Though I didn't let on, my gut was churning.

Go home, it warned me. *Turn around now.*

But I was ignoring all the red flags, doing my best to pretend everything was just fine.

It was early afternoon, but the sky was already gray and the clouds hung stiflingly low.

I was glad we'd ditched our city dresses and heels for more sensible and layered hiking attire and flat boots.

A storm was coming. The swells rushed in, crashing furiously on the rocky shore. The howling wind whipped everything into frozen icicles and the seagulls screeched as they got whisked up by the strong currents.

I brushed the long hair strands off my face, wondering about my crazy decision to come here and invite my BFF to join me.

"Maybe they made a mistake, Asha," said Katy, as if reading my mind. She took out the crumpled photo from her pocket. "Maybe this wasn't meant for us."

"They paid up, and they were generous, weren't they?" I said, pushing my fears to the back of my mind. "It had to be for us."

But it hadn't been an ordinary order for an ordinary cake.

I knew it as soon as I saw the gruesome image.

The unsigned message that had popped into my bakery's inbox four days ago had come with something extra.

A photograph of a dead man. A naked corpse on a desolate beach.

A shudder went through me as I stared at the picture in Katy's hand.

The sand dunes and cactus in the background reminded me of a remote area I'd been to before. One at the Mexican border where only outlaws dared to go.

It was this photo that brought Katy and me to this small town of Trembling Cypress Bay, off the Oregon coast. It was a place so remote it felt like the end of the world.

We were waiting for the next ferry on the town's fishing jetty, trying not to get soaked by the ocean spray crashing around us.

Underneath the muddy water near the pier, long strands of dark green kelp waved madly, like those wacky inflatable air dancers you find at county fairs.

It was like even they were warning us to stay away.

I pulled the jacket zipper up to my neck and curled my toes in my boots. The humidity on the West Coast soaked right into your bones and, I swore, chilled your blood.

We were a long way from home and our upscale New York bakery.

"When someone promises a weekend at an exclusive resort, I expect Laguna Beach or Cancun," grumbled Katy, "not a dinky little fishing village in the middle of nowhere."

She poked me with her elbow.

"If they lied about this, how do we know they're not lying about everything else?"

She was right.

I had no idea what to expect.

Minutes after we got the cake order, they, whoever they were, sent a ten-thousand-dollar retainer. An electronic transfer from an anonymous payee, explained our bank.

Who pays that much money for a Dulce de Leche cheesecake?

Then came the message.

We were to hand-deliver the cake to a luxury retreat on an island off the Oregon coast. Another twenty thousand dollars would be ours if we served the cake for dinner the first night and stayed the complete weekend at the resort.

The signature line simply said, *The Host, a friend of Madame Bouchard.*

That, I knew, was a call for help.

I could use thirty thousand dollars to expand the Red Heeled Rebels bakery and buy my chef team a set of new industrial-strength mixers. All I had to do was serve my cheesecake and stay the weekend at a resort? That would be the fastest money I'd ever made.

Of course, I said yes.

The money was nice, but as I stood on this remote ocean front at the other end of the country, I felt a knot forming in my stomach like those kelp strands under the sea tangling into a gnarled mess.

My mind swirled with unanswered questions.

Why did they invite us? What did this exclusive island retreat in Oregon have to do with the photo of a dead man?

I wondered if I was going to regret my decision to come.

To be continued....

＊—■—＊

Continue the adventure!

MERCILESS GAMES, the next book in this series, will give you more spine-tingling intrigue, mystery, and lurking killers who Asha will ferret out in the end.

Get the book here.

MERCILESS GAMES: www.TikiriHerath.com/Mysteries

＊—■—＊

Seven strangers are invited to an exclusive writers' retreat on a remote island off the coast of Oregon.

Their stay will be at a hundred-year-old lighthouse revamped into a luxury ocean-front getaway for the discerning and wealthy literati who shy from publicity.

Asha arrives on the island, believing her job is to cater to this sagacious celebrity party.

But before the weekend is over, an unseen killer will attempt to murder them, one by one.

With their phones taken away and their only connection to the mainland cut off, panic sets in on the island. Everyone suspects each other and a chilling realization dawns on them.

They are all connected by one horrific incident in the past they'd rather forget.

The mysterious killer has only one stipulation—delivered by an anonymous message on a bathroom wall. If Asha can identify the true motivation for these assassinations, the remaining guests will be spared.

Knowing there is now a target on her back as well, Asha races against the clock to crack the killer's code before more innocents die.

But are these seven guests as innocent as they make out to be?

✦━━━✦

What readers are saying:

"Hooked right from the start!

"The atmosphere on the island added so much to the story. It gave it an Agatha Christie vibe."

"Well-thought out and compelling!"

"I enjoyed being on the edge of my seat not knowing what was going to happen next. Loved the twists and turns. Kept me guessing!"

✦━━━✦

Get the book and find out what Asha and Katy confront next. Available around the world, on Amazon stores everywhere.

Get the book here.
MERCILESS GAMES: www.TikiriHerath.com/Mysteries

◆——◆——◆

Available globally in e-book, paperback, and hardback editions on all Amazon stores. Also available for free in libraries everywhere. Just ask your friendly local librarian to order a copy via Ingram Spark.

Author's Note

Dear friend,

Thank you for reading this book.

Did you enjoy the story?

Would you like to help other readers meet Asha and Katy, and follow their adventures? If you do, tell your fellow mystery fans about this book and share on social media. Leave an honest review on Goodreads, Bookbub, or your favorite online bookstore.

Just one sentence would do. Thank you so much!

One more thing.

If you'd like to learn the backstory of Asha, Katy, and Tetyana, flip to the end of this book to learn about the spin-off series that tells their stories.

The Red Heeled Rebels international crime thrillers is the origin story. It spans four continents, features the back stories of everyone in this found family, and shows how they all met.

Don't forget your exclusive book gift!

HER DEADLY END is a short but twisty thriller about an unusual murder-suicide case that Special Agent Tanya (Tetyana), Asha, and Katy accidentally stumble upon while vacationing in Paradise Cove. It's a pulse-pounding, nerve-shredding mystery of a devious serial criminal stalking a small seaside town in Washington State.

Click the link below to get your gift.

HER DEADLY END: A gripping thriller with a twisty end

My best wishes,
Tikiri
Vancouver, Canada

PS/ If you didn't enjoy the story or spotted typos, would you drop a line and let me know? Or just write to say hello. I would love to hear from you and personally reply to every email I receive.

My address is: Tikiri@TikiriHerath.com

Debate this Dozen

Twelve Book Club Questions

1. Who was your favorite character?
2. Which characters did you dislike?
3. Which scene has stuck with you the most? Why?
4. What scenes surprised you?
5. What was your favorite part of the book?
6. What was your least favorite part?
7. Did any part of this book strike a particular emotion in you? Which part and what emotion did the book make you feel?
8. Did you know the author has written an underlying message in this story? What theme or life lesson do you think this story tells?
9. What did you think of the author's writing?
10. How would you adapt this book into a movie? Who would you cast in the leading roles?
11. On a scale of one to ten, how would you rate this story?
12. Would you read another book by this author?

The Reading List

T he Red Heeled Rebels universe of mystery thrillers, featuring your favorite kick-ass female characters.

Tanya Stone FBI K9 Mystery Thrillers
www.TikiriHerath.com/Thrillers
NEW FBI thriller series starring Tetyana from the Red Heeled Rebels as Special Agent Tanya Stone, and Max, as her loyal German Shepherd. These are serial killer thrillers set

in Black Rock, a small upscale resort town on the coast of
Washington state.
Her Deadly End
Her Cold Blood
Her Last Lie
Her Secret Crime
Her Dead Girl
Her Perfect Murder
Her Grisly Grave

Asha Kade Private Detective Murder Mysteries
www.TikiriHerath.com/Mysteries
**Each book is a standalone murder mystery thriller,
featuring the Red Heeled Rebels, Asha Kade and Katy
McCafferty. Asha and Katy receive one million dollars for
their favorite children's charity from a secret benefactor's
estate every time they solve a cold case.**
Merciless Legacy
Merciless Games
Merciless Crimes
Merciless Lies
Merciless Past
Merciless Deaths

**Red Heeled Rebels International Mystery & Crime - The
Origin Story**
www.TikiriHerath.com/RedHeeledRebels

The award-winning origin story of the Red Heeled Rebels characters. Learn how a rag-tag group of trafficked orphans from different places united to fight for their freedom and their lives, and became a found family.

The Girl Who Crossed the Line

The Girl Who Ran Away

The Girl Who Made Them Pay

The Girl Who Fought to Kill

The Girl Who Broke Free

The Girl Who Knew Their Names

The Girl Who Never Forgot

The Accidental Traveler

www.TikiriHerath.com

An anthology of personal short stories based on the author's sojourns around the world.

The Rebel Diva Nonfiction Series

www.TikiriHerath.com/Nonfiction

Your Rebel Dreams: 6 simple steps to take back control of your life in uncertain times.

Your Rebel Plans: 4 simple steps to getting unstuck and making progress today.

Your Rebel Life: Easy habit hacks to enhance happiness in the 10 key areas of your life.

Bust Your Fears: 3 simple tools to crush your anxieties and squash your stress.

―――✦―――

Collaborations

The Boss Chick's Bodacious Destiny Nonfiction Bundle
Dark Shadows 2: Voodoo and Black Magic of New Orleans

―――✦―――

Tikiri's novels and nonfiction books are available on all good bookstores around the world.

These books are also available in libraries everywhere. Just ask your friendly local librarian or your local bookstore to order a copy via Ingram Spark.

www.TikiriHerath.com

Happy reading.

Asha Kade Private Detective Murder Mysteries

How far would you go for a million-dollar payout?

The Books:

Merciless Legacy

Merciless Games

Merciless Crimes

Merciless Lies

Merciless Past

Merciless Deaths

◆——◆

Each book is a standalone murder mystery thriller featuring the Red Heeled Rebel, Asha Kade, and her best friend Katy

McCafferty, as private detectives on the hunt for serial killers in small towns USA.

There is no graphic violence, heavy cursing, or explicit sex in these books. What you will find are a series of suspicious deaths, a closed circle of suspects, twists and turns, fast-paced action, and nail-biting suspense.

www.TikiriHerath.com/mysteries

⟡———⟡

A newly minted private investigator, Asha Kade, gets a million dollars from an eccentric client's estate every time she solves a cold case. Asha Kade accepts this bizarre challenge, but what she doesn't bargain for is to be drawn into the dark underworld of her past again.

The only thing that propels her forward now is a burning desire for justice.

⟡———⟡

What readers are saying on Amazon and Goodreads:

"My new favorite series!"

"Thrilling twists, unputdownable!"

"I was hooked right from the start!"

"A twisted whodunnit! Edge of your seat thriller that kept me up late, to finish it, unputdownable!! More, please!"

"Buckle up for a roller coaster of a ride. This one will keep you on the edge of your seat."

"A must read! A macabre start to an excellent book. It had me totally gripped from the start and just got better!""

A brand-new murder mystery series for a pulse-pounding, bone-chilling adventure from the comfort and warmth of your favorite reading chair at home.

Can you find the killer before Asha Kade does?

To learn more about this exciting series, go to www.TikiriHerath.com/mysteries.

Sign up to Tikiri's Rebel Reader Club to get the chance to win personalized paperback books, chat with the author and more.

Available in e-book, paperback, and hardback editions on all good bookstores around the world. Print books are available for free in libraries everywhere. Just ask your friendly local librarian or your local bookstore to order a copy via Ingram Spark.

Tanya Stone FBI K9 Mystery Thrillers

*S*ome small-town secrets will haunt your nightmares. Escape if you can...

The Books:

Her Deadly End

Her Cold Blood

Her Last Lie

Her Secret Crime

Her Perfect Murder

Her Grisly Grave

A brand-new FBI K9 serial killer thriller series for a pulse-pounding, bone-chilling adventure from the comfort and warmth of your favorite reading chair at home.
Can you find the killer before Agent Tanya Stone?
www.TikiriHerath.com/thrillers

FBI Special Agent Tanya Stone has a new assignment. Hunt down the serial killers prowling the idyllic West Coast resort towns.

An unspeakable and bone-chilling darkness seethes underneath these picturesque seaside suburbs. A string of violent abductions and gruesome murders wreak hysteria among the perfect lives of the towns' families.

But nothing is what it seems. The monsters wear masks and mingle with the townsfolk, spreading vicious lies.

With her K9 German Shepherd, Agent Stone goes on the warpath. She will fight her own demons as a trafficked survivor to make the perverted psychopaths pay.

But now, they're after her.

Small towns have dark deceptions and sealed lips. If they know you know the truth, they'll never let you leave...

Each book is a standalone murder mystery thriller, featuring Tetyana from the Red Heeled Rebels as Agent Tanya Stone, and Max, her loyal German Shepherd. Red Heeled Rebels Asha Kade and Katy McCafferty and their found family make guest appearances when Tanya needs help.

There is no graphic violence, heavy cursing, or explicit sex in these books.

The dogs featured in this series are never harmed, but the villains are.

To learn more about this exciting new series and find out how to get early access to all the books in the Tanya Stone FBI K9 series, go to <u>www.TikiriHerath.com/thrillers</u>

Sign up to Tikiri's Rebel Reader Club to get the chance to win personalized paperback books, chat with the author and more.

Available in e-book, paperback, and hardback editions on all good bookstores around the world. Print books are available for free in libraries everywhere. Just ask your friendly local librarian or your local bookstore to order a copy via Ingram Spark.

The Red Heeled Rebels International Mystery & Crime

The Origin Story

Would you like to know the origin story of your favorite characters in the Tanya Stone FBI K9 mystery thrillers and the Asha Kade Merciless murder mysteries?

In the award-winning Red Heeled Rebels international mystery & crime series—the origin story—you'll find out how Asha, Katy, and Tetyana (Tanya) banded together in their troubled youths to fight for freedom against all odds.

The complete Red Heeled Rebels international crime collection:

Prequel Novella: The Girl Who Crossed the Line

Book One: The Girl Who Ran Away
Book Two: The Girl Who Made Them Pay
Book Three: The Girl Who Fought to Kill
Book Four: The Girl Who Broke Free
Book Five: The Girl Who Knew Their Names
Book Six: The Girl Who Never Forgot
The series is now complete.

An epic, pulse-pounding, international crime thriller series that spans four continents featuring a group of spunky, sassy young misfits who have only each other for family.

A multiple-award-winning series which would be best read in order. There is no graphic violence, heavy cursing, or explicit sex in these books.

www.TikiriHerath.com/RedHeeledRebels

In a world where justice no longer prevails, six iron-willed young women rally to seek vengeance on those who stole their humanity.

If you like gripping thrillers with flawed but strong female leads, vigilante action in exotic locales and twists that leave you at the edge of your seat, you'll love these books by multiple award-winning Canadian novelist, Tikiri Herath.

Go on a heart-pounding international adventure without having to get a passport or even buy an airline ticket!

What readers are saying on Amazon and Goodreads:

"Fast-paced and exciting!"
"An exciting and thought-provoking book."
"A wonderful story! I didn't want to leave the characters."
"I couldn't put down this exciting road trip adventure with a powerful message."
"Another award-worthy adventure novel that keeps you on the edge of your seat."
"A heart-stopping adventure. I just couldn't put the book down till I finished reading it."

❖———❖

Literary Awards & Praise for The Red Heeled Rebels books:

- Grand Prize Award Finalist - 2019 Eric Hoffer Award, USA

- First Horizon Award Finalist - 2019 Eric Hoffer Award, USA

- Honorable Mention General Fiction - 2019 Eric Hoffer Award, USA

- Winner First-In-Category - 2019 Chanticleer Somerset Award, USA

- Semi-Finalist - 2020 Chanticleer Somerset Award, USA

- Winner in 2019 Readers' Favorite Book Awards, USA

- Winner of 2019 Silver Medal - Excellence E-Lit Award, USA

- Winner in Suspense Category - 2018 New York Big Book

Award, USA

- Finalist in Suspense Category - 2018 & 2019 Silver Falchion Awards, USA

- Honorable Mention - 2018-19 Reader Views Literary Classics Award, USA

- Publisher's Weekly Booklife Prize - 2018, USA

To learn more about this addictive series, go to **www.TikiriHerath.com/RedHeeledRebels** and receive the prequel novella - **The Girl Who Crossed The Line** - as a gift.

Sign up to Tikiri's Rebel Reader club and get bonus stories, exotic recipes, the chance to win paperbacks, chat with the author and more.

Available in e-book, paperback, and hardback editions on all good bookstores around the world. Print books are available for free in libraries everywhere. Just ask your friendly local librarian or your local bookstore to order a copy via Ingram Spark.

Acknowledgments

To my amazing, talented, superstar editor, Stephanie Parent, thank you, as always, for coming on this literary journey with me and for helping make these books the best they can be.

To my fantastic international team of beta readers who helped me through this adventure, who cheered me on as I toiled, and who gave me their feedback, thank you. In alphabetical order of first name:

Blessmore Chikwakwa, Zimbabwe
Carolyn Pennett-Staresinic, Canada
Cyndi Wannamaker, Canada
Laura Edwards, USA
Michele Kapugi, USA
Natasja Smith, South Africa
Stephie Smith, USA

To all the kind and generous readers who take the time to review my novels and share their honest feedback, thank you so much. Your support is invaluable.

I'm immensely grateful to you all for your kind and generous support, and would love to invite you for a glass of British Columbian wine or a cup of Ceylon tea with chocolates when you come to Vancouver next!

About the Author

Tikiri Herath is the multiple-award-winning author of international thriller and mystery novels.

—◆———◆———◆—

Tikiri has a bachelor's degree from the University of Victoria, Canada, and a master's degree from the Solvay Business School in Brussels, Belgium. For almost two decades, she worked in risk management in the intelligence and defense sectors, including in the Canadian Federal Government and at NATO in Europe and North America.

Tikiri's an adrenaline junkie who has rock climbed, bungee jumped, rode on the back of a motorcycle across Quebec, flown in an acrobatic airplane upside down, and parachuted solo.

When she's not plotting another thriller scene or planning an adrenaline-filled trip, you'll find her baking in her kitchen with a glass of red Shiraz and vintage jazz playing in the background.

An international nomad and fifth-culture kid, she now calls Canada home.

To say hello and get travel stories from around the world, go to
www.TikiriHerath.com